VINES & FLORETS

BLOOD, BLOOM, & WATER BOOK FIVE

AMY MCNULTY

Snowy Wings
PUBLISHING

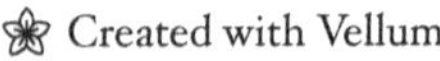 Created with Vellum

CHAPTER ONE

"This horse is dirty!" Hya, clutching the plastic miniature brush with a decade or more of coarse, nylon mane and tail hairs in its bristles, paused in her mane-styling work. Her nose wrinkled.

The My Little Pony in her hand had seen better days, sure, but I liked to think the dirt streaks and the scuffed cutie mark were signs of a life well lived. Well, okay, that pony hadn't lived a life of any sort. But when I'd been Hya's age—or younger, really, thank goodness my sister hadn't experienced half of what I had before the age of nine—it had been a warrior in many a battle amidst the fallen leaves outside.

"That's because she's seen more than her share of battles." I took the pony from Hya and danced her across the hardwood living room floor over which most of my childhood toys were now scattered. Kicking the pony's forelegs into the air, I made a neighing sound. "We'll save you, princess!" My voice was high-pitched. "We'll stop the faeries from hurting you or anyone else!"

My heart sunk to even speak the words in play.

Hya giggled and took the pony back. "Faeries don't hurt people, silly pony." She started styling the frizzy mane again.

But they did. So could vampires and merfolk, but faefolk in particular...

1

"Where are your games?" Behind me, Ash was making a racket sorting through all of my well-worn toys. He picked up a T-rex and made it buckle a little halfheartedly, but he'd been clearly searching for some "vintage" handheld video game system or something.

"You *have* games," I told him. I frowned as I watched him chuck the dinosaur aside and examine my toy cars. There was still bits of grass stuck in the wheel well of my remote control dragster. He went to work picking the withered blades out. Maybe the twins were a bit old for these toys. I'd played with them for years beyond the age of nine, but most kids weren't like me.

"There's nothing but kid stuff here," said Ash sourly.

"Kid, you're nine years old," I pointed out. I took hold of the discarded T-rex. His paint was cracking in the uneven surfaces. Too much time spent soaked in the bath.

I let out a roar and made the dinosaur's open mouth munch on a lock of Ash's short, brown hair. Squinting his hazel brown eyes, he whapped at the toy to get it off.

"Mom said *annoying your brother* isn't playing," said Hya matter-of-factly. She spoke as if she'd been told that many a time and was now lording it over me because she could legitimately lecture someone else.

Scooting closer to her twin, she sat on her knees beside him. They were really an echo of one another, as identical as fraternal twins could get. Hya's brown hair fell down to her shoulders, the length allowing for more of its wavy thickness to become apparent. Their eyes were the same shape and color, and they were both the same rosy shade of pale. Even their button noses and chubby cheeks made it seem like they'd been poured from the same mold.

They were the perfect blend of Dad and Noelle, though Dad's dark hair had won out against the natural pale, white blonde of Noelle and my step-sister, Ember. Though these days, Noelle dyed her graying hair a platinum silver.

"Okay," I said, flicking my own dark hair—a richer, deeper brown more like my mom's and sister Ivy's—over one shoulder. "I'm sorry. How about I tell you a story instead?" I wiggled the T-rex in the air in front of them.

Hya leaned against our brother. He flinched at her weight against his arm but didn't move. "Is it a good one?" she asked, hugging my pony to her chest.

Ash snorted.

I arched a brow at him. "It involves scary monsters and brave girls and blood and magic and... death."

Ash's eyes widened at that, the little smug expression on his face melting.

Hya frowned, her own excitement waning then waxing with each descriptor I'd given her. Still, she seemed riveted.

Was it time for them to know? I'd been a year younger when I'd *lived* it.

I strained to hear signs that Dad or Noelle were listening nearby, but a tool clanged out from the garage and I knew Dad was probably tinkering with his latest acquisition, some old motorcycle that Noelle had called a death trap. Upstairs, the hardwood floor creaked, and I figured Noelle was still in the master bedroom, getting dressed for an evening out.

Dad better get inside and get showered before they had to go, or he'd find himself at the wrong end of one of Noelle's lectures.

"When I was eight, ten years ago," I started, lifting up a plush calico cat I'd gotten because it had reminded me of Blossom. My ancient kitty lived at Mom's townhouse, sleeping away twenty-three hours of the day. "A handsome faery prince became my friend."

Ash snickered, but Hya's jaw dropped. While they were nearly identical, Ash had gotten all of the skepticism and Hya all of the imagination. She reminded me of myself at her age, but she was more innocent, less brash.

"Little did I know," I said, "my sisters had already been cast under spells—by a vampire prince and a merman one." I found appropriate toys to represent all of them. Ivy was a dark brown squirrel, Ember another one of my ponies. Dean Horne the vampire royal was a classic, shiny car, along with Calder Poole the merman prince as a shark missing a fin. I hadn't selected my faery prince yet.

"They fell in love, and they built armies, deciding that only one could prevail." I gathered a bunch of toys behind the shark and the car, then made the squirrel and the pony cuddle up with them—the pony with the car at first, the squirrel with the shark.

Hya laughed and Ash rolled his eyes. "Why would *princes* fall in love with our sisters?" He said the word "sisters" like it was gum found on the bottom of his shoe. It was an endless source of frustration that he had four of them, even if Ivy and Ember hadn't grown up with the twins at all.

"This house," I said, gazing back and forth and gesturing around us. "It was built on magical land."

"Oo," said Hya.

"Right." Ash crossed his arms tightly over his chest.

"My sisters didn't know that at first," I said, "but just living here—they became potential *warriors*. They were called 'champions.'"

Ash let down a little of his defenses. "Did they fight?"

Nodding, I made the squirrel and the pony clash. "With fire and ice and trickery that only vampires and merfolk could teach them." I had the squirrel give out a tiny cry, then clack against the pony again. "*Noooo*," I had the pony say.

Hya giggled, lending her own pony to the skirmish. "No annoying your sister!" she shouted in her own high-pitched pony voice.

"So who won?" Ash asked, straight to the point.

"Did you forget about somebody else?" I asked with a smile. The smile dropped shortly. This hadn't been a game. I sighed and picked up the cat.

"While my sisters were fighting, and falling in love with each other's princes..."

"*What?*" said Ash, genuinely taken aback.

"Oh, oh!" said Hya, dropping her pony to the ground and squeezing her thighs. "Did the princes really get the princesses to switch sides?"

"The *champions*," I corrected. "But yes. It turns out both

princes were in love with the other prince's champion, and to win the war, they had to first take their true love away."

Hya gasped, but she seemed delighted to see the squirrel head over to the side led by the car, the pony to the shark.

Maybe the "true love" bit was laying it on a bit thick, but…

It didn't really feel *inaccurate*, either, from what little my sisters had let me see of that side of them.

"While they fought and they clashed, the champion of bloom plotted her own win." I picked up the cat. I still hadn't chosen the faery prince.

Hya did that for me, picking up a Wolverine action figure.

I had a sudden feeling that Orin would have been flattered, though the short, burly, hairy superhero looked nothing like the prince at all.

"Did the faery prince love her too?" she asked.

I winced. "No, no—not like that. I was only eight, and the faery prince wasn't interested in romance with anyone."

"With *anyone?*" Ash asked, cocking his head.

I nodded.

He grinned. Finally someone he could root for, and it was *him* of all people.

I took the Wolverine from Hya's hand and stared at it, as if I could work through my feelings with him instead of the real thing. My therapists had tried back then. I'd found the only way they'd really let me move on had been to eventually admit it had all been a fantasy in my head.

If only.

"The faery prince was tricky, and he was plotting against the vampires and merfolk before they even noticed," I said. "Eventually, he named me his champion and promised me one day I'd be a princess if I would defeat my sisters."

Hya frowned. "Like… fighting?"

"Like fighting." I sighed. I made the cat go up to the squirrel and the pony and offer them each a kick.

"Who won?" Ash reiterated.

"Well..." I frowned. How much could I tell them? "Technically, Ivy." I lifted up the squirrel. "As the champion of blood."

"Gross." Hya's shoulders bobbed, her nose wrinkling.

Ash's brow drew together. "And who... died?" He said that last word quieter.

Chewing on my lip, I picked up the shark, turning it over in my hands. Then I pushed aside some of the toys that I'd gathered behind him, then one behind the vampire car as well, and even more from the pile to represent the faery army I'd never explained to them.

"So many," I said softly.

"A prince?" asked Hya, a little bit of sorrow in her voice, too.

I nodded. "Just one."

She let out a sharp breath. "Is that why Ember doesn't have a boyfriend, even though she's so old?"

I chuckled. "You don't *have to* have a boyfriend, even when you're twenty-eight," I told her. "And twenty-eight is not *old*."

"Ivy has a boyfriend." Ash cringed.

She sort of did. We all thought. Even Dad and Mom and Noelle thought so... But no one wanted to come right out and ask her.

Except Ash, apparently.

"I don't know if she does," was all I said.

Ash rolled his eyes. "Then she gets awfully *mushy* with her *friend*." Leave it to the boy's cootie detector.

"Ashwood? Hyacinth?" Noelle's heels clomped down the wooden staircase. "Autumn, have you put in the order for the pizza yet?"

Oops. Forgot about that. Babysitter 101. Feed the kids.

"Not yet," I said, dropping the Wolverine and the cat as I stood from the ground. History. It was all ancient history. So why did it still make me so queasy?

"Pizza!" shouted Ash, jumping to his feet.

"Can we get the cheesy, cheesy, cheesy bread?" Hya was on her feet now, too, tugging on the green button-up shirt I'd left unbuttoned over my white tee underneath.

"That sounds like it might be one too many 'cheesies.'" Noelle appeared from the hallway, fixing an earring on a pale ear that almost got lost in her silver hair, pulled back into a bun. She looked around and frowned. "This better be cleaned up before you all go to bed."

The room *did* look like a twister had gone through the box of toys Dad had kept for me all these years. He'd brought it up from the basement before disappearing into the garage.

"Cheesy bread! Cheesy bread!" Hya whirled around the room and latched on to her mom's skirt. Noelle practically barreled over, working to extricate herself and smooth down the black material.

Behind me, Ash was already putting the toys back into the box without a word.

"Autumn, if you don't order soon, the kids are going to get antsy. *Antsier.*" Her pale hazel eyes widened, her head tilting slightly toward Hya, who continued to dance around her. "Antsy" referred to the sole hyper child she'd birthed. Perhaps all those years raising me with half-custody should have prepared her for that, though. "If they have to eat while you wait, make sure it's a healthy snack—where's your father?"

As if on cue, something metallic clashed in the garage.

Noelle rolled her eyes. "Working on the death trap again, I see."

"Death trap, death trap, death trap!" said Hya. I went to grab my phone off the nearby coffee table to order the pizza, the pre-programmed frequent order making it as smooth as telling it "order pizza" and the "forty minute" wait time counter popping up. Taking care not to wear out the delicate plastic hinges, I folded my paper-thin phone in half and stuck it in my jeans pocket.

"Mom, Autumn told us about vampires and mermen and faery princes!" Hya said, twirling in front of her mom.

"She did, did she?" Noelle frowned at me over her head, rubbing her neck. There was a faint set of dual puncture scars there, just like there was on mine, faded enough to be mistaken for freckles or moles on first glance.

"Besides the *princes*," said Ash, all matter-of-fact, "it was about sisters fighting to the death! *My* sisters!" He stared pointedly at Hya, a mischievous grin on his face.

"Not *me*!" she said, poking her head around Noelle's legs and sticking her tongue out at him.

"I'll have to fight you myself!" said Ash, chasing after her.

Hya squealed and they both darted down the hallway, into the dining room, and through the kitchen.

"No running inside!" Noelle cried. "Outside—and just for twenty minutes!"

She spun on me, her eyes narrowing.

Noelle had been unconscious during the worst of it, oblivious for the rest. She didn't have firsthand knowledge of a thing to do with what had happened. All she had was a set of scars on her neck from a vampire bite, a memory of a woozy feeling from its venom, the sight of a bed and breakfast destroyed, and the word of her husband, kids, and even husband's ex-wife that magic was real, and this had all really happened.

It'd be enough to make the most cynical person believe her entire family was out to gaslight her.

But for Noelle, family had won out.

"I don't think it's appropriate to discuss that with them," she said, her voice clipped.

I twirled a lock of hair around one finger. "It was just a story. Like a fairy tale."

Noelle pursed her lips. "A fairy tale based on your experiences?"

I bit my tongue.

Noelle sighed, massaging her temple. "Autumn, if you need to talk to someone about it again—"

"*No.*" Wincing, I took a step back. "I'm old enough now that they'd think I was psychotic if I kept insisting it was all real."

Noelle nodded, her gaze fixed over my head at the window overlooking the front yard. Late April in the Midwest, and the weather had decided to go for one of its warm spells instead of its late winters this year. The front yard was vibrantly green, the sun, though about to set, still shining in the twilight.

"Maybe you just need more friends," said Noelle, completely out of the blue.

"What?" I asked, wondering if I'd heard her wrong.

Noelle rubbed her puncture mark scars again. The more she rubbed, the more evident they became. I realized with a start she must have tried to cover them with concealer, so they were still a point of fixation with her. I rarely wore makeup to begin with, so I certainly wouldn't bother with concealer on my neck, but now she was making *me* rub my scars self-consciously.

"Your father and I have you watch the twins almost every weekend you're here," she said.

"It's fine," I said. "You can have a date night."

"But I feel bad—like we're taking advantage of you." She looked me up and down, as if my jeans and other casualwear would reveal it all. "If you have plans with friends, just let us know and we'll hire another babysitter or ask Lacey if she might come over." Lacey was Noelle's best friend and the mother of Ember's best friend, too.

"Lacey's a grandmother," I said, making Noelle's nose wrinkle just like Hya's so often did—Noelle and Lacey *were* the same age. "She's probably exhausted from looking after Journey's kid."

Noelle crossed her arms, ignoring the loud swear my dad let out from the garage as something else clattered to the ground. At least he would never get the death trap *running* at this rate.

"A young woman your age should have friends," she said.

"I do!" I protested. I struggled to think of a name that wasn't so obviously an online moniker, like my best friend—okay, online only, but still—PonyFan42U. "Scarlett," I said quickly, remembering the name PonyFan had given me once, though only when I'd pressed.

"Who's Scarlett?" she asked. The rest went unsaid. Why hadn't she met this supposed friend?

Noelle didn't put much faith in online relationships.

"And... And Alan!" I added, scrambling to deflect with someone she'd actually met. Alan Parr. We'd played together a little bit as kids. He'd been held back in school about five years ago, so we'd been in the same grade for a while.

"You still hang out with Alan?" Noelle's guard looked to be dropping.

"Well, um, yes… Sure." *In class*, I didn't add.

"Did he ask to you prom?"

My eyes widened. The room went silent, punctuated by distant, happy shrieks in the yard and more clangs from the garage.

"Why would he ask me to *that*?" He had a girlfriend. And prom was the last thing on my mind.

"Because prom is a rite of passage for any teen. Most teens, *well-adjusted* teens, want to go." Noelle shook her head, and it was that "well-adjusted" dig that made it so I couldn't bring myself to protest. "I think I should talk with your father and Glory about your lack of friends."

"I don't have—I don't have a *lack* of friends," I sputtered, darting past her and into the kitchen.

Dad shuffled inside from the garage just as I walked by, a streak of grease on his cheek as he wiped his hands on a rag. "What's eating you, sport?"

I swirled on him and practically *hissed*, not doing much to prove to any parent I was *well-adjusted*.

Dad shirked back.

"Autumn, don't just walk away from—*Easton*!" Noelle stumbled to a stop in the kitchen. "We have to be there in twenty minutes! What are you doing?"

"Getting ready." Dad chuckled.

"How are you going to *get ready* from *that*?" She gestured at his grimy T-shirt, his holey jeans, the dirt all over him.

"One leg at a time," Dad said, running a filthy hand through his salt-and-pepper hair.

Noelle practically shrieked when he moved toward her to try to kiss her, but I knew it was only because of the dirt and grime.

Opening the sliding door, I stepped outside as they kept bickering, the warm evening air like a balm to my face.

With a roar, Ash leaped out at me from around the corner of the house.

I jerked in place, my hand on my heart, a sheen of sweat dripping down my temple.

You killed them, I reminded myself, a not-so-infrequent mantra in my head. *You may not have dealt the blow, you may not have made the wish, but all those people—Ember's boyfriend—are dead because of you.*

Magic is gone from the world because of you.

My brother and sister laughed, unaware of the battle inside my head, running around the yard with all the innocence children their age should have had.

CHAPTER TWO

"Don't you think she's being ridiculous?" I tried to keep my voice down—the kids were in bed down the hall, supposedly sleeping. I munched on a cold piece of pizza as the story kept spilling from my lips to the phone I'd slipped into its dock on my end table. Above my bed, it projected the video from Seattle, two hours behind us, the sun still streaming through the window behind my older sister. Old school, Ivy had her end of the feed set up through a computer, and she folded her hands across the desk in front of her, the dynamic, angled cut of her dark bob crossing over one of her bright blue eyes as she readjusted herself in her office chair.

"Maybe," she said. "But you have to think about it this way: She's worried about you. We all are."

Letting out a big sigh, I tossed the crust of the pizza into the greasy box I'd stuck on my desk chair across the room. It was about as much use as the thing ever got.

"I'm fine," I said. I lied. Mostly fine. And that was good enough.

My stomach felt heavy, and I couldn't be sure if it was because of the excess pizza or the subject matter we were discussing.

"But you told the twins about what happened?" Ivy's thick, red lips frowned. If I hadn't known for sure that vampires didn't exist,

I'd wonder if someone had bitten her enough times to finally change her. Ashen and gorgeous, my sister exuded all the calm confidence that her vampire friends had once had.

"Not *really*," I said. "It was just a story to them."

Ivy scratched at her own neck then. We'd both been bitten by the same fledgling vampire mermaid at one point or another: our step-sister. "I did wonder if they should ever know... But I agree with Noelle. They're too young right now."

"*I* was younger than them when *I* found out." I flung back on my patchwork quilt and stared up at the projection on my pastel green ceiling.

"And we all feel awful about that." Ivy sighed and offered me a flittering smile. "Ember and I—we were kids, too, practically. Just like you are now. And you should be out there, having fun."

I'd forgotten. Ivy may have understood the whole uptight step-mother thing better than anyone else I could think to vent to, but a.) she'd only lived with her a year and b.) she'd had tons of friends. She still did. Ivy was one of *those* people.

Rolling over, I picked at a piece of lint on my comforter, offering my back to the projection. Ember was actually more like me. She'd only ever had a handful of friends and was plenty happy entertaining herself if need be.

But Noelle was Ember's *mom*, and Ember was almost every bit as uptight and "perfect" as her, so there was no way I'd vent to her about it.

"I don't care about prom," I mumbled.

"That's fine," said Ivy. "It was one of my favorite memories of high school myself, but it's not for everyone."

I growled and rolled back over to stare up at my sister. "I'm fine at home. There's nothing *to do* in town anyway."

"My friends and I didn't need anything special." Ivy shrugged. "Do the kids still hang out in Standing Springs Park?"

"You mean by the lake the merfolk used to swim in? I honestly don't know."

Everything came back to them. The vampires had won, techni-cally, so there'd been only one loss—their leader, and no one really considered it a loss, especially since she'd threatened Noelle and the twins before they'd been born. But the faefolk and the merfolk... So many of them had faded into nothingness before Ivy and Dean had swooped in to save the rest by making them human.

Too late for all of them, though.

"Well, it doesn't have to be there." Ivy tucked a stray strand of her sharp bob behind her ear. "There have to be geek kids around, too."

"Geek kids?" I narrowed my eyes up at my sister.

"You know—you like all that geeky stuff. Movies, TV shows, comics. Like Or—" She stopped herself.

"Orin?" I finished for her.

She frowned. *Of course* he would be the first "geek" who'd popped into her mind, despite the fact that it had been a decade. Ivy's friends didn't have fun interests like mine did.

And I had plenty of friends. Who cared if they were mostly online?

Groaning, I decided I'd had enough of everyone examining Autumn Sheppard under the microscope. "How's work?" I asked.

"Fine. Just fine. My work never ends." Ivy's grin practically stretched off her face. "Which reminds me—how're *your* post-school plans going?"

"Something like yours," I muttered.

"Are you still going to community college?" she asked.

The way she said it—as if *she* hadn't done the same. Well, after a year in the Peace Corps and another year just traipsing around the world.

Mom and Dad had been on edge the entire time, insisting on phone calls at least once a day.

That, and the community college she'd gone to had wound up being in Seattle, not our hometown. But whatever, a tech degree was a tech degree. She didn't get to lord it over me for staying local.

"Yes," I said shortly. "Mom said I could stay with her full-time, even if Dad and Noelle think I should be going somewhere else and living on campus. It'll be great. I'll still have my kitty and my routine." *And my safety net*, I wanted to add. How to explain a panic attack triggered by faeries to some random roommate?

"Do you know what field yet?" she asked, leaving any criticism left unsaid just yet.

I shrugged. "Starting with IT, but I don't know. Definitely not medical." Ivy was a phlebotomist. The career choice from the champion of blood. Rich.

Something crashed through my phone's speakers, like a glass shattering far off behind Ivy.

"Uh-oh," she said. "Just a sec."

She got up from her desk and opened her bedroom door, heading off down the hallway. Some muffled voices echoed out from behind her and I closed my eyes, almost drifting off, when I heard the shuffling of footfalls from the phone.

"Hey, Autumn!"

A bright and cheery, almost singsong voice snapped my eyes open. Long, golden hair over one shoulder, a colorful dress with what looked like illustrations of a scroll—or, as the visible bit of wording explained, the U.S. Constitution. Zelda Horne, former vampire, current elementary school teacher, and one of Ivy's housemates.

"Hi, Zelda." I waved. I didn't even care that she'd see me lying down on the bed. I was too tired to get up and besides, Zelda was like Ivy's fourth sister.

"Sorry about that." Her plump lips shifted into a wince. Her skin had a tan sheen to it despite the fact that the warm weather was still in its early days for the year, like she'd been enjoying her ability to hang out unimpeded in the sun in the past few years, weather be darned. "I was making dinner and I dropped a measuring cup. Shattered it, actually. Your sister is cleaning it up for me and told me to say *hello* after I bandaged myself up." She lifted her hand, showing off a rather large bandage wrapped around her index finger. "Cut myself picking up the pieces, and you know I can't stand the sight of blood." She made a choking sound in her throat.

The talk about dinner made me hungry again despite the

bloating sensation in my stomach and I got up, heading across the room for the rest of that cold piece.

"What's for dinner?" I asked, trying to think of what else to talk about. I couldn't remember if I'd ever attacked her when she'd been a vampire and I'd had the powers of the champion of bloom. All the wan-faced 1940s-style bloodsuckers kind of melded into one mass in my mind. At least the two former vampires Ivy still cared about had updated their wardrobe.

"Well, it *was* going to be Yorkshire pudding," she said. "A favorite of Ivy's from her travels—her and her comfort food." She rolled her eyes just as I sat back on the bed, stuffing the last of the crust in my mouth. "But then I realized even as I went to measure the flour that we didn't have enough eggs. I texted Dean—oh." She turned her head. I didn't hear what had caught her attention. "That must be him now." She turned back to face the camera. "Ivy told us she wants to have you come visit after graduation. We'd love to have you here!"

"She does?" That was news to me.

"Of course!" Zelda clasped her hands together and practically bounced on her heels, like she was addressing one of her students. "We'd love to have you for a couple of weeks. Even a month! There's so much to do in Seattle, and even if Ivy will be at work and Dean has the local branch of the moving company to worry about, I'll be off for the summer, so we can have plenty of time to catch up."

I offered her a flittering smile. Spending a month halfway across the country mostly getting to know a former vampire I wouldn't even be keeping in touch with if it weren't for Ivy's bizarre insistence on living with the two of them was not my ideal last summer before college.

Then again, it could get me out of helping out Mom and Noelle at Noelle's supply company, which, though it meant I wouldn't have to go out on any crazy adventures, was promising to bore me to death before classes started this fall.

"Maybe," I said. "I'll talk to Ivy and my mom." Dad wouldn't care either way, I was sure of it. A month in Seattle would beat traveling solo around the world for a couple of years in the stress-your-parents department anyway.

Ivy popped back into the bedroom doorway. "Dean's back with the eggs."

Zelda's eyes sparkled as she turned to the camera. "I'll leave you two to it, then. Bye, Autumn! Keep up with your studies!"

"How's Dean?" I asked Ivy as Zelda shuffled away.

We all had a sneaking suspicion Ivy was dating him again, which bothered Dad the most, but he felt he couldn't say anything since she was well into adulthood and she'd spent all that time apart from him to get to know herself a little better. Even if Dean, now technically a twenty-seven-year-old, a year younger than Ivy, had been born sometime in the 1920s.

What father would approve of his young daughter dating an old man?

"Fine," said Ivy, a smirk dancing on the corner of her lips.

Mom and Noelle sometimes thought maybe Dean and Zelda were the couple—they'd known each other since the '40s, after all, and they had all that baggage. Ivy had been the one to move in with *them* after a few years. Dean had bought the house after leaving town. Horne Moving Co. was still a thing with his former brothers and sisters—but they'd taken the show on the road, each opening up a branch in different parts of the country.

I thought maybe Dean and Zelda viewed each other more like siblings.

No one had the guts to ask.

"How's Alan?" Ivy asked.

Again with the Alan thing. At least it sort of made sense since Ivy had been good friends with Alan's older sister, Paisley, back when Ivy had been local.

"Fine, I guess," I said. "I see him at school sometimes, but we don't hang out anymore."

Ivy frowned.

I rolled my eyes. "He has a girlfriend. And whatever, I got over my crush on him like four years ago. Catch up, big sis."

"Well, we should have plenty of time for that if you do come this summer. I was going to ask you, but I heard Zelda getting to it first."

"Yeah..." I said, torn. Half of me thought it might be fun, but then I'd have to... you know, leave. Vacations were hectic enough. I liked my routines. I mean, not too many years after *all of that*, after the end of magic, there had been the pandemic and lockdowns, so I'd gotten even more used to it.

Staying home suited me just fine.

It was safe at home now. I knew my routine.

"Well, think about it," said Ivy, settling back down in front of her computer. "I'll let Mom and Dad know."

"Ive, Zelda told me you—oh, hello, little Autumn." Dean stood in Ivy's open bedroom doorway now, adjusting his tie. For a second, I had a flashback to him as a vampire, though the suit was decidedly tighter, more modern, and he wasn't wearing a hat that looked like something out of *Who Framed Roger Rabbit*.

"Not so little anymore." I flexed my puny arm at him, as if that would prove anything.

He chuckled. "Maybe not. Time flies... when it moves at all for you." A sheepish grin made his handsome face light up, his chiseled features, his pale brown hair complementing a healthier if still somewhat fair complexion. He even had a bit of stubble on his cheeks.

Ivy looked over her shoulder at Dean, then back at the camera, back and forth quick again. "We should get going," she said. "It's Zelda's turn to cook, but she always needs help." As if on cue, there was another shattering sound in the background, and both Ivy and Dean winced. "That's why I give her the easy recipes," Ivy added.

"I think 'easy' for Zelda might be a frozen meal," said Dean.

"Enjoy your dinner," I said, trying not to laugh. Zelda was a nice woman. She didn't deserve to have anyone laughing at her behind her back.

"Thanks, and, Autumn—I know she's frustrating, but Noelle has a point. I really wish you would do *something* fun before you graduate. Prom or not, just... Let yourself enjoy the last little bit of your childhood."

I opened my mouth to protest that I was eighteen, but she held up a hand.

"Just think about it. Love you, kiddo."

She was starting to sound like Dad.

"Love you, too," I said, reaching for the phone and switching off projector mode before hitting *end*.

I stared at the phone screen, swiping left and right, taking note of the few messages from my online friends.

PonyFan asked if I had any plans for my last summer before college because she'd just proposed a road trip with friends, but her parents had refused. They were practically keeping her under lock and key until she got to campus. She was a high school senior, too. A more "well-adjusted" one by the sounds of it, if staying home all summer was a disappointment. That and the fact that she had friends with whom she wanted to go on a trip to begin with.

Probably working at my step-mom's, I wrote back after telling her that was too bad about her parents and her trip. Before waiting for a reply, I slipped the phone into its charging dock and got up, deciding, though it was Friday night and even Dad and Noelle weren't back quite yet, it was time to get ready for bed.

CHAPTER THREE

Lunch at Union High School went either one of two ways for me. Hiding in the courtyard behind my favorite apple blossom tree or pining for the comfort of said tree as I stared at it through the cafeteria window, wishing it weren't pouring out just now.

At the end of a long table, the other people didn't bother me, leaving a wide berth four seats long between me and their large group. Freshmen, I thought. Or maybe sophomores. I didn't recognize any of them anyway.

The buzz of cafeteria conversation melted into an incoherent mess as I tapped my phone screen with one hand and held my sandwich with the other.

"Now *here's* someone who surely has the free time."

Jolting, I looked up, just as a chair loudly scraped against the linoleum floor.

Mikayla Jacobs slipped in the chair right across from me without making a sound. It was her boyfriend, my childhood friend and *maybe* former long-term crush, Alan Parr, who moved the chair beside her with enough ruckus to wake the dead.

The heads of the group at the other end of my table all turned toward us, taking me in with their analyzing stares for the first time. Putting the rest of my sandwich back into my open lunchbox, I sunk into my seat, wishing I had picked out something to wear that would let me blend into the beige-colored wall behind me. A thin, forest green sweater and a pair of jeans was too flashy just then.

"Mikayla," I said, nodding. "Alan. Um, hi?"

They didn't speak to me that often. Not outside of class, anyway. And certainly never Mikayla.

Mikayla flicked her straw-blonde braid over her shoulder, leaning forward and unintentionally giving me a good shot of her cleavage with the buttons undone down the front of her white, crinkly blouse. The guy a few chairs down from me seemed to zero in on it, too. "Autumn Sheppard, you've just been drafted."

My throat closed up like a vise, my eyes darting to Alan for help. He shrugged, his brow lifting almost apologetically. His light brown hair was so close-cropped against his tanned skin, he could probably etch designs into the fuzz like some kind of scalp labyrinth. "I told her you wouldn't be interested."

"Interested in what?" I folded up my phone and slipped it into my back pocket. I may have wanted to sink into the floor, but that didn't mean I wanted to be rude.

The group beside me had gone back to their conversation, the pressure of their curious gazes fading.

"Emergency Round 2 Prom Committee," said Mikayla, her hot pink lips parting into a Cheshire cat grin.

I laughed. Then I realized she wasn't joking.

"What does that even mean?"

"So, like, there was this Prom Committee put together earlier in the year..." Mikayla looked over her shoulder and lowered her voice, as if about to be busted. "And they totally bombed it. No coordination, never meeting—then one big massive argument about the theme."

"Okay..." I wondered where she was going with this.

"Jenna insulted Parker's taste in fabrics, Chloe told Becca, who told Maria that Chloe thought Maria's ideas were 'insipid'—she likes that word lately. Anyway, bottom line is: They imploded." Mikayla tossed her braid over her shoulder. "And Mrs. Burke knew

I needed this big project for my college applications—well, there's more to it than that, but it's a long story—and she knew I could handle stepping in, so... I'm in charge of Prom Committee now." She parked the tips of her fingers on her chest with a flourish. "I passed earlier in the year when I thought I might do yearbook, but that didn't work out with my part-time job at the time, so... Here we are. Date's been picked out and everything. We just need to come up with the theme and bring it all together."

"I'm not going to prom," I said, gripping my napkin between both hands. "I don't have a date."

Mikayla rolled her eyes. "I'm not asking you to go, I'm asking you to help with the planning—and you don't have to have a date to go." She threaded her arm through Alan's. "I'd go looking my red-carpet best whether or not this dork had asked me."

She would.

"I don't... I mean, I have to babysit a lot. For my brother and sister." Noelle would kill me if she knew I was using that as an excuse.

"Every single day?" Alan asked. "I thought you spent half the time with your mom." He turned to his girlfriend. "The twins are her dad and step-mom's."

The napkin was beginning to shred between my fingers. "Well, when I'm at my dad's," I muttered. The weekends only, really. And not for that long, not even every weekend.

"Autumn Sheppard, if you go through your entire high school career without a single extracurricular activity to show for it, what kind of memories are you even going to *have?*"

My full name kept falling too easily from Mikayla's lips.

"Classes," I muttered. "Homework. Lunch."

Alan laughed. Then his face fell. "You're serious."

Mikayla reached across the table and stilled my hand from pulverizing the last of my napkin into pulp. "You need this, girl. More than anyone." She gripped my hand harder, making me think maybe she needed it more. "Please. All of my close friends picked a side in the implosion—none of them will help."

Forcing a smile onto my face, I extricated my hand from hers. I had several options here, and now that my well of excuses had run dry, I felt like all I had left was to turn tail and hide.

"It's nice of you to think of me," I said, quickly zipping up my lunchbox, full of my half-eaten meal. *When you're out of other options, apparently.*

"Alan says you're very creative," Mikayla said. She wouldn't let this go. "I remember that myself—your first year here, you wore all those colorful outfits."

I grimaced, my hand still on my lunchbox zipper. My fashion choices as a kid might have been a bit bold, and I'd still been experimenting with rainbow colors and bright tulles and all of that by the time I'd enrolled in Union High.

A few weeks of pointed stares and giggles not-so-skillfully stifled behind hands had fixed me of that.

I gestured at myself. "I'm as dull as dishwater these days."

"Not just your clothes. What about the faeries?" Alan asked.

He didn't *look* like he'd meant to shoot me straight in the heart there, but that was what he'd done.

In some more vulnerable moments as a kid, I'd told Alan a bit about what had happened—the good parts, if there had been any, really. Before it had all gone to heck.

"What does that have to do with this?" I snapped.

Alan winced. "I thought they were pretty creative stories."

"My shrinks beg to differ."

Our voices were rising, and that crowd was staring at us again.

Gripping the handle of my lunchbox, I jumped to my feet and turned around, though my attention was still directed at Alan and Mikayla. "Sorry, and thank you, but sorry—"

"Whoa, watch it!"

My blood ran cold and I shuddered backward.

"Hey, Joel," said Mikayla from behind me. There was a silky, smooth tone in her voice that I'd have suspected was meant to be flirtatious if she weren't sitting arm-in-arm with her long-term boyfriend.

Or maybe it still was meant to be that way.

Joel Serafin, debatably the hottest guy in school.

I was on the "yes, he is" side of that debate.

There he stood. Holding his lunch tray full of spaghetti high over his head and looking down at me with a curling lip and dark eyes that seemed cold, flat, like I was gum under his shoe.

Or just a dolt who'd almost knocked into him while he'd been carrying his lunch, I supposed.

"Sorry," I said quickly, and if I weren't imagining things, the hotter my cheeks grew, the softer his expression did, the less tense his muscles as he lowered his tray and moved it out of the way.

"It's... It's fine." Joel let out a deep breath and behind him, some of his buddies called his name. A table of burnouts, people too cool to take school so seriously but clearly trying to take not-being-serious a little too seriously, awaited him, a single empty seat at the end of the table.

A gorgeous girl dressed in black, her black hair framing her heart-shaped face and olive complexion, stared back, her eyes narrowing on me.

With a jerk, my gaze turned back to Joel, but that was no better.

His dark, wavy hair was almost black, settling in disorganized layers all over his head, a single piece over one eye. His complexion was fair, but nothing like that of the vampires'. More like he was just one sunny day away from turning as tanned as the nearest jock, but he went to great pains to avoid even the slightest bit of color. Tall, he had a slight build, like he worked out when you weren't looking and had at least managed to sculpt those arms into firm, bulging lines. He seemed into, like, retro '90s fashion. Baggy flannel and cargo pants far too wide for his legs.

He certainly didn't seem to mind dressing to stand out.

"Did you pick out a topic for your English essay yet?" asked Mikayla behind me. She was talking over my head to Joel.

"What? Oh." Joel blinked, clutching his tray. "No."

I used the distraction to slip around him, pinning my back to the wall, jolting as I got a whiff of whatever deodorant or after-shave he used. It smelled... heavenly. Like a fresh breeze and warm cotton and a valley of wildflowers.

My toes and fingers tingled and I realized with a start I was stopped, pinned against the wall, just gazing up at him.

"Autumn, you're *on* the committee," said Mikayla, my presence not at all forgotten, apparently. "I'm putting down your name."

"Oh, no, I—" I gazed up and caught Joel's eyes again. He continued to study me, and I had no idea how to read what he was thinking just then. He no longer looked at me like I'd almost plastered marinara sauce all over his grunge T-shirt and open flannel shirt—which I *had* almost done—but he didn't seem to know what to make of me, either.

Me, the girl trapped between his tall body and the wall, just *standing* there.

"Yeah, sure, okay," I said quickly, my senses returning to me. Whatever got me out of there faster.

It was only when I was out in the mostly empty hallway that I realized what I'd just done.

CHAPTER FOUR

At least Noelle should be happy if I told her about this.

My number hadn't changed since middle school, which was a pity. If it had, Alan presumably wouldn't have given the information to Mikayla, who'd then texted me immediately.

A meeting time and place.

Today. After school.

I had my own car—a hand-me-down from Noelle, a sleek, all-business navy blue compact about five years old—so I didn't have the excuse of rearranging any pickup to get me out of it.

Monday was a Mom day, so I wasn't expected home to watch the kids after Dad dropped them off. Though my sisters had often had to pick me up when they'd been high school seniors and I'd been in elementary school, Dad's job had become more flexible over the past few years and he always got the twins from school.

Still, that meant I couldn't make dinner for Mom when she got off work. But she wouldn't mind. Besides, since she was Noelle's secretary—had been for almost a decade, since the previous one had been a vampire planted there for somewhat nefarious reasons —telling her would mean the news would soon enough travel to my step-mother, too.

And then they could both rejoice that strange Autumn was *doing* things that normal teens did.

Or that they did on paper, anyway. I had a feeling if "signing up for Prom Committee" was top of the "high school experience" charts, Mikayla wouldn't have been scraping the bottom of the barrel by enlisting me. She definitely wouldn't have been so pushy about it.

Letting out a tight breath, I read Mom's reply. *That's great, honey! So glad to hear you're having fun. Don't worry about dinner. I'll pick us both up something on the way home. Unless you go out to eat with your friends! Then don't worry about it. You can have what I bring for leftovers.*

Yeah, I wasn't about to have dinner with these "friends."

PonyFan had texted me during the school day, so to distract myself from the mess I'd gotten myself into and slow down the inevitable, I slipped down an empty hallway and opened her message.

Did you see they're rebooting Adventure Time? She punctuated the message with emojis of a sword, a dog, and a sequence of one red and one purple heart she often added to any good news.

What? I wrote back. I searched the news, and sure enough. One of my favorite childhood cartoons was coming back—and starting the canon anew.

You didn't set a search alert to the news? PonyFan was replying right now.

I checked my notifications, and yeah, there was something. I hadn't noticed. *Been... busy today*, I wrote.

Uh-oh. What does that mean?

Was it so weird that I might have been busy on occasion? Then again, I had made a point of typing in that ellipsis.

Why not spill the whole story? That was the beauty of online friendships. All the support and none of the embarrassment that came with interacting with people face-to-face. *So there's this guy. Out of my league.*

PonyFan didn't write anything back, like she knew I wasn't finished. I almost put the phone away, but I figured I couldn't leave her hanging.

I bumped into him at lunch. Like, literally. Might have knocked his tray toward him and peppered his shirt with spaghetti sauce in the ensuing mess. So I exaggerated a little. Painted a messier picture. I may as well have drenched him for how embarrassed I was feeling.

She finally started typing again. *Do you like him?*

That was the first question she had?

I sent a winking emoji. Yes, I could confide in her, but I'd hardly admitted it to myself. He was cute. Drool-worthy. He may have featured in a daydream or two, but I knew not to waste too much time on something that was never going to happen. *Does it matter? Out of my league.*

Well, I mean… I just thought it would make the whole thing worse. If you liked him.

He doesn't even know I exist. I avoided the temptation to add, "Though he probably does now."

No one is out of your league, FreeFall. "FreeFallFly" had been my screen name back when we'd first started messaging. It was supposed to be my own original pony character. She was really the only one who still called me that, though.

Snickering, I typed back, *Not even Chris Hemsworth?*

I said, 'No one is out of your league,' not 'No one is too old for you.' Besides, the Young Avengers should be more your style. No boomers. So late 40s was a "boomer" to PonyFan—or was he in his early 50s by now? Either way, he was technically a millennial.

You liked Black Widow! I typed back with a vengeance. She was barely younger than Hemsworth. PonyFan liked girls mostly, I knew that. She'd been crushing on Black Widow while I'd been crushing on Thor during our pre-teen years.

I like Marilyn Monroe, too, but that doesn't mean I'd seriously consider dating her. If she were alive. And over a hundred.

Okay, well, I solemnly swear not to date any actual boomers. Or whatever generation came before that. I thought briefly of my sister with Dean and the fact that he'd been born probably somewhere around the same time as Marilyn Monroe. I shuddered. And Orin had made Dean look like a baby, but I'd never liked him like that.

He'd been the cool older brother, the guy who'd had the patience to listen to me ramble about all my favorite shows and books and even engage me in bolstering my imagination. Of course, that had all been in the service of *using* me like a pawn. A murderous, vengeful pawn.

Well, that had brought back a well of terrible thoughts. My endorphins utterly crashed, I typed out "gtg" and slipped the phone into my back pocket. Readjusting my backpack on one shoulder, I took a deep breath before popping back around the corner and making my way to the art classroom.

Mikayla's voice echoed over the large space, though my brain refused to focus on the words as my cheeks flushed when every set of eyes in the place turned toward me.

At least there were only four other people.

Mikayla. Alan. And two other girls I didn't recognize—no, I'd had a class with one of them last year. She'd even been my lab partner. Prae Kharti.

Still. Not exactly a packed room. No wonder Mikayla had gotten desperate enough to recruit me. This was not the type of activity the typical teen did. The last committee's implosion testified to how devoted they'd all been to that.

Well, as long as my parents thought it was...

"You're late," said Mikayla, those hot pink lips in a tight line.

"Sorry," I said. "Had to go to the bathroom." Where I'd stayed an extra few or five or ten minutes to wait for the noise to die down outside and gather my courage to venture into the halls of Union High after school.

"Well, take a seat." Mikayla gestured to the gigantic art classroom—with its easels and clay and paint stains all on display—like there'd be a shortage for spots.

"This is Autumn Sheppard," Mikayla said to the two girls I wasn't that familiar with.

"I know," said Prae, her posture open, as if about to welcome me into a warm embrace. She was pretty in that kind of "girl next door" way. Long, thick black hair that cascaded down one shoulder in waves. Dark brown skin with just the slightest flaw here and there—marks from past and current battles with acne. But she didn't wear makeup to try to cover it all. Her charcoal black eyes were round beneath rimless glasses, and though she tried to drown it under a baggy sweatshirt, she was clearly hiding an hourglass figure. "We've had classes together."

Multiple classes then. Noelle did often say I had my head in the clouds.

I slipped onto a stool across from her and the other girl, sliding my backpack onto the table's rough wooden surface.

"Oh, good, so you know Prae. And this is…" Mikayla started. "Oh my goodness, I'm so sorry. I've forgotten already."

"Tia," said the other girl. She didn't offer a last name.

She had one of those faces… It was strange. At first, walking in, I'd hardly spared her a glance, but now, really looking at her, I felt like she was peering into my soul.

I shuddered at the sense of familiarity that washed over me but brushed it away. I was positive we'd never been in classes together.

Medium brown skin that was truly flawless. High, sharp cheekbones, a narrow nose, and warm brown eyes that would look too large on any other face—but they fit hers perfectly. Her coiled black hair was pulled back into a ponytail, her delicate hands crossed carefully on the surface of the table. Her jacket was almost like faux leather, a thick, roughened untreated version in brown that might have looked more at home in a steampunk version of a Renaissance Faire. She was thin—almost *too* skinny—beneath that jacket.

"Right. Tia," said Mikayla, oblivious to the way Tia's eyes were boring into me. "She just transferred."

Ah, that explained why she wasn't familiar. Though it didn't explain why her face was vaguely ringing some bells.

"A month and a half before graduation?" I found myself asking. I almost bit my tongue to try to stop the foolish question from escaping my lips, but it was out there.

Tia shrugged. "My cousin and I move around a lot."

Cousin? Now that was a question I was mildly curious to pose, but I'd hate if someone pried that much into my family history.

"Tia's parents passed ten years ago," said Prae, answering the question I hadn't even asked. "She was raised by her older cousin." Prae took Tia's hand in hers atop the table and squeezed.

Tia offered her a smile, but it was tight, the clear result of too much effort.

"Yes, that's, well..." Even Mikayla had the sense to look flustered for once. "We're so sorry to hear and so glad Prae roped you into—er, *recruited* you for this committee."

She stared at us from the front of the room, at Alan at the table behind the rest of us. She rolled her eyes and gestured for him to join us as she stepped back to the teacher's desk and grabbed a stack of papers.

With a screech, Alan shoved his stool back and slid in beside me, offering me a crooked grin. "Forgive my girlfriend. She's a little uptight."

"You think?" I blurted out.

Mikayla frowned as she approached the table. "Alan Parr, if you're whispering because you don't want me to hear something, you'd better hope it's because you're planning the next romantic date you have in store for me and you just want it to be a surprise." Her eyes narrowed as she passed out a piece of paper from her stack to the other four of us. There were still at least a couple dozen copies in her hand. She'd clearly been hoping for more turnout. She read off the top one, walking back and forth.

Alan scratched the back of his neck as he centered the paper in front of him on the table. It was a highly organized outline of the meeting's objectives, down to the minute.

Uptight was only the half of it.

"Since *someone* was late," Mikayla said, pausing in her pacing to direct a furrowed brow my way, "we'll skip the beginning, the history of the prom at Union High, the past few years' themes." She grinned broadly at us. "Alan was kind enough to lend me out to my childhood friend, Karl, last year so I could attend. It was 1920s-themed. I had this sparkly, frilly flapper dress... Not that *everyone* dressed to match the theme, mind you, but I think as members of the committee, this year we definitely should."

I raised my hand halfway up. "Unless we're not going, of course?"

Mikayla frowned at me, but it was the way Tia's head snapped sharply to me that almost made me jump off my stool.

"We could always use your help to make sure things are going smoothly," said Mikayla. "Chaperoning the refreshments table, taking tickets—that type of thing."

"But you said..." She *had* said I didn't have to go even if I helped with the committee at lunch. Right? Maybe not in so many words.

Mikayla's pink cheeks reddened and she slapped the pile onto the table. "Autumn, look around you! I've spent days trying to get my friends, my classmates, Key Club—*anyone* to sign up to help and this is all we've assembled! *This!*" She gestured at each of us pointedly, as if we were truly the bottom of the barrel.

"Kay, calm down," said Alan.

She shot him a look intended to melt his flesh from his bones and he folded in on himself. "Right. Your application. Got it."

"Application?" Prae asked.

Mikayla took a few deep breaths, her eyes closed, doing some kind of weird, new-age waterfall-like movements with her fingers in front of her face. Then she took one more deep breath and opened her eyes. "My top choice school had me on a waitlist," she said. "I had a callback and another interview, and I might have talked about how I was going to be in charge of the Prom Committee—you know, to show off my leadership skills. Mrs. Burke had asked me that morning if I'd be interested in taking over after the whole previous committee's... *implosion*... So anyway. That sealed the deal for me." She nodded, as much to herself as to anyone, and picked up her stack of papers again. "Let's see... 4:05, yes, let's brainstorm themes for the prom. We have four weeks, people, to get this done." She sounded like a stage manager.

Her college days might have hinged on this, but I was only here as a last resort. Oh, if it weren't for Noelle and Dad and Mom and even *Ivy* laying into me about spending more time with friends, I'd be out the door about now.

"Under the sea?" ventured Prae.

The edge of the paper curled in my fist, the crinkle echoing out against the vast, empty space of the classroom.

Alan came to my rescue. Sort of. "Autumn has a thing about mermaids."

Tia cocked her head, observing.

"A thing?" asked Prae.

"It's not... *a thing*," I said. "I just don't like... Don't like thinking about them." Because my actions had led to the deaths of a bunch of merfolk. I couldn't even bring myself to ask Ember if any merchildren had been among them.

I didn't want to know. I *couldn't* know or I might just collapse.

"Just mermaids?" asked Tia. Her lips pursed.

"Yeah, anything *else* we should know about that triggers yours fears?" Mikayla added, exasperated. "Clowns?"

Alan chuckled. "I'd be all for a clown-themed prom."

"Don't you even *joke* about that," snapped Mikayla. She massaged her temple with one hand.

Prae practically bounced in her seat. "A horror-themed prom *could* be pretty cool. Not just clowns. Serial killers and demons and—"

"Stop! Stop, stop, stop." Mikayla threw her stack of papers back on the table and clutched the edge of it, rocking back and forth as she tried to catch her breath. "This is not a haunted house. This is prom. The only prom most people will get to have in their lifetimes." She stood up straighter again, the beauty-queen smile on her face so fake, you could practically imagine the Vaseline on her teeth. "Think beauty. Loveliness. Happiness." She gestured with each word as if a hand model presenting the next item in a showcase.

"The forest," said Tia softly. "Woods. Trees. Nature."

"Yes," said Mikayla, her voice still deliberately airy. "Yes, that's the right train of thought. What could we do with a forest theme?"

"Woodland creatures?" Alan asked. "Like deer and rabbits. My dad even shoots some squirrels."

Mikayla slapped her face. "We're *not* doing a hunting theme."

"Sprites?" asked Prae. She looked back and forth between all of us.

Tia looked stone-faced at me.

"Little elves in the trees?" Alan asked. "Like the cartoon cookie men?"

"Faeries," said Tia softly, her face not turning from me at all.

"*That*'s it!" said Mikayla, clapping her hands together.

Only her voice was like a hollow echo in my head.

My skin felt flush, my head lightheaded. The way Tia's eyes bore into mine...

A king had looked at me like that once. A queen had promised me a life as a princess, living in a kingdom of endless forest.

Without telling me that forest would grow and engulf all of humankind.

Mikayla was up at the chalkboard, writing down, "Faery. Woodland" at the top, but I was shoving my stool back, my weak knees practically unable to hold my weight as I grabbed for my backpack.

Tia's gaze never left me.

"Where do you think you're going?" Mikayla snapped. "We've just started. We have to take a vote, brainstorm decoration ideas, put in an order for supplies—"

"I have to go," I said, turning on my heel.

"You've only been here ten minutes!" Mikayla cried.

But my heart was thundering so loud as I reached the classroom door exit, I couldn't hear anything else she shouted after me.

CHAPTER FIVE

I made a beeline for my car, my hands actually shaking as I walked and tried to fish my car fob out of my backpack at the same time. The pack, hanging halfway off one shoulder, swung wildly as I fumbled to clutch it against my chest.

There was a bite in the air as I stepped outside, the spring warmth retreating today in favor of a gusty, overcast early evening.

The parking lot was largely empty now, thought there was a straggler here and there, a few dressed in practice uniforms. As I neared my navy blue car, I hit the *unlock* button and the headlights flashed.

"Autumn!"

Just ignore her, just ignore her.

I had nothing against Prae, but the sooner I got away from here, the better I'd feel.

"Autumn, wait up!"

Opening the driver's side door, I let my backpack slip off my shoulder and tossed it across to the passenger seat. Only I forgot to zip it up after taking my key fob out and things scattered everywhere. Hair ties, tampons, cough drops, a pack of tissues, and even the charger for my phone, which settled obnoxiously below the brake.

Cursing, I leaned over to fetch the cord, still standing outside of the car.

Someone grabbed my arm and I spun around, my hands shooting out.

As if I were going to shoot vines at an attacker. Not a bad instinct to have back during the supernatural war that had raged on unnoticed under the vast majority of the world's noses. Not so appropriate to do to a nice classmate of mine ten years later.

Only it wasn't Prae.

Prae was back by the sidewalk, discussing something with Tia, both of them turning to glare at me every few seconds as if I'd lost my mind. No, if I was right about who Tia was, she could tell I hadn't. That look meant something else.

Pure loathing.

But more importantly—Orin had me in his grip.

My heart thundered, time seeming to slow down. Even through my sweater, his hand felt heavy, oppressive on my arm.

"You..." I stumbled to speak, to say anything more. "How... Why...?"

A twinkle danced in Orin's hazel brown eyes, the same effortless charm relaxing his warm features that had convinced me he'd been my cool, older-brother-like friend a decade back. It was subtle, but he'd aged—actually *aged*, after a thousand years of life. No more did specks of green dance in his wild, brown curls. There may even have been a white hair or two instead.

But there was just something heavy about the stubble on his once clean-shaven oak brown cheeks, the way his smooth skin seemed sunken, weighed down.

The dark bags under his eyes, which I'd never before seen.

"Hello, love." His attitude didn't seem as worn-down as the rest of him—but then again, he was a master of appearing nonchalant about world-shattering things.

I ripped my arm out of his grip, and he let it go.

Fumbling for my phone, I whipped it out, wishing I'd taken Dad's warnings seriously and carried the pepper spray he'd gotten me even to school.

"I'll call the police," I said, holding the phone out above me, as if to keep it from his grasp. Despite what I knew about magic being lost, I still braced myself for a gust of wind to tear it from me, to take my last hope away.

Orin gently directed my arm down again, gripping me by the wrist and clearly able to knock the phone from my grasp if he so chose. He *was* a head taller than me.

"No need for that," he said, his cockney English accent still in place, though I couldn't have told you how he'd developed it since he'd lived in the woods here in Midwest America for so long—long before there'd even *been* an America bulldozing itself across the land.

My gaze flicked behind him, where Prae's brow narrowed even more in concern.

I was clearly panicked and this man was manhandling me...

She stepped off the sidewalk, but Tia grabbed her arm, speaking to her. Prae kept looking over her shoulder at me, fumbling through an oversized tote over her arm as Tia spoke.

Tia *was* a faery. They *were* working together.

I hadn't been crazy for that to pop into my mind and send me scurrying out of that Prom Committee meeting.

"I'll scream," I said. "Prae... Prae will be a witness for me and you'll get arrested..." I winced, remembering my vow to only call the police if the situation truly warranted it. But this *did* warrant it. He'd *tricked* me! He'd almost gotten me killed—almost made me kill my sisters! The whole world!

None of which I could remotely begin to explain to a cop.

Slanting away from me, Orin let me go. "Just give a moment of your time, love. That's all I ask." He gestured behind him. "It won't be just you and me. Tia, too."

"Your *cousin?*" I sneered, cradling my phone.

He nodded. "Yes. She's actually my cousin. Her parents vanished with most of the rest of our kind."

Prae and Tia were headed toward us now, Prae's kind and open expression a contrast to the way she gripped something tight and stiffly against her side.

Some kind of spray bottle, I noticed.

So some of us were more prepared than others—and the one who'd actually been in a supernatural war was the one lacking.

"Everything all right?" Prae asked. "Autumn, Tia said you'd know her cousin? That he probably just wanted to say *hi*?"

Swallowing, I let the hand clutching my phone fall to my thigh. "I... I do. He used to... *babysit* me."

It was the best I could come up with.

"Oh." Prae's expression brightened. "You darted out of there so quickly, I thought something was wrong, and then you were shouting..."

"I startled her, that's all," said Orin. "She's a bit narky, then, understandably."

Prae blinked hard, staring up at the handsome former faery prince. It was the voice that had done it. I was watching her melt into goo in real time.

She tucked a strand of hair behind her ear. "You're British?" she asked.

Tia's eyebrow quirked as she crossed her arms tightly over her chest. She didn't speak with a foreign accent, which made me all the more certain Orin was just messing with us all. Though his parents *had* spoken more regally, like posh Londoners.

My stomach clenched at the thought of them, but they were dead now. Not even vanished like the others—dead before it had come to that.

"English specifically," said Orin, winking at her. "Don't get 'Britain' and 'England' confused, love."

English, my butt.

"I would never," said Prae, chuckling nervously, as if that even made sense.

She was lost—hard. *Ten years too old for you*, I wanted to tell her. *No, make that a thousand.*

"My cousin thought I might run into Autumn when I transferred to Union High," said Tia, speaking up for the first time since joining us. "Of course, I didn't realize when he came to pick me up today that Autumn and I would have attended the same meeting." Her perfectly even lips curled up into a devious smile, and I had *every* reason to believe she'd somehow found this out about me.

Had I been foolish, letting my guard down, just because I hadn't seen hide nor hair of a supernatural creature for more than half of my life thus far?

It had been a decade, but memories of it all haunted me daily. My palms sweated now as I remembered the warm *surge* I'd experienced when shooting out vines that seemed to have endless potential for growth.

I'd hurt people with them. Ember. Even Ivy. And Noelle... When she'd been carrying my baby brother and sister.

"Yes, well... It's been great." I turned on my heel quickly, yanking the charger out from under my brake before sitting down behind the steering wheel. "Got to go."

"What should we tell Mikayla?" Prae asked. "We still have work to do."

"I'm too busy to help," I mumbled, grabbing for the open driver's side door.

Orin shifted so the edge of the door clanked up against his hip. I tried pulling it shut again, hoping he'd move, but he just kept letting it crash against his side.

Tia turned to Prae. "Autumn and I will be there tomorrow," she said. "Just tell her we had to go home early."

"Tomorrow?" I pulled on the door again. Orin's slim hip was taking a beating.

"Yeah, Mikayla wants us to meet every day after school this week," said Prae. She shrugged as she slipped her bottle of pepper spray back into her tote. *No! Don't lower your guard around this guy!* "I'm counting it as community service hours. My mom and dad are strict on everyone in the family volunteering—and helping the school counts too."

"A verifiable saint, you are," said Orin, purposely leaning harder against the door as he fluttered those eyelashes down at the rather short-of-stature Prae. I kept nudging him with it.

She melted, clutching her tote to her chest as if it were a

stuffed animal. "Oh, uh... It's... I mean, my parents *make* me, but yeah, I get why. I try to give back." She tucked her hair back behind her ear again and I finally pulled so hard on the door, Orin stumbled a little.

He recovered smoothly, though, running a hand through his hair. "Be seeing you around, then, love, when I bring my cuz to and from the school."

"Yeah. Uh, okay, that'd be great. See you tomorrow, Tia, Autumn." Prae nodded at both of us in turn.

The door still wouldn't shut with Orin in its path, but Prae was walking away, oblivious to the fact that I was pummeling her crush with however many pounds of solid steel.

The door thumped and thumped against him every slow, steady step she made back to the school.

"All right, blimey!" Orin spun on his heel to face me once Prae had retreated indoors, his hand shooting out to stop the door from slamming into him one more time. "Get the hint. I can't let you leave without talking to me."

Still gripping the door, I at least stopped moving it, my gaze turning from Tia to Orin and back again.

Tia frowned. "You don't remember me exactly, do you?"

I blinked. "No..." I admitted. At first, it had been just Orin and me for so long. By the time the other faeries had come along, they'd spent so much time as little hand-sized creatures, I couldn't say I'd committed their features to memory or anything.

But there was one thing I knew... There hadn't been what I'd call faery children.

"Let me guess," I said. "Like Orin wasn't a twenty-year-old local bookstore owner, you're not a teenager at all, are you?"

Tia smiled, and for once, it didn't look like a cat about to pounce on her prey. "No. But I figured I could still pass for one." She gestured at her body, then at her cousin's. "Some of us are aging a little better than others in this new, magic-less world."

She *did* look like a teenager. If she was hundreds of years old at minimum, but she'd started aging ten years ago, there should have been *some* sign she was human now. Maybe she hadn't taken it as hard as Orin seemed to have.

But she still looked as regal and beautiful as the faeries always had in my mind. I closed my eyes and clutched the steering wheel, counting out my breaths to avoid the onslaught of anxiety gripping at my chest.

"I homeschooled her to catch her up with human subjects," said Orin, breaking through my concentration entirely unhelpfully.

"And he introduced me to every movie and book under the sun," added Tia. She didn't seem too pleased.

I tapped my forehead over and over against the steering wheel before snapping upright and opening my eyes. "So glad for you both." The key fob clutched in my hand, I stuck it in and hit the ignition button on the dashboard. "Now please go live your human lives somewhere far out of my sight."

"*Cheeky*." Orin *tsked*. "We need to have a proper chat, all right?"

"Don't care." I tapped my fingers on the steering wheel, staring straight ahead. "Try my sisters. Maybe they can kick your butt again."

"Ouch." Orin placed a hand over his heart. "You *do* know I let them win, yeah? That I didn't want my parents to rid the world of humanity?"

Tia *hmm*ed as she looked around. "I still don't know. The planet might have thanked us for that."

Orin smacked her shoulder lightly. "Forgive her," he said. "She's still learning to embrace the lives we've got."

"Well, I'm sure a therapist would love to hear it," I said, grabbing for the car door again. "Good-bye."

"Autumn." Orin stepped closer, once again sacrificing his hip to the edge of my car door. "Did Ember ever tell you about our final conversation all those years ago?"

I let the door rest against his hip. "No..." There was a lot my sisters hadn't told me about their own battle scars. They'd treated me like a kid. I supposed I had been, but... I wasn't anymore.

"I told her magic still exists—and I've spent the past ten years confirming that to be true."

I hesitated, the hum of the car's engine carrying out in the silence between us.

"How?" I asked.

Orin gripped my car door tightly, leaning forward. "Come with us for a cuppa. I'll tell you everything. Including my theory about how we can bring our fallen back from the void."

A gust of wind whipped out across the parking lot then, jostling my open car door even harder against Orin's side, but he remained still, staring down at me.

The wind had once been his to command. Right now, battering against us, it made me feel the gravity of his words—the power in them.

Because if I could bring back the merfolk, even the faeries who'd vanished alongside them...

If I could bring back Ember's high school boyfriend...

Maybe I wouldn't feel so guilty anymore.

CHAPTER SIX

I nursed the chocolate shake Journey's dad had served me almost as soon as I'd walked in. "The usual?" he'd asked.

I'd nodded, unable to do more than offer a flittering smile.

He'd only just served it to me when the door to the diner opened and in stepped Orin and Tia.

Orin smiled broadly, his hands stuffed in his pockets. Tia hugged herself tightly, taking in the place, but the only other customers just now were a man and a woman over in the corner opposite of me, more than halfway through their meal.

"Take a seat anywhere," Mr. Slowe said from the window that led back to the kitchen. Since his daughter had become a mother and an accountant, he'd had less help around the place. It wasn't a matter of family being cheaper, he'd told me one afternoon, but of family being the only ones he could really rely on to do it right.

Ember had told me that according to Journey, staff turnover was high because her dad was too demanding. He was still on her case about inheriting the family business—or at least convincing that husband of hers to take over if she didn't want to.

Her husband was a commercial pilot, though. One who knew *nothing* about Journey's brush with death as a vampire, so Ember said.

I couldn't blame her from keeping it a secret. Her parents had never found out, either. Noelle confided in her best friend about just about anything—but not something as strange as all that.

"I have to say," said Orin as he slid into the booth across from me, "despite owning a shop down the road for oh-so-many years, I've never had a chance to sample this place's... offerings." He cleared his throat as the door to the back swung open and Mr. Slowe stepped through.

"Friends of yours, Autumn?" he asked. He was a big man, built something like a linebacker. His close-cropped black hair was almost nonexistent on his scalp, partially due to hair loss and partially because the color blended in so well with his dark complexion.

"Acquaintances," I said, offering him another flittering smile.

He frowned as he gazed at Orin, but the tension in his shoulders relaxed somewhat when he took in Tia. Perhaps he figured she was more my age—even if she wasn't at all.

"What can I get you?" He grunted. He didn't bother pulling out a notepad—he got it right every time.

Orin reached for the laminated menu behind the napkin dispenser and grabbed it gingerly by the corner, as if it were covered in slime.

Mr. Slowe's chest rumbled, but Orin didn't take heed of it.

"Your finest..." Orin's lip curled. "Your finest... steak and eggs. Rare. Runny."

Tia flinched. "A salad. Vegan."

"Dressing?" Mr. Slowe asked.

"None," she answered simply.

"Drinks?" he asked both the former faeries.

"Tea's fine, mate," said Orin. "Iced, hot, whatever—though my cousin likes hers especially sweet."

Mr. Slowe grimaced, looking to me with his head cocked as if to ask why this guy was so strange, but I had no answers I could give him.

My stomach rumbled, though I wasn't sure I could handle a meal right now. "Scrambled eggs and toast," I said between sips of my chocolate shake.

At least that—that mild sweetness, the so-cold-it-almost-hurts tang—felt right.

Something felt right with the world.

Once Mr. Slowe had walked away, heading back toward the other two in the diner, Tia rolled her shoulders with a jerk. "I don't know how you can stand to eat animals products." She spoke to Orin, but her gaze flicked to me as well.

"We're human now, cuz. Get used to it."

"I've been *getting used to it* for ten years now." Tia scratched a long nail on the surface of the table. So she wasn't handling life as a human well, after all.

"There are humans who are vegan, too," I pointed out, almost as a defense of humankind. Even if it didn't apply to me.

Orin smirked. "Don't tell her that. Or she'll just use it against me."

"I already knew," said Tia. "How else did you think I knew the word 'vegan'?" She practically *sneered* at me, her deep eyes shooting daggers.

Sorry I spoke to you.

I sipped at my shake.

"So why here?" asked Tia. "Why did we have to meet here?"

The straw stopped picking up any shake, my sucking sounds echoing out against the metal cup. This whole place was intentionally designed to look something like one of those classic 1950s diners that had been kitsch longer than they'd been the actual trend.

"You suggested the woods," I said, referring to the long stretch of woods that circumvented much of the town, passing behind Dad and Noelle's place, wrapping around the small lake at Standing Springs Park.

"Yeah? We've got a nice place there," Orin said.

Tia snorted. "If there's *one* thing I like about human existence, it's walls with a little more insulation than that shabby cabin."

Orin nudged her. "Hey, with a fire roaring, that place is downright paradise."

"Yeah. For you. There's *no* room for me." Tia turned a rather pompous smile on me. "I *made him* get us a condo as long as we moved back here. He can go play recluse in his cabin whenever he wants, but I need my space."

Mr. Slowe passed by on his way to the kitchen again, and our table went quiet as he brought over Orin's and Tia's drink orders, two sweet teas, by the looks of it.

Tia took to hers greedily, reminding me of a hummingbird consuming nectar as she sipped on the long, paper straw.

"Don't you miss the woods?" I asked her.

She stopped drinking then, peering at me out of the corner of her eye. "I miss my family more."

Mr. Slowe hummed from the kitchen, the grill sizzling as he got to work. The couple in the other corner of the place got up. They were probably around my parents' age.

"Thanks again, Phil," the man shouted back at Mr. Slowe. "Delicious as always. We left the payment and the tip on the table."

"Take care," shouted Mr. Slowe.

The woman waved good-bye, and they both stepped out, getting into the only other vehicle out there beside Mr. Slowe's, mine, and the green smart car that had to be Orin's.

It was even quieter now, the noises from Mr. Slowe puttering around the kitchen loud enough that they no doubt drowned out our conversation from his ears.

"All right," I said. "I'm listening. You have until the end of this meal to convince me you have a plan, or I never want to see your faces again." I looked pointedly to Tia. "I don't care if you just *transferred*. Transfer again. Go away."

Tia cradled her glass of mostly just ice now, squeezing so hard, it looked about to crack. "Look, here, you little spoiled brat—"

"Now, now," said Orin, putting a hand on his cousin's shoulder. "We're not enemies here. We never were."

Tia poked at her ice with her straw. "If we never were enemies, then why did she ever surrender?"

So that was it. Yes, I blamed myself for everyone's deaths— because if I'd never become the champion of bloom, the war wouldn't have ended, and two sides wouldn't have been declared the losers, some saved only by Ivy and Dean's wish that supernatural creatures no longer exist and thus no longer be targeted by the magic erasing every faery and merperson. But there was the fact that if *I* hadn't surrendered, the faefolk specifically never would have lost.

I didn't feel bad about *that*. "Because your queen and king and prince, for that matter"—I shot Orin a dirty look—"tricked me, and though I feel bad about *most* of their deaths, I would choose the rest of world over letting the faefolk win any day."

Mr. Slowe must have flipped over Orin's steak then, the sizzle crackling out even louder than his humming.

"That aside..." Orin made a gesture as if picking something up and tossing it to the other side of him. "You know who can bring back souls who've passed through to the other side? I'm not talking about the proper dead—my parents are gone, and we're all the better for it." He looked at his cousin pointedly, but she just stared straight ahead, neither confirming nor denying what he'd said. "But those who vanished right into thin air? Those aren't the regular dead. Their bodies left with their souls. And I have it on the down low that *angels* can send their magic to the realm where they all are and yank them back here again."

"Angels," I said. The disbelief was evident in my voice.

The swinging door to the back popped open and Mr. Slowe hustled into the dining room, his melodic tune still humming over the air. "Here you are. Eggs and toast." The steam rising off my plate was making my mouth water. "Steak and eggs. Vegan salad." He leaned against the booth behind me, his other hand on his hip. "Anything else I can get you?"

"I'll take some water," I said.

"More tea, thank you," said Tia, offering him the first real smile she'd offered anyone all day.

Mr. Slowe practically melted under it. "Sure thing, sweetheart."

I raised an eyebrow as he took her empty glass. Tia was gorgeous, sure, but didn't he think she was younger than his daughter? And he was happily married, to boot, as far as I could tell.

I shook my head and dug in. These faeries and their effect on people.

It was another minute or so before Mr. Slowe came back with the tea and water and then bussed the table the other customers had used, pocketing the cash they'd left behind.

He hummed the whole while, and Orin and Tia both started eating. Orin with absolute *relish*, Tia shoving at the leaves in her bowl as if hoping to uncover some rare, succulent truffle she'd have no hope of finding in this place.

Finally, Mr. Slowe carried a bin of dishes to the back, using his back to open the door, and the door swung shut behind him.

I took a bite of my toast, relieved to find my appetite not too diminished after all. Orin was being ridiculous. And I would never need to see him again after this. "I'm surprised these *angels* didn't get involved in your supernatural war," I pointed out, almost chuckling. Almost.

"Angels are big picture," said Orin, nonplussed. "Like *gigantic* big picture. Cosmos, infinity, and all that." Orin spoke between bites and gestured his fork around. "They couldn't care less about who controlled this measly planet in one tiny, miniscule corner of the galaxy."

"A planet full of beauty and possibility," said Tia, finally sampling a bite. She chewed it, but slowly, as if it were an entirely unpleasant experience. "Squandered by humanity."

Orin rolled his eyes. "Yes, yes, we know, cuz. But to angels... Well, it's more of a place of exile, considering the most powerful of them can fly between the stars, see things our little brains can't even imagine."

"Exile?" I asked, putting down the crust of my toast.

"Ah, you caught on to that." Orin tilted his head. "Yes, the only angels we have any hope of reaching, I'm afraid, are the children of the fallen ones."

A single, skeptical laugh escaped my mouth. I looked from one cousin to the other. They were *good*. Still no tell that they were tricking me. "Fallen angels?"

"Exiled to Earth." Orin nodded.

I took a sip from my ice-cold water. He was really going forward with this.

"But Ivy and Dean wished all magic out of existence," I said, trying to poke holes in his outlandish theory. "The magic of the consummate lands, or whatever you called it. They saw to it. You two are proof of that."

Orin tapped the edge of his plate with the tines of his fork. "No, no, no. Their exact words were for *supernatural creatures to become human*," he said, as if that explained anything. "Not for the eradication of all magic. You sisters really didn't pay attention to these details, did you? Got to think before you speak, all right?"

I frowned. As if he had any right to lecture any of us about anything.

"Okay..." I said, rubbing a finger through the condensation on the side of my water glass. "So, by that logic, fallen angels should now be human, correct?"

"They're not supernatural," said Tia smugly. She set her fork down, her salad only half-devoured. "They exist outside of Earth's *nature* entirely."

"That..." Okay, they were starting to make sense, but it still felt like a stretch. "Supposing *that*'s true, well, they're exiled, aren't they? For what?" I tried thinking over the religious stories I knew about angels. "For siding with the"—I pointed to the floor—"the guy below against the big guy above? Seems like they might not be the helpful sort."

Orin snickered and leaned back in the booth, his arm stretching out behind his cousin. "The fallen angels I have in mind didn't fight firsthand in a celestial war. Those were exiled so long back, they have descendants. Tia and I—well, we think maybe one of *them* can be persuaded. They're not heartless, fallen angels. Far from it. The ones who fought against the *big guy in the sky* did so precisely *because* they wanted more freedom, a wider variety of experiences. I imagine it'd be a bit boring just mucking about in perfection for eternity. Great happiness only comes when you've also experienced great sadness."

I swallowed, not sure I agreed with the truth of that.

"Say I believe you," I said, the words less sarcastic out of my mouth than I'd thought they'd be. "Why did you never mention them to me?"

Orin shrugged. "I never mentioned werewolves to you, either, but that doesn't mean they didn't exist."

I stared at him—at Tia. Waiting.

"They didn't," said Tia curtly.

Orin nudged her shoulder again and Tia bounced, but her expression didn't budge from utter stoicism.

"Point is, there was never a way for fallen angels to get involved," said Orin, pushing aside his mostly empty plate and leaning his forearms on the table. "They can't just turn their powers on and off like that, even if they know about their family history. Whichever one of us won was really none of their concern, even if they would be rightly brassed off. But what could they do about it?"

"So why do you think they could now 'turn their powers on'?" I asked.

Tia smiled, then, and the devious curve of her lips was so much less friendly than it had been when speaking to Journey's dad.

"Because *you*, child, will activate one's abilities."

I blinked. "You sound as if you've actually found an angel. Like you have a specific one in mind."

"We have," said Orin. "We do." He took out a napkin from the dispenser, wiping his lips with it and elongating the suspense.

I had to count the breaths in my head to keep from screaming at him.

"And you're going to seduce him for us."

CHAPTER SEVEN

I laughed. Chuckled so hard and so wryly, even Mr. Slowe's humming stopped from the back of the restaurant.

My face fell at how unamused Orin and Tia seemed to be.

"You're *serious*," I said, my voice lowering.

Mr. Slowe's humming started up again, followed by the clink of dishes.

Neither former faery spoke.

"I'm a *high school senior*," I said, licking my lips, as I found my throat suddenly dry. "Not some experienced sexpot."

"Well, we need a high school senior girl," said Orin. "Cute. Able to turn on the charm. An older *sexpot* wouldn't be appropriate. The target is a high school senior, too."

I blinked—hard, staring at Tia. "A fallen angel... high school senior?"

She shrugged. "Like we said, the ones on Earth now are *descendants* of the angels. He's not actually older than eighteen like I am, if that's what you're worried about."

Though I knew they could only see the upper half of me, I gestured at myself. "But still... You thought I could turn the head of a *descendant of an angel?* Why not *you?*" I stared pointedly at Tia.

Orin grimaced. "We thought about that, but my cousin... just doesn't have what it takes."

Tia frowned. "Our kind doesn't *fall in love* usually. Few of us are interested in such things."

"Your parents?" I asked.

"Faefolk reproduce through different means," said Orin simply. "More like flowers than mammals."

"Which is why though there are a few scattered here and there, I worry our kind will once and for all truly die out, human now or not," added Tia. She stared down at her half-full iced tea.

"That's not fair," said Orin. "There's IVF and all sorts of human ways—"

"No," said Tia simply. "Not for me." She picked up her salad fork, but she wasn't using it for eating. "My child will be born of the bloom, as it was always meant to be."

I opened my mouth. Shut it. Then opened it again. "Is your aim the resurrection of those lost or... getting your powers back? Because I can tell you right now, I couldn't care *less* about you getting your powers back. In fact, I hope you never—"

The fork shook in Tia's hands.

Orin put a hand on her shoulder. "My cousin's opinions are not mine. But we both agree—yes, we want our friends and family back." He shook his head out a little, letting the dark curls dance over his brow. "You want them back, too, right? The merfolk sentenced to a punishment beyond their crimes. I mean, they *were* trying to flood the world, but surely, the *children* don't need to pay for their parents aiming to throw a spanner in the works."

Tia's grip loosened, the tension in her shoulders relaxing.

I wasn't ever going to be foolish enough to take a faery at their word, though.

They wanted their powers back.

They weren't going to get that.

But back to that other problem. Running my hands through my hair, I leaned back in my seat. "I wish I could help you, but I've never... I've never even been to a dance. I've never had a date. You're asking the wrong girl. And besides, what would *seducing* this guy have to do with—"

"'Seducing' may have been the wrong choice of word," said Tia, snapping her harsh look to the former faery prince. "But the thing is... We need the angel to fall in love."

Orin shifted awkwardly in the booth and reached into his back pocket, producing a creased and scuffed little spiral notebook. He flipped through the pages and pages of copious scribbles in smudged black ink. "We've spent the last ten years not just checking in to make sure our kind left got settled, but researching the descendants of the angels. Their abilities lie dormant, and may always do so throughout all of their lives—unless they experience true love."

I scoffed.

But Orin didn't seem to notice. He stopped at a certain page. "See here. In the fifteenth century, Jeanne D'Arc in France—"

"Joan of Arc?" I repeated.

Orin's eyes narrowed. "As I said. Her leading the French troops is well known to this day, but her divinity... Well, the evidence that she displayed some celestial abilities was hidden away. She was rewarded with sainthood, but sometimes there's such a thing as *too* much evidence. No need to test the populace's faith if it's all right there as plain as day."

Mr. Slowe burst out from the back, rubbing his hands on his apron. "Anything else I can get you kids?"

"No, we're finished," said Tia, stacking her bowl and Orin's plate and shoving them toward the end of the table. "Just the check, thank you."

Mr. Slowe started gathering everything he could handle, leaving behind only the drinks. "Three separate checks?" he asked.

"One will do." Orin dug in his other back pocket and produced a wallet, then a steel-black credit card.

Mr. Slowe's eyes popped when he saw it, but he took it without a word as he balanced the dishes and shuffled away.

"I see humanity hasn't been too much of a struggle for you," I said, guessing the card meant something like a high credit limit. Noelle had one for her business only and was sometimes a little *too* proud to show it off when she judged a meal with my parents a business expense.

"I was here a long time before that," said Orin, his eyes twinkling. "Had enough to keep a failing business afloat, didn't I?" The nearby bookstore he'd once run. It actually still appeared to be there, but it was never open. Never.

"He owns the building," Tia said, as if reading my mind. "And he still pays to keep the lights on in the place."

"My cats need *someplace* to call home, don't they? They much prefer my stacks of bookshelves to the dull condo. And they won't leave well enough alone at the cabin." His eyes sparkled. "Even without the shiny colors, that ball still attracts them. Little paws bobbing it this way, knocking it that. Troublemakers, the lot of them."

Shiny-colored ball? I cocked my head.

Tia played with the straw in her drink. "He lost one cat to old age and he replaced it with *three* kittens."

"They're proper cats now," he said, flipping through the pages of his notebook once more. "Have to pay someone to check in on them and feed them when I'm out of town, but it's worth it." He looked up at me and smiled. "Nothing like a bookstore cat, eh?"

I thought of my own Blossom at home. Noelle had had a cat once, too, but he'd been Ember's and she'd taken him with her after school. He'd only lived a short while after that. But I liked to think he'd preferred living his last few years that way. Quiet. Just him and Ember. Noelle's house had become rather noisy toward the end there.

I took a sip of water and shook my head. *Focus.*

"Joan of Arc is partly famous for her virginity," I said. "So say I believe you that she was genuinely celestial and history just rushed to cover that all up." I did know firsthand that magic was—had been—real, after all. "Where does true love come into play?"

Orin looked up from his notebook and tossed his hair back. "A virgin she may have been. But that doesn't matter. It's an awakening of the *heart* that activates the magic."

"So... Joan's true love was her God?" I asked.

Orin shrugged. "Perhaps. Or perhaps there was a person on this Earth who inspired her desire to move mountains. Perhaps she took a lover and history wrote that out, too. Requited or not, virgin or not, every instance of celestial activity we've uncovered can be traced to a descendant of an angel experiencing what fallen angels all found it worth falling to Earth for: Emotion. Love. Despair. Even hate."

"By that logic, I could get this guy you have in mind to *hate* me, too," I pointed out.

"That wouldn't activate the powers we need. Besides, then he wouldn't be likely to help us—you—would he?" Tia said through clenched teeth.

"That's right. Love." Orin slapped his notebook closed and pushed it across the table toward me. "Love is the way."

Mr. Slowe came back from the back of the kitchen, ringing up our transaction at the register near the door.

My hand touched the top of the notebook. I was sure it was filled with more examples like Joan of Arc. It wouldn't matter. Orin couldn't prove any of this was real—not with scribbled messes like the rantings of a madman on a wall.

Mr. Slowe came over with the card and receipt, a bright look on his face. "I hope you'll come back here," he said. "Any friends of Autumn are especially welcome."

Tia smiled warmly at him and he practically flushed. Orin took his card and scribbled on the receipt with an offered pen, leaving, I noticed, a tip more than twice the cost of the bill.

"Absolutely," said Orin. "Thank you, sir. What a fine establishment you have here."

He slipped the paper and pen toward Mr. Slowe and the older man's eyes practically bugged out of his head.

"Thank *you*, sir," Mr. Slowe said. He chuckled and tucked the receipt away. "You be sure to say *hi* next time you stop by. I'll make sure I give you something extra special." He winked and started whistling, heading back behind the swinging kitchen door.

"I do hope it's not a free bucket of lard," said Tia, her nose wrinkling. She sipped the last of her tea before adding, "This whole place reeks of it."

Orin clamped his lips together and leaned back into the booth.

I shoved the notebook back to him, not even having bothered to lift the top page.

"It would be *easier* for me to inspire someone to hate me," I said simply. "At the most—if I was very, very lucky and got some wicked makeover and some lessons in how a normal girl acts, I could maybe, *maybe*, score a date. But if your plan depends on getting someone to experience *true love* for me, you're out of your minds."

"Oh?" said Orin. "I think you're underestimating yourself."

I rolled my eyes. "Okay, look, whatever examples you've found in that notebook—I take it they're not everyday occurrences, right? No angel DNA activating powers in half the population?"

"There aren't *that many* descendants," said Orin curtly. "There's another factor, how both mother and father have to have a high percentage of DNA from a seraphim angel—"

"That aside," I said, not ready to get into the nitty-gritty of angel hierarchy just then. "Angel-humans fall in love, right? Get married? Have babies?"

"Yes," said Tia.

"So how often is this love considered *true*?" This was like something out of a fairy tale. "If I even managed to get this guy to fall in love—and that's a big *if*—it's going to be a high school love at most. Shallow, fleeting... Maybe a lucky couple makes it, a life with their high school sweetheart." I shook my head. "But my parents couldn't even make *college* sweethearts work, and they at least were out of their parents' houses when they met."

Tia gripped her glass a little too hard again. "We *need* this to work—"

Orin raised a hand, cutting her off. "How about this, love? How about you don't worry so much about *forcing* the love to happen and you just start off as friends with this boy, okay?"

I opened my mouth to respond—that was impossible for me, too. Unless we chatted online, but even then...

"You're thinking too hard again, eh?" Orin made a little spinning gesture with his finger. "I can see all those gears turning in your head." He laid his palms flat on the table. "Please. Just try it. Friends, okay? That's not so bad, innit?"

Did he know whom he was talking to? "Why me?" I asked, quieter.

"Why indeed?" asked Tia, her brow furrowed.

Orin let out a deep breath. "You're the only one who'd understand. You're the only one who wants what we do. You like boys, yes?"

My eyes stung as I felt heat rushing to my cheeks. "Yes..." I mumbled.

"So we're not asking the impossible of you, right?" Orin prodded.

"Not in the loosest possible sense." I rubbed my water glass, the condensation having faded and my fingers squeaking on the warming surface.

"Your sisters—they fell in love at your age, too. With princes, no less," said Orin. "For you, I've got an angel in mind. Bit of an upgrade, if you ask me."

"They weren't me."

"Nor would I expect them to succeed." Orin reached over and took my hand off my water glass, offering it a squeeze. His sly smile was disarming, friendly. "This mission is too important for a typical teen. But *you*, Autumn Sheppard, are no average teenage girl."

He said that as if he meant it in a good way.

Tia scooted out of her booth, and Orin slid out after her.

I didn't move to follow them.

"Think about it," said Orin, nodding to the notebook he hadn't taken back. "You can just start as friends, all right?"

No, it wasn't all right. It wasn't all right at all.

I sighed. Out of the corner of my eye, a dark purple vehicle pulled up into the lot in a spot not too far from our booth at the window. "Is this boy even *local*?" I asked. I wasn't sure that would make it easier. "If not, maybe I can approach him online—"

"He's at the school," said Tia bluntly.

I startled, my head whipping up to her. "What kind of coincidence is *that*?"

Orin gestured around him. "Consummate lands. The kind of magic that was here sometimes attracts his kind." He shrugged. "If I'd have known that, I wouldn't have bothered searching the world to discover where the various lines of angels had settled. But it all led us back here. To you. The only girl in the world who can help us see this through."

I swallowed, looking away again.

"We'll talk again soon, then, all right? You just think on it. Think about what success could mean—not just for you, but those you hold dear." Orin rapped his knuckles against the table and the two of them turned.

My hand settled on Orin's worn notebook, and then I stood. "Wait!" I said as they reached the door. "You didn't tell me who—"

But the words died in my throat.

In the little vestibule between the outer doors and inner doors that led to and from the diner, Orin and Tia stood face to face with my step-sister.

Ember Goodwin.

CHAPTER EIGHT

Ember, her long, almost-white blonde hair swept to one side in a ponytail that fell across her chest, stumbled back into the outer door.

Orin was talking to her, Tia standing to his side with her arms across her chest, like his silent bodyguard.

I opened the inner door, cramming myself in with the three others lingering in the rather small vestibule.

"Autumn?" Ember's brown eyes widened, her oval face slack.

"Now we're well in it, I figure. We were just—" started Orin.

"Go," I told him. "Just go. I'll talk to her."

Orin raised an eyebrow and held up his hands in surrender. He headed toward the door, and Ember, still clearly dumbfounded, slipped aside to let the former faeries pass. Tia narrowed her eyes and gave us both an "I'm watching you" look as Orin held the door for her and the two headed to their small car.

Ember didn't say anything, her gaze fixed on watching them go.

Then she spun on me.

"What are you doing with them?!" The words practically spilled out of her mouth, each one full of force and accusation.

"It's complicated," I managed.

"I imagine." Now it was Ember's turn to cross her arms. She was half a head shorter than I was, and there was just an airy, princess-like softness to her at all times, even when she and I had been fighting, so it was less intimidating than she probably intended it to be.

The door opened behind me.

"You kids forgot your notebook," came Mr. Slowe's deep, hearty voice from behind me. "Ember! What are you doing in town?"

"Thank you," I said quietly, taking the worn-down scribbles of a mad faery from Mr. Slowe's outstretched hand. I filed back into the diner, and Ember stepped in cautiously behind me, checking left and right.

Then her frown vanished and she offered Mr. Slowe a hug. "I'm staying with my mom and the twins for a month," she said. That was news to me. She stepped back from the hug. "Sort of a last-minute thing. I'm off to Florida for another Atlantic exploration for a few months starting in late May, and I thought I'd use the free time to hang out with the family." She shot me a wary look, her gaze settling ominously on the notebook in my hand.

I shoved it into my back jeans pocket, even though half of it still stuck out.

"Journey and Lacey will be so glad to see you!" he said, referring to his daughter and wife. "And little Jerrica! Wait until you see how big she's getting." Speaking of his granddaughter, his face melted into happiness as he hooked his thumbs under his apron straps.

"I just texted Journey," said Ember, smiling. "We're definitely going to hang out."

"Good," said Mr. Slowe, stepping back to let Ember farther inside. "She misses you, always traipsing around to different under-water adventures—moving off to Chicago."

"I'm a marine biologist," she said. "That kind of thing kind of comes with the territory. And there aren't exactly aquariums posting jobs around here." She laughed.

My hand rested on the notebook sticking out of my back pocket, partly to make sure it didn't fall out and partly because... I felt the weight of her life choices. Did she miss being a mermaid, having free rein of the lakes and oceans? Was it some sort of way to still feel connected to that part of her... to the prince who'd vanished to save her?

I felt more determined than ever to see Orin's plan through. It was ridiculous and I had no hope of success... But I had no other way to try to bring back those we'd lost that day.

"Well, come on in," said Mr. Slowe. "I hope to see plenty of you while we have you in town."

Ember looked up at me. "Well, I was going to get dinner to go for the family..."

"I'm with Mom today," I told her simply. "And I already ate." I was eighteen now, so there was no court order saying I had to split my time between Mom and Dad, but I still did. More or less. More casually, without specific set days. Sometimes, when I wanted some peace and quiet, I'd spend a few extra days at Mom's.

Ember's hand shot out to grab mine. "You know what? I'll put in the order and have some coffee here while I wait. Autumn will sit with me and have dessert."

"But I don't—" I started.

Mr. Slowe chuckled. "Come on now. Sit at the counter and I'll give you both a slice of apple pie on the house." He winked at us. "I won't tell anyone about Ember eating dessert before dinner if you don't."

"Sounds great." Ember's hand squeezed mine. "Thank you so much." She practically dragged me over to the counter, causing me to stumble behind her, as far away from the opening overlooking the kitchen as she could seat us.

Taking a steeling breath, I sat on a stool, wincing as the spiral of the notebook poked into my butt. Carefully removing it from the pocket, I tucked it on my lap, under the counter, as Ember grabbed a menu and started up an order large enough to feed ten, let alone five of them.

"Ash won't eat the chicken," I told her when she got to the kids' meals. "It's mac and cheese he likes the most."

Ember nodded thoughtfully and still ordered double the chicken, but she added two orders of kids' mac and cheese, too.

Squeezing the notebook with one hand, I rapped the counter

with the fingers of my other, staring off at a faded illustration on the wall of a bunch of teenage girls in poodle skirts.

Ember finally sat down beside me, putting the menu back in its holder.

"So." She crossed her hands in front of her on the table.

I didn't say anything.

Mr. Slowe came back with a pot of coffee and Ember turned over the mug that was waiting in front of her. I shook my head when he offered me the same.

"What else is new in Ember Land?" Mr. Slowe asked, and though I could tell Ember was grimacing at the continued interruption, she covered it well. All the more time for me to gather my thoughts.

"Nothing much. My brother and his wife had a second baby." That was her older half-brother on her father's side, of course. "Oh, and I decided I'm getting another cat when I get back from this trip. Mom offered to cat-sit at her house whenever I'm going to be gone for more than a few days."

"Another kid for Auntie Ember to visit, huh?" Mr. Slowe put the coffee pot down. "And for you... a cat. They're cute and cuddly, sure, but what would your *boyfriend* think about that? He a cat person?"

Ember slunk into her seat.

"Girlfriend?" Mr. Slowe asked.

She shook her head. "No one right now. Um..." She cleared her throat, cradling the mug of steaming coffee in her hand. "Too busy." She took a sip of it, straight black.

Mr. Slowe offered a "hmm" and went over to the fridge behind the counter, where most of the desserts were on display. Taking out an apple pie missing a single slice, he grabbed two small plates from under the counter, too. "You about broke my nephew's heart all those years back, you know that?"

Ember's eyes practically bulged out of her head. "How... How is Dante? Journey doesn't talk about him much. With me, anyway."

"Fine, just fine. Want these warmed up? Ice cream?" he asked. Ember and I both shook our heads, me because I was eager to get out of here, and her probably because she was in no mood to prolong the conversation. "He's working as a waiter in Brooklyn, trying to be the next big thing, like every other upstart. Got some bit role in an off-off-Broadway play, though."

"That's great!" Ember said. She seemed genuinely happy as Mr. Slowe slid the slices in front of both of us and went to put the rest of the pie back in the fridge. "I'm really happy to hear."

Mr. Slowe raised an eyebrow. "Got himself a fiancée. Journey tell you?"

"No." Ember's shoulders slouched, but she recovered quickly, straightening her back. "I'm happy for him." She sipped some more of her coffee then, with renewed focus.

Mr. Slowe chuckled and headed back to the swinging door to the kitchen. "Just waiting on my invite to *your* wedding, Ember."

"You'll be waiting another few decades, then, at least," said Ember softly, her tone cheery but forced.

The swinging door clanked back and forth, Mr. Slowe's melodies filling out the place again.

Ember had always been awkward around guys—around anyone, other than her best friend—too. Sure, she'd dated more than I had —but not until her senior year, if I remembered correctly.

I wasn't about to count the few weeks she'd dated Dean as the champion of blood because I knew how disastrously that had ended for her. But then there'd been Calder, and then after a few months of mourning, Dante Johnson, Journey's cousin. But that had only lasted about a month before Ember had told him she couldn't do it. That she hadn't been ready to move on. But then, that summer, before she'd left for college...

"Didn't you date some guy named Joe, too?" I asked.

Ember, who'd been gulping another sip of coffee, spit it back into her cup.

She wiped her lips and shook her head at me. "Why on Earth are you asking me that?"

I shrugged. How to begin to explain? If she knew it was to help in a plan proposed by Orin, she wouldn't help me.

"I'm just wondering if I'm misremembering."

Ember flushed. "No, you're not. I did. We were total opposites, and it was never serious for me, but..." She was sputtering now. "Why am I getting the third degree here from him—from *you*? *You* owe me an explanation, missy."

I started digging into my pie with gusto, stuffing my mouth. It was so good, though, I almost felt my guard melting away.

Ember leaned forward and snatched the notebook out from my lap.

"Hey!" I protested, but she was already flipping through it.

She cocked her head. "What *is* this?" She looked a little wary, like she'd just realized she might have been holding the manifesto of a serial killer.

I snatched it back and clutched it to my lap, harder this time. "None of your business."

"Excuse me?" Ember raised a brow. "Do you want me to tell your dad? Is it *his* business what his daughter is up to with the faery prince who nearly killed his wife?"

"He didn't *almost kill her*."

"Oh, right. That was *you*," said Ember, bitterness coating her voice. She stabbed her pie a few times.

We were at a stalemate, both stuffing our faces with pie, Ember gulping down her coffee like it was a chore instead of a pleasure.

My mouth was dry, but I didn't want to speak up, to ask for anything to drink. I just finished my pie and dropped my fork down to the plate with a clatter.

"Don't tell my parents I was with them, okay? They'll just worry." I moved to stand up.

Ember grabbed hold of my elbow. "I'm sorry, okay? I shouldn't have said that."

I ripped my arm out of her grip. Then I sighed. "You weren't wrong."

"You were a kid," she said softly. "*He's* the one responsible. He's a manipulative monster, Autumn, and if you think I'm just going to *let* you do anything with him—"

"You don't get to *let* me do or not do anything," I said. "You're my step-sister, not my guardian." I narrowed my eyes at her.

"Besides, it sounds like he came to you for help and you wouldn't do it. So you had your chance. Now it's up to me."

Ember's head flinched back slightly. "What are you talking about?"

I sat back down at the booth, lowering my voice. Mr. Slowe's kitchen was drowning in noise, from his singing to the sizzling to the fan, but I didn't want him to overhear.

"He said he told you—about angels."

Ember blinked over and over. Then she laughed. "I... I guess? Like right after it was all over. But I'd trust him about as far as I could throw him, which"—she gestured at her arms, thin and willowy beneath a pale red blouse—"is not far."

I clutched the notebook tighter. "What if I believe him?"

Ember opened her mouth and I shook my head.

"No, listen. I know not to trust him. I do. I'm still wary around him, and I'll be careful, I swear."

Ember's lips settled into a thin line. "What did he ask you to do?"

I wanted to tell her. The words were rushing up and into my mouth, but my neck and ears felt impossibly hot, and a shortened version of the truth came out instead. "Make a friend."

"Make a... friend," she said, as if that were the strangest thing she'd ever heard. "With an angel, I presume?"

"Yes." *Only I don't even know who he is yet.* "And then we can ask him for help."

"Him?" Ember lifted a brow and cradled her coffee cup in the air in front of her.

She'd caught that.

"Yes, and well, I... My only friends are online. I haven't been alone with a guy my age since like... ever." Alan didn't count. His or my parents had always been around when we'd hung out together.

"Not everyone is a social queen bee." Ember took another sip and then put her empty cup down on its saucer. "You don't have to have dated before leaving high school. I wish someone had told me that was normal back when I was your age. I might not have rushed headfirst into..." She left the rest unsaid. Dean had been her first boyfriend. And Dean had always preferred Ivy, had only needed Ember for the vampire-mermaid-faery war.

"Yes, well, I never minded it before. Now I'm supposed to make this guy—" I stopped myself.

"Make this guy…?" Ember prompted.

"Make him like me," I admitted. Let her take that either way. "And first, he has to actually look at me." I winced.

Ember did, studying me for a while. "I see a beautiful young woman, creative, charming, funny—any number of people would like to be your friend. I wouldn't be against you setting out to make a new friend. But I don't like that *he*'s telling you what to do. What do you expect this *angel boy* to do for you?"

"Bring them back," I said quietly, digging my finger into the small space inside the notebook's spiral.

"Bring who back?" said Ember, picking up her fork to finish her pie.

"The faefolk, the merfolk—anyone who disappeared before Ivy and Dean could turn them human."

Ember's fork clattered to her plate, her already pale skin growing somehow more ashen. "He's *lying*," she said, her voice croaking.

"I believe him," I said. "I *have to*. Don't you see? I have to at least try."

"No, you don't." Ember put her hand atop mine under the counter. "Autumn, we can't get back those we lost. And even if we could, no one expects *you* to take that burden on yourself."

I stood again, forcing her hand to fall.

"Yes, but no one but me would do this, either. No one else *could* do it. And the least you could do is not stop me from trying."

Ember opened her mouth, and the swinging door opened again, Mr. Slowe coming back in with two large takeout bags in either hand.

"Don't tell anyone," I whispered. "Not my parents—not Ivy. And I promise I'll keep you in the know."

Ember's posture deflated.

"You're going to be here the next few weeks, right?" I said, louder this time. "We can get together a number of times."

"The Goodwin-Sheppard family order," said Mr. Slowe, placing the bags on the counter in front of us. "Can I get you girls anything else? More coffee?"

"No, thank you," I said. "But thanks for the pie." I turned on my heel, but then I spun one more time to lock eyes with Ember. "Trust me. Trust me because this is your *only* chance to see him again."

Ember blinked, staring down at the crust of her pie.

"See who again?" asked Mr. Slowe. "Is your little sister acting matchmaker for you?"

"Yes," I said before Ember could give him a non-answer. "If she'll let me."

Ember had no response.

CHAPTER NINE

"After you two left yesterday, Mikayla had another idea."

It was between second and third period, and Prae had somehow found me on my way to French and was pulling a stack of papers out of her backpack.

Tia lingered behind her silently, apparently having been located and dragged along with Prae before I had. She stared at me the whole time, a dead-eyed look on her face.

"She loves the forest and faery idea"—this comment, Prae directed at Tia over her shoulder and Tia offered her an imitation of a smile—"but she also had one of her own: Angels."

Tia snorted, raising an eyebrow at me.

My mouth gaped open. "That's... a coincidence?"

Prae frowned, clearly not following, but handed me a third of the giant stack of papers she'd withdrawn, handing another third to Tia.

"Yes, well, personally I prefer the forest theme." She tilted her head slyly at Tia. "Did you... tell your cousin about it?"

"About prom?" Tia shrugged. "Sure."

"I just thought, well... *Anyway*." Prae tucked a strand of hair behind her ear. "Our task today is to pass these out to as many students as we can and get a vote on it."

The last part was hard to hear over the burst of laughter from a group of students passing by. One clipped me with his backpack and I stumbled, almost dropping the papers.

"Watch it!" shouted Prae after the retreating figure.

Heat rising to my face, I hunched over in response, trying to hide behind her. But she was a head shorter than me.

The guy, some blond guy in a letter jacket, just looked over his shoulder and frowned, not saying a word before turning back to the conversation he was having.

I was used to being ignored. After being teased so much for standing out as a kid, I preferred it that way.

"Rude," said Prae.

My eyes scanned the top of the stack of papers.

What should our prom theme be? The student body decides!

Underneath were blank check boxes next to the themes "Heaven and Angels," "Forest and Faeries," and "1980s." No one had even mentioned that one to me. I wondered who'd thought that up. If I were choosing, I might have preferred the 1980s, the eclectic fashion, the wild hair... I used to *like* dressing like that, and I wouldn't actually stand out if everyone else was, too.

"Oh, that one was mine." Prae used a pen she'd been holding and tapped the "1980s" theme.

Tia frowned. "Where do they turn in the ballots?"

"They fill it out then and there and give it back to you." Prae passed us both an extra pen.

"This seems time-consuming," I pointed out. "I thought Mikayla said the timeframe was kind of tight. Didn't she seem fine with the forest theme yesterday?"

"Well, maybe if two-fifths of our Prom Committee hadn't *left early*, I could have had some help reining her in." Prae jerked at her sleeve cuff. "Trust me, this vote thing *is* saving time. She can't pick one—and I convinced her talking about getting the student body involved this way would look good on that resume of hers or whatever she's so worried about."

"It's fine," said Tia before I could retort. "In fact, that works out perfectly."

It... did?

"Meet me here before lunch," she said, looking straight at me.

Prae seemed to take that as an invite for her, too. "Good idea. Good way to reach a good chunk of the student populace. I'm sure we'll go through our stacks in no time."

Grimacing, I did a quick flip through my stack. "It would have been easier to do an online poll."

"And fewer people would have participated," said Prae. "You really don't like talking to people, do you?"

I frowned, stuffing the pile into my backpack. So this was it. An ice breaker? Was the angel going to be at lunch?

"Tia—" I started, but she was already down the hall, her stack of papers clutched to her chest, her movements graceful and poised, like a rich person's secretary on a mission.

"She could use some more friends, too," said Prae. "A bit aloof, don't you think?" She whispered that part to me. "Not at all like her cousin."

I cringed. "Yeah. Okay, see ya."

I spent all of French and World History in a fugue state. Only when called on once in history did I even manage to think about anything but the pit in my stomach—but only because I'd blurted out that "Persia" instead of "Prussia" for an answer and had managed to make half the class laugh at me.

By the time the end-of-period bell rang, I was already packed and rushing out into the bathroom, every murmured conversation, every giggle like an indictment of my every move.

Shoving open the bathroom door, I clutched the edge of one of the sinks and counted my breaths.

And I was supposed to talk to these people about prom?

I was supposed to... make some guy my friend?

What if it was that jock who'd just slammed into me and then turned his head over his shoulder when Prae had called him on it and sneered, like *I* was the bother?

What if it was someone who *had* a significant other already— what if he wasn't even into girls?

Ivy could have done this—and not even felt bad about making someone fall in love with her. She probably wouldn't have even had to try, and she might not have even loved him back the same way.

Ember might have struggled, but if the guy was cute enough, she probably would have thrown herself into the task headfirst, spouting something about destiny or what have you.

Ember... hadn't said anything to anyone, as far as I knew. Neither Dad nor Ivy had sent me any panicked messages, so I guessed that meant Ember was choosing to believe in me.

Because I may have been her only hope.

The door swung open with a clatter, the buzz of conversations from the hallway flooding into the room for a moment before the door swung just as wildly back into place behind Tia, the stack of papers from Prae at her hip, her pen in her hand.

"Joel Serafin," she said, without preamble.

"What?" My mouth went dry.

"The angel you need to get to fall in love with you."

I choked, my grip slipping on the edge of the counter.

The hottest boy in school. The too-cool-for-school type. The one with that gorgeous goth girl hanging all over him—the one whom I'd almost drowned in spaghetti sauce just yesterday.

"No," I said, backing up from the mirror. My face was ashen— my expression horrifying. But that only made sense because that was definitely what I was experiencing just then.

"Impossible," I added. "This will never work."

A harried gush of breath escaped Tia's lips as she jiggled Prae's papers in her hand. "You're going to use this as an excuse to approach him."

I scoffed. "Yes, because he and his friends *so* seem the type to give a rat's behind about prom."

"Most of his group plans on going," Tia said. "We've been following the boy around town for a few weeks now to confirm."

"What are you, stalkers?" I said, my voice a hushed whisper. I only thought then to check the stalls for feet. No one, thankfully.

Tia's lips pursed. "We wanted to be sure. And, might I add, the child is entirely dull. Hard to imagine the celestial power in his DNA, but both his parents are descendants of seraphim. Still, he likely has no idea. The adults usually wait until their children are old enough to handle the news. You need not be so intimidated by him."

"Easy for you to say. You're the gorgeous girl who thinks nothing of stalking!"

The door opened behind Tia and a tall girl took a step in, looked between Tia and my face and must have been horrified at what she saw there. She took a few careful steps back and retreated outside.

I laughed sourly. "I radiate friendliness, as you can tell. Totally approachable."

"The angel child isn't exactly what I'd call 'gregarious,' either," said Tia. "His social circle is small." She grabbed me by the arm. "We've ascertained he does plan to go to the prom, and he already has a date. You will get him to break off that date and go with you."

The sounds escaping my lips were growing more animal-like and less like laughter. "Are you *kidding* me?" I swung my hands out wildly, wincing and cradling one after smacking the porcelain of the nearest sink. "So you do expect me to *seduce* some guy. And not just *any* guy. A guy with a girlfriend who wouldn't even look my way if I were passing out a million dollars."

"You exaggerate," said Tia. "And I didn't say he had a girlfriend. He has a date to the prom. If necessary, my cousin and I can incapacitate—"

"No, no, no, no." It was my turn to grab her. "What do you mean, 'incapacitate'?"

"Not murder, if that's what's gotten you so worried." Tia put the hand clutching a pen on one hip.

"Well, that's one small thing to be thankful for." I massaged my temple and started pacing the small length of the bathroom. "Wait a minute—if he's interested in someone else, can't we just wait for him to fall in love with her to awaken his power?"

"He won't experience true love with her," Tia said simply. "He's known her so long, it would have shown itself already. Besides, if he awakens his power due to someone else, you'll have no connection to him, no means by which to ask him for our favor."

"Well, I could be his friend," I said. "Like you said... Start as a friend." I bit my lip, halting my pacing as I tried to psych myself up for this. "Yes, his friend, and he falls in love with someone, and then I can be like, 'Hey, do your buddy a solid? Bring some faeries and merfolk back from the dead?' Yeah. Yeah, that could maybe... I mean..." I tugged on my hair, looking at its dull, brown color in the mirror. "I could dye my hair black, stand out a bit more, but not like stand out *too* much, you know? Then—"

Tia grabbed my elbow, and this time succeeded in directing me toward the door. "Be yourself," she said simply. "Your acting skills leave too much to be desired."

The door opened just as we approached it, Prae on the other side. She beamed as her eyes caught the stack in Tia's hand.

"I was wondering where you two got off to. Ready to get this Prom Committee stuff out of the way? We really do need to get to ordering and designing after school if we're going to get everything we need to transform the gym in time."

"Yes," said Tia, standing behind me to open my backpack and pull out the stack of papers I'd stuffed in there. Frowning, she stared at the creased and wrinkled mess and swapped it for the neat and tidy stack she'd held in her own arms, shoving that one instead in my hands. "We were just discussing that." Tia dropped the pen Prae had given her on top of my stack.

I opened my mouth to protest, but Prae held the door and started babbling as Tia gave me a firm push into the hallway.

"Let's get this done fast, then," said Prae, "so we still have time to grab lunch." She stopped, pulling her phone out of the tote bag hanging from her arm. "Let me just text Mikayla that we're taking care of fifth period lunch."

Tia didn't stop, and we were down the hall, heading toward the raucous laughter and conversation buzzing out from the cafeteria.

"I can't do this," I said, instinctively grabbing for one half of the wide open door frame.

"You ate lunch here yesterday."

Tia had seen me? Of course. Admitted stalker here and I'd been one of her and her cousin's targets.

"Only because it was raining out," I protested. "When it's not too cold or wet, I eat out—"

But Tia gave me another shove and I stumbled forward, stopping just shy of slamming into this blonde girl's back at the end of the line to get food. She looked over her shoulder at me and sneered but turned back to the girl in front of her, about to speak again.

"We're with the Prom Committee," said Tia, turning on that insincere charm. She handed two wrinkled papers from the top of her stack to both girls in turn. The commotion got the guy in front of them to turn around, and he got a paper, too. Tia fished out a pen from her pocket and passed it to the first girl. "We're taking a vote." She looked over her shoulder at me just as Prae walked in and settled beside us.

"Looks like Tia's got the line covered," said Prae. "Mikayla and Alan are going to wander the halls and grounds, looking to catch anyone who doesn't eat in the cafeteria."

I scanned around the vast, crowded space. Some students ate elsewhere. Students like me since the sky was clear today. Students like the ones Joel Serafin hung out with...

"You two start in the back corner," said Tia, that false smile on her face as she kept handing papers down the line, already collecting completed forms from the first three and moving that pen along. "Catch the ones who left the cafeteria—I think I saw a group of them just outside that back door, out on the stairs."

"The stairs?" Prae seemed as confused as I was. "Mikayla and Alan will get the students not in the—"

"They'll miss these," said Tia, still expertly conducting her paper collection and disbursement. "They're tucked out of the way."

Prae frowned but headed toward the back door. She'd only gotten a few steps before Tia called out, "Make sure to bring Autumn with you."

Prae lowered her voice as I pulled up alongside her, almost hard to hear over the din in the cafeteria. "I have an idea what weirdos might have taken their trays out into a darkened stairway. They're only in the cafeteria when they think they might get caught in an area that's off-limits." Her lips pinched as she shoved open the door. "I'm not sure they'd care about prom, though. Still, we can say we asked."

The lights were off in this part of the hallway, the noise from the cafeteria fading as the door shut behind us.

Prae clutched her stack of papers to her chest and stepped forward. "Hello? Anyone back here?"

A high-pitched laugh broke out and then cut itself short.

"You lost?" said a girl. Her voice was alto, with a bit of one of those goosebumps-inducing vocal fries.

We stepped around the corner, to the back stairs. Overhead were red emergency lights only, flickering in this forgotten staircase that I thought only led to some janitor closet and roof access on the floor above.

Scattered amongst the stairs were two girls and three boys, a group I'd seen around on occasion before even yesterday. Not too often in the cafeteria, like Prae had said, but then again, I wasn't there too often myself.

"We thought we might find you here," said Prae, clearing her throat and tossing a lock of hair over her shoulder. She couldn't meet their eyes, but I did—looking at everyone but him.

If I remembered their names right, there was Rick something, a guy whose dark hair was buzzed on one side and completely over one brown eye on the other. He lined his eyes with mascara and had black nail polish, his outfit such a mass of black that it was hard to tell one piece from another.

"You interested in prom?" Prae asked, handing Rick the first paper. He took it, balancing his half-eaten lunch on one knee, his sole exposed brow furrowing.

Below him a few steps was Sabine, a beautiful girl with close-cropped dark hair she'd dyed a pastel pink. She was kind of the baby-anti-goth but somehow still fit in so perfectly with them. She wore a Lolita dress in a pale rose that complemented her deep brown skin, along with white tights and pale pink lace-up ballet-slipper shoes.

"Of course," she said. "I'm going Elegant Lolita for that." Her voice was higher-pitched. She hadn't been the one to ask if we'd been lost. She took a paper from Prae's offered hand and squinted at it. It was probably hard to read in the dim light.

"What is this?" asked D. I was sure his name was "David" or "Dan" or something, but he only answered to the one letter. He frowned as he snatched the paper from Prae. He was lanky, pasty, but his peach skin tone was more yellow than white. He had bright red hair that was clearly a dye job, as it clashed with his dark brown eyebrows.

"Just a quick survey." Prae handed a pen to Sabine. Then she nudged me.

The other two were closer to me on the stairs.

I focused on the girl in front of me, Estelle. She was Filipino American, and her long, black hair was pulled up into two braided buns on either side of her head—more like cat ears than Princess Leia, though. She'd been the one to shoot me a death glare for nearly knocking into Joel yesterday, and she was giving me another one now, her hand extended. She was wearing fingerless fishnet gloves, the rest of her outfit a mix of blacks and royal purples, a frilly blouse with puffs and ruffles and a faux-leather skirt along her shapely, long legs. Her smoky eyeshadow was thick, lending a harsh glare to her otherwise flawless face.

"Well?" she said, that vocal fry at work with just the one word.

Flushing, I handed her the top of my stack and the pen. She frowned as she strained to read it in the light. "A survey?" She snorted.

"Oo, forest and faeries! I love it." Sabine scribbled away, handing the pen behind her to Rick and the paper back to Prae. "Maybe I could save the Elegant Lolita dress and go with one of my more forest-y dresses." She smacked Estelle on the shoulder. "Oh! That one inspired by *The Secret Garden*!"

"Wear what you want," said Estelle, her thick lips in a thin line as she scribbled on the sheet in front of her. "I'm going to show up in whatever I want ready to break hearts, regardless of the *theme.*" Sabine burst into giggles and Estelle folded her paper, practically flicking it back to me before handing the pen up above her.

Prae collected the paper from Rick, waiting on D to make a selection. Instead of filling in the circle next to his choice, he started writing—or drawing—something that was taking him a few moments.

"Well?" asked a smooth, silky voice. "Don't you have anything for me?"

My head snapped up.

Joel had my pen in his hand, his hand held out to me, waiting. From where he was seated on the stairway, just above my head height, it was like he was reaching down, waiting for me to grab his hand, to take me up and far away.

The red overhead light flickered over him, and I knew, despite the fact that part of me had hoped they'd been wrong all along, I was looking at a fallen angel.

His bright eyes looked friendlier today, devoid of any of the annoyance they'd held for me yesterday.

He was still wearing something that made him look like a 90s throwback, but I couldn't take it all in. I couldn't look away from his gaze.

Numbly, foolishly, instead of handing him a piece of paper like he clearly expected, I put my hand in his.

CHAPTER TEN

The laughter—both high-pitched and lower register—was what snapped me back to the moment. I'd put my foot on the first step, the toe of my sneaker dangerously close to toppling over what had to be Estelle's discarded lunch tray.

"What do you think you're doing?" Estelle wasn't laughing. Far from it.

My eyes blinked rapidly and I stepped back down, my hand only belatedly slipping from his.

I jolted to find his hand tighten around mine for a moment, not expecting to find the resistance when I went to pull myself back.

He smiled and put his other fist—still clutching the pen—to his lips, as if attempting to hide his amusement.

Then he let me go.

"Autumn...?" Prae asked.

Scrambling, I whipped the top copy of my stack up at him, not even looking to make sure he took it. But he must have. The paper vanished from my limited frame of view.

Sabine snorted and nudged Estelle. Estelle smiled, but it was as fake as Tia's might have been as she glared at me.

"Heaven and angels?" came Joel's warm voice.

I snapped back to look at him.

He held the paper in front of him, though his eyes caught on me, his face soft, open.

"Prom themes," said Prae quickly, by way of explanation. She held out her hand to D up above her, but he was focusing on his paper laid out on the step beside him, scribbling with the pen.

"Oh, that's *boring*," said Estelle. "Vote for 1980s like I did and let them get on their way."

"Forest and faeries!" pouted Sabine. She looked up at Rick above her. "What did you vote for?"

He shrugged and shoveled a mouthful of potatoes in his mouth with his fork. "Whatever was on top," he said, his voice muffled by the food.

Sabine poked his knee and shook her head. "You should have asked *your girlfriend* if you didn't care. If we wind up with a dull theme because of you, you're buying me a new dress to make up for it."

Rick practically choked on his mashed potatoes. "Your dresses are like a hundred dollars!"

Sabine smoothed her pink skirt. The closer I looked, the more apparent the idyllic design featuring storybook rabbits was. "Well, if I'm forced to go as an *angel*, I'll need an all-white dress. And maybe some wings while I'm at it. Now that I think about it, a heaven theme might be fun..."

Rick moaned and stabbed his potatoes once more.

Joel finished marking and folded up the paper, handing it back to me, and then the pen. When I went to take the pen from him, my hot, flush face forcing me to focus on a spot on the stair above his shoulder, I found it difficult to wrench away.

"You don't talk much, do you?" he asked. "I think you saying 'sorry' yesterday was the only time I've heard you speak."

My gaze met his, and I was all too aware I was tugging on the pen above Estelle's head. But he wouldn't let go.

"Are you finished?" Prae asked D, tapping her foot.

"Just a sec." His mouth split into a wide grin and he kept scribbling.

"What's your choice?" Joel asked, and I realized with a start he was still speaking to me.

Still demanding that I *say* something.

The longer I went without speaking—especially after him pointing out how little he'd heard me say before—the more ridiculous I looked.

And I *needed* to speak to him. I needed to make friends with him.

What was wrong with me?

"Angels," I croaked out, though I hadn't given it any thought until that moment.

"Mine, too." His smile could melt ice floes.

He finally let go of the pen and I tumbled backward, causing Estelle to snort, the first time she'd seemed genuinely amused since we'd intruded on their dark and reddened getaway.

"I just need yours back," said Prae, standing on her tiptoes as she tried to get a look at what D was doing.

"All right, all right," he said, folding up his paper and handing that and then the pen down to Prae. He grinned like a cat who'd found himself in a room full of rats. "Thank you, Prom Committee," he said, far too sweetly.

Both Sabine and Estelle laughed at that, and Prae was already down the hall, heading into the light.

"Autumn?" she asked, turning on her heel. Her figure looked angelic itself just then, the distant light framing her at the edge of the darkness.

I was still stuck to the spot, staring up at Joel again.

"Autumn?" he repeated, as if wondering if that was really my name.

Estelle attempted to elbow his shin up behind her, but all she did was smack her elbow against the stair. I noticed the sharp pain cross her face as she'd probably hit her funny bone, but she bit her lip and cradled her arm to her, saving her expression to shoot me another death glare.

"Autumn Sheppard," I said, at least able to remember my own name. I clutched the stack of papers to my chest tightly.

"Joel Serafin," he said.

"I know," I said, like a freak.

"You know my name?" he asked.

As if anyone in school didn't. Even the cheerleaders thought he was hot—I'd hear them talk about him from time to time—he was just too weird for their tastes. Nerd girls liked him. Jock girls liked him. Gay Key Club guys liked him. There wasn't a type of person interested in boys I hadn't overheard talk about him on occasion.

Except no one would have ever heard me talking about him, of course.

I'd intended to admire him from afar—I'd only seen him around once every few days—and then taking this crush with me to the grave.

Or so I'd planned anyway.

"Yes, wow, you're so unknown around here," said Estelle, her vocal fry now pitched with pain. "So impressive that she knows that. Don't you have more surveys to pass out, Prom Committee?" She blinked her eyes rapidly at me, fluttering her eyelashes.

Prae tilted her head, indicating for me to follow her.

"Yes, um, right." I spun on my heel, the squeak of my sneaker on the tile so loud, it actually made Sabine wince as it echoed throughout the empty hallway. I ran after Prae, barely slowing my pace as I caught up to her. In fact, she had to speed walk to match mine.

I shoved open the cafeteria door and fled inside, for once, the raucous endless buzz of conversation, the press of the throng of students all around me, a welcome respite.

"What was that all about?" Prae asked as the door swung shut behind her.

"What was what?" I asked, realizing I could barely hear her over the thunderous pounding of my heart.

Prae *tsked* as she unfolded the piece of paper on top of her stack. "Never mind. Oh, look—gross!"

She showed me the paper D had been working on so long. There was a drawing of cartoonish people kissing, the girl drawn so comically hourglass, she'd have collapsed under the weight of her giant hips and chest held together by that tiny waist. *Whatever gets me laid*, he'd written under the "1980s" option.

Prae wrinkled her nose and crumpled it up, heading straight for a garbage can and chucking it inside.

"*Some people*," she said, straightening her back. "Come on." She shuffled the other two papers she'd collected to the bottom of her pile. "We have so many of these to hand out yet."

"Yeah..." I said after Prae's retreating back. But she was already at the nearest table, commanding everyone's attention, passing out fresh sheets of paper to everyone within reach.

I stood frozen to the spot, thinking, barely moving out of the way when someone came over to dump the contents of the remainder of their tray in the can beside me.

"How'd it go?"

Tia swooped in as silent as a ninja on my other side, making me startle and snap back to the moment.

"Why didn't you come with me?" was all I asked.

She shrugged. "I figured Prae would do a better job of drawing them out." She nodded at the third member of the Prom Committee team in the cafeteria, already collecting half the papers she'd just passed out and making sure her pen passed from one person to the next. A smile lit up her face—she seemed more relaxed here than she'd been in the hallway.

Still, compared to don't-talk-to-me Tia and I-can't-talk-to-you me, she had to have been the best option for breaking the ice with that group.

I supposed Tia's choice made sense, in a way.

"I made a fool of myself," I said.

"But he'll remember you?" she asked, rolling her pen around on her bottom lip.

"Oh, he'll remember me, all right."

I stared at the top of my stack and unfolded the top piece, the one Joel had handed back to me.

He'd checked the "heavens and angels" theme just as he'd said he'd had.

But under that were ten numbers.

"He gave you his phone number," said Tia—and if I wasn't totally mistaken, I'd say I'd detected a hint of amusement in her statement.

That made one of us.

All I felt was panic.

CHAPTER ELEVEN

I flipped through Orin's notepad with one hand, petting Blossom with the other. She was purring despite the fact that Orin was sitting on the other side of her, at the edge of my bed. Her animal instincts weren't telling her to be wary of the former faery prince who kept sneaking a little pet under her chin.

"You're not going to find what you're looking for in there." Tia sat in my desk chair, the desk itself strewn with junk that buried my laptop somewhere in there.

One page had a drawing of a flower, surrounded by notes about secret meanings in paintings.

"There's nothing here past the nineteenth century," I said, flipping to the end of the book.

Orin dragged the notepad closer to him. "Miracles got harder to hide in more recent years," he said. "So we figure there may have been less of them. Besides, we had enough data. As long as we located a potential mark—"

Tia let out an audible breath. "Angel."

"Right." Orin folded the cover over his notepad. "I didn't find information on how people made the angels fall in love. Seems self-explanatory, innit?"

Beneath my fingers, my tri-colored Blossom stretched out, her eyes still closed, and nudged her forehead against my thigh.

I checked my phone screen. 8:00. "My mom's going to be home any minute now," I told them. Tuesdays, she had Book Club, sometimes here, but more often at friends'.

"Then enough faffing around," said Orin, taking his notepad and slipping it in the front pocket of his green checkered button-up shirt. "Or we can leave you to it on your own. Less embarrassing, I imagine, innit?"

"*No.*" My stomach hardened as I clutched the thin phone tightly in my palm. "I wouldn't know what to say."

"Start with *hello*," Tia suggested. From the mess behind her on my desk, she handed me the prom theme vote paper Joel had filled out.

The one with his number.

I logged into my phone with my thumbprint, distracted by a waiting message from Ember.

Orin scooted closer and looked but didn't say anything.

"I have to respond," I told him clumsily. She'd asked if "he" had done anything worrisome, and I could only assume she'd meant Orin. "Or she may tell everyone else about this."

Everything's fine, I lied to her. Well, no faery was putting me in jeopardy or anything. Just emotional jeopardy.

"I thought she might take it better than the others—so long as it came from you." Orin grinned and pulled his own phone out of his pocket. He had the latest, top-of-the-line iPhone. It was so thin, it almost looked like you could crumple it up like a piece of paper. My Android phone's hinges were already cracking a bit at the corners, bleeding into the screen subtly. He tapped at his screen, his attention focused on it.

"I wouldn't count on her keeping quiet for long," I said. "She's only in town a month—I doubt she'll just keep it to herself when she leaves and can no longer show up at a moment's notice should I need her for anything." I sent Orin a piercing look at that.

He stood, slipping the phone back into his pocket and pantomiming washing his hands of the affair. "I don't blame her, love. Though that makes me certain we have a shorter deadline than we thought."

I snorted. Then I paused, my hand clutching the top of Joel's paper. "What, you expect him to fall in love with me—before Ember leaves town?"

"I *was* going to suggest before the end of summer," said Orin. "Before life's plans inevitably send the two of you separate ways."

"Even that's four months," I said. "I can't make anyone—but especially Joel Serafin—fall for me in four months!"

"Did you expect us all to be patient enough to wait *years?*" Tia swiveled in the chair and took hold of a magical girl anime figurine collecting dust at the back of the desk. "The boy has plans to go to school out of state. Unless you change your own plans and follow him there—which might prove difficult this late in the school year —we knew your best opportunity for this was closing fast."

"But I can't... We're in *high school!*" I protested.

"And you'd rather you spend the next few *years* of your life chasing a boy around the country, rather than focusing on your own life goals?" Orin picked a stuffed rabbit off of my book shelf and wagged it at me. "We don't want *you* pining after a boy. We need him to pine after you."

Jumping up and leaving my phone behind, I snatched the rabbit from Orin and the anime girl from Tia and then tossed them on my bed. Blossom startled, but only enough to keep one eye open an extra beat.

"Fine. Four months," I said, picking up my phone again.

"Four weeks," said Tia. "If that's when your step-sister leaves and might tell everyone. It'll only be tougher with all that atten- tion on you—on us."

I laughed dryly. "This isn't happening in four weeks. We're not even going to be friends in *four weeks.*"

"Four weeks is when the prom is, right?" Orin asked Tia.

Tia shrugged and nodded.

"Excellent! He'll take you to the prom and that'll be the night."

"I'm not going to..." I started.

Both former faeries turned their gazes on me.

Right. I had a mission. And prom was potentially the most normal thing about it.

I slowly—one careful digit at a time—added Joel's number to my contacts, brushing aside a message from PonyFan asking what I was up to—as if she expected the answer to be anything but "spending the night curled up at home as always." If Joel had *really* wanted me to text him, he could have asked to wave our phones together and gotten the contact information that way. But then he'd have had to explain that to his friends, and Estelle, for one, would clearly have taken issue with that.

"Let me guess," I said, my finger hovering over the *save* button. "Estelle is that not-his-girlfriend prom date you mentioned?"

Orin and Tia exchanged a look.

"Does telling you *yes* or *no* make this more dodgy for you?" Orin asked.

"Just tell me the truth," I said.

"Yes," said Tia sharply. "And she clearly wants it to mean more, but she and Joel have... a difficult relationship. Their parents are practically pushing them together."

I froze. Orin smacked Tia on the shoulder.

"And you forgot to tell me this because...?"

"Parents can't stand in the way of true love," said Orin. His eyes took on a dreamy, faraway quality.

I refrained from commenting on that. Orin clearly still wasn't in touch with his newfound human reality.

Beside the fact that Joel could have almost anyone he wanted in school, having to fight someone so close in his social circle for his attention was beyond anything I'd ever pictured myself signing up for.

Had a part of me been happy to find out my target was *him*, my only crush for the past few years?

Sure.

But a crush was only safe when there was no shot of it ever working out for you. Ever.

"Well?" Tia said. "Do you want our help or not?"

Feeling as if I were going numb, I opened up a message for my new contact and started typing.

Hi.

That was it. That was as far as I got.

Orin leaned over my shoulder. "Well, it's a start, innit?"

How are you? I typed next.

Orin took a sharp breath in, pursing his lips. "Is this a text or a letter between an old-timey soldier and his sweetheart back home?"

Groaning, I lay back in the bed and stared up above. I thought briefly of the video chat I'd done with my sister, but there was no way I was showing him my face via my phone.

"How about 'thanks for the number' to start?" offered Tia.

Moaning, I brought my phone screen up above my head, deleting the *How are you?* And replacing it with Tia's suggestion.

But I couldn't hit *send*.

The former faeries just stared at me.

Grabbing my pillow and burying my head into it, I hit *send* without looking and tossed the phone down at the end of the bed.

Blossom had had enough of the noise, and she jumped down. I peeked out from under the phone to watch her stretch like a yoga master, first her front legs and then her back, before she sauntered out my bedroom door and to the second-floor hallway.

The phone buzzed.

I didn't move.

Orin grabbed it for me, and since it hadn't gone to sleep yet, he didn't need my thumbprint to read anything.

"'Who's this?'" he read.

Right. Forgot that part.

"How many girls did he give his number to today?" Tia asked, disgusted.

Burying my face in the pillow more, I felt hot all along my neck and hairline.

"This is hopeless."

"'Autumn,'" said Orin slowly, and I realized he was typing my answer in for me.

I shot up and snatched the phone from him, but he'd already replied.

He'd added a heart emoji to the end of my name. *A heart emoji.*

I growled.

But Joel was already typing.

Just messing with you, he wrote. *I figured it was you. Or a wrong number.*

I frowned. He was either entirely too smooth or this was going far too well. Suspiciously well. He didn't mention the heart emoji.

"Now what?" I asked after reading his response aloud.

The cousins stared at one another, seeming to have some kind of conference in their heads.

Orin pulled his phone back out. "I have a few romcoms on here."

Tia snatched the phone from him. "We don't have time for that."

My eyes bulged. What was I *doing* asking these two for help? They didn't know how to win a guy's heart any more than I did.

Tia seemed to have picked up on my wavering confidence. "Just... ask him to hang out."

"And do what?" My throat was growing dry, this task growing more and more ridiculous by the minute. "It's going to seem like I'm asking him on a date."

"You *are* asking him on a date," said Tia sharply.

"You said friends first was fine!"

"That was when we thought we had four months, not four weeks." Tia looked down sourly.

I stared at the screen. Joel was typing again even without my reply. He'd probably seen I'd read his message and then hadn't even begun to respond and was thinking about what a clod I was right this very minute. "Look, if I could get this all done fast, I would want that, too! I want this nightmare over with. I want to stop feeling so much guilt. But I just *can't*..." I stopped myself.

We're hanging at Standing Springs Park right now. Want to join us?

Orin's breath came heavy over my shoulder. "And that's how you ask someone to hang out without it explicitly being a date."

Tia perked up.

Joel and his friends, no doubt.

Estelle at the very least, if she was still determined to win his heart herself.

I checked the time. 8:18. On a school day.

"My mom wouldn't let me—" I started.

"Nonsense," said Tia, jumping to her feet. She snatched the phone away from me and her fingers moved like miniature cheetahs across the screen. "I'll go with you."

"Hey, wait a second—" I said, but she handed me the phone back before I could even begin to try to steal it back.

The screen was open to the message to Joel, but another reply popped up on top of it.

Mom.

I clicked it. There was a message from a minute ago *I* hadn't typed, explaining how I was hanging with my new friends at the park tonight.

Mom had responded. *Thanks for letting me know. Be careful and don't stay out too late, sweetie. You have school tomorrow. Be back by ten.*

And under that message, "my" response to Joel.

I'd love to, Tia had written. *I'll be there in twenty.*

Below that, Joel had written. *Cool.*

And he'd ended the message with two black hearts.

CHAPTER TWELVE

"I thought this was where the high schoolers hung out when there was nothing to do," I said, staring out the windshield of my car at Standing Springs Park.

There was a "lake" in the middle that was more like an overly large pond, considering Lake Michigan wasn't that far away. A little island stood solitary in the middle of the lake, and at the back was the endless array of pine trees and oak trees and everything else that made up the woods. In the front was the "beach," though it was more of a long strip of dirty sand. I couldn't picture anyone sunbathing on it, even in the summer. There were some grassy areas, some rocks, a few worn-down park benches, and an area for a bonfire. That was what raged now, a collection of vague figures around it, some wearing the Union High letter jacket colors in red and navy—even a few Central High jackets in purple and gold.

This was a full-on party on a school night.

People my age cradled red Solo cups, and I knew that no matter what the stakes, I wasn't about to let someone convince me to take a sip of whatever was floating around in those.

Tia unbuckled her seatbelt. "And there's so much to do in town now?" It didn't seem like a question.

"Well, I mean—the Internet has everything. Who'd even want to leave home?"

If I didn't get motion sick playing VR games for long, I could point out you could "travel" to some pretty amazing places without leaving home.

But that was beside the point. We were here now. Doing what teens in town still apparently did. A ritual passed down from one class to the next, as I recalled this was a favorite hangout spot for Ivy and her friends, too.

Tia was out of the car, so, sighing, I knew it was time for me to get out, too. I checked the phone one more time for any instructions on how to find Joel, but the messages had stopped. My finger lingered over the black hearts.

"Come on," said Tia, opening the driver's side door for me.

Stuffing the phone into my back pocket, I followed her out, making sure to lock the door. I shivered as I dropped my keys in my other pocket.

"I should have worn my jacket," I protested. Hope was flooding my body, like it was the perfect excuse to turn around, go home. Yes, I was working against the clock, but this was hopeless to begin with.

Tia shifted out of her tan-colored faux leather and handed it over. She was wearing the same Renaissance-Faire-like white blouse she'd had on earlier in the day.

"What if you get cold?" I asked.

"I'll step near the fire." She tilted her head toward the roaring bonfire some distance away. "The angel is more likely to be skulking in the shadows. You're going to need it."

Frowning, I slipped on her coat and felt at least somewhat better. Had to figure the stalker would know everything about his habits.

Our feet scuffled over the gravel in the parking area, our footfalls growing quieter as we reached the grass and the noise from the gathering grew louder. There was music blaring, too, a heavy bass beat soaring out over the crisp evening air.

"Ladies," said a guy wearing a Central High letter jacket. He turned around to a keg positioned on a withering tree stump near the edge of the fire and quickly filled two red cups up with a yellow liquid, waving them in our faces. His smile was broad, his blue eyes hardly leaving Tia's impassive face.

"Thanks." The corners of her lips curled into that little forced smile of hers as she took both cups. She shoved one at me.

I tilted it toward me. It smelled like raw bread dough. "I don't want—"

"Take it," she hissed. "Just cradle it." She lifted her head, leading the way toward the fire, ignoring the question from the bulky blond Central jock who wanted to know her name.

The warmth from the fire hit my face like a cuddly blanket and the tension in my shoulders eased somewhat as we neared it. The cup did prove something of a crutch for me as I hugged it to my chest with both hands, scanning the sea of faces for anyone familiar.

I'd thought Joel and his friends too "alternative" to be hanging out with people like these. So many letter jackets—those were the jocks. A few girls I recognized as cheerleaders. Most people I didn't recognize at all. People laughed, drank, talked—made out. I was quick not to look too long at any of those pairings. Almost out of habit, I lifted the cup to my lips, only to stop myself before I tilted the liquid down my throat. The scent alone was enough to snap me out of it.

"Keep your wits about you," Tia managed to say over the din, the crackling of the flames.

I jumped as a branch snapped and fell lower down the pyre, my vision going black. A memory of a ball of flame—red one moment, purple-ish the next—soaring toward me, Ember as the champion of blood...

"Focus," said Tia.

I blinked, and the park cleared in my vision.

"Well, if it isn't *Autumn Sheppard*."

I jumped again. One of the couples making out on a log next to me broke apart. Mikayla and Alan.

"And Tia..." Mikayla seemed unclear on her last name. "I thought you were *too busy* after school to help out. Seems you found time for fun today."

"We passed out your survey at lunch," said Tia, cradling an elbow and holding her Solo cup with a touch of elegance, as if it were a glass of wine.

"And didn't show up after school to help us tally the results," Mikayla said, sending us both the evil eye. "Heaven and angels won." She flung back her braid. So even without Joel's vote—as I'd kept that one.

"I still think it should have been heaven and he—" started Alan.

"*Anyway*," said Mikayla, clutching her knees in front of her. "Prae and I—and Alan," she added belatedly, "did a lot of the ordering. The school gave us a strict budget, but it'll work." She offered a flittering smile at Tia. "Prae actually had the idea to kind of incorporate the forest into our idea of heaven. Otherwise, it would have just been an all-white color scheme and clouds. Kind of dull."

"I'm sure," Tia pretended to take—or actually took—a sip of her drink.

"I was like, 'Bambi's mom goes to heaven!'" said Alan. His face was flushed and his voice a bit loud, an empty red cup on the ground at his feet. "My dad has some hunting trophies—"

Mikayla squeezed his arm. "And I nixed that. No dead animals. Least of all real ones." She rolled her eyes. "No, it's more like light and airy, faery angels mixed in with the more traditional ones. Heaven is a slice of undisturbed nature and all that."

I squeezed my cup, the material buckling too easily to my force. I couldn't quite picture this—it was the gym. What more could we do besides hang up streamers? But I nodded along.

"So *anyway*, I thought I'd let you know I used your suggestion, too. 1980s didn't quite mesh, though." She shrugged. That had been Prae's idea.

"Great," said Tia. She looked around the crowd, clearly not fully engaged in the conversation.

Mikayla seemed undeterred. "It'll take a couple of days for everything to arrive, but it's not like we can *actually* start decorating until the night before. So our next task, besides designing the tickets and selling them, is designing the whole look of the gym. A blueprint, if you would."

Tia snapped back to the conversation, grabbing me by the arm and directing me toward the edge of the fire. "Down there," she whispered into my ear. There was a path leading down a slope to the sandy strip in front of the lake.

So that was where she judged Joel to be.

"So you need us back tomorrow, I take it?" Tia asked, directing Mikayla's attention solely to her.

This was my chance.

I briefly caught Alan's eyes as he slipped an arm around his girlfriend and squeezed her to his side, her continuous babbling more like background noise than anything he was actually paying attention to. He nuzzled Mikayla. She just pushed at him and kept talking.

"Yes, the both of you. Some of us need to be in charge of tickets, some decorations—"

Taking a deep breath, I found a collection of empty and half-empty red cups atop a picnic table just at the edge of the path leading to the beach and dropped my cup there. A guy in a Union High letter jacket sitting on top of the table glanced at me over his shoulder but didn't say a word, turning back to petting the brown hair of the cheerleader who was talking on the bench below him, her body between his outstretched thighs.

My face flushed at the thought of how easy all of this seemed to everyone but me.

Friends first, I told myself. *Sure, these faeries are expecting the impossible from you, but no matter how quick this has to get done, you have to start as friends.*

Squeezing my hands into fists at my sides, I headed down the path.

Maybe they won't be there, I told myself, a twisted bit of hope that actually spurred my steps on faster. *Maybe they left early. This doesn't really seem their scene any more than it is mine.*

But that hope died out as I stumbled the last few steps down the slope, the thundering party music behind me drowned out by another tune, this one less danceable, somewhat retro and familiar, but I couldn't place it. Nonetheless, the familiar tittering giggling drew my attention to the darkened forms gathered around someone's projected phone screen, and they were dancing around the phone's holographic image of stars swirling around a galaxy.

Sabine and Rick—I could identify her even before my eyes adjusted to the darkness based on the Lolita dress she wore.

A cloud of steam brushed past me and I jumped, turning to find Estelle vaping on a rock. I cringed, and she seemed to notice, taking another suck on her death stick and exhaling pointedly in my direction. "It's vapor," she said.

"It's poison," I said back.

She raised an eyebrow, a couple of silvery bracelets hanging off her wrist sparkling in the moon's reflection off the lake beside us. "Better the rot in my lungs than the rot in my soul being stuck in this place."

She took another inhale and I shuffled away, closer to the water's edge.

The island in the middle of the lake seemed closer now, just a short swim away.

Ivy had told me about the merfolk alcove under it, a sort of mimicry of a little castle, where the merfolk had once gathered for dinners and events and other essential gatherings.

Their actual house had been amazing—water worked into its very floors, according to Ivy—but I'd never seen it before we'd burned it down.

We, as in the bloom. I hadn't been there personally, but Orin had told me about it, had convinced me to give the order, so to speak—the faefolk's attempt to rid the merfolk of their stronghold.

It had worked, for a time. The merfolk had had nowhere else to retreat to on land and they'd moved around in RVs. I wondered why they hadn't just retreated here, to their underwater sanctuary. But I knew they wouldn't have stood even a chance of winning if they'd just gone into hiding.

"You the one Joel was texting?" Estelle asked, breaking me from my thoughts.

I turned, unsure what to say. I didn't want to fight with her over him—I still felt like a trespasser in *her* social circle.

"He was being coy about it." She laughed, but her throat caught on the sound. "He'll break your heart, you know."

"I don't... I mean..." I wrung my hands.

"You hope you'll be special." She took another inhale of her cartridge. "But you won't be. You're not. Whoever wins his heart can't be just *anyone*."

She was making the prospect of intruding on her life more and more tantalizing.

"He's over there," she said finally, and then I realized over the distant beat of the bass, the clearer sound of the couple's music, there was laughter—and splashing.

I narrowed my eyes, trying to get a glimpse. Two pale figures popped out at the edge of the little island, one letting out a, "Whoo, it's cold!"

That sounded like D.

"Told them it was too cold to go skinny dipping," said Estelle. She coughed and slammed a fist against her chest.

Skinny dipping?

If I'd stood there thinking about it, I never would have had the courage.

But time was short, and I had no idea what I was doing—so I figured I may as well dive right in.

Both metaphorically and literally.

"What are you doing?" Estelle asked, flicking off her cartridge.

Tia's coat dropped to the sand beneath my feet, followed by my sweater, my undershirt, and then my shoes, and socks, and jeans.

The underwear could stay.

"He doesn't like *desperate*," said Estelle. Her voice quavered, despite the fact that she seemed to be trying to convey a lie about how little she cared.

But I was already at the edge of the dry sand, goosebumps

popping out all at once all over my flesh the instant my bare foot hit the water.

CHAPTER THIRTEEN

"You're going to get pneumonia!" Estelle shouted.

Somewhere beside her, Sabine let out another one of her shrieks.

I couldn't hesitate. Hesitating meant I'd stay still. Get cold. Think too hard.

Die of embarrassment.

I knew how to swim—unlike my older sisters, I'd never experienced what it meant to be a mermaid, but the water felt good, the exercise natural. I didn't play a lot of sports, and the most exercise I usually got involved chasing the twins around the yard, but right now, with an almost heavenly light at the tunnel carving my way through the force of the water, I had a goal in mind.

"Sheppard? Is that you?" Genuine surprise threaded Joel's voice.

"Who's that?" added D. "The chick you texted?"

Their conversation died out into murmurs I couldn't entirely hear as I butterfly-stroked one foot after another. But as I put the sandy shore behind me, I heard cheers spurring me on. None with my name—Sabine and Rick probably didn't remember it.

But I was getting their attention now.

I reached the edge of the shore, my foot kicking against the angled slope that would take me up on land.

I hesitated.

And that was my mistake.

All at once, the chill of the water hit me. The ridiculousness of what I'd just done. The *desperate* quality to it, as Estelle had reminded me.

The fact that I was about to climb out of here in nothing but my soaked and clingy underwear.

I blinked, my mind racing desperately to remember what underwear I'd even bothered to put on today. Gray boyshorts and a mismatched white bralette.

Go, Autumn. Negative one for my skills in the seduction department.

To be fair, I'd never thought it'd get far enough I'd have to worry about him seeing my underwear.

"Need help?"

Crouching at the edge of the shore, Joel leaned down and held out a hand.

His half-smile seemed strained, like he was fighting to contain the more natural depth of his happiness.

His dark hair was even darker in the bright moonlight, straighter, too, slicked back messily against his forehead and scalp.

His pale face seemed to actually glow.

And he was missing a shirt. My eyes darted dangerously below and I found that Estelle wasn't quite accurate when she'd called it skinny-dipping—he had boxer shorts on. Green ones in a plaid pattern.

I needed to stop staring.

D saddled up beside him, bouncing back and forth on his feet and rubbing his bare arms. "It might be warmer in the water," he said. He had boxer shorts on, too, his frame so skinny, it looked like a tepid breeze might send him flying.

"She didn't swim this far to not check this place out," said Joel. He studied me, cocking his head, as if to wonder why I *had* swum this far.

I took that hand again and let him pull me out, the force of his yank enough to lift me up and out of the water entirely.

Stumbling as I regained my footing, my free hand smacked straight onto Joel's chest.

I looked up, his hand still on mine, holding my arm up over my head.

My forehead hovered mere inches before his nose. I found myself stepping up on my toes, the sand digging in between the crevices, lifting my body so my lips hovered exactly where they needed to be to line up to kiss him.

"You okay?" he asked, letting me go but putting a steadying hand on my bare hip. His skin was warm against my clammy skin.

"Yeah, uh, sorry. Thanks." I practically dug at my cheek to brush a clinging wet strand of hair aside as I lowered myself to my feet and took a step back.

"Who even *are* you?" D asked.

"Autumn," said Joel, shooting D a look. "Remember her from earlier? The survey about prom?"

D lifted an eyebrow. "*You* move fast."

Joel chuckled and I threaded my hands together in front of me, swallowing.

I shouldn't care that he "moved fast." I *needed* him to move fast. But something Estelle had said needled at me, like the most I could hope for here was to be some short flirtation before he moved on to the next girl who caught his eye.

My neck and ears flushed. I was still unsure if I'd really caught his eye.

"Hi," said Joel, his smile dazzling, as if we were only just meeting for the first time this evening.

"Um... Hi?" I offered back.

I really had no idea what we were doing.

"Well, I guess that means I'm not wanted," said D, shaking his limbs out and rotating his head side to side.

"No, you..." I started, my heart thundering at the idea of being left alone here on this little island with Joel, even if that could only help what was supposed to be the aim of this whole evening. "I mean, Estelle told me you were out here, and I just wanted to see you—I mean, the mermaid alcove for myself."

"The what?" Joel laughed.

Nice save, I told myself sarcastically.

I flexed my fingers, my teeth beginning to chatter. "It just... It looks like a place mermaids might gather," I mumbled.

D wiggled his eyebrows. "Yeah, a freshwater mermaid who lives in a lake that freezes over in the winter." He dove in, submerging himself completely, and then popping his head back up. "You coming?"

"We can wait a minute," said Joel, his gaze flicking to me out of the corner of his eye.

I crossed and rubbed my arms, suddenly far too aware how little a wet bralette disguised anything.

"Suit yourselves," called D, his firm, steady strokes taking him back to the shore.

"You cold?" Joel asked.

"No," I lied. It was so obviously a lie since my teeth clicked before and after I spoke the word.

Joel chuckled and held a hand out toward me. "I guess we should follow him, then."

I hesitated, and that was when my mind raced, the cold seeping down into my bones.

I grabbed his hand and he squeezed, rewarding me with a sense of warmth that was just enough to still the shaking of my limbs.

"One, two... Three!" He jumped, and I did, too, just behind a beat, as I was slow to follow along.

We both dove off the narrow sediment slope, submerging fully into the water.

It was harder to see under the water, the dark of the night obscuring an already hazy sight, but he was there in front of me, our hands still clasped together.

And somewhere far beneath him, at his feet, was a light.

He seemed to notice it, too, his head snapping downward.

Then we both popped up above the water's surface, our hands unclasping as we paddled to stay upright.

"Did you see that?" Joel asked, pausing in his paddling just long enough to brush some of the hair out of his eyes.

"The light?" I asked.

He nodded. Then, without saying more, he dove again.

I kept paddling in place, checking over my shoulder.

D had reached the shore to the park by now, his jubilant screams echoing out over all the raucousness as he stood straight on the shore and jumped some more in place, swiping some clothes off the log on which Estelle had been sitting. Estelle herself was at the edge of the water, her arms crossed tightly over her chest.

"Come on!" she shouted.

Joel popped back up beside me, startling me. "There's something down there."

"Joel!" shouted Estelle, practically as loud as her lungs might have been able to. "Come on already! I want to go home!"

Joel cupped his hands over his mouth, his legs doing all the work to keep him upright. "Go with D!" he shouted. "I'll see you tomorrow!"

The sight of Estelle turning sharply on her heel and clambering up the slope to the bonfire was hard to miss even from our distance.

The guys were laughing, Sabine shouting something at them as D chased Rick and shook out his wet hair, sprinkling him.

"You better not get *me* wet!" Sabine said.

Eventually, they joined Estelle up the slope, vanishing from sight entirely.

Joel and I paddled, the movement keeping my skin from growing too clammy.

"Sorry," he said, "but I didn't think they'd have the patience to wait for me."

"Wait?" I asked, my limbs tingling from the effort of staying afloat.

He took my hand again. "You've got to see this. Hold your breath."

I cocked my head but expanded my lungs almost as far as they could go.

We dove, Joel leading the way.

He dropped my hand underwater to swim deeper, toward that light we'd both noticed.

It was coming out from between several holes in the rock beside us, like the "roots" of the island that anchored it into the lakebed.

Ivy had described the merfolk "castle" beneath the island in Standing Springs lake.

I'd pictured a fairy tale castle made of sediment and rock.

This wasn't that, but it was clearly an open space, a place where there'd once been life.

Joel poked his head through a hole in the rock, as if it were a window, then looked back at me and waved me on to follow him.

We swam around and found a larger hole, more like a door, but my chest was burning and I shot back up to the surface.

The chill night air felt good on my lungs as I paddled just above the water's surface. I checked the shore, but there were no more figures there, the bass music from the bonfire the only sound besides the crickets nearby.

I gazed down, looking for Joel, assuming he'd soon follow me.

But there was no other movement than my own.

"Joel?" I called out to the night air. As if he could hear me.

Adrenaline shot through my system, as I paddled in circles—looking for Joel, for Tia, even for Orin, though he wasn't even along with us. Then again, he *had* "observed" Joel enough to learn an awful lot about him.

Where was that conniving, spying former faery prince now?

With a slap to my face, I centered myself and took a deep breath. *He better not be playing a trick on me.*

Swimming faster than I thought possible, thrusting hard with each kick until my legs began to burn, I aimed for the large door-way-like hole in the rock where I'd seen Joel last.

I swam inside, and for a moment, I was awestruck. The wide, open space was lit by what seemed like luminescent moss balls glowing brightly along recesses in the cavern walls, floating up and down, up and down. Along the edge there were rocks throughout that reminded me of backless chairs, with the middle left open for milling or dancing—if that was what merfolk did. And at one end, there were several larger, more ornate stone seats, like thrones, nestled in an alcove that drew the eye, even through the blurriness of viewing it all through the water.

A lost kingdom for a lost race of creatures.

I wondered what it had looked like full of life, an underwater ball.

Here I was, a wreck at the idea of stealing someone else's date for prom—of going to prom at all—and yet daydreaming about the beauty of a fairytale ball.

A bubble caught my attention, over by the "throne" area.

I swam, my lungs starting to burn, but I had to check it out.

I could see him.

In a narrow pathway between the rock, a body was floating.

His bare foot was stuck down a crevice.

Joel, lifeless, was completely passed out.

CHAPTER FOURTEEN

There was no time. My lungs ached, my vision darkening, but he'd been here longer.

But if he hadn't been able to remove his own foot...

No. I have to be able to do this.

With a power kick from my legs, I went lower and grabbed him by the ankle, heaving.

A shot of pain rounded my shoulders, but I pulled. Because I had to.

With a dye of red spraying across the water, the foot came loose.

I didn't think. My head was spinning. I grabbed hold of him around the side, slipping my shoulder under his arm, and shot forward through the nearest hole large enough. Pushing him sideways, we just managed to fit through. If we'd gotten caught again...

I couldn't think of it.

I shot up, Joel's limp form weighing me down, dragging me under, but my legs were pumping beyond their limits, the moonlight so close within reach.

No time to even dwell on the fact that this would be so much easier if magic were still real.

We burst through the surface, and I gasped, struggling to breathe again.

Joel's head limped beside me, and my eyes widened.

"Joel?" I asked, slapping his cheek. Every movement I made was sluggish, my energy spent.

No. I had to have more energy. I just had to.

Heaving him behind me, I made for the sandy sediment on the little island and dragged him onto land.

I turned immediately to him, calling his name between heaving breaths, slapping him.

I put an ear to his chest, my own heartbeat so loud, I couldn't tell if he had one or not.

"No, no, no, no."

CPR. I could do this.

Clutching one hand over the other, I pumped on his chest, trying to hum the right tune to measure out the thrusts, but it seemed hopeless. Tears streamed down my cheeks, I could barely keep from collapsing, my teeth chattered—but I had to keep going.

I couldn't remember if you were still supposed to do the mouth-to-mouth part or not. Seemed like someone had told me once that was no longer necessary, but by everything that was good in this world, the compressions alone weren't working.

I had to try something.

I took a deep breath and then pulled his jaw apart, smashing my lips against his and blowing as hard as I could.

My vision going black, I would have thought I was hallucinating, but as I pulled back, he seemed to glow.

A faint, white light, shining out in the moonlight.

I put my mouth to his again, not even taking a breath, and *felt* it this time. The warmth, the light—the life.

It was too much for me.

I collapsed on his chest, just as he shot up, twisting, vomiting out lake water.

Relieved, I rolled back onto the sand, my breaths raspy and mixed, for reasons I didn't understand, with laughter.

Joel heaved once more and sat up straighter, his breaths heavier than my own as he stared at me.

"What... happened...?" he choked out.

I couldn't talk. My lungs wouldn't let me.

"Autumn?" he asked. "Are you all right?"

I nodded numbly.

"Did you... Did you save me?" He wiped his mouth.

Again, I nodded, staring up at him. His light was fading now. He regarded his hands and flexed his fingers, touched his chest, as if he couldn't believe he was inside his own body.

"My ankle," he said.

I glanced down, remembering the blood.

Then I shot up, fighting back a bit of vertigo as I leaned on my elbow. His ankle seemed fine.

"The water... must have washed the blood," I said between breaths.

"So I *did* hurt it," he said, lifting his foot and rubbing his ankle. "I was exploring and it got stuck and..." He frowned.

"Is it broken?" I asked.

"No, it's..." His face grew paler, which I hadn't even realized was possible. "Fine. It can't be."

He stood up, then, with strength a guy who'd just been on death's door should *not* have managed.

"What?" I asked, strangely jealous of his energy.

"I..." He scrambled to my side, placing a hand on my shoulder. "Never mind that. Are you hurt? You're cold."

His hand was so warm on mine.

I fell against his chest, my cheek on a spot just above his somewhat sculpted pec. If I'd *planned* it, it wouldn't have gone so well, but I was out of mental energy to even care.

"Autumn?" he asked.

"I'm... okay," I said. I didn't feel so at all. "We need... We need to get back to shore. Call an ambulance. Maybe... Maybe I can swim."

"No," said Joel, his tone brokering no argument.

"But you—you passed out," I said. "I should be the one to swim back. Maybe they can send a rescue."

Joel's hand wrapped around my shoulder, and he embraced me.

Actually *embraced* me against him tighter. "No. We can't. My parents are doctors, they'd find out—they can't know. They wouldn't... They can't know."

My face was flushed as I inhaled the scent of him. Warmth, like freshly washed sheets hung out to dry on a sunny summer day.

"Dry drowning," I said between breaths. "Sorry you'll get in trouble—I will, too. But we have to go to the hospital. Both of us. My sister almost drowned once. It's not something to take lightly."

"*No*," said Joel, his voice dark and stern.

Surprising me.

I leaned back and stared up at him. His lips were in a grim line, and he looked away the moment my eyes met his, a muscle in his jaw clenching, as though the sight of me pained him.

"I can heal you," he said simply. "I healed myself—and I can heal you, too."

"Joel...?" I asked, drowsy. He wasn't supposed to know about his angel DNA. Right? He wasn't supposed to have powers—not until he met the one. The one I was foolishly, clunkily aiming to be.

His lips brushed my forehead. "Thank you," he said.

And then he lit up, glowing.

I closed my eyes, but not because I was overwhelmed by the brightness. Because I needed to fall back against his chest, feel his warmth around me.

Visions danced behind my eyes. A warm, sunny day. Running through the grass, barefoot.

Laughter in the air and a song on my lips.

———

I shot up.

I was dry—mostly. The limp clump of hair down one shoulder was still damp.

I was wearing clothes—my clothes.

And I was back on the shoreline, the thumping of that bass

beat louder, the glow of the bonfire behind me and the murmur of conversations ringing in my ears.

I patted my body and realized my underwear was still wet beneath the clothes, but nothing ached. *Nothing.* My muscles reacted promptly to every moment. I felt like I could run a thirty-mile marathon.

"Joel?" I looked around.

He'd swam us both to shore, dressed me, and... left me?

I shot to my feet. No mistaking the fact that I felt like a million bucks. Common sense nagged at me that I was still in danger from my brush with death, but I'd never felt healthier.

I took a deep breath, and the air felt sweet on my lungs. Nothing rattled.

Fishing my phone out of my pocket, I brought up the last message with Joel. Those black hearts.

Where are you? I wrote.

There was no reply, so I jogged up the slope to the bonfire, looking for him there.

The crowd had dwindled quite a bit, the fire dying down.

Mikayla stood and stretched, twisting her hips back and forth as she parked her palms on the small of her back. She stopped and frowned, looking at me. "Did *Autumn Sheppard* go for a swim? In *April?* You've got to wait until summer if you're going to risk that around here."

I gripped her by both arms and she let out a little cry. Alan froze, staring at me. I wondered if I looked as wild as I felt just then. "Did Joel Serafin come by here?"

"Joel was here?" Mikayla peeled my hands off her arms. "What do you need him for?"

"Yes or no!"

Alan snapped back to life, sliding an arm around his girlfriend and shooting me a curious look. "His friends went to their cars a while ago, but I didn't see him with them."

"It would have been after that," I said, staring at my phone screen.

He'd written back. Thank goodness!

I'm fine, he wrote. *Don't worry about me. But please leave me alone.*

I blinked hard. Huh?

That message would have made more sense *before* this evening. When him sharing his number might have turned out to be a mistake—or a joke. But he'd seemed to be really flirting with me. And I hadn't... I'd *saved* his life!

I typed back a simple, *Why?*

It bounced back, a message appearing that he'd blocked me.

"No, no, no, no." The phone slipped out of my grasp.

"Are you okay?" Alan asked.

My gaze darted around the campfire as I snatched up my fallen phone. "Where's Tia?"

The screen indicated it was already ten. I was supposed to be home—I quickly dashed off a text to Mom that I was running late and didn't wait for her reply.

"You're looking for everybody tonight, aren't you?" Mikayla shrugged. "Tia walked away from us a while ago. I assumed she went to find you."

I darted for my car, looking left and right, finding unfamiliar faces everywhere I turned. The Central High guy who'd offered me a drink as I'd arrived smiled as he saw me. "Your friend have a boyfriend?"

"Huh?" I was breathing raggedly, despite the fact that I'd been feeling better than ever just minutes before.

"The chick with the scowl you came in with? I saw her get in a car with a guy. I don't know. Kind of looked like her. Could have been her brother."

Orin? But why would they leave me? They're the ones who...

"Yes," I snapped, scrolling through my screen. I didn't have a way of reaching them. Why hadn't we ever exchanged numbers?

Probably because I didn't consider them my friends.

"Yes, what? Brother or boyfriend?"

"Boyfriend," I said because I was not playing matchmaker for Tia—and she didn't seem like she'd be interested, anyway.

"Ah. Of course." He made some noise, probably packing up the leftover cups, but I was still glued to my screen. Mom wanted to know if anything was wrong and if I was on my way.

No. Getting in my car. Can't text while driving, I wrote back.

"What about you?" the guy asked. "You seeing anyone?"

Second choice. Very flattering.

"I, uh... Yes," I lied.

And then it hit me. I lowered my hand, tearing my eyes from my screen.

Whatever had happened—they didn't need me anymore.

Joel clearly had magic. Perhaps he already had—either the true love requirement was an inaccurate guess on Orin's part or...

He'd already met his true love.

He'd seemed to know what he'd been doing when he'd been healing me, hadn't seemed shocked that he could *heal me* at all.

Feeling numb, I tucked my phone into my pocket and fished out my keys, making for the door.

The faery cousins were likely on top of it.

Maybe they'd just needed to confirm. Maybe they'd been watching me almost drown, had witnessed Joel's magic, and now they were done with me.

Just like Joel... Was he scared I'd figure him out? Was he appalled at the sight of me, now that he'd seen me in soaked, dull underwear, with a soaked, bird's nest of hair, looking like I was on the verge of death?

The drive home was quiet, the sinking feeling in the pit of my stomach surprising. I'd never wanted this. Never would have stepped outside of my comfort zone to risk humiliation—to risk my life for a guy who had plenty of better options.

So why did it feel like I'd just lost something?

CHAPTER FIFTEEN

Wednesday, I went to school. I didn't see Joel—or Tia, but I didn't even see Joel's friends, either. But it wasn't like our paths crossed often.

After school, at the Prom Committee meeting, Prae reported that Tia had called in sick.

I went through the motions of looking over Mikayla's sketches for the prom décor, then sitting with Prae at a computer in the library to help design the tickets. But I wasn't much help.

Fortunately, Prae wasn't as obnoxious a partner as Mikayla might have been and we got the ticket design done for the printers, after Mikayla made a few "helpful" suggestions.

Thursday was much the same. Tia was a no-show at Prom Committee, and Mikayla brought in a giant stack of crisp, white stock paper she'd gotten the tickets printed on the night before.

"I saved some money in the budget by telling them we'd cut them ourselves," she said, plopping the stack down on the art table in front of Prae and me. She frowned. "I wonder if Tia caught something the other night at the park."

"You all went to the park together?" Prae asked, already picking up a chunk of the stack and sliding it into the art room's sole paper cutter behind her.

"Well, we saw each other there. Just a Central-Union High

post-game thing. Not a big deal." Mikayla had a laptop in front of her and was peering at the screen, typing awkwardly with mostly her pointer fingers.

I hadn't even known that was what that had been. Did Joel and his friends care about sports?

"I'm surprised Tia knew about it," said Prae, making another cut in the next stack. "Being new and all." She was frowning. I wondered if she'd wanted to come.

You could have taken my place there. I could have done without the lingering ache in my chest whenever I thought about it.

"Alan, Autumn, help me with this."

Stifling a groan, I got up from my chair and joined Alan standing behind Mikayla to peer at her screen.

"'Prom Court Vote,'" read Alan out loud. Mikayla was working on a website builder, and this page had a write-in voting form.

"Prom King and Queen are so old-school," said Prae, making another chop with her cutter.

"That's why it's 'Prom Royalty,'" Mikayla said, straightening her back and typing away. My phone buzzed and since Mikayla wasn't paying me much attention, I pulled it out, my heart thundering.

With something like hope. Ridiculous.

"Whatever gender wins, the top two will be the top royals, labels of their choosing," said Mikayla, typing away. "Then the next four will be part of the Prom Court."

"It's just a popularity contest," said Prae sourly.

I brushed aside a message from PonyFan—wondering where I'd been the past few days, if I was okay—and found a message from Ember.

Headed to your dad's tonight? she'd written.

Great. If I went there, she'd be there, and I'd get the third degree. But yeah, that was the plan. Dad and Mom would both think it was weird if I stopped switching it up. I didn't have Orin's brainwashing powers to back me up on that like Ivy had once had.

Yeah, I wrote back. *But late. Busy with Prom Committee.*

Well, this committee was proving a good excuse. Mom had even been so glad to see me "hanging out with friends" Tuesday night, she hadn't gotten too mad at all about me returning home half an hour late. *"I appreciate you texting me to let me know,"* she'd said. *"You're eighteen now, so that's all I need. The courtesy to know you're safe."*

I didn't recall her being so lax with Ivy after *she'd* turned eighteen and before she'd moved out of the house, but then again, that had been not too long after the whole nightmare at the bed and breakfast by Mom and Dad's college.

Ten years had passed. Maybe she was ready to let that tension go.

I wondered if I would ever be. If Orin and Tia would hurry up and get Joel to do what they'd told me they wanted him to do...

"Earth to Autumn? Hello?" Mikayla looked up over her shoulder at me. "We're voting here on allowing the Prom Court. Prae says it's too old-fashioned—"

"It celebrates social hierarchy," she said, cutting another stack.

"And *I* say it's an essential tradition that can be tweaked to modern sensibilities," snapped Mikayla. "What kind of prom would I be in charge of if we didn't have Prom Royalty?"

"No one will care," said Prae.

"Well, the vote is two to one so far," said Mikayla, elbowing Alan.

"Uh, right. I vote for Prom Royalty," said Alan, snapping up straight. "Babe, can you even *be* Prom Queen, though? Since you're on the committee and all?"

"What would *that* matter?" Mikayla rolled her eyes. "Anyway, I don't *care* if I win." Her lips pinched as she started one-finger typing again.

Well, *I* actually didn't care. But it seemed like one more thing that would prove a hassle. "I vote 'no' with Prae, then."

Prae stopped with the paper cutter blade halfway to the next stack and beamed at me.

Mikayla bristled. "Guess we'll just have to ask Tia to be the tiebreaker."

"Tiebreaker for what?"

Tia walked into the art room, her head held high, and a sashay to her step like she were a debutante making a grand entrance. She was wearing a tan blouse with ruffles at the neckline, along with a pair of brown slacks that hugged her thin frame.

"Tia, you're better? You didn't come to class this morning." Prae cocked her head.

"That time of month," she said, as cool as a cucumber. Alan reddened beside me, like it was something his delicate ears didn't want to overhear.

"*Okay*, well…" Mikayla tossed her shoulders back. "Glad you made it. Now *please* explain to these two that we need a Prom Court because it's tradition and it's a tradition we can remake and—"

"Yes, I vote for Prom Court," said Tia, a hand on her hip as she saddled up next to me.

"Yes!" said Mikayla, focusing back on her screen and typing away—as fast as her two fingers could.

I rolled my eyes at Tia. I wanted to *thank* her for the extra work, but we had more important matters to discuss.

"You didn't text me," I said.

"Been busy," Tia replied. We stood there in silence a moment, the squeak of the hinge on Prae's paper cutter and the *clack, clack, clack* of Mikayla at the keyboard the only sounds.

Alan cleared his throat. "Babe, can we sit?"

Mikayla waved a hand over her shoulder, her focus still on the computer. "Yeah, yeah, go help Prae with the tickets."

Alan wandered over to Prae, but she was just about done with the cutting. Tia and I moved over to the corner of the art room, out of Mikayla's sight and far enough not to reach Alan's or Prae's ears.

"What happened?" I hissed under my breath.

I wanted not to care. I really did.

"The angel saved you—after you saved him." She lifted an eyebrow. "Didn't know you had that kind of athleticism in you."

"So you were watching the whole time?"

"Of course. Had to make sure things were going smoothly."

I leaned back against the paint-splattered wall. I couldn't tell if it was an intentional design to be artistic or just the result of decades and decades of sloppy painting in this room. "Well, so then you saw. Joel has magic—you were right that it can still exist, but you were wrong about the true love thing. So wrong."

"I don't think so."

"Well, either you were wrong or he already met his true love. The fact that he…" I checked to make sure no one was watching and lowered my voice even further. "He used magic. And he didn't flip out about it."

Tia's lips pursed. "That depends on what you expected his reaction to be. Maybe he knew about the angel DNA earlier than we expected. Maybe his parents told him now. Either way, he's acting differently. His whole family is. That's why we went back into surveillance mode."

"Stalking, you mean?"

She didn't comment on that.

"Okay, who knows anything about marketing?" Mikayla announced, loud enough to hear. "How do I get everyone to vote in this online poll? Or should we pass out paper ballots, too?"

"Then people can vote twice." Alan chuckled.

"Without authentication and with the use of multiple devices, people can already vote twice," added Prae. "Not only is it a popularity contest, but it has the potential to be rigged to begin with—"

"Make an announcement and send an email," said Tia loudly. "And speak to the principal about getting it on the school website. Everyone has to log in there to turn in assignments."

"Yeah," said Mikayla, typing away. She jumped up from her chair. "Alan, let's go see if the principal is still here!"

He shrugged and let go of the pile of tickets he was straightening.

Prae frowned. "I really think you should talk to someone in IT club about authentication protocols. Maybe limit it to one vote per school login—"

"That's way beyond me," Mikayla said, taking Alan by the hand.

Prae sighed. "Then let me ask. We should stop there first before we get it on the school site."

And just like that, they were gone, leaving Tia and me alone in the vast, empty art classroom.

"Well?" I asked. "When you stalked him... What did you find out?"

Tia frowned. "Surveillance was... tricky."

"What do you mean?"

"His behavior is erratic."

No wonder she hadn't shown up proudly proclaiming they'd taken care of everything. Even if Joel had his powers, there was still the matter of convincing him to use them for us. That was supposed to be where I—friend at minimum—came in handy. But now he'd blocked me.

"His parents increased security."

"Increased security?" I cocked my head. "An alarm system...?"

"Yes, shutters closed, gate now locked around the perimeter..."

"Do they live in this neighborhood or in the White House?"

Tia smirked. "Orin wondered the same thing."

Great. I didn't want to remind anyone of Orin. The faery had been too important to me during a formative time, I supposed.

"So... We decided that his 'classmates' should go in and check on him."

"Classmates, meaning...?"

"You and me."

I scoffed. "You haven't even said two words to him, right? And me... Me, he..." Letting out a heaving breath, I pulled out my phone, swiping away some message notifications, and showed her the end of my interaction with Joel Serafin.

Instead of growing as frustrated as I was, she positively lit up. "This is perfect!" she said. "Don't you see? He's trying to stay away from you."

"Yeah..." I tucked my phone back in my pocket. "I got that..." My stomach sank. "I figured it was because I could tell people about what he did. Not that I have proof or anything—or that I *would*—but he doesn't know that. Maybe he just figures it's better if he stays away, doesn't subject himself to questions."

"No, because *you* caused the change in him."

"The... change in him..." It wasn't a question, more a baffled repetition of her statement.

"He didn't have powers before that night!" she said. "This explains everything."

"It does?" I dry swallowed, my throat scratchy. "But... But then that would mean..."

"You *are* his true love, just as Orin hoped you could be!" This was the most enthused I'd ever seen Tia, her eyes sparkling. "He was right!" She laughed, actually laughed, a light and airy sound. "He was actually right."

I, on the other hand, felt entirely weak. "No. That doesn't make sense." My knees wobbling, I let a shaky hand trace the nearest tabletop and collapsed into a chair. "He barely knows me."

"That's not how true love necessarily works." Tia was pacing now. "Don't you believe in love at first sight?"

"Not really, no. Not *true love* anyway." My hands were still shaking on the table surface. Could such a thing be true? And *for me?* The girl who could barely string two words together around another human being, let alone her crush?

"All your human stories talk of it," said Tia, still pacing. Well, hardly *all*, but Orin had probably fed her a good dose of movies and books that did just that. Though the way she spoke... It was almost dismissive, as if she were merely quoting Orin and not wholeheartedly believing it herself. "So the problem now is simply getting him to *accept* this and directing that magic where we need it."

"Whoa, whoa, back up." I gestured both hands in the air. "I..." I clutched my chest. Was this love? True love? Did it matter what I felt, so long as he felt this love for me?

But why me?

What was so special about *me?* I knew I wasn't hideous or anything, but cute or not, the fact that I had no friends generally kept the boys far away from me.

I wasn't particularly smart or funny or unique—that part of me had worn away when I'd stopped dressing in bold, bright colors in order to better blend in.

The only thing *remarkable* about me was something I shared with my two older sisters, so that hardly made me one-of-a-kind. And it was something almost no one knew about, not unless...

"The consummate lands?" I asked out loud. The world felt weightless beneath my feet.

Tia stopped moving and whirled on her heel, the joy vanishing from her face. "What did you say?"

"I still live at my dad's half the time. That was the prerequisite for becoming champion of the bloom." My nails dug into the jeans on my thigh. "A person steeped in the magic of the land where all that blood was spilled originally between faefolk and merfolk, right? Where the pact was made?"

Tia crossed her arms. "What of it?"

"Orin said... He reminded me that Ivy and Dean wished for no more supernatural creatures, but that wishing magic away entirely wasn't part of that wish." I took a deep breath. "So those lands... They could still have meaning. I could still be imbued with some kind of magic. Enough to... Enough to attract an angel? To wake up the primordial magic in his DNA?"

Tia's eyes narrowed.

I stood, the chair scraping harshly on the hard floor. "You didn't reach out to me just because you knew me. You wouldn't risk the revival of your species on something so simple. It'd make more sense to try to convince some gorgeous girl who actually would normally *have a shot* at winning the likes of Joel Serafin's heart."

Tia's jaw flinched just slightly, and I knew. She'd probably brought the point up to Orin herself.

"But Orin had a theory that me being steeped in that magic... That there was something about me that would mesmerize him, one source of magic to another. Right?"

She didn't respond.

"And... And... It wouldn't matter that he'd never look my way without such a thing. Is *true love* even a part of Orin's theory at all or is it just some kind of magic attracted to magic?"

"Love is a part of it," said Tia bluntly. But that was all the information she had to offer.

Slinking around the table, I grabbed my backpack. "I'm sure. Maybe those other angels really fell in love. Or maybe this kind of *true love* for an angel requires the presence of magic." I slung the backpack over one shoulder, going quiet. "Whatever the case, you lied to me."

Tia scoffed, tossing her arms out. "Does that matter now? We're so close. Do you want to bring our lost ones back or not?"

"*Your* lost ones," I pointed out. "I only... I only felt bad about some of them. The kids. The merfolk, mostly. You and your kind... You've been around long enough. Too long, if you ask me. Long enough to figure out how to fool stupid humans time and time again."

"We didn't *fool you*," she snapped. "The boy is clearly besotted with you. What more could you want?"

I was already at the classroom door, clutching the doorjamb with one hand. "Real love," I said, my voice hoarse. "Maybe I've always wanted that. But that kind of thing doesn't happen this quickly."

I left before she could spew more reassurances and lies.

CHAPTER SIXTEEN

An open notebook on my thigh, with notes from some class last week. My tablet opened to a textbook page. I had to keep nudging the screen awake. A pen in my right hand.

All just part of the façade, to give me an excuse to be on the weatherworn wrought-iron bench in Dad's back yard. The one that overlooked the treeline to the woods where the consummate magic ran deepest, where Orin had a cabin tucked away somewhere near the stream that led to the lake at Standing Springs Park.

It was all connected. Just as I was, and I always would be if I stayed here, in this town, with no plans to leave it.

Ember and Ivy had moved on, left the magic—and all the turmoil that had come with it—behind.

Well, except for the occasional visit.

"Boo!" Hya leaped at me from behind, wrapping her arms around my neck and practically strangling me.

She'd been quiet shuffling her way back here to me. Either that, or I'd been too lost in my thoughts to notice her coming.

"Hyacinth, leave her alone! She's studying!" Ember called out from nearer the house, then she uttered a little shriek herself as Ash let out a battle cry and must have tackled her.

"Choking..." I said, shifting Hya's small arms farther down my chest and away from my windpipe.

Hya giggled and let go, dropping back to the ground behind the bench. No wonder it had felt like an elephant weighing me down. She'd gripped on to me and lifted her feet off the ground.

I turned around to watch Hya run back toward the sliding glass door leading inside. Ash was whacking Ember's thigh with what looked to be a karate chop. His mom had torn him away from some fighting video game to play outside and get fresh air about an hour ago, which meant he was likely to be demonstrating his virtual moves to whichever sister was within reach for a while.

The sliding glass door yanked open and Noelle poked her head out. She had an apron on over her fancy blouse and pressed slacks that looked more at home in a boardroom than a house.

"No hitting your sisters!" she screeched. "Inside. Now!"

"Oh, *Mom*..." said Hya.

"It's getting dark and dinner is almost ready. Autumn!" Her voice grew louder. I actually shuddered, coming back to life. "You'll strain your eyes in this evening light. Come inside!"

The kids' voices echoed inside, and the door slid shut. Chewing my lip, I closed my notebook and folded my tablet cover over the screen. Then I sat there a moment longer, my mind empty, my unused things gathered on my lap.

"You weren't studying at all, were you?"

I jumped on the seat and spun around. Ember had done an even better job of sneaking up on me than Hya had.

"Huh? I, oh..." I stared down at the pile in my lap.

"I noticed you never wrote a thing. Never turned the page."

"I thought you were playing with the kids."

"I was..." Ember came around the bench to sit beside me. "But since I'm apparently the only one who knows what kind of trouble you may be getting yourself into, I couldn't help but keep a vigilant eye on you."

I chuckled without meaning to. Dryly, sardonically. "You should have put your *watchful eye* to use two nights ago."

"What happened two nights ago?" Ember spoke so quickly, her

voice raising to the point of hysteria, that I actually let out a little yelp.

"No-Nothing." My stammer gave it all away.

Ember grabbed on to my arm, squeezing so hard, it almost hurt. "*Autumn*, I can still tell everyone—"

"All right, all right." I yanked my arm out of her grip. Then I spilled it all—for real, this time—explaining the "true love" goal instead of the friendship, and how ridiculous I'd been to ever believe in it.

When I finished, Ember rubbed her temples, letting a quiet breath escape her lips.

"Well, first off, you *are too* someone special whom someone will be lucky to fall in love with someday, so don't sell yourself short there," she said, straightening up. "But also don't try to *make love happen* with some guy just because *Orin* tells you to—"

"He wasn't just *some guy*," I said, my voice cracking. "I actually *did* have a crush on him. I'll admit I never even dreamed it might actually go anywhere, but I thought... I thought maybe it had all been for a reason. Maybe I've liked him for a few years because it was all for this moment. Maybe there was some cosmic force beyond my understanding..." I squeezed the pen tightly in my hand. "But that was stupid. If that were the case, like a quarter of the school would be destined to have him fall in love with them."

"A popular boy?" Ember asked. I'd left that part out. When I nodded, her lip turned up in half a grimace. "So that's why you think the only way he could actually have fallen in love with you is because of..." She gestured at the woods behind us.

The consummate lands. The magic spilled here a millennium ago to consecrate the battle between supernatural creatures.

"Angels, huh?" Ember stared straight ahead.

"Now I'm wondering what else is real and just didn't choose to play a part in this war. Witches? Zombies?"

Ember wrinkled her nose. "Not zombies, please. I wonder what power they'd bestow their champion."

"Champion of rotting flesh," I said, letting go of my pen and holding my arms out stiffly in front of me, my hands flopped downward. "The champion shoots out powers of decay."

Ember shuddered and squeezed the edge of the bench below her. "Ew, no, no, no."

We both laughed softly, and I let my hands fall. Then the air went quiet between us, the gentle rustle of the leaves of the trees in front of us the only sound.

The sliding door opened some distance behind us.

"*Girls!*" shouted Noelle, clearly frustrated. "Dinner. Come on!"

The door didn't shut, and I imagined she was hovering inside the doorway.

Ember turned over her shoulder. "Just give us a minute!" she shouted. "We'll be right in—start without us."

It was my turn to peek at Noelle. Her pinched expression softened somewhat as she looked back and forth between us. "Five minutes," she said. "I'm not heating anything up for you." The door shut.

Ember laughed. "As if we couldn't just heat it ourselves."

We shifted to face one another on the bench.

"I'm sorry about ever hurting your mom," I said, not able to look up at Ember. "I didn't mean... I mean... I knew I'd hurt *you* if my attack succeeded, so it's not any better. Not that I wanted to *really* hurt you, just enough to make you... To make you..."

Ember took my hand and squeezed it. "It's okay," she said. "Back then, we all did things we regret. And you have the most excuse—you were a kid."

"I wish you all would stop saying that," I said, still unable to look her in the eye. "You make it seem as if I should just forget and move on, but I... I can't."

"I know," she said softly. Her hand fell and she clutched the jeans at her thigh. "It hasn't been easy for any of us."

"Maybe for Ivy," I said, peeking at my step-sister to find her with wet, dull eyes.

Ember shrugged. "She knew the merfolk, too—and she felt bad about Calder at the end. She still feels it. She's just better at distracting herself."

"Are she and Dean dating again?" I asked, my curiosity getting the better of me.

Ember grinned, wiping her eyes of tears not quite shed. "You think if she were, she'd tell *me*?"

"Touché." I straightened the pile of things on my lap for lack of anything better to focus on.

Another bit of quiet fell between us.

"Ember, I still don't want any of them to know about this—"

"Okay," she said. "It's your story to tell. If it's over, there's no need for me to interfere with that."

The spiral of the notebook dug into my skin, and I remembered the scribbled notes in Orin's notepad—which he seemed to have taken with him the other night.

It hadn't all been written to trick me. The way Tia had been acting—they did genuinely believe that Joel was an angel who could bring those lost to the orb's final wish back from non-existence.

I was proof that Joel had the power to heal.

That magic was real.

Ember cocked her head. "This *is* over, right, Autumn?"

I took her by the hand. "Come with me—after dinner?"

"Where?" Ember asked in a flat tone of voice, her eyes narrowing.

"To seduce an angel."

CHAPTER SEVENTEEN

"Well, we're not getting beyond that." Ember clutched the steering wheel of her dark purple car a little too hard and leaned down to get a better look at the house in front of us.

Most of it was obscured by a gate—a shiny, dark gate that looked as if it hadn't even been through a single rainfall yet.

"They did add more security," I mumbled. I checked my phone in my hand. "This is where Google says he lives."

"Not even an angel family can make themselves safe from Internet searches," Ember murmured. She turned to me. "Well? What's the plan?"

I unbuckled my seatbelt, ignoring the incessant dinging as I opened the passenger's side door and shut it behind me.

Ember rolled down her window as I approached the intercom. It seemed fancy. A touch screen was hidden from the elements behind a crisp, clear, plastic box.

I opened the box and started tapping at the screen. "Hello?"

Ember shut her car off and opened her door, gazing left and right over her shoulder as she stood behind me.

"You think they're watching nearby?" she asked under her breath.

I elbowed her just as the screen came to life. It showed a man. Gray threaded his long, black hair, which somehow he pulled off with all the finesse of a Greek god. He was thinner than a god might be, though, more trim, his tall body perfectly fitted in a sleek, gray suit that complemented his golden peach skin. His thin lips looked thinner as they didn't budge from the grim line in which they'd settled themselves. "Can I help you?" he asked dryly.

"Um..." All of the bravado I'd summoned darted straight out the proverbial window.

Ember pushed me aside a little, coming off too strong herself, too frenzied. "My sister is, uh..." She looked to me and whispered. "What's this kid's name?"

"Joel—" I started.

"Joel's friend from school," Ember finished quickly. "He's been out a few days, and she was worried..." Her flash of energy crashed and she wrung her hands.

This was one set of circumstances in which the more sociable Ivy would have probably shone for both of us awkward dorks.

"I've never seen you before." He angled his body backward from the camera, worrying his brow.

"I've... I've never come over before. We've never been introduced." I stuck a lock of hair behind my ear, then jutted my hand out toward the camera as if asking for it to shake my hand before realizing how foolish that was. "Autumn... Autumn Sheppard."

The man's eyes widened and his arm shot out, perhaps to hit a button on whatever device he was using to video chat with us. "My son is ill but doing fine considering, thank you, good-bye." The camera cut out.

"Well... That's that, I guess." Ember bounced a little in place and leaned toward her car. "Let's go."

My feet shuffled slowly toward her, but I kept looking back at the video screen. At the gate that Tia had told me was brand new. I could hardly make out the house behind it, though it was clearly two stories. "They're hiding... from *me*."

Ember jingled her car key in her hand. "The guy's dad did change when you said your name. Not that he was entirely *welcoming* from the start."

I looked around. Besides this large gate in front of the driveway, there was a smaller gate at the end of a walkway a couple dozen feet away. A sign posted on it instructed anyone approaching the gate to walk over to the driveway and contact the residents via the touch screen there.

"I'm sure that's connected to their security, too," Ember said. She looked up, then nudged me, lifting her hands just slightly to point out the cameras clearly zooming in on us from all angles. "And they're surely watching us right now—if they have a special interest in you."

"In keeping me away, you mean." I chewed my lip, then turned on my heel and opened the passenger door of Ember's car. She sighed audibly with relief and got behind the steering wheel, turning on the car and backing us out in a few smooth, graceful moves. "Let's not mess with this. Even if they're really angels, they don't want you near them. We have to respect boundaries."

My eyes widened at that. "If they're really angels, that's all the more reason why I *have to* get near him!" I clutched Ember's arm. I hadn't yet put on my seatbelt and the warning was ringing in both of our ears. "Don't you see? Pull around the block and park."

Letting out a great breath of air, Ember did as instructed after rounding the corner down the street. With the car in park, she turned to me. "Whatever you have planned, you're just going to have to wait until he shows up at school."

"He might not go back to school if he's avoiding me. There're only a few weeks until graduation. If his parents have his back, maybe they can work out some home study for the last few weeks."

"You really think he won't finish high school with his friends because he met you?"

"Yes? Maybe? If I awakened his powers like... *Tia and Orin* seem to think." I didn't even like saying their names. Ember similarly shirked, though she'd never spent more than a minute around Tia. "Maybe that triggered something his whole family doesn't like. Joel's dad didn't send us away until he asked who I was." The more I babbled, the more this was making sense—to me, anyway. "If I were any other friend of Joel's, he might have let me in. Makes me think he won't keep his son locked up away from human contact entirely."

"So...?" Ember cocked her head.

"So I sneak in—in the back of someone else's car."

Ember frowned. "Whose?"

"I... I don't know yet." None of the options I could think of seemed right. I wasn't friends with his friends. He wasn't friends with someone who might help me, like Prae. Tia made the most obvious choice, but I didn't want to talk to her. Besides, she had trouble acting human, and with Joel's potentially-angel dad on high alert, something about her might set off alarm bells in his head.

Mikayla and Alan... They'd ask too many questions. Or Mikayla would, and Alan never did anything without Mikayla.

"There's another problem," Ember said. "Another friend *may* get in the gate, but they'll see you jump out from the back seat."

"Well, I... I have to try!" I leaned back in my seat and crossed my arms stubbornly over my chest. How pathetic was I to keep pushing where unwanted? But I needed to. If he couldn't help me —if he *wouldn't* help me—I'd walk away and leave him alone.

But I couldn't live with myself if I didn't even ask.

"Not tonight," said Ember, oblivious to the dark turn of my thoughts. "After our visit, they would be too suspicious. But tomorrow, have someone text him, try to draw him out of his house."

"Who?" I asked. "I don't really know any of his friends."

"Figure it out. Or move on from all of this." Ember started up the car again and looked over her shoulder before pulling away. With movements that lacked energy, I buckled up. I couldn't just move on. "But if he's like most teens—he won't be able to stay cooped up inside forever. Not if it can be helped."

"*I* could," I mumbled, finally bringing up my text message from PonyFan and telling her I was sorry for the late reply, but I'd been really busy.

Ember squeezed my knee. "But you're not like most teens, Autumn."

She didn't emphasize whether she meant that in a good or a bad way.

———

Lunch. Friday afternoon. I clutched my tray in front of me, having left my thermal lunch bag at home.

I figured hunger would force me into action if I chickened out. Standing at the end of the line, scanning the crowded room for familiar faces, I was still close to chickening out.

There was Prae, in the corner of the room, at the end of one table... Next to Tia.

Of course.

Tia could help me with this. She *would* help me with this. But I couldn't even look at her without reminding myself that with the former faeries' help, I would always just be a tool, one they'd be using in ways I'd be slow to figure out before it might be too late.

"Autumn Sheppard!"

That had to be Mikayla.

I turned in the opposite direction to find her and Alan at the end of a table packed with rowdy students. Alan was practically a different person, a broad smile on his face as he laughed and playfully shoved a lanky guy sitting next to him.

New tactic. I crossed the room to her, being careful not to smack anyone in the crowd with my tray. There were three empty seats at the end of the table, and I sat down next to Mikayla.

"Have you seen Prae or Tia?" she asked. "I thought we'd—"

"They're busy," I said, picking up my fork to twist some noodles around it. No sauce, lots of parm. Small salad, Italian dressing, and a side of garlic bread.

"Oh." Mikayla's shoulders slunk. She had her back to Prae and Tia, so I hoped she didn't wind up inviting them over. "It's just, the prom is coming up soon and I wanted to discuss after-prom plans."

"After-prom?" I asked, after swallowing a mouthful of noodles.

"My mom and I stayed at this darling little place right near my backup school, and she talked it over with the owners, and they said they'd *love* to rent the whole thing out for prom weekend, and I thought it would be cool if, like, as a reward, the whole Prom Committee stayed there." She counted off on her hands. "I thought I'd extend an invitation to the Prom Court, though chances are, most of the Court will have their own plans by then, but that might be good, because it's kind of small, and I think they said eight was the max we could book it for."

"Eight?" That would be a pretty small hotel.

"Four rooms with two each max. If we have a few extra, the owners said we could bring sleeping bags and have a third person in each room on the floor or the couch."

"There are only four rooms?" I asked. A growing pit wore at my stomach, my fork clattering back to the tray as my appetite left me. "What's your backup school?"

"Fowles University. It's—"

"Oh, I... I know where it is."

Alan, laughing at something his friend beside him had said, turned his head to face us, his smile dropping. "Babe, what are you talking about? Your after-prom plans?"

"Yeah." She nudged me. "I'm inviting Autumn, even if she's such a Scrooge about prom. Because *she's coming to help with tickets* at the very least, right?"

"Ri-Right," I said. If Joel wasn't still locked up by then, I at least knew he had plans to be there. I *had* to go now.

"Oh, but..." Alan sucked in a harsh breath. "Babe, I didn't tell you. That place... You know how people *died* there, right? In a gas leak?"

So I was right.

Mikayla frowned. "Yeah... The owners admitted that. Something in the basement *exploded*. But it was ten years ago, and they totally rebuilt the whole building. They weren't there when it happened, but they'd loved the place and were too sad to let it just go..." She winced. "Might be part of why they're still able to fully book so close to the date. They admitted not everyone was keen to visit such a place, even if rebuilt from the ground up."

"I... I was there," I said, threading my fingers together and resting my hands on the table. "During the... explosion."

Mikayla's jaw dropped. "What?"

"My sister had a college visit." My throat was dry, and I licked my lips before continuing. "She didn't wind up going there, partly because... Because..."

"Oh," said Mikayla. Her voice was so quiet, it was hard to hear over the shrieking conversations around us. "That's awful. I'm sorry."

"You didn't know." I picked up the slice of garlic bread and tore into it, trying to focus on it and not my memories.

The sight of the owners' bodies in the basement, sweet lies in my ears that they were just sleeping.

The faeries, sucking on their blood.

Mermen flopping about in several inches of water, leaking out from the water heater. Vampires poofing like magic from one side of the bed and breakfast to the other.

Battles outside, inside... Everywhere around us.

Freshly turned vampires mad with thirst for blood.

"Well, Mom and I... We already booked it? I don't think they do refunds, and I was hoping to get everyone who goes to chip in."

"It's fine." I waved her concerns away. "Please don't change your plans for me."

Mikayla went quiet—for probably the longest I'd ever seen her—and lightly patted my upper arm. "But I do want you to come. Maybe we can do something else later to celebrate with Prom Committee?"

"Sure," I said, swallowing. I shifted in my seat, scanning the cafeteria to find Prae and Tia. They were both gone.

"Well, you're welcome if you change your mind," said Mikayla. "Like I said, even if I extend an invitation to members of the Prom Court, most are likely to already have plans. I doubt we'll have the full eight even."

"How many people are on Court again?" I asked.

"Six," she said, straightening her back and shoving her half-eaten tray farther away from her. She pulled a purse out from under her seat and took her phone out. "King and Queen or whatever titles the top two would like, then the four runners-up. Not split into any gender." She unlocked her phone with the speed of lightning and tapped away. "Prae's IT friends got it all squared away for us. Did you vote yet?"

"No." Totally forgot about that.

She pinched her lips. "Everyone got an email in their school account. Just click on the link. I'm in the top ten. Alan, too." She lowered her voice. "About a third of the potential vote is in, and yes, as administrator, I can take a peek at the results."

So she wanted me to vote for her—and Alan, I presumed. She showed me the screen and it looked like every student got to vote for two. She logged into some management console and showed me the result.

Trailing neck and neck for the top two spots were Wyatt Lim, the hottest football player and our team's star quarterback—even *I* knew that and I hadn't been to a single game—and... Joel.

Of course. Gorgeous, aloof Joel.

I didn't even see Estelle or any of his other friends on the list, though Mikayla scrolled through quite quickly. Surprisingly, Tia was there, toward the bottom. Tia Morgan? I didn't know what last name she and Orin bothered using. Unless that was a different Tia. I mean, how could *this* Tia impress enough people to earn votes? I didn't have any classes with her, but surely, I of all people would know her "surname" more than anyone at school.

"Do you think he's even coming?" Mikayla asked, bringing the list back up to the top and tapping on Joel's name. "I wonder if we should have Court alternates if anyone voted in doesn't buy a ticket."

"I think he is."

Mikayla's face popped up from the screen as she grinned at me mischievously. "That's right. You were looking for him the other night. Any special reason why...?"

"Oh, not with me." I put the last of the garlic bread down on my tray when I realized I was squeezing the crust into tiny, flaky pieces. "With Estelle Do. I think. Prae and I surveyed them for prom theme, and that's why I know." That sounded plausible. Right?

"Oh...?" Mikayla didn't seem convinced. "Well, I guess that makes sense."

A lightbulb went off in my mind. If I could spin this right, this could be an effective segue into getting her help drawing Joel out of his house. I had a better shot with her than any of Joel's friends.

"Say, you keep worrying the Prom Court might have plans after prom," I said, my voice catching on a few of the words. "Why not contact the potential winners early to see? That way, you can weed out anyone who doesn't want to chip in, or..."

Mikayla chewed her lip. "Well, I mean, the vote isn't even half in. I don't want to get anyone's hopes up..."

I doubted most people on that list cared half as much as she did.

"I'll go," I said, surprising even myself. "To that bed and breakfast after prom."

Alan frowned. "But—"

"It's *fine*." I grabbed the edge of the table. "I need... I mean, I need to move on sometime. Besides, it's a brand new building, right?" I did my best to smile.

Mikayla tapped her lip. "You *do* know Joel is probably not going to come, even if he does show to the dance."

Was I that transparent?

My eyes widened. "I mean, he has a date. So yeah."

"The Court can bring their dates if there's room." Mikayla's eyes twinkled at me. "It's just... I can't picture him there, can you? Him or Estelle."

"I guess not." I scanned the cafeteria for signs of either of them, but it was a nice day, so his friends were either outside or in the hallway again.

He was probably still MIA.

"Isn't Serafin out sick?" Alan asked. He scratched the back of his head. "Might not even show to the dance, after all."

"Oh, that's weeks away. I doubt he'll be sick for *weeks*." Mikayla fluffed him off. That made one of us.

She stared at me. "Well, how about this? I'll ask *him* alone in advance. With numbers like these, it'd be weird if he didn't make it into the top six by voting's end." She grinned wickedly and started typing.

"What are you doing?" I asked.

"Texting him, of course," she said. "We're not super close or anything, but I know he's on our group chat. How else do you think we both wound up at the same party?"

Oh. Yeah, there was that.

I put a hand on her forearm. "Do you mind not mentioning that the whole Prom Committee is invited?" I asked.

She cocked her head at me. Alan frowned.

"Oh, and... One more thing," I added, taking a deep breath before I launched into the latest plan formulating in my mind.

CHAPTER EIGHTEEN

"You know, he's not going to show." Mikayla took a sip of her Frappuccino and stared over her cup at the door behind me.

Cradling my iced green tea latte, I had my back to the door and a hoodie worn up to cover the back of my head—in case he saw Mikayla and hightailed it out of there when he figured out the "friend" she was with was the person he was avoiding the most.

"Thank you for trying." My hands were growing numb clinging to the drink for so long.

"If my cover is we were assigned to be partners in physics"—I'd asked her if she'd had any classes with him, and that had been it—"wouldn't it make more sense to go to his house if he's been sick?" she asked.

"His house is like a fortress. I couldn't sneak in with you. Too many cameras."

She arched an eyebrow at me. "It sounds like you've given that some thought. Care to share what went down between the two of you?"

"Nothing," I said quickly—too quickly.

"Well, at the very least, I got to help you pick that out." She nodded to the emerald dress in a long, plastic bag from the women's clothes store a few spaces down the outlet mall on the seat beside her. I'd asked Dad and Noelle and they'd said I could charge it to them.

They were ecstatic I was going to prom, even if it was "just" to help with committee and without a date.

I flushed thinking of myself all dressed up. And in... green. Maybe she'd just been being nice, but Mikayla had said the color complemented my skin tone. But it did make me think, with a shudder, of my history as the champion of bloom.

"I picked my dress out ages ago." So she'd told me—and she'd told me the next bit she was no doubt about to launch into, too. "White with sequins on the bodice, and a long, tulle skirt—oh, it'll go so nicely with the heaven theme. Who'd have thunk."

She would have *thunk*. Because she'd been the one to suggest the heaven theme, and after it had already seemed like we'd settled on forest and faeries alone.

I took another long sip of my drink.

"Who's doing your hair?" she asked.

Another thing to worry about. "My... My step-sister, I guess?" She'd still be here by the time prom rolled around. She was due to leave for the Caribbean the following week.

Mikayla frowned. "Well, I hope she's good at it because booking this close to the date at a good salon would be practically impossible." She took another sip of her drink and sat up straight. "Well, *there's* a sight."

Despite my whole plan to keep myself hidden until he was within arm's reach, I turned to look over my shoulder. Out in the parking lot, a group of teens spilled out from two cars—one a shiny Ford Explorer, the other a somewhat worn-down burgundy sedan. D stepped out from the driver's side of the sedan, Rick and Sabine behind him—Sabine looking especially standout today in a bubblegum pink Lolita dress and bow that perfectly matched her hair—and from the newer car, out stepped Estelle from the passenger's side and from the driver's... Joel.

My breath caught at the sight of him, though I knew he couldn't see inside like I could see him.

He wasn't dressed in his usual retro grunge look.

Instead, he wore a simple white cable-knit sweater and beige cargo pants. Estelle visibly recoiled a bit when he slipped in beside her—and she took in his look as if she were seeing him for the first time and couldn't believe what she was seeing, either.

But it worked on him. Anything would, really. It somehow made him like New England fall model chic.

A little more... *angelic* and less *rebellious*.

"New part of plan," I said, hopping to my feet and sipping the rest of my latte as fast as I could. "I'll head to the bathroom for a while, let him get seated, and then show."

Mikayla's eyes widened. "But the physics partner thing was just a cover *for you*. What am I supposed to do?"

"You'll think of something. You're clever like that."

"Autumn Sheppard, I gave up a date night to help you with this. You can't just—"

I bolted down the hall, tossing my cup in the recycling as I passed, and retreated into one of the bathrooms before locking the door behind me.

Now to wait.

I pulled my phone out of my back pocket to check the time. There were messages from PonyFan and Ember, the former sent a couple of hours ago and Ember's pretty recent.

PonyFan was just telling me how bored she was and how she'd binged two seasons of *Game of Thrones* over the past few days. We'd both been too young to watch it when it had been the big thing.

I keep meaning to watch that, too. But if my dad's journey from super fan to former fan is any indication, expect the ending to let you down, I wrote to her quickly, dismissing the message and bringing up Ember's:

Mom told me you went prom dress shopping with a friend. Is that what you're actually doing?

Yes, I typed back. *I'm going to help with Prom Committee stuff.*

Ember started typing back. Then she stopped. Then started typing again. *Hmm, okay, but is that ALL you're doing?*

Time to fess up? Would she freak and tell Dad and Noelle?

I may have drawn the angel out to meet my friend, I wrote back.

We're in a public place. I figured he wouldn't run away. But he brought his friends and I'm hiding in the bathroom.

AUTUMN!

She took a while to write back, though she was typing the whole time.

Fine. But get out there! Don't leave your friend to deal with your messes. Be careful. Watch for Orin nearby. Where are you? I'll drive and meet you.

I'm fine, I typed back. *No faery in sight.*

She started typing back, but I was faster.

Gotta go.

Right. It'd been seven minutes. Surely, that was more than enough for the whole group to get drinks and settle down. I slipped the phone back into my pocket.

My hand hovered on the handle, but then I caught sight of myself in the mirror.

Flinging my hood off, I fluffed at my hair, finger-combing it but not that effectively taming the strands.

There were slight bags under my eyes, and with the hair and sloppy hoodie, I looked wild, manic.

And I wanted to talk to *him*, the would-be model?

The door handle jiggled behind me, and, finding it locked, I heard the person try the door beside me and go inside that single bathroom instead.

Taking a deep breath as my hand hovered over the handle, I opened it up and stepped outside.

Rick and Sabine were seated at the next table over from Mikayla, sharing the booth seat beside her. They were staring at each other, Sabine laughing, Rick's arm around her, so they didn't look up to notice me.

D had his back to me at the table on the other side of Mikayla, and Estelle was nowhere to be found, though the coffee cup without an owner on the table across from Rick and Sabine might have been hers.

Across from Mikayla, Joel sat, clutching a short hot drink, a plate with a sandwich on it in front of him. His back was to me, and Mikayla had a plastered-on smile as she clutched her cup and nodded, then her gaze darted up and she spotted me.

Joel stopped talking, then checked over his shoulder to see what had gotten her attention.

His body tensed the moment he laid eyes on me.

I slipped into the empty seat at the table beside him before he could blink.

"We need to talk," I said, hushed.

Sabine's laughter cut short as both she and Rick turned to look at me and their friend.

Joel darted up from his seat, taking all of his friends aback. "There isn't a physics project, is there?" he asked Mikayla.

She winced. "I really *did* want to ask you about the bed and breakfast trip—"

"Will *she* be there?" He thumbed a hand in my direction, addressing Mikayla only, as if I weren't there at all.

"Um, maybe?" Mikayla leaned toward me, as if eager to hand off this conversation.

"Then no."

His face was tight, his eyes cold.

Despite it all—despite the fact that actually *falling in love* wasn't the important thing here—his look hurt.

"Whoa," said D around a mouthful of brownie. "Did we miss something? This have something to do with why you're 'sick'?" He made quotation marks with his fingers around the last word.

Joel took a deep breath and closed his eyes, as if fighting to stop himself from screaming.

You and me both, buddy. Why was he so *angry* with me?

"What's going on?" an alto voice with a vocal fry asked from behind me. "You're in my seat."

Right. The coffee cup in front of me. With the name "Estelle" written as clear as day upon it.

"Joel, what did she do to you?" Sabine asked, her usually sunny disposition replaced with a darker look.

"I didn't *do* anything," I snapped, feeling the pressure of all these eyes on me. Even the businessman a few tables over was looking our way, the barista wiping tables across the café pausing long enough in her arm movements to stare over at us. "Unless you count *saving his life*."

Joel opened his mouth to say something, but he snapped it shut.

He wasn't going to deny it, then.

"What is she talking about?" Estelle crossed her arms.

Joel ran a shaky hand through his wavy hair. "No-Nothing. I'm leaving. You coming?"

D was chewing wildly. "Give me half a minute, bro..."

But Joel was already halfway toward the door, pulling a key fob out of his hand. Estelle arched a brow but didn't say anything more, just reached across me with all the force of someone about to slap me and grabbed both her drink in front of me and Joel's from the table beside me. Joel was already out the door.

"You *really* messed things up for him," she said dryly, her fish-net-stocking fingerless gloves clutching a coffee cup in each hand. "Not that I'm complaining."

She left the café before I could retort, turning around and slamming her back against the glass to open the doors.

D was still chewing two tables down from me, loudly and hurriedly. "Guess he's not going to finish that," he said, snatching Joel's discarded plate and starting on the chicken salad sandwich.

"He's really leaving," said Rick, staring out the glass front of the Starbucks. Sabine was similarly stunned into looking out, and I watched, too, as the Ford pulled out of the parking lot, stopping just long enough to pick up Estelle, who had to juggle one cup against her chest to open the door before getting inside. They drove off almost the second she'd shut the door behind her.

"Well, that was..." Mikayla's voice seemed strained. "Um, so, my boyfriend is waiting on me?" She spoke as if it were a question. "Nice... Nice hanging with you, Autumn. See you Monday." She stood, smiling politely at the three remaining classmates and shooting me a bit of a suspicious look.

"Yeah, thank you for meeting me." We'd come in our own cars, so she wasn't my ride or anything. Best to let her go. "I really appreciate it."

"I expect you to put in one hundred and ten percent now," she said, and she could only be referring to the committee. As she grabbed her shopping bags and empty coffee cup, she beamed more broadly at Rick, Sabine, and D in turn, though her merriment faltered slightly at the sight of D wolfing down Joel's scraps. "Don't forget to vote for Prom Court," she said. "And get your tickets—you can buy online and pick them up at Will Call. I thought about just digital check-ins, but who doesn't want a paper ticket for their prom scrapbook, you know?" She was coming to life again a bit, her mind focused on something she could actually take charge of once more.

"Yeah, of course," said Sabine sweetly.

Mikayla nodded and headed to the trash before exiting the café.

"Oh, she forgot one—" said Sabine, starting to get up. Mikayla had left behind the clear plastic bag that showed off my dress.

"That's mine." I felt my face flush as I drew everyone's focus once more.

Sabine slowly nodded, looking over at the dress on the bench beside her. "Nice. Prom?"

"Yeah…" I tapped the edge of the table, ignoring the mild vibrations in my back pocket I knew indicated a text message.

"You got a date?" D asked between bites. I couldn't look at him because he hadn't learned, apparently, not to talk with his mouth full.

"I'm just going for Prom Committee. I guess I'm going to be on Will Call."

Our tables went quiet a moment, Sabine taking a sip of her drink and clearing her throat a little, D still chewing loudly.

"How'd you save Joel's life?" D asked after a moment. "That's news to me."

"And to me," said Rick.

Sabine nodded. "He's been weird the past few days. Said he

caught a bug, but whenever we went to his house, he seemed fine. Well, not *fine*, maybe. Uptight."

"Anxious. Pacing," added Rick. "Bored out of his mind." So Joel's parents *had* let friends come visit him.

"Tonight he says he's feeling better and maybe we can all hang out, but he has to meet this girl for a class project first," said Sabine. She looked at me, cradling her cup in both hands, as if waiting for me to fill in the blanks.

"That was me." I sighed. "Mikayla wanted to talk to him about after-prom because he's probably going to be on Prom Court"—D snorted at that, but I continued, undeterred—"and I... asked her to draw him out from his house for me."

"She *did* seem a bit out of her depth," said D, slurping his iced coffee. "Then you come out from the bathroom and ambush him, like—*bam*!" He grinned wildly at me. "You've got guts, girl." He gave me a onceover, as if taking me in for the first time.

"So... the life-saving thing?" asked Rick. "It was when we left the two of you in the lake, wasn't it?"

Sabine's mouth gaped, as if it were just clicking into place. "He's been weird ever since!"

"Yeah, I..." My gaze was fixed on the table in front of me. "He got stuck under the water. I pulled him out."

This time, Sabine gasped so loud, the employees chatting behind the counter all stopped, staring at us.

"You *what?*" Sabine said. "He never told us that!"

With an audible growl, the businessman looked up from his phone and stood to go, collecting his garbage and then gathering all his things. I guessed we were being too loud for him.

"Why did he keep that from us?" D asked aloud. "That's... oh."

"Oh?" I prodded.

Rick and Sabine exchanged a look.

Sabine spoke, straightening the bow on her head held on with an elastic band. "Joel's parents are, like, *super* strict."

"Overprotective," mumbled D through the last few bites of Joel's sandwich.

"They're both doctors," added Rick. "So they're too busy to

keep a close eye on him usually, but I can see why he didn't want them to know he almost drowned."

"But to not tell us?" Sabine rolled her eyes. "It's not like we would gossip about it. We'd know it couldn't get back to his parents."

My brain whirled with what else to say. I couldn't talk about the healing he'd done... "I wanted him to go to the hospital," I said. "He seemed fine, but you know—just to be sure."

Sabine nodded. "But he didn't want to go, right?"

"Right." That part was true.

"Because his parents would *definitely* find out if he did," said Rick. "But still... Seems a bit risky after almost drowning."

"Well, uh..." I didn't want them to think he'd actually been at risk, not since the healing magic would have taken care of any danger an average human being would have faced in the same situation. "Maybe I'm exaggerating. He didn't almost die or anything."

Sabine let out a little "hmm." "My best guess is he's terrified you'll tell his parents either way—or tell anyone and that it'll get back to them."

Chances were, based on how his dad had acted around me, they already knew. And were upset for reasons Sabine couldn't possibly imagine.

Had they not wanted their son's powers to ever activate? Why? Would it be such an awful thing to be able to heal with the flick of a hand?

Then again... Maybe they knew what I wanted from him. Maybe they were against bringing people back from the... Well, not *dead*. Wherever they were, the way they'd disintegrated into thin air—that hadn't been a normal death.

"Still, bit of a douche move, don't you think?" D said, his sandwich finished at last. "Not to tell her about his parents? To give her the cold shoulder like that?"

"He blocked me on his phone," I said to try to gain more sympathy. They could be the *ins* I needed to get close to him again. "Without even telling me why, he just told me not to get in touch with him again." I bit my lip. "I know it's... *creepy* of me to ignore such a request, but I just wanted to know why."

Sabine and Rick exchanged a look.

"I get it," said Sabine. "He owed you at least that much."

"Don't take it personally," added Rick. But it very much was personal. It was only *me* who could have activated those powers in him, probably because of me living on the consummate lands. Not this true love garbage Tia and Orin had tried to sell me on.

"If I were you, I wouldn't give him the time of day, either," said Sabine. "Not if he treated *me* like that."

"I know." I swallowed. "I just really needed to talk to him, that's all. For some closure," I added quickly.

Sabine and Rick had a wordless conversation again, then both turned and stared at D.

Somehow, he was on the same wave length, too.

"Oh, no," he said. "She wouldn't want to anyway."

Blinking rapidly, I took him in. He'd deflated, lost some of that overconfidence. "Wouldn't want to what?"

"D isn't going to prom," she said.

"Correction: I'm down for whatever after-parties you go to. But what's the point of the dance itself? Gyrating like a bunch of lemmings to some dumb pop music? No, thanks."

"You said you didn't have a date." Sabine tapped her cherry-blossom-pink nails against the cardboard of her cup.

"Yeah, but I don't..." I frowned. D. There was something about him that repelled me just slightly, even if he wasn't bad-looking beyond all the grease and the obnoxiousness. But that was a *lot* of grease and obnoxiousness to get past. "Are you asking me to go with you?" I could barely get the words out.

The corners of his lip twitched. "I know, right? You wouldn't want to anyway. Forget they even asked. It wasn't *my* idea—"

"Okay," I said. "If you can get me alone with Joel for even just a minute, I'll go to the prom with you."

"You... You will?" D drew his head back quickly. Then he recovered, the shock smoothing into a bit more bravado. "I mean, of course you would. Like, ironically, right? That's the only way to go."

My stomach sank. If someone had told me a week ago I'd be going to my senior prom—let alone with David or Dan or whatever his name was as my date—I would have thought they were joking.

"Ironically," I agreed, though I wasn't sure that was the right word. "And I really do have Prom Committee stuff to deal with, so, like... I mean, maybe we should just meet there."

D frowned but nodded. "Yeah, whatever. But if this is all so I can get you alone with my *gorgeous, douche* friend, the least you could do is pay my way." He snatched his cup and sucked on the straw until it echoed into the plastic, rattling the remaining ice cubes around. He was staring at my dress on the bench across from him in such a way that my skin crawled a little. Like he was picturing me in the dress—though I had to admit that wasn't *too* skeevy. Better than other things he could be picturing.

And my parents thought prom would make for a good memory for me?

I'd have had a better memory of the night if I spent it at home.

CHAPTER NINETEEN

Working alongside someone you didn't trust—and couldn't explain to anyone precisely *why*—was getting old.

But Tia's bemused silence over the past few weeks was even more unnerving. Like she didn't mind that we'd stopped working together to get Joel to grant our wish.

Because she probably knew I had a plan of my own and approved of it.

Anything the former faeries approved of was suspect, but I couldn't see their angle. They wanted their friends and family back, and that was reason enough for them to let me try this. Though something still felt... off.

"Thanks for the ride," said Prae. It was a warm May day and we were on a backroad, so she'd lowered the window on the passenger side of my car and was making little airplane-like movements with her hand out the window. "My parents are out of town this weekend. And I have a license, but we don't have an extra car."

"No problem."

"One week until the prom, huh?" Prae let out a sigh that was one part relief, one part anxiety. "These past few weeks went by in a blur."

Tell me about it.

I'd given up on meeting with Joel at school. He was gone more days than not, apparently arranging some kind of online learning situation with most of his teachers, according to his friends. D had messaged me I'd get my "promised time" with Joel on prom night itself because no matter what was going on at home, he wouldn't miss that. I'd given in and stopped needling him for help. Ember knew about the whole scheme, so there was no need to rush quite so much now. Besides, as more and more time passed, I had less and less faith I had a shot at all.

D and I hadn't spoken in about a week, since I'd texted him that I'd taken care of the tickets and to meet me at Will Call the night of.

He'd just sent some weird GIF I didn't recognize of a green-faced cartoonish man saying "alrighty then" in reply.

I wondered if he, Rick, or Sabine had told Joel or even Estelle about D and I going. If they hadn't expected D to show at all originally, surely the subject had come up.

"Oh, do you mind stopping someplace? It's on the way." Prae pulled her hand back into the car and started shuffling through her tote bag. She rattled off directions and my blood went cold.

Just down the street from the Slowe family diner. The town's only bookstore.

"The Hollow Tree?" I asked. "They're closed."

"No, Tia's cousin owns it." Prae sat back up again, holding some papers she'd fished out of her bag. "I was telling her about the paper I'm working on for European History and how I'd like more sources—really *old* ones, you know? To give the paper more credibility—and she said her cousin's store has some options."

Clenching my jaw, I took the turn off the road near the highway that would lead to the isolated road with hardly any businesses on it. "And did she wonder how you'd get to the store?"

Prae looked sheepish, probably thinking I was chastising her for making me run errands with her rather than forcing me to confront the faeries I'd successfully ignored for weeks. "Well, she offered me a ride when I told her my parents were out of town and I'd just planned on getting a bus, but then she texted me right before Prom Committee that she had to get home early, but that her cousin would still be at the store after school."

"Of course he would." I'd figured I'd been too lucky to have her absent from Prom Committee today. But she *had* been present for some meetings the past few weeks, so I hadn't read too much into it.

I should always read *everything* into the behavior of faeries.

The log-cabin-like Hollow Tree popped into view on the left side of the road and I turned on my blinker. There was one car in the gravel parking lot, and I recognized it as the green smart car Orin drove.

Otherwise, the store looked as abandoned and forgettable as ever.

"The light's on," Prae pointed out as we pulled into the spot right in front of the store. No point in hiding.

The "Open" sign was flipped over on the door, too. The whole place would be quirky—intriguing, even—if I didn't know who owned it. Ivy had worked here briefly when she'd been my age, but she'd quit when she'd gotten clued in to how the faery prince owner had been manipulating things. When I'd thought of him as the cool older brother I'd never had—and he'd managed to use his brainwashing powers to convince my parents he'd be the best babysitter—we'd hung out here a few times.

Customers almost never walked in here. The few who did had called ahead to pick up specific books.

It was a money pit, but I suspected it was mostly a place for Orin to store a giant collection of books he could pretend he'd be willing to part with.

"Thanks for taking me," Prae said as we both got out of the car. She fished through her tote bag and produced a wallet, then flipped through the contents of that. "I can treat you to dinner someplace if you want."

I fluffed her off. "Don't worry about it. It's been a while since I've been here."

"Oh, kitty!" Prae pointed to the sole window at the front of the store. Beyond the too-tall bookshelf that blocked half of the view inside and the messy stacks of books clearly in need of dusting was a curled-up pile of fur. The light filtering in from the early evening sun speckled all over her coat, highlighting the dots of orange throughout the black.

"A tortie," said Prae, closing her fist into the air in front of the window, as if she could pet her through the glass.

I opened the door and a bell jingled overhead. "I hear there are two more."

Prae's eyebrows shot up and she scrambled inside. "Did Tia tell you that? What happened between you two? You've both been acting kind of cold to each other. First, you go off to parties together, then you hardly say two words to one another..."

"Nothing," I mumbled. "We've just been busy, that's all."

"Hmm..." Prae seemed to be thinking that over as an excuse. I didn't think it passed muster, but it at least got her to drop the topic.

Once the door shut behind us and the bell stopped jingling, we stood in the entryway to utter silence.

Prae winced and took a few steps inside. "I guess we can just start looking?" She disappeared down an aisle consisting of two bookshelves packed tightly together. I could only spot the top of her dark hair as she walked away.

Most of the shelves were crammed with books, and they certainly looked, for lack of a better term, *lived in*. Someone had read each and every one of these books, had transported themselves to another world for a few hours. Spines were cracked, pages yellow, designs seemingly out of date.

Closer to the door was a stack of newer, crisper books with spines still intact, though that may have been because there were doubles or even triples of each title. I picked one up and flipped it open. These "new" books were from ten years prior.

"Hello, ladies."

I snapped my eyes up to find Orin coming out from the room behind the register. He stood at the counter and started stroking a pile of fur I hadn't noticed before, this one entirely orange-striped.

"Hi." Prae popped out from around a shelf and brightened. I'd almost forgotten about her obvious crush on the man. "Tia sent me to—"

"Ah, yes, brilliant." Orin stepped out from around the corner, a finger in the air. "She told me to escort you to firsthand accounts of World War I." He hovered beside her, almost but not quite, touching her back and directing her to the stairs. "Our non-fiction is largely on the loft."

The small, rickety stairs were a disaster waiting to happen and definitely some violation of the ADA. Prae babbled on about her project as her feet clomped up each step, continually looking behind her to make sure Orin was still following, and smiling wider each time. Orin, for his part, treated her as his favorite customer, returning the smile and engaging her in conversation that continued until they were both out of sight and up on the second small story.

Waiting for the inevitable shoe to drop, I stepped toward the register and offered my hand for the tabby to sniff. He did, opening one sleepy eye to check me out first, then, once he'd closed the eye, he stretched out on the counter, showing me his belly.

I knew better than to touch it, though, offering him face, head, and a little bit of back scritches instead.

To the right of me, an all-black fluffball made its way down a precarious obstacle course consisting of shelving, stacks of books, and the top of an armchair.

"You must be the third kitten," I said, knowing full well they weren't kittens anymore. The three of them looked to make an amazing trio, though, and they seemed as well cared for, as Feilia, the fluffy long-haired Maine Coon I'd remembered from the store, had been.

I'd never fully understand these former faefolk.

Maybe it was just humans they thought nothing of trampling all over.

The black cat walked behind the counter and toward the back room. Then she stopped and looked over her shoulder at me, as if to ask me to follow along.

Don't mind if I do.

No one awaited me in the back room, no Tia to make her plans for this whole setup clear. There were countless boxes and more books—and far too much dust on every surface.

The cat jumped up onto the small folding table half-covered with books and then launched up onto a nearby shelf, settling into a nest-like blanket someone had placed for her there.

"Did Daisy lead you back here?"

I spun on my heel. Orin stood in the cramped doorway, Prae nowhere to be found.

"If that's the name of this fluff, then yes." I shuffled around the table to pet the black cat. She performed her inquisitive sniff of my hand and then approved.

"Cumin is the orange cat and Rosie the tortie." His grin was broad, lighting up his eyes in a more genuine way than his "customer service" expression he'd showered on Prae out in the store.

"So you got me here," I said. "And I presume left Prae to browse books for a while so you'd get me alone." I couldn't look at his face, so I looked everywhere else around the room. At the cat. The stacks of books. The mug of half-drunk tea on the table next to... Orin's notepad.

Giving Daisy one last pat, I pulled out a chair at the table as far as it would go in the cramped space and sat down to snatch the notepad. "You let me take this home," I said, flipping slowly through the pages. "But then you took it away. Hiding any more secrets in these pages?"

"Secrets?" Orin chuckled. "I'm an open book these days."

I rolled my eyes at him and kept looking at the pages.

"Surely, Tia told you I figured out true love isn't a factor in all of this."

"That's where you're wrong." Orin took the seat across from me. He leaned over to tap the top of the page I had opened. "It's definitely a factor. Have a gander. None of these angels got their powers because of the consummate lands. None of them were even *near* this place. So there had to be another reason, and true love is it, all right?" He leaned back, crossing his arms over his chest.

I frowned, trying to decipher the page I was on. Tristan and Isolde. "I thought they were figures from myth…"

"Myths have their roots in human experience," said Orin.

With a half-hearted shrug, I shut the notepad closed and nonchalantly pulled it closer to me, sliding it on my lap. He didn't protest.

If he didn't mind me studying it, then I had to believe I wouldn't find anything more incriminating in there. Ugh. The mental gymnastics I had to go through with these former faefolk.

"I'm doing fine on my own," I said.

Orin cocked an eyebrow. "I can see that. That's why my auntie and uncle are back from the nowhere realm they were sent, and my people are no longer practically obliterated. Proper jammy."

"I didn't *say* I'd accomplished the task. But I have a plan."

"Yes, go to prom and corner the angel boy there." Orin tilted his head. How they knew the exact details of my plan I couldn't say, though I'd mentioned under extreme reluctance to Prae that I was going to meet D there for a casual thing when she'd prodded this past week. So that had definitely gotten back to Tia. But the rest of it? Even though they were always observing, surely some of that was just them putting two and two together. "Why not corner him at school all the sooner?"

"I thought of that," I said. "But he's hardly there. Since you're being *so* helpful, do you have any bright ideas for getting him to not walk away from me the moment he sees me during prom?"

"No…" Orin scratched his cheek. Well, what was he criticizing me for, then? "I'll give you until prom to try things your way. But we needed to touch base, and I figured you'd throw a wobbly if either Tia or I just showed up at your place again."

"You mean, *my parents* would." And I hadn't been away from one or the other of my parents for long the past few weeks after school.

Orin held both hands up in surrender.

"Okay," I said. "So you know what I've been up to, apparently. How about you? Learn anything else by stalking lately?"

"No one's getting in that house," said Orin, as if he'd actually considered sneaking into it. To be fair, so had I. "Not without a ruckus we'd rather avoid. So Tia and I tailed his parents. Well, me for the most part, when Tia went to school. Though she's after the angel's mum right now."

"What?" I asked. "How does that help?"

"They're still going to work," said Orin. "And anyone is allowed in a hospital. In fact, seeing familiar faces there for a week or two is pretty unremarkable, if the staff assumes you're there to visit a patient. We figured the more we learn about what they know, the easier it'll be to navigate around the barrier they've put up between the two of you."

I squeezed the notepad in my lap, the spiral wire digging into my palm. "You've put some thought into this."

"While you've been going to school and therapy, I've spent the better part of a decade getting a crack on and figuring this plan out." He bent over to scratch the tortie cat's chin and I realized I hadn't noticed her slipping back here. I frowned at his flippant attitude toward what I'd been up to, as if it weren't *his* fault I'd been in therapy to begin with. The cat jumped up into his lap. "I'm not giving up now, when it's all so close within reach."

I waited for him to continue, wondering how long Prae could be caught up amongst his history books. Quite long, actually, now that I thought about it, given the packed-to-the-brim state of his shop.

"Something dodgy about the parents," he said softly. "More than we were expecting, even."

"What do you mean?" I asked. Then again, it sort of clicked. Parents typically didn't install expensive, high-tech security systems because their sons didn't want one girl they'd sort of flirted with to leave them alone. If it *was* serious, the first step was usually involving the police, but if the whole situation revolved around angels and magic...

It'd make sense the parents wouldn't call the authorities.

"I think you've figured it out," said Orin, observing me. It had never been faeries who could read minds—that had been merfolk.

Though the way my sisters had described it, it hadn't been as simple as reading thoughts.

"They've told their son he's an angel," I said. "What are they afraid of? He can heal... That's as much as I know. But what if he can't actually bring people back?"

"He can," said Orin firmly. "He might not know it yet, but I'm sure he can. With you at his side—"

"With the magic of the consummate lands, you mean," I said dryly. "It might have helped to know I actually had a shot with him —because of forces beyond my control."

"Is that what this is about? You insisting it's all about the consummate lands, that you're unworthy of an angel? It definitely helps—magic like that will call supernatural beings like a moth to a flame. But, love, so far, he hasn't exactly been cracking boyfriend of the year. He'd be lucky to have you after this is all over."

I weighed the benefit of pursuing this conversation further.

There wasn't one.

The former faefolk weren't my friends. I'd known that before all of this, and I knew it even more now. I just had to remember that.

"Why do you think Joel's parents are keeping him from me?" I asked. "Did you learn anything from tailing them to their workplace or did *you* waste your time, too?"

"Touchy, yeah?" Orin confined a laugh to a mild snort. "I managed to get into his mum's office one afternoon—nothing too much of note, but there was this." Orin shifted in his seat and the cat let out a little irritated chirrup as he pulled his phone out of his cargo pants pocket and brought it up to the table. Tapping away at it, he brought something up and then turned the screen to show me.

It was a picture of a desk, fairly neat and tidy, generally unremarkable, a thin, high-tech monitor on screensaver and a desk phone beside it.

"What am I looking for?" I asked, leaning over the table for a closer look.

He tapped the picture of the monitor, the screensaver in

particular. At first glance, it seemed like one of those generic vista screensavers that came as default with a lot of programs. On closer inspection, there was something in the reflection of a dark patch of grass on the screen. Something behind the monitor in the room.

"What is that?" I asked, wondering why he hadn't just snapped a picture of the item in question.

Orin swiped the screen again and showed me a picture of the office's small window, a display box on the shelf below the sill.

An empty display box. Black base, clear stand holding up nothing, clear dust cover on top.

"Did you take whatever was—" I started.

But Orin shook his head. He flipped back to the picture of the monitor, this time zooming in to the questionable spot.

The image was pixelated, so it was hard to see clearly, but whatever it was was red. Something red—sitting in that same display case.

"It's invisible to the naked eye," Orin explained. "At least for those of us without angel blood in our veins. But I took off the top and touched it—it's there, all right."

"What is?"

"An angel feather," said Orin, his voice taking on a reverent quality. "And judging by the reflection its magic failed to take into account to consider when in stealth mode, it's blood red."

The shop bell rang. Either Prae had stepped outside or The Hollow Tree actually had another customer.

"Autumn?" a far-too-familiar voice rang out. Ember. "Autumn, are you in here?"

"Autumn?" another semi-familiar voice, a woman, joined her.

A child squealed, and both cats in the room perked up, their ears twisted backward as they turned their heads in unison toward the door leading to the shop. Heavy, uneven toddler-like footfalls preceded the squealing of a third cat.

"Looks like we have company," said Orin.

CHAPTER TWENTY

I darted up, still clutching Orin's notepad as I swept past the former faery prince and out into the bookstore proper.

"Ember?" I called out. Orin's third cat was on the register, its back arched as it batted downward with a paw. A small child with a deep brown complexion was jumping up on the balls of her feet trying to reach the animal as Journey Slowe pulled her back. Journey's long, brown coiled hair was pulled back into a high ponytail, her dark eyes narrowed as I stepped out from the backroom—no, as Orin stepped out behind me. She looked like an older clone of her daughter.

"Cumin!" said Orin, pushing past me and even bumping me along the way. He swept the orange tabby up into his arms and rested him against his chest. The cat purred loudly and rubbed the top of his head against Orin. "Not used to much company," he said. "Especially kids."

"At a bookstore?" offered Journey dryly. "Store cats are usually a little friendlier."

We were caught in a silent standoff, Journey's kid's attention diverted as she padded her toddler feet off to a sunny spot by the window, climbing up onto a plush chair. A waft of dust puffed into the beam of light as she moved to reach a big picture book with a faded cover that was on display.

Footfalls pounded down the steps. "Autumn!" Ember, wearing a pale blue sundress, took the rickety stairs two at a time. "We were headed to Journey's dad's place and saw your car out front—"

Of course. I should have figured that was a possibility. But I hadn't known Ember would pass by this way right at the exact right time.

Orin bent over and spoke in soft tones to his cat, letting him jump from his arms and head into the backroom. As he disappeared into the dim light, three sets of shiny feline eyes stared back at us. It was kind of eerie.

"I'm just giving a ride to a friend," I said, clutching the notepad against my thigh.

Behind Ember, Prae took the stairs down at a much more reasonable pace, a couple of thick books clutched to her chest, her face painted in curiosity.

"Prae, that's my step-sister, Ember, and this is her friend Journey and Journey's daughter." I gestured around the store.

"Her name's Jerrica," said Journey. She looked from Prae to me. "Hi, kid. It's been a while."

"Hi." I shuffled my foot across the scuffed wooden floor awkwardly.

Ember wove her way around tables stacked with books and jutting displays and made it to the counter. She paused, staring daggers at Orin, then rounded the counter and grabbed me by the forearm to drag me around with her.

Orin stepped back, his hands up in a form of surrender.

"I'm fine," I whispered under my breath. Prae was making her way to the register, clearly observing us. Jerrica was flipping through her storybook and not paying attention at all.

Journey knew about the supernatural, and she had even once been a vampire—I wondered if that meant Ember had now filled her in on what I'd been up to—but I hoped the presence of the other two would keep Ember from making a scene.

Ember's gaze darted to the notepad in my hand—she'd seen it with me in the diner a few weeks back—and she ripped it out of my grasp before I could blink.

"Hey!" I shouted, following her around the store. So much for not making a scene.

Prae let out a little awkward laugh and put her giant books down on the cashier's counter with a clunk. "I'll take these." Her voice was warm, even flirtatious. "Thank you so much for your help."

Journey shook her head and stared hard at Orin. "You can't help yourself, can you? All those charms and lies just spilling out of your mouth."

"Nice to see you again, too, Miss Slowe." Orin rang up the first book. "Always a pleasure."

I ceased hearing their conversation because Ember had stopped in the corner of the store, allowing me to scramble up to her.

She flipped through the notepad, holding it up to the beam of light, and furrowed her brows.

"What are you doing?" I hissed.

She spun on me. "I should ask you the same thing."

I reached for the notepad, she shimmied away. I tried again and I was grasping air, the woman having spun away like some dancer.

Jerrica giggled from behind me somewhere, her attention now on my frustrating sister.

"Fine!" I stopped, lowering my voice when I caught Prae's head turning toward us. "Then *you* study it to see if he's hiding anything more from me."

Ember tilted her head, clutching the notepad to her chest and leaning closer to me—but still keeping the notepad just out of reach. "I thought you weren't working with them anymore."

"I'm not," I said, clenching my jaw. "I have a plan I came up with without their help—but I figure it can't hurt to see what they can offer. We want the same thing."

"*Do* you?" Ember asked.

"We do," I said. At least on that, I was sure. Mostly sure. I leaned in closer. "Just... I need a minute with him. Trust me, okay? I need you to trust me to handle this. It's the only way to get them back."

Ember's shoulders slunk, her face focused downward.

Jerrica toddled up beside her and grabbed her by the wrist of the hand not holding the notepad. "Auntie Emby! Spin again! Let's spin again!" She tried spinning in place like Ember had but immediately crashed into a stack of books, sending them scattering across the floor. Jerrica laughed, but Ember caught her before she toppled over, too. Jerrica set to work gathering the books.

"No," Ember said, straightening up. "Let *him* clean it."

Jerrica clapped her hands together then knocked over another stack of books beside her on purpose. Cat hisses rung out from across the store space.

"Oy!" shouted Orin. "Watch it, maybe, all right?"

Ember took the still-giggling Jerrica by the little hand, then spun on me, pointing at me with the notepad. "We're talking about this at home." Darn. It *was* a Dad's house night.

But at least she was heading out.

Journey joined them near the door and took Jerrica's other hand.

"Darling little girl," said Orin, a smirk only just slipping past his lips. "Real chip off the old block."

Journey sent him a look that would have had mere mortals fleeing, then the bell rang out overhead and the three left the shop.

Of course, though Orin was mortal now, he wasn't any *mere* mortal. He'd lived too long as an immortal.

Prae clutched her books to her chest, and Orin stepped out from behind the counter.

Two furry heads poked out around the counter behind him at his feet.

"Gone already? Not too concerned then, were they?" He tucked his hands into his pockets.

Prae looked from Orin to me and back. "Did you used to date one of them?" she asked the former faery.

I snorted. "Yeah, and he was a real disappointment all around." I took hold of Prae by the elbow and directed her to the door. She was hunched over slightly, her head drooped, as if I'd just blown her fervent dreams.

Good, if they involved hooking up with Orin. That wasn't going to happen for more reasons than one.

The skittish tortie jumped up on a shelf beside us, seemingly out of nowhere.

Remembering the sweet bookstore cat before, Feilia, and the times I'd spent here, scratching her chin while I'd flipped through chapter books about daring adventures and kickbutt princesses, I reached a hand out to let her sniff it.

She did, hesitatingly, and seemed to approve—headbutting my palm until I gave her behind-the-ear scritches.

"Hi, baby," cooed Prae.

Rosie jumped back, her back arched, and ran off, disappearing amidst the chaotic shelves.

"She's sensitive, that girl," said Orin by way of explanation. "I think only those who've danced with death might earn her sympathy."

Prae blinked rapidly, staring at me.

Scowling, I opened the door, the bell sending what sounded like a stampede of cats scurrying, though I doubted it was more than the three.

Prae stepped outside. "What was that about?" However, I didn't follow her, letting the door shut between us.

"Red feather," I said, flinging my hands in front of me as if telling Orin to "hit me" with the details. "What's it mean? Go!"

Orin's head snapped back as if I'd managed to surprise him. He, who'd never so much as blinked as his plans had unfolded around him.

But he recovered quickly, quirking his lips up into a smile. "Well, I can't say for certain—"

"Theory, then."

"My guess is it can only be seen by those with angel DNA—maybe even only those with the purest form. And it was once white—or black, if it came from a fallen angel originally," he said. "And that it turning red was some kind of indicator."

Prae shuffled to the front window and I could see her peering inside the shop, stepping up on tiptoes.

"An indicator of what?" I asked, my voice harsh and low.

A gleam beckoned in Orin's eye. "That one of their powers is activated."

Well, that would explain why his parents had put their son on lockdown, if that feather had turned red the night I'd saved him from drowning. But it didn't tell me anything I didn't already know.

What I didn't know was how I was going to convince him to use those powers for my benefit.

CHAPTER TWENTY-ONE

The last week before prom flew by. With seniors due to finish a few weeks early, classes were winding down. It wasn't that surprising for teachers to assign more "fun" activities without the pressure of preparing for final exams.

Prom Committee was more work than my classes were, and even that was at an end—mostly.

There was still tonight. The prom itself.

"Up or down?" Noelle asked. It was early afternoon on the Saturday of prom, and I was seated in front of the deluxe double wooden vanity in her and Dad's room.

Mom was downstairs, visiting with Dad, while Ember was somewhere in the back yard with Ash, Hya, and Jerrica. Mrs. Slowe and Journey had dropped by this morning and were out picking everyone up some lunch—though not from their family diner, for once. Mr. Slowe apparently was not to be told of their incognito excursion.

"Whatever you think is better," I said, getting a good look at the array of makeup, serums, hair creams, bobby pins, and whatever else Noelle had pulled out for today.

"Up is easier to handle at the dance," said Noelle, picking up a hairbrush. "Though it's harder to pull off and a little painful."

I tried not to let out a gasp as she roughly ran the brush

through my long locks. I checked the time in the mirror's reflection from the alarm clock next to her bed. 1:00. I was supposed to get to the gym several hours early to help with the finishing touches of setup. We'd already been there half the night after school to get it all ready.

It had seemed almost perfect. But Mikayla didn't accept "almost perfect." You'd think this was a sport and some talent scout was due to attend the big dance, to offer her acceptance into the college of her choice merely on tonight's "performance."

Without warning me, Noelle swapped the hairbrush for some kind of spray and sprayed my head as if it was a fire extinguisher and my roots were on fire.

I coughed, my eyes growing watery, but before I could even comment on it, she'd swapped the spray for the lid from a jar of goo and was dipping both hands in it and then spreading the goo on my scalp, working her way to the ends of my hair. It felt like she was going to rip the hair out by its roots.

"Should have said 'down,'" I said, mumbling.

"You still would have gotten all this conditioning." She grabbed my head and straightened it so I looked forward. "Now hold still."

I let her do her magic.

"So if you're bringing your dress to the gym and getting ready shortly before the dance, when are we getting pictures of you, hmm?" Noelle asked, now working through it all with a comb.

My head bobbed with every tug. Beauty was painful.

"I'll make sure we get pics," I lied. Well, Mikayla was bound to, anyway. A commemorative photo of the ragtag Prom Committee.

My phone buzzed on my lap and I quickly logged in to check the screen, trying to be subtle as I angled it so Noelle wouldn't pay it much mind.

It was from PonyFan. Today was her prom, too. She almost hadn't gone but had decided she may as well "get the experience." She, unlike me, had a date. *Just a friend, though*, she'd told me.

Scratch that. I did have a date. The thought of it made my stomach sink. *Me, too*, I wrote back. *Well, kind of a friend.*

You have a date?! She wrote back, surprised. *Why didn't you tell me?*

I shrugged, though I knew she couldn't see it, earning me another chastising from Noelle to stay still. She was sectioning the hair off into multiple ponytails now, affixing each so tightly in place, my scalp was straining.

Sort of last minute, I wrote. Though we'd sealed the deal weeks before. It just wasn't something I'd run and message PonyFan about. *But it's no big deal. I have committee stuff first. We're just meeting there—not going out to eat or anything.*

She was typing, but it took her a while to send her reply. *When did this happen???*

She knew about Prom Committee—I'd talked about it with her before, and how I couldn't believe I'd been roped into it, but it had at least gotten my parents off my back. So she meant the date.

A couple of weeks ago, I wrote back, stretching the truth a little. One of the kids let out a particularly high-pitched joyous squeal that carried through to the front of the house.

I can't believe you didn't tell me earlier! she wrote quickly. *What's their name?*

Noelle was now weaving braids into the various ponytails she'd crafted from my hair. Since when did we care about names? I'd never asked for her date's name. What would it matter? It wasn't like we even knew each other's classmates.

I don't know, I wrote back, and it wasn't a lie. I'd never pressed to learn D's actual name.

You... don't... know? She added a few confused faces.

I sent a winky face emoji with its tongue hanging out.

"What do you think about this?" Noelle asked. She'd capped the braids at both ends and was now arranging them atop my head loosely. With the way she looped it, I felt vaguely like a faery princess, a braid wrapping tightly around each ear to join up in a coiled-braid bun at the back.

"Beautiful," I said, my smile wavering. It *did* look nice, but the thought of "faery princess" ate heavily at my mind.

I quickly typed out, *Have fun*, ready to end the conversation since a fluttery feeling in my stomach was leading to twitchy muscles. I added a kissy face emoji.

She typed, *You, too, Miss Mysterious.* She added a series of hearts, black, purple, black, black.

Sure. Fun. That was the aim of tonight for me.

I'd ask her to send pictures, but neither of us had ever shared pictures with one another. She knew my name was Autumn, followed a number of my profiles, but neither of us were big on appearing in videos online or even images, like everyone else seemed to be.

Orin's last text in the list popped briefly into my vision—Tia and I had exchanged numbers after the meeting at The Hollow Tree—before I flipped the phone over on my lap, tapping one socked foot against the carpet anxiously.

Daddy Bird has one, too, he'd written. "Bird" was how he'd decided to refer to the angels in texts. *It's not visible, but he keeps staring at the same spot every time he drops by his office. Another one of those empty display boxes. Like he thinks it's going to change or something.*

He'd asked for updates for the movements of "Baby Bird" at school, but I had nothing for him. Joel had spent half the week out, and the other half not appearing before my sight. The only reason I'd known he'd been there at all was because every so often, D had texted me.

My gorgeous friend you're using me for is here today, he'd written two days before. *Still got a bug up his...* He'd included an emoji of a peach, I assumed to mean rear end. *You really did a number on him, huh?* He'd written next. *I still think cornering him at prom is best. Fewer places to run.* He added a laughing emoji.

"There." Noelle patted both sides of my head, having finished sticking me with more bobby pins than my hair had any right to be able to hold. Before I could comment, she was back with a spray, forcing me to snap my eyes tightly shut and bite my tongue.

"Perfect," she said, beaming into the mirror once I finally opened my eyes. I smiled back at her, tears welling. Whatever she'd last used stung. "Now the makeup." Noelle pulled out a drawer and removed package after package of new sponges and makeup brushes.

I winced. Makeup made my face feel itchy.

"I'm surprised you didn't want to get ready with some girl-friends," continued Noelle, rubbing a wedge into a pale cream-colored primer or foundation or something. She'd already had me wash my face this morning.

"You're surprised?" I couldn't help replying.

Frowning, Noelle went to work, spinning me around by the shoulder and tilting my head up. "I was sure you and the other girls on Prom Committee might have wanted to get together for lunch, since you're all missing out on dinner like most kids."

The wedge attacked my face and pulled on my skin. She kept going back for more of the cream and I had no idea where my skin was putting it all.

"Mikayla wanted to do something special with her boyfriend."

"That's the one dating Alan Parr?"

I was surprised she'd remembered that. "Yeah. She's cool," I added. We weren't exactly matched well, personality wise, but she wasn't mean and she *had* done me that favor.

She'd just about *died* when Prae had told her I was going to prom with D, and I'd explained it had "sort of happened" after she'd left us at Starbucks.

"Bit of a downgrade from your aim of Joel Serafin, if you ask me," she'd said, her eyebrows shooting up to the sky. But she'd bit her lip before adding, *"Then again, he's taken, isn't he?"*

"I'm glad to hear you get along," Noelle said. Now she got a new wedge and dipped it into something else, spreading all the goop around on my face even more. "What about *your* date, huh?"

I never should have told them I had one.

"It's nothing," I said quickly. "Casual. He's meeting me there because I have Prom Committee."

"Hmm," said Noelle, finally swapping the wedges for a brush. I stretched my mouth to both sides and felt the foundation caking and cracking, like I was fighting to break through a sheet of ice on my face.

"Stop that," said Noelle, though not too meanly. She was more concerned with staring at a large palette of eyeshadow colors she had. "Your dress is emerald green," she said. "And you have brown eyes and hair, and a somewhat pale complexion..." She was talking more to herself than me. "Let's go with a forest green. Don't often get to go with bright colors—and I can blend it with some browns to make it look softer, more natural."

I shrugged. She knew better than I did.

First, though, she picked up what looked like a coloring pencil and asked me to close my eyes. "Your father would really like to meet your date," she said, drawing along my eyelash line.

"It's not... We're not..." I started. "It's not like that," I said to put an end to it.

"Well, let's hope so. He's worried about your trip afterward."

I'd told them it had been near Fowles University. I hadn't told them it had been the same place where Noelle had gotten the blood sucked out of her and there'd been a few bodies in the basement. Technically, it wasn't *the same* place anymore.

"He doesn't need to worry," I assured her. "D isn't coming with me."

I opened my eyes as Noelle stepped back to find her nose wrinkling.

"D..." she said.

I'd told her the name before and she'd had the same reaction every time. It *did* seem a little pretentious to lay claim to a single letter of the alphabet.

She dipped a small sponge on a stick into the green eyeshadow. "I wish you'd gone on birth control," she said. "It's helpful with cramps, too, you know."

I felt my skin blush, but I couldn't see my cheeks going pink in the mirror under the layer of caked-on goop.

"I'm not... Like I said, he's not even coming. And we're casual. I swear."

"Well, you should bring some condoms just in case." As if she *wanted* to kill me, she walked across the room to her bedside dresser and pulled out a pack. I didn't realize she was even at risk of getting pregnant at her age. "Put these in your bag," she said, tossing an attached strip of four—*four*—of those squares on the vanity in front of us.

I just stared at her, wide-eyed.

"Oh, come on," she said, laughing. She didn't often laugh alone with me. "All the girls got 'the talk' before prom, and you can never be too careful. Easton said he'd let me handle it, but maybe we should get your mom in here and we can do it together—"

"Nope," I said, quickly grabbing the strip. The wrappers crinkled in my hand. Why were these things so noisy? "It's fine. Let's move on."

Noelle chuckled again and asked me to close my eyes. She went to work with the shadow, pausing to dip the little sponge every few moments.

"Well, at least you're having a normal high school experience," she said. I was surprised because all I heard from her was how I wasn't *normal* at all because I had so few friends. She didn't say that exactly, but she certainly implied it. "Not having any supernatural myths come to life around you," she added.

Oh. *That* kind of normal.

My hand squeezed the wrappers. Panicked at the sound, I let the strip go.

Noelle stopped applying eyeshadow, and I peeked to see her grimace.

"I'm sorry to bring up bad memories," she said softly.

Right. Memories. That was all that was bothering me.

I shook my head and a car pulled into the driveway. I couldn't see it from where I sat, but I heard it.

"Must be Lacey and Journey back with lunch," Noelle said. "We're almost done."

She went to work putting on the finishing touches and the front door opened, Journey's voice carrying throughout the house and the sliding back door opening as the sound of three screaming children joined them.

"There." Noelle beamed at me and directed my face back to the vanity mirror. "Gorgeous."

I supposed I did look beautiful—otherworldly, not quite me. The green eyeshadow was almost smoky, definitely more forest green than bright green in color.

She handed me a tube of unopened lipstick. "This color should look good with the look, but no sense in applying it before eating." It was a shade of red called "wine." I knew I'd never put it on if she was relying on me to do it myself. The makeup I had on itched enough as it was. I added it to the strip of condoms I was apparently supposed to stick into my duffel bag for the night.

"Now don't go messing up your..." She looked at me. I was in a gray tracksuit. "Hair," she finished, "before tonight."

"Thank you," I said, offering her a flittering smile as I tried to look anywhere but at the pile in my lap.

Noelle lit up and patted my shoulder. "You're going to have an amazing time tonight. I'm so proud of you for getting out there."

My smile struggled not to fall, but I locked eyes with her in the mirror and bit my lip, nodding.

She cupped my chin briefly. "Careful about that lip biting when you've got your lipstick on."

She walked off, her voice carrying down the hall as she struck up a conversation with Lacey, and I sighed, standing up and walking over to my room, my phone in one hand and the collection of wrappers and lipstick in the other.

Hya practically barreled into me at the top of the stairs on her way to the bathroom. Flinching, I clutched my fist tighter so she wouldn't see what I'd crammed in there.

"Ooo, a princess!" she said, stepping back and taking me all in. Then she laughed. "A track-star princess!"

"Ha ha," I said. "I'm putting on my princess dress later at the ball."

"'*The ball*,'" Hya singsonged back to me, prancing around and clutching an imaginary skirt around her.

Ash slugged up the stairs, pounding with each step. He stopped at the top of the stairs and nodded, almost appreciatively. "What's that?" he asked, pointing to my clutched fist.

I looked down and panicked, though only the tip of the lipstick tube was visible. "Lipstick," I said quickly, tucking the hand behind my back.

"Yuck," Ash said. Probably because Hya had gotten into Noelle's makeup supply more than once a few years back and drawn red streaks all over both of their faces.

"Munchkins, wash your hands!" called Dad up the stairs. He clutched the bannister at the bottom, and his already amiable face lit up even more as Ash moved around me. "You look beautiful, Autumn. Just beautiful."

"Thanks," I said, cringing. He meant well, but I was starting to feel the spotlight on me from all this attention and I didn't like it.

I darted forward as one of the twins turned on the sink in the bathroom.

"No-o," Hya said, making a one-syllable word into two. "I got here first and I have to pee."

"Then let me just wash my hands first," Ash snapped back.

Downstairs, little Jerrica's laughter drowned out whatever else the twins were going to argue about.

I got into my room and shut the door behind me, leaning against the door and letting out a deep sigh.

My fist untightened and I looked at the collection of wrappers and lipstick and shuddered, scrambling to an outer pocket of my duffel bag and tossing it all in there, zipping it up tight. I'd just throw it out, but sometimes the twins had garbage collection duty and I didn't want them rifling through there. Maybe someone else at the bed and breakfast would need them anyway.

I checked my phone again, but the only update was from Mikayla, saying she was already on her way.

Time to grab some lunch and get moving.

———

Ember hadn't stopped chewing her cheek the entire way to school. Since Mikayla's mom had ordered a shuttle from prom to the bed and breakfast for at least those of us on the Prom Committee, I hadn't wanted to drive myself and leave my car at school all weekend.

Besides, I knew Ember would want the time to check in with me.

"So this boy—this angel—is going to be at the dance," she said, tapping the steering wheel at a stoplight.

"As far as I know." I wrung my hands in front of me. My duffel bag was atop my feet, which were still in sneakers, my garment bag draped over the back seat behind us.

Ember sighed. "Autumn, I'm supposed to leave for my research trip next week—"

"Supposed to?" I asked. "No, it'll be fine. Go."

Though I didn't say that if I managed to succeed this weekend, she might not *want* to. Not if there was everything to catch up with her lost merman prince.

I rubbed at my neck where Ember had bit me all those years ago, almost subconsciously.

Ember glanced at me before the light turned and started the car up again, clutching her steering wheel.

"I know I was your age when... When everything happened," she said. "And I felt so grown up—but I wasn't, Autumn. Not enough to handle all that."

I shrugged. I didn't want to get into the fact that I'd been even younger. Maybe a youth steeped in supernatural warfare had better prepared me for this at this age.

"I can't just *leave you* with you in the middle of all of this."

"I'll be fine," I said. "Besides, I want to talk to Joel once and for all this weekend. If he can help me, maybe he'll do it as soon as he can. If not... If not, then..."

"Then your involvement in all of this is over." Ember's jaw clenched. "It's one thing for you to flirt with some boy you like, but this whole..." She gestured wildly with one hand. "This whole thing reeks of faery. No offense."

"Reeks of faery...?"

"Orin was always so calm and friendly," she went on. "But he was always manipulating us behind the scenes. He was always working for his own ends. Even with how old Dean was—is—Orin was older than him by a mile. I don't like that he was the prince you were stuck with."

I chuckled dryly. As if he'd been the last muffin in a baker's dozen and he'd been bran and prune flavor.

"This isn't a laughing matter." Ember worried at her bottom lip. "I should tell our parents—or at least Ivy."

"No. Don't," I said quickly. "Ivy wouldn't understand."

"And I do?"

"You do," I said softly. "Because you feel it too—the guilt. The desire to bring them all back."

"Well, not *all*, I suppose…" Ember went quiet for a bit. "But, Autumn, I don't trust Orin and his cousin."

"Did you make any sense of anything in his notepad yet?" I asked. It wasn't the first time I'd asked since she'd taken it from me a week before.

"No… But he could have written that notepad precisely to help trick you. It's all about true love awakening an angel's powers, and it doesn't even mention the magic of the consummate lands, like you figured out."

I nodded. "Because he wanted me to think this was some special destiny and not just… another occasion for him to use me." I was surprised to find the pressure of tears welling behind my eyes. "I don't care if he's using me, Ember. We want the same thing."

"Do you?" Ember asked.

"He wants the faefolk back," I admitted. "He probably doesn't care about the merfolk. But there's no way just one kind is returning. I don't even think he'd care about stopping the merfolk from returning, so long as everyone's powers were still gone—"

Ember slammed on the brakes, sending me flying forward, my seatbelt digging into my chest. A car behind us honked and swerved around. Shaken, Ember pulled off to the side of the road. We were only about half a mile from the school now.

"What was that?" I asked, my heart still hammering in my chest.

Ember roughly shifted the car into park. "Where's the orb now?"

"Huh? Oh, the orb." That round ball made of three sections, one each for blood, bloom, and water. Orin had kept custody of it when he'd pretended to be a neutral party, and it had been integral to Ivy and Dean making their wish, and to each of us making our vows to fight as champions. "I don't know."

"Ivy and Dean held it last." Ember was talking now more to herself than me.

"Why does that matter? What power would the thing still have?"

"I can't say for certain, but Orin was always one step ahead of us. It's too important not to know its whereabouts. I have to ask." She reached into the console and pulled out her phone. It was thicker than most, an unbendable older model.

I reached over and grabbed her hand. "No! What are you doing?"

"What I should have done two weeks ago. Let Ivy and Dean know about this."

"And what are they going to do? Hop on a plane and be here in a few hours?"

Ember raised a brow at me, as if that were obvious.

"*No*," I said. Somewhere amidst my own messages was a cheerful message from Ivy telling me to have fun tonight and send her some pics. She was out of the loop and I wanted to keep her that way. "Ember, you promised me."

"To let you handle this by yourself, when the faery prince is up to his old tricks again? Not happening." She tugged her phone out of my grip.

"Just one more night, okay? Just give me tonight. I have a plan."

Ember sat stiffly for a moment and then practically tossed her phone into the console. "This is a mistake," she said as she looked over her shoulder and put the car back into drive.

The car went quiet, as I didn't have a retort for her.

"Oh!" I said after a moment. "Shiny-colored ball."

"Huh?"

"Orin mentioned it. The orb... I think it's at his cabin."

Ember growled. Actually growled as she squeezed the steering wheel tighter. "Of course he has it."

"If they have it, they can't have a use for it, surely. If they could have done this without me, they would have."

"Maybe we should ask Ivy and Dean what *they* think."

"You promised," I said, though maybe she hadn't technically said those words. "Give me tonight."

Ember didn't look entirely convinced. Time was running out. Soon my whole family would know what I was up to. I needed to enact my plan fast.

If Joel was even willing to talk to me.

My stomach sunk as Union High finally came into view. I wondered how many other teens who went to prom dreaded it like I did.

CHAPTER TWENTY-TWO

"Autumn Sheppard!"

Mikayla came shuffling toward me almost as soon as I stepped inside. Her hair was in curlers, and she had on tight, pale pink leggings and a sweatshirt about the same shade to match. "There's a problem with the Prom Court vote!"

Oh, that. She was so worried, I'd thought the gym had burnt down or something. The thought wasn't too far off from what had happened at a dance my sisters had gone to. "Really? Did you ask Prae to contact her IT friend who set it up?"

"She did—or she asked the communications teacher to look into it, and they outsourced—I don't know." She stomped her foot. "Oh, I knew we should have done paper ballots. Outreach may have been limited, but we had a pretty good vote for prom theme." She was gesticulating so wildly, I had to lean back out of her flailing hand's range. "I love your hair, by the way. Good makeup, too." The panic slid off her face for one second as she tapped a finger to her lips and examined me. Then she shook her head, as if remembering herself. "The problem was some kind of login error, despite this whole 'only one voting login per student' spiel Prae gave me. Multiple votes from single students went through, skewing the results. If they're to be believed, Joel Serafin got more votes than we have students to become Prom King."

So it was he who'd won in the end? Despite barely showing his face around school the past couple of weeks. I wondered if he'd mind having Wyatt by his side for dual Prom Kings.

Mikayla's voice grew quieter and she slipped an arm through mine—the one not carrying my duffel bag over my shoulder and the garment bag over my forearm—as she led me toward the gym. "You don't think she sabotaged this on purpose, do you? She did give me that speech about it being archaic and a *popularity contest*." She spat the words as if they weren't genuinely true.

The lights from the gym flooded the hall, more than the afternoon sunlight trickling in through the nearby windows.

"I doubt it," I said, unable to picture Prae conspiring with multiple people along the way.

"Hmm..." began Mikayla. "But there's just something *too convenient* about all of this."

We walked into the gym together, still arm in arm, and Mikayla looked around to take it all in, as if this were her first time seeing it. In the shine of the bright overhead lights, I knew it wasn't quite the same experience that others would have tonight laying eyes on it for the first time, but it was still worth a double-take or two. Not to toot the Prom Committee's horn, but Mikayla and Prae and Alan had really pulled it off. Tia and I had helped, but we'd been... preoccupied.

"Oh, drop that here. We'll grab it and change in the locker room in a bit." She gestured to a little travel suitcase on wheels with a pink floral design I had to assume was hers with a garment bag lying on top. I put my stuff next to hers and then she took my arm again, as if we were old friends and she was giving me a tour.

There were fake trees around seven feet tall lining the walkway, each strung up with fairy lights at this very moment by Alan, who nodded at us as we entered. He had on track pants and a plain black T-shirt. Between the trees were fog machines that were not yet turned on—to give it that "heavenly cloud feel," as Mikayla had put it.

Mikayla kept leading me down the path of trees to the larger open area, complete with the dance floor we and a few of the maintenance people had lain out last night. Paper clouds decorated every so often with golden, paper halos in front of strings of lights dotted the walls, the ceiling strung with white, twinkling icicle lights. Between those were origami stars, all made from white. Mikayla had managed to rope a few of her friends into helping fold those, and the maintenance team had hung them with a cherry picker last night.

Mikayla dropped my hand. "You know what? Straight-up faeries and forest would have been better after all. What was I thinking?" She smacked her own forehead.

"It's beautiful," I said, grabbing her arm and gently moving it down from her head.

"But with a forest theme, we could have just done green," she said. "And vines and flowers—"

"It's fine as is," I said, interrupting her. The words "vines and flowers" had acted like a kick to my stomach, reminding me of the little florets I had grown on my own hands, infant flowers that had blossomed to birth faeries.

But I'd... I'd only been summoning them, right? From wherever they'd been hiding out all these years. Something Tia had said a few weeks ago, about how faeries reproduced, made me shudder all the more.

Mikayla snapped me out of my dark thoughts. "Oh! We forgot the trash cans."

To the side was a table for refreshments, the ladle, napkins, and Solo cups already at the ready, as well as one of those office water dispensers to the side for those who didn't want punch.

She started shuffling off behind the giant screen we'd decorated with silhouettes of angels that would lead to the hallway and then out to the kitchen, where some of the kitchen staff were supposed to be meeting with us to get the punch, cookies, and veggie snacks ready. I went to follow after her, but I stopped in front of an angel's outline drawn on the screen. My hand reached for its wing, where we'd glued an assortment of craft store feathers. They were white, naturally, but for a moment, I pictured the one beneath my fingertips as red. Blood red.

My heart sunk at what could even be the meaning of it.

Mikayla's shout of "*What?*" carried into the gym from down the hall. Over by the entrance to the gym, Alan looked up from his task of stringing the trees with lights but shrugged when I locked eyes with him. I headed behind the screen and down the hall to investigate on my own.

Prae and Tia were in the low light of sunlight filtering in from the windows behind them, Mikayla on the other side of them. And behind them... Orin.

"My cousin knows all about tech things," said Tia, her voice brokering no argument. She didn't look to have done her hair or makeup any special way—but she'd never need it. She was natural, gorgeous. And unlike the rest of us in sweats and leggings and workout clothes, she was in tight faux black leather pants and a flowing deep green blouse. "Prae gave him the logins and he fixed it."

Prae smiled sheepishly. Her hair was affixed tightly into a bun above her head, with two curls on either side of her face hanging down. She had on thick makeup, but it looked nice on her, hiding the bags under her eyes and the little marks I knew usually dotted her skin. "No one else seemed to be making any headway."

"But this doesn't *make sense*," said Mikayla, scrolling through her phone screen and frowning.

My gaze darted to Orin, who was dressed in a tuxedo in white and gray instead of black. He looked like a million bucks, his thick curls dancing off his cheeks at the slight bob of his head.

"You dressed up?" I said.

"Chaperone," he said with a wink. "Tia told me they were short."

"Oh. Great." I crossed my arms and looked at Tia, too, but she ignored me. We were at an impasse again, but we'd never quite crossed the line into enemies.

Not yet.

Not unless Ember's theory proved to be true and they were holding on to the orb for nefarious reasons.

That had really bothered Ember. She hadn't seemed... entirely herself when she'd dropped me off. I chewed on my lip. Good thing I hadn't bothered with the lipstick.

"But... But..." Mikayla stared at me, as if I'd had anything to do with this vote or the fixing of whatever technical problem had plagued it. "You won second place. You're Prom Queen."

"*What?*" Now it was my turn to blink rapidly and stumble backward. Then I laughed awkwardly, the joke becoming clearer. "Ha ha. Very funny."

"I'm serious!" Mikayla flipped the screen around and practically shoved it in my face.

At the top was Joel Serafin, with six hundred and seven votes, and below him was Autumn Sheppard with five hundred and ninety. Below that was Wyatt Lim, with five hundred and eighty-seven.

"No, no, no, no," I said, shaking my head. Panic flooded my voice and I knew I sounded as high-strung as Mikayla did. "There has to be some mistake, I don't think more than ten people here *know my name*, let alone—"

My head snapped up. Tia's cousin had fixed it.

Fixed it so I'd get a dance with the Prom King.

It was my turn to slap my forehead as Mikayla scrambled to take her phone back.

"Well, I'm still in Court," she said, as if that were all that mattered at the moment. "And Alan." She smiled. "It's fine. It's fine. Just surprising is all."

She started walking away, muttering to herself as she stared at the screen.

"Wait, Mikayla—" I started. This was the stupidest plan. They'd announce me, then all but, like, three people would say, "*Who?*" and then they'd ask their friends if *they'd* voted for "Audie Sleppard" and not a single person would get the name right, let alone agree they'd voted for me. Maybe some would recognize my name from my tragic past.

"You know, the girl who was in that gas explosion a few towns over? Like ten years ago? No?"

Was that my best hope? To hope everyone chalked it up to some weird tragic sympathy vote, though I was sure the incident was far from the front of anyone's minds?

"No," I said simply, glowering straight at Orin, well aware Prae was still within earshot. I clenched my jaw and my fists, biting back the words I longed to scream out.

"The people have spoken," said Orin simply. He smirked.

"I *had* a plan," I said. "One that doesn't thrust me into the spotlight."

Right. The spotlight. My knees shook. I was growing nauseous.

Prae looked from him to me and back again. "Congrats, Autumn? I guess? I thought you didn't care about such things, either, but apparently, you led some kind of campaign—"

"I *don't*!" I said, stumbling against the nearby wall for support. "I didn't. There's still clearly a mistake. I shouldn't have a single vote there at all."

"That was Tia," said Prae, shrugging and offering the former faery woman a sly smile. "One single vote. I told her it must have been mine."

"And I asked her why she voted if she was so against such a thing," Tia said dryly.

Prae laughed. "Well, as long as it was happening... Mikayla sort of pressured me to log in and 'vote for her and Alan,' and I figured I'd vote for Alan, but I'd add Tia, too. Since the two of them didn't *force me* to vote at least." She turned to me. "Sorry, we were only allowed to vote for two."

"I know," I said. I'd voted for Mikayla and Alan under similar duress from our forceful leader. "It's fine. I didn't want this."

"Yeah..." Prae didn't seem to believe me. Why would she? How else could I have pulled this off in her eyes if I hadn't launched a massive secret campaign? She cocked her head and looked at Tia. "I'm surprised you got just *one* vote. I know you're new here, but you..." She gestured at her. At Tia's supermodel coolness. Yeah, she definitely had not had just one vote when I'd gotten a peek at the tally a few weeks back. "You turn a lot of heads," she said, to put it mildly. "Frankly, I'm surprised you hang out with me so much." She laughed nervously.

"I'm a good judge of people," was all Tia had to say to that.

Orin threw his hands in the air in surrender as my glare locked on to him. "I fixed the numbers issue with the voting. Honest. The two votes per student was mixing up with the directive that there be only one ballot allowed per student and a little tinkering here, a little tinkering there and, bob's your uncle, everything's ace."

I didn't even care what Prae thought anymore. I stepped forward, grabbed Orin by the wrist, and dragged him farther down the hall, away from the gym. Once we rounded the corner, I said, "Explain."

The devious smile on Orin's face said it all before he even spoke. "We saw an opportunity."

I gestured for him to go on.

"There really was a problem with the program. Prae asked me to help, and wow, lo and behold, my cuz is popular at this school full of children."

It dawned on me. "*Tia* got second place."

"Swapped your name with hers," said Orin, nodding.

That at least made some sense. Even if she was aloof—maybe *because* she was—maybe she'd charmed almost six hundred students without even trying to.

But... huh? Someone had still voted for me?

The thought of one person who'd actually wrote my name into the ballot was more shocking than the fact that I'd won second place. Because I'd immediately known *that* couldn't have been true.

It had probably been Tia trying to get me into Joel's orbit and failing miserably, or maybe Alan or Mikayla being nice. Whatever. I had bigger problems at hand.

"Okay, well, I didn't know she'd become *that* popular with her too-cool-for-school mystique." I thought over the way she'd charmed everyone in the cafeteria when we'd been conducting the prom theme survey, and I supposed she had a way about her. Maybe she'd demonstrated it even more when in classes. But that aside... "And even though she's only gone here a few weeks, I'd *still* bet people would be less apt to question her winning than they would me."

"Will you stop getting so hung up on who gets to be Prom Queen Polly?" Orin blew out a breath that made the hair over his eyes dance. "There are more important things at stake here."

"Yeah, and thanks to you, my plan of cornering Joel alone at some point and doing things *quietly* isn't going to pan out."

"You think he wouldn't see that coming and walk away? Especially once he figures out you were hooking up with his mate?"

"I'm not *hooking up with*—"

"Point is, if he steps out on the Prom Court dance, he'll look a right git. He won't run screaming while you talk to him as you dance together because all those eyes will be on you."

My heart beat rapidly at the thought of "all those eyes."

"So, yeah, how about a, 'Thank you so much for figuring out the flaws in my bright idea and coming up with a better one before it all went to pot,' all right?" Orin winked and started walking back toward the others.

Yeah. Thank him. That sounded about right.

I thought suddenly about Ember's theory, that the orb still had an important role to play. "Hey, Orin?"

He stopped.

"That cat toy you mentioned your kittens messing with at the cabin..." What was I going to do? Accuse him of hiding the orb outright?

Orin glanced over his shoulder. "That old piece of useless junk?"

It *was* the orb. But he was right. What use was it now?

What did I want to say to him about it, then? I couldn't let him know about Ember's suspicions.

"Say, did that fair-haired sister of yours set a deadline yet?" he asked before I could say anything more. "Before she spills the beans to the rest of the fam?"

Why was *he* bringing up Ember now?

"She gave me tonight," I said, my voice cracking just a little.

"Then let's hope you deliver. For all our sakes." Orin gave me a little salute, his lips pinched as he held back a smirk before he shuffled down the corridor once more.

Clutching my sweaty palm against the smooth material over my thigh, I watched him until he turned around the corner, picturing those little stabbing wooden spears the faeries used to use and wishing I could send a wave of faefolk at him to poke and pinch him over and over.

———

"Nguyen, Nguyen…" I said, rifling through the 'N's in the stack of Will Call souvenir ticket envelopes. "Here we are."

I handed the couple their tickets and the girl returned a broad smile, sliding the tickets out of the envelope as she and her date made their way to the line. Alan was by the door with a couple of the teacher chaperones checking tickets—either on phones or the paper versions. A lot of people still wanted the paper souvenirs for their scrapbooks or memory boxes. Mikayla had been right, after all.

The deep bass of music spilled out from the darkened gym, the white and green lights along the walkway of fake trees sparkling out here into the hallway from the opened doors.

Tia and I had been at it for half an hour already, Prae and Mikayla somewhere between the kitchen and refreshment table to make sure everything went smoothly with the food and drinks. The kitchen staff had surprised us with some sandwiches for dinner and then we'd changed.

Well, everyone but Tia had changed. She didn't look sloppy— far from it—but she didn't look dressed up, either.

"That green brings out the brown of your eyes," said Tia, not even bothering to look at me as she spoke. She smiled, and it seemed a little too devious. "Reminds me of a faery princess."

I scowled and took a look at the velvety dress I'd picked out with Mikayla's help. It had broad straps that completely covered the shoulders but a wide-open neckline. The velvet bodice cinched in a bit at the waist, then poofed out into a softer, broader skirt with hints of green tulle fabric peeking out at the hemline.

It did look slightly like Tinkerbell's dress, now that I thought about it.

"I thought faefolk were all about shades of brown," I said out of the corner of my mouth as another group stepped in from outside, their laughter echoing out down the hall.

"Earth tones," said Tia, a hand on her hip. "And that includes green."

I got ready to greet the next bunch to approach the table. Then my insides turned to jelly.

It was Joel—and all his friends.

Sabine was wearing the angel Lolita dress she'd thought of buying—she'd worked fast since knowing the prom theme. White, faux feathery wings were strapped to her back around the arms like a backpack.

"Tickets, please," she said, bringing her phone out of the little clutch purse on a golden chain and showing me the screen.

For a moment, I didn't move. Behind Sabine and Rick were Estelle and Joel.

Estelle looked beautiful as usual, but she also looked like she hadn't made much of an effort, unless "grunge goth" had been the aim of her look. Fishnet fingerless long gloves gave away to a frilly white blouse and a black leather skirt over more fishnet stockings and some silver-studded black boots. Her dark hair was messy, and her makeup thick, particularly the eyeliner. "Let's just go inside," she said, her nose turned up just a little as she slipped an arm through Joel's. "Who cares about souvenir tickets?" She scoffed, earning her a glower from Sabine as Tia smoothly reached in front of me to rifle through the envelopes and pull out the one I was supposed to have been searching for.

My gaze was still locked on Joel—and for a time, his was locked on me, too.

His dark hair had softened somewhat into malleable waves I just wanted to reach over and run my hands through.

He had on a white dress shirt and dark navy tie that matched the dress pants he'd paired with them, but he'd foregone the dress jacket entirely. His hands in his pockets, he tore his gaze from me and his Adam's apple bobbed as he swallowed, letting Estelle lead him away without a word.

My stomach fluttered, the butterflies traveling upward through my chest.

"Thanks," said Sabine, snapping me back to the moment. "You two look nice," she added.

"Thank you. You too," I said, trying not to think about the mess Orin and Tia had gotten me into—the one that would *make* that boy look at me. I shook my head. No, that was... In the past few weeks, my own passions had cooled somewhat. Surely. But just being so close to him had stirred something in me.

It was just the magic of the consummate lands between us.

I needed to ask him to help me, to plead my case, but then... But then we would go our separate ways.

Without the magic that had chosen me for reasons entirely beyond my control, I was nothing special. I didn't fit in with anyone here, didn't deserve a second look from someone like him.

"How much longer do you have?"

A deep voice focused my attention. Sabine and Rick were already over by Alan.

In front of me now was D, his hair a bit messy, a loose red-dotted tie around his neck, sporting a stiff, yellow dress shirt and brown corduroy pants. He'd put about as much effort into dressing up as Joel had, but for some reason, he hadn't really pulled it off as well. His clothes looked less lived in and more yanked from the back of the closet, complete with wrinkles he hadn't ironed out of the shirt.

I looked to Tia for help. She offered none.

"We're supposed to stay here until half an hour after the dance starts," I said.

D's expression grew pinched. "What am I supposed to do until then?"

"You can go inside. There are refreshments and you're free to dance with whoever you want—"

D rapped his knuckles on the table between us. "Yeah, yeah, I know. You just need my help." He looked over his shoulder, but the hallway was empty. How to tell him I didn't really need his help now? No. If my own plan worked, I could leave before the Prom Court was announced. I'd have to at least try. "You don't seem so busy. Why don't we get the little meeting with pretty boy over with so you can chuck me aside already?"

"Chuck you aside?"

Tia finally spoke up for me. "We have to stay here. Just hold your horses and man up, big boy. Go nurse your fragile ego over in the corner if you must."

I jolted. I didn't think D would take that well.

On the contrary, he couldn't take his eyes of Tia.

"*Hello*," he said. "And you are?"

"Not interested," said Tia plainly, tossing her shoulders back. Under her breath, she muttered, "Child."

"Tia," I said, half to annoy her and half to give D someone else to focus on.

"So *you're* Tia," said D, sliding around the table. There were chairs behind us that we hadn't had much chance to use and he took the one for me and pulled it closer to the former faery. "I've heard more than one person talk about you."

That would confirm her winning second place. This was all doomed to backfire spectacularly, but then again, what were they going to do? Investigate the voting process? Rescind the title from me? The title meant nothing, and by then, I'd have had my chance to speak with Joel.

"Joy," said Tia dryly.

"I like how little you care about all this." D was sitting on the chair backward, leaning his forearm across the top of the back of it.

Tia's sigh was drowned out by more conversation echoing down the hall as the door outside opened again and more students filed in.

It was still twenty minutes until the dance officially started. Fifty minutes until Tia and I could wrap up here.

"I don't care about dances, either," said D. "What do you say maybe after I help our mutual friend out here, you and I head somewhere a little more... inspiring?"

But at least Tia had shifted the focus off me for these last fifty long minutes.

CHAPTER TWENTY-THREE

"Prae, squeeze in closer to Autumn. Alan, wipe that goofy grin off your face. No. Leave that spot for me, remember?"

Mikayla's voice was tense. We were at the professional photography station she'd had set up and she was standing beside the photographer we'd hired with the prom budget, doling out the instructions the photographer herself would usually be the one to relay.

"Yes, I think that's good. Why don't you go over to your friends and I'll take it from here?" The photographer, a middle-aged woman with mostly gray hair pulled back into a messy bun, slid the cats-eye glasses that dangled around her neck onto her face and leaned toward the camera screen.

Huffing, Mikayla practically tripped in her two-inch stilettos as she padded over the canvas taped to the ground and took her place between Alan and Tia.

Behind the photographer, in a dark corner, D picked at the paint on the wall.

"Son, are you joining them?" the photographer asked.

"No!" Mikayla practically shouted. She pursed her lips and studied me, as if I'd dare to correct her. "We can get photos with our... *dates* alone after. This is Prom Committee only."

The music echoing out from the gym was a soft ballad, the

words in Korean, but the melody sweet enough to convey the romantic message of the song.

D swallowed his laughter. "Take it down a notch, Kayla. I won't ruin your pretty picture."

Mikayla scowled and fluffed her hair over her shoulder.

Prae leaned closer to me and whispered, "They used to date. In middle school."

That was news to me, but I hadn't known either of them in middle school.

"Okay, bright smiles," said the photographer, directing us all back to the task at hand. "Say, 'heaven cheese!'"

That actually got most of us to laugh out loud. Not Tia, of course, and Mikayla seemed flummoxed, but the photographer snapped the picture.

"One more!" said Mikayla, snapping the spaghetti strap of her soft pink dress. "I wasn't ready."

The photographer took a second picture and then we dispersed, Mikayla holding on to Alan's wrist so they could take their couple photo.

Prae leaned into the hallway and shouted, "Okay!" before a guy in an ill-fitting powder blue tux that popped against his dark complexion shuffled into the room.

"Tia, Autumn, this is Samar. We're just friends," she added quickly. "We grew up together."

I hadn't noticed her meeting up with a date, but we hadn't been working the same part of prom setup after our sandwich dinners.

"Excuse me," said Tia solemnly, not even bothering to pretend to have social skills as D sidled up between us, running a hand through his greasy red hair. "I have somewhere to be."

I opened my mouth, about to follow her down the dark hallway, when a heavy arm draped around my shoulder. I winced, sliding out from it.

D smelled strongly of musky cologne. Maybe Tia hadn't wanted to give him any more chances to flirt with her. "Friends, huh?" he said. "Better than a partner in crime."

Prae laughed nervously, as if she had a clue what he was talking about. "Wanna get a pic for our parents?" she asked her date.

Samar blinked, and I realized he was staring after Tia, who'd just vanished from view.

"Uh, yeah," he said once he realized Prae was waiting for a reply.

They went off to step to the side of the white sheet acting as the background. Alan had his arms clasped around Mikayla's abdomen in front of him, and she folded her hands prettily over his to perfectly show off her corsage.

D stepped in closer. "You about ready to do this? Or do you want a picture together, too?" He grinned lopsidedly.

"Let's go," I said, tugging on my skirt to straighten my bodice and wipe off the perspiration that was forming on my palms.

D and I walked down the darkened hallway, the music from the gym ahead thundering out with bass. Since no one expected stragglers to crash this late, no one was there to accept tickets and students had the freedom to wander out into the hallway and out the front door for some fresh air. As we neared the walkway of lighted trees, D leaned over and raised his voice. "Maybe we shouldn't walk in together," he said. "In case Joel is watching." He pointed to a corner of the room, behind the screens we'd set up, where the maintenance people had shoved and packed up all the bleachers. "I'll bring him back there." He winked. "Just be careful. It looks like the perfect spot for make-out central."

Like the chaperones would let *that* happen.

D fixed his tie a little straighter and stepped inside. I counted to thirty and did the same.

The path of lit-up trees was almost otherworldly in the dark. For a moment, I staggered, my heart clenching at the sight of the green, glowing lights, my mind racing with visions of floating faeries. The music was loud in my ears, my heart moving in time with the rapid beat. Though the soft white glow of all our heavenly lights and stars waited up ahead, I moved forward through two of the trees, the rough cloth-like texture of some of the leaves scuffing against my face as I took a deep breath and squeezed through.

No one was around to see me.

With the bleachers up ahead, I scrambled, my stiff ballet flats clomping against the unprotected gym floor in this part of the building, but the music drowning out my illicit escape from the decorated areas of the gym.

I reached the bleachers and clung on to a metal beam, practically tumbling forward. I'd hardly had a chance to catch my breath when I saw some figures so entwined, they looked like one amorphous blob just a few feet in front of me. So D had been right.

I whipped around so they wouldn't see me and settled for sitting on the floor, clutching my legs to my chest and leaning my forehead to my knees. The skirt was rough but soothing somehow against my skin.

Deep breaths. In and out. Memories of all my mistakes from ten years ago—ruining Ember's car, nearly knocking Noelle down the stairs, wrapping my vines around Ember's throat—surged like a tidal wave before my eyes. It was a wonder she even forgave me and trusted me to get this done.

I didn't have faith I'd get this done.

I had a pair of tenuous allies, but I'd never fully trust them. Not to mention they'd gotten me into this mess to begin with, and it was about to get much worse if I didn't convince Joel to help me before the Prom Court announcements were made and I had time to get Mikayla to let me drop out.

Vague memories of a happier Ivy headed to her own prom, posing for pictures in front of our house with her friends... Ember had gone, too, with her boyfriend that second half of her senior year, Journey's cousin, though her own enjoyment had seemed somewhat subdued.

I'd envied them, had thought they'd looked dressed up like princesses, just like Hya had called me earlier today.

What a joke. It was all just a veneer, a shiny, pretty lie.

Well, maybe not for Ivy. She'd been made of different stuff. I shouldn't have even *been* here—

Behind me, the heavy breathing and smacking was interrupted by a series of coughs. "Give me a second," said a familiar alto voice with a touch of a vocal fry.

Estelle.

That meant...

I jumped to my feet, my ankle tilting sideways and causing me to stumble, slamming loudly into the bleachers with a clanging bang that echoed as the folded-up bleachers vibrated.

"What the...?" said Estelle. "Hey, who's the pervert?" She stepped out from the shadows, a scowl evident on her face in the meager light. "*You?*" She swayed slightly, her eyes widening.

The form behind her shifted, and a sudden wave of vertigo took me over at the thought of finding Joel here. With her.

As if... As if he owed me loyalty.

As if... As if we were actually in love.

CHAPTER TWENTY-FOUR

"I'm just waiting for someone," I said, leaning back on my sore ankle. I winced. It hurt, but at least it didn't feel like it was sprained, just a little stretched too far in one direction.

"Yeah, sure," Estelle spat. "Because Joel rejected you, so you've already moved on to the next guy?"

The form behind Estelle was growing closer, stepping out into the dim light.

My heart thundered.

"What's going on?" asked an unfamiliar voice.

Then Wyatt Lim came into view.

Wyatt Lim?

What was she doing with him?

And why, of all things, was a rush of relief soaring through my entire body, from my head to my toes?

"Sorry," I mumbled quickly, spinning around—and running straight into a broad chest.

Stumbling backward, I rubbed my sore nose and looked up.

There were two people on the other side of me. A few feet back, D, looking a little sheepish, and right in front of me, the person whose chest I'd smacked into: Joel.

Estelle cleared her throat behind me. "Oh. Done dancing with half the girls in school?" she asked dryly.

Joel didn't respond to her, though. Didn't react to the fact that she was coming out from behind the bleachers with Wyatt.

He just stared at me, the white light from the dance floor some distance behind him, seeming to cling to him like some kind of full-body halo.

His skin was flushed, probably from the dancing, his lips slightly parted.

"Why are you here?" he asked. His eyes locked with mine, and I knew he meant me.

Estelle didn't take it that way, though. "I'm passing the time while you ignore me." She flung a lock of hair over her shoulder.

"Hey," said Wyatt, clearly hurt at being described as "passing the time." "Why do you always have to be such a—"

The music grew especially loud just then, drowning him out.

"Excuse me?" Estelle turned on Wyatt, her eyebrows narrowing, and launched into some kind of tirade, but she was drowned out by the music, too. Wyatt strode purposely back toward the dance floor, and Estelle launched after him.

"Oh, no, you don't walk away from me after calling me that!"

All of my plans of cornering Joel alone fleeing from my addled mind, I stepped to the side, leaning against the wall as I just stared at him.

"Well, uh, that wasn't what I meant to show you," said D, shoving his hands in his pockets.

"It's fine," said Joel, his eyes never leaving me as he stepped closer. "Estelle and I are just friends."

"Tell *her* that." D hooked a thumb in the retreating girl's direction. "I'd wager that little show was for your benefit as much as for her idle boredom."

Joel finally looked away from me and blinked, as if only just now remembering where he was. "Did she ask you to get me to show me that?"

"No." D shrugged. "I guess I don't know for sure she wanted you to see her." He shuffled forward and stood beside me, leaning against the wall. "No, it was *my date* I promised to go fetch you for."

Joel's hand clenched into a fist at his side, his posture stiffening slightly. "Your date?"

He was getting caught on the wrong point entirely. Hadn't he wanted me to leave him alone?

D offered him a sly grin as he slid an arm around me. "That's what happens when you don't see what you have right in front of you." His powerful cologne made my eyes water.

Joel's Adam's apple bobbed.

"Only messing with you, dude," said D, laughing, though there was a strain to his voice. He backed away from me. "Lighten up."

"But you came with *him*?" Joel asked, turning on me.

Why was this conversation focusing on all the wrong things?

"Well, I met him here," I said. "I needed D's help—"

"You don't *know his name*?" Joel tossed out at me.

D and I exchanged a look. Was Joel angry at D for taking his reject to this dance or me for not taking D seriously as a date?

"Technically, I guess," I admitted.

D sniffled and shrugged. "Devon," he said quietly.

I blinked. That was a pretty nice name. Why did he go by "D"?

"But you—" started Joel.

"Hey!" shouted someone, getting all of our attention. "What are you kids doing back here? Stick to the dance floor."

A teacher. Mr. Foster, I realized, as the stout man with the thin, greasy hair neared. If only I'd thought to put Orin to good use and have him be the chaperone patrolling this area.

Mr. Foster frowned as he took in the sight of D, Joel, and me. Nothing untoward was going on—it would be weird if it were—so he probably felt he couldn't do much else, other than gesture back to the twinkling lights. "Whatever dramatic romantic entanglement this is, keep it to where we can all see you."

Cringing, I stepped past D, leading the way before either boy could say anything. I didn't trust D not to make some bitingly unfunny comment.

Tears pricked the sides of my eyes just slightly as my head filled with failure.

I couldn't do this. I couldn't do any of it. I hadn't even said more than a few words to Joel, hadn't begun to explain to him what I knew, what I needed him to understand about me.

I had never been up to this task, no matter if there was no one else for the job because no one else of the right age lived on the consummate lands and spent half her nights seeped in its magic. I chuckled darkly to myself, thankful Orin hadn't resorted to manipulating a little kid again, considering the twins and their full-time status at the house. It had to be the *romantic* aspect of this mission, though I may as well have been a little kid myself when it came to my ability to charm anyone.

I reached the screen and stepped around, settling for a dark corner by the trash can filled with used Solo cups and napkins. Behind me, Mr. Foster stepped through, shaking his head, the two boys slower to appear from the other side of the screen.

"Hey, everyone!" A series of taps on a microphone and Mikayla's voice took over from the music. I blinked through unshed tears to see her standing on the platform next to the DJ we'd hired with the prom budget. "Everyone!" she said, louder this time as the room took a bit to quiet down. "I just want to pause this dance for a moment while we announce Prom Court!" She grew excited like a cheerleader on the last word, and half the crowd let out a whoop or a cheer.

My stomach sank, and my eyes locked with Joel's as he and D stepped around the screen.

"Counting down to the top two royals, I'll begin with places six and five on the court." Mikayla's smile was evident from here. "Neck in neck"—sure, because everyone she'd cajoled into voting for her, she'd made vote for her boyfriend in the same breath— "Alan Parr and Mikayla Jacobs!"

Someone operating a spotlight off to the side of the room pointed it at Alan on the dance floor. A number of the crowd clapped. I spotted Prae with her date, both offering a polite round of applause, but Tia and Orin were nowhere to be found.

"Come on up here, babe!" Mikayla said.

Alan endured some wolf whistles and jostling from a crowd of boys as he approached the stage, and Mikayla elevated up to her toes to give him a big kiss on the cheek before draping a sash she'd fished out of a box behind her over his chest and then doing the same for herself. They were white and read "Prom Court" in golden, cursive lettering.

Joel swallowed noticeably as he stepped past me, no longer willing to be in my presence, I supposed. D and Mr. Foster lingered behind me, their attention on Mikayla.

The cheers died down and Mikayla turned back to the microphone. "In fourth and third place, we have Ellie Brooks and Wyatt Lim!" She gestured out to the crowd in front of her as if a game show host.

The cheers were louder now, screams from the girls around Ellie—a redhaired cheerleader with natural makeup and a pale, fit, leggy frame—and hollers from the jocks currently gathered around Wyatt. Estelle was a few feet back from them, and she rolled her eyes as she walked away from the ruckus. She ran into Joel and they both stopped for a moment, but though Estelle clearly spoke, Joel just brushed past her and headed toward the pathway of trees that would lead to the front door of the gym. To the exit.

Wyatt and Ellie already had their sashes draped over them by the time Mikayla's voice drew my attention back to her.

Joel was leaving. My plan had failed miserably, and now it would even cause Orin and Tia's ridiculous machinations to fail.

But wait, he *knew* he was going to be on Prom Court. Mikayla had told him. And he was still planning to walk away?

"And now... Your Prom Queen and King, in second and first place, respectively..." Mikayla laughed a little nervously, as if she, too, was anticipating the fallout, though she couldn't have suspected Orin had manipulated things to work out in my favor. "Autumn Sheppard and Joel Serafin!" She gestured out at us again.

The spotlight scanned the dance floor again and again. At one point, it passed right over me as people cheered without much enthusiasm, but those cheers also broke into murmurs. "Over there!" shouted a gravelly voice, and I realized Estelle was smugly pointing down the path of trees toward Joel, who was making his exit. The light caught Joel halfway down the path of trees.

"Joel?" Mikayla called out into the microphone. "Joel, you need to get back here!"

Estelle speed-walked down the path and gripped Joel by the arm tightly, practically dragging him back into view.

"Good going," said Mr. Foster beside me. I supposed at least *he* knew who I was.

"Dang," said D. "How'd you pull that off, Sheppard? I didn't know you were popular."

I cleared my throat and clutched my dress skirt with both palms. I wasn't, but I couldn't argue with it.

"Who's Autumn Sheppard?" a girl's voice carried out over the dance floor, but it was quickly drowned out by a series of cheers—particularly from the cheerleading squad—as Estelle dragged Joel farther and farther onto the dance floor. The spotlight followed him the whole time up to the DJ podium, where Alan, Ellie, and Wyatt stepped aside as Mikayla put a golden sash over his head and then a costume crown atop it. Estelle watched and smiled smarmily up at him. When Joel turned toward her, she flipped him off.

With friends like her...

"Shouldn't you be going up there with him?" Mr. Foster asked.

Mikayla turned to the microphone. "Autumn?" she prodded.

Right.

The cheering for Joel died down, replaced by more whispers and murmuring. Already, this sham would be falling apart as people compared votes. I had to get to Joel and fast. It was all riding on this spotlight dance.

The spotlight scanned the crowd and *again* moved slowly over me without stopping at all.

"Go, Autumn!" shouted Prae, cupping her hands over her mouth.

"Over here!" shouted Mr. Foster, waving his arms and no doubt trying to be helpful.

The spotlight spun toward him, then stopped on me.

I took a careful step forward, but not before lifting my arm up to block out the light, my eyes watering. Through the blaring light, everyone looked like shadows, like frightening silhouettes.

I felt an arm slip through mine and startled.

"Come on, Shep." D's voice carried a spark of amusement. "Everyone's waiting for you."

"Is she dating *him?*" said a hushed whisper from somewhere in the crowd. D wasn't hideous or anything, but her tone seemed to indicate that he was.

"No wonder I haven't heard of her," said some guy.

D just waved out at the crowd as if we were a couple of Hollywood stars heading down the red carpet. He thrust out his chest and patted my hand as if proud to be my escort.

I wanted to sink into the ground.

We got closer to the stage, but every step was its own kind of agony, that spotlight causing the temperature around me to rise.

"Wait, is that the girl from the gas explosion?" said someone else right as I reached the stage.

"Gas explosion?" echoed D, but I didn't have time to reply. Alan reached a hand down to me, and Wyatt moved to do the same, then stepped back, a frown creasing over his face.

Right. That whole thing over by the bleachers. I was sure he hadn't had any opinion of me until that moment.

But Alan was enough to hoist me up on his own.

"Congrats!" said Mikayla, her smile so wide, her teeth were practically half of her face. She draped a golden sash over me. It read, "Prom Royal" in white lettering, now that I got a closer look at it. "And your crown." She settled a costume crown to match Joel's atop my head. It was slightly too big for me, settling sideways over my scalp.

I blinked, letting the moisture that had accumulated during my spotlighted walk to the stage trickle down my cheeks. Joel looked straight ahead, stiffly, his fist clenching at his side.

"Gentlepeople, your Prom Court!" Mikayla shouted, stepping back to gesture to the line of us, and then at herself.

Cheers and clapping picked up, though there were more than a few claps that seemed to be polite and formal.

"I can't believe you'd go this far," said Joel between gritted teeth. I was the only one who'd heard him, I was certain, and his words were like an icy slap to my face.

"And now, a special dance for the Prom Court members!" continued Mikayla. "Everyone, please clear space in the middle of the dance floor and wait to join in until the next song." She nodded toward the DJ, a burly guy in his twenties, I'd guess, who nodded back and flicked some dials and knobs on his equipment.

A ballad started up, one I hadn't heard before.

Mikayla and Alan brushed past me on the stage, Alan jumping down off the podium and holding his hands up to grab Mikayla by the waist. He brought her down and swirled her around for a moment above him, to the cheers of the crowd, particularly a group of girls I knew were Mikayla's friends. Probably the original Prom Committee.

Then Alan and Mikayla kissed just before Alan set her down, and the crowd went absolutely wild.

Laughing, Alan whisked her off to the center of the dance floor and they began to sway, her arms tightly around his neck, his clasping around the small of her back.

Wyatt and Ellie looked at each other and shrugged, then Wyatt jumped down and helped Ellie down after him. Ellie tumbled—perhaps intentionally, judging by her exaggerated reactions—and then planted a quick kiss on his lips, too.

As far as I'd known, they weren't dating. Either that, or Estelle had been messing around with a guy who wasn't single.

"*Hey!*" shouted a guy from the crowd. "That's my girlfriend!"

"Oopsie," said Ellie, shrugging.

The crowd went wild, and the two hit the dance floor with broad smiles in much the same pose as Alan and Mikayla, though perhaps just the slightest more distance between them.

"We're not doing that," Joel said under his breath.

As if I was going to ask him to.

He strode forward without looking at me and jumped down.

All hope I had for ever getting his help had vanished.

He hated me. He really hated me. I didn't deserve *that*—well,

maybe not until my fishy appearance as Prom Queen at his side—
but it was clearer than ever that I'd never deserve his love.

Forget love, even his friendship, which all of this rode on.

"Come on, *Your Majesty*," said Estelle from below me, her voice
cracking.

"You can do it, Shep!" D winked at me and clapped.

I jumped down after Joel, landing perfectly on my own two feet
without any assistance.

I *had* spent time as a child being carried around by those who
flew.

Before Joel could protest or walk away, I slipped my hand in his
and spun him around, my forcefulness working more in my favor
than any particular advantage in strength.

He stumbled, and I grabbed him on the shoulder, bringing our
clasped hands out to the side as if about to waltz—which would
not at all fit with the gentle, swaying crooning of the music.

Joel blinked rapidly, his crown slightly askew from the movement, but now a perfect reflection of mine. I started swaying with
him, moving my feet only slightly, the bee-like murmurs of the
crowd around us dying out as they faded to mere silhouettes in a
circle around us. The spotlight flicked over us to the other two
dancing couples and back.

"Stop," Joel whispered. His shoulders drooped, and he swallowed hard as his gaze fell.

I stopped moving us. In this single moment, he didn't seem to
hate me. He seemed... hurt. As if I'd broken his heart somehow.

"I need your help," I said. "Please. Please hear me out, and then
I won't ever bother you again."

Joel's jaw clenched and he looked me straight on. "If I help
you," he said, "I'll die."

The world seemed to fall out from under me.

CHAPTER TWENTY-FIVE

Now I was petrified, but Joel was the one to lead me in a dance once more as the spotlight fell on us, settling his free hand on my waist and guiding me across the dance floor in what might have been some semblance of a waltz after all. That led to some cheers, and even a bit of laughter.

"What do you...?" I tripped just a little on my feet but recovered quickly, turning it into a smooth, twisting trot. "What do you mean?"

"You know what I am."

"I... I do." That would make it easier than the whole "convincing him he's an angel" obstacle I'd originally pictured in this plan. "And I need you to right a wrong."

Joel offered a darting gaze. "Whatever you want from me, I beg you. Don't ask. Don't even *think* it."

"You don't even know what I want to ask."

"I know that you used me from the start." His Adam's apple bobbed as he let go of my waist and spun me around by the hand.

"*Used* you?" I twirled back into his arms, this time, landing against his chest, much like Ellie had done with Wyatt. I gazed up to find his lips a hair's breadth from my forehead. The air between us was hot, his scent like cotton drying in the sun. "I... I hardly have spent any time with you. You invited me to be friends and then I saved your life—and you shut me out.”

He pushed on my arm gently, putting a small swath of space between us. We were closer than we had been originally, though, his hands falling stiffly to my waist and mine on his shoulders.

“You won’t admit you approached me with the intention of using me?” He spoke softly, and we were just far enough from anyone else that I was sure no one would hear us.

“I...” I chewed my lip, searching the crowd for Orin or Tia, but whether or not they were there, I couldn’t tell. The mass of people just looked like formless, mocking shadows, the echoes of their whispers traveling out across the music. I gripped on to Joel’s shoulders tightly. “I never thought I could *use* you. I hoped you would help me. I didn’t know—”

“That I would die? The more I use the power, the more my... hidden nature will dominate my cells. If you knew what I was all along, you must have known of others like me.”

“Others?” I thought about Orin’s notes. Joan of Arc. Tristan. Lady Jane Grey. Alexander the Great. Famous for their remarkable feats and then...

Their untimely deaths.

“No,” I whispered harshly.

Orin had *known*. He must have known that all along. Of course the former faeries would keep that from me. Just like they kept everything else I might *disagree* with from me.

“Then I can’t...” My palms felt sweaty, like they were in danger of staining his shirt. “You can’t help me. No one can.” My voice cracked, and I blinked hard, holding back tears.

The bodies, the destruction... The water heater gurgling and the flopping merman tails in the basement flooding. The human victims, drunk dry for their blood.

Joel reeled back a bit, practically stumbling. Without speaking, he reached out and wiped a gentle thumb against my cheekbone, wiping away a tear.

Our eyes locked and my heart thundered. A fluttery, tingling sensation spread out from my core to my fingers and my toes, a sudden flush spreading throughout my body.

My legs went weak, and all the racing, guilty thoughts went quiet.

The soft, slow song headed into its final bars.

Joel leaned down and kissed me.

It wasn't anything like the first time our lips had touched, no sense of urgency or panic behind the contact.

This was euphoria. This overwhelming sense of all the shadows around us fading into nothing, the gasps and murmurs so far beyond us. His hand reached up to gently cup the back of my head as we came up for breath, my gasp as if resurfacing from our time together almost drowning, but then he kissed me again, and everything around us faded to nothing.

Together, we felt as one.

The music faded, and a thumping beat took its place.

I staggered backward, Joel's gentle grasp caving to my force.

My heart thundered so loudly now, it was practically all I could hear in my ears. My feet slipped as I stumbled, the conversations wafting from all around me growing louder, clearer.

"Who even *is* she?"

"Did she just *kiss* him?"

"Did *he* kiss her? But she's—"

"Who even voted for her? Do you know a single person who knew her name before this?"

But none of it—none of it—mattered as much as the fact that my greatest heart's desire would put him in danger.

He grew smaller and smaller in my view as I backed up, his figure darker as the spotlight framed him in shadow and the crowd filling up the dance floor between us.

His eyes glinted from the sparkling white lights above him, his hand reaching out toward me.

I spun, nearly barreling into someone.

"Autumn, are you all right?" It was Prae.

Nodding, doing my best to keep the tears from falling, I

stepped past her, squeezing my way around dancing couples. The music blasted in my ears, the darkening of my vision zeroing in on the one thing to offer any relief, that path of green light out of the gym.

Fumbling past the last of the crowd, I clopped my heavy shoes down the path, practically running by the time I reached the hallway. I turned sharply toward the front door, desperate for fresh air, and ground to a halt when a flood of laughter floated to me from that direction. The front door was propped open, a group of people lingering nearby.

I turned again, running down the hallway, stopping suddenly as I found the locker room where Mikayla, Prae, and I had gotten changed earlier. I flung myself inside, not even bothering to hit the light switch by the door.

I didn't know how long I stood there, leaning against the wall, taking deep breaths as my mind raced with everything and nothing all at once.

What had that been about?

Of course I couldn't ask for his help if it put his life in danger, no matter what. But what I'd felt... It had *hurt*. It still did. I clutched at my heart over my bodice, the velvet soft material cushioning my fingertips.

The thought of losing him *hurt*, like he meant something more to me than he should have.

Did the magic of the consummate lands drawing him to me affect *me*, too? Was this... Was this what love felt like?

But how?

He'd done little but push me away.

I didn't like this. This wasn't what love was supposed to be like.

The door to the hallway opened and I gasped, the lights flickering on. I raised my forearm to shield my eyes as my vision adjusted to the stark, bright light.

"Autumn? I thought I saw you headed this way." Prae spoke softly and took a few steps toward me, taking me by the elbow and directing me to sit on one of the benches in front of the lockers.

She slid my overnight bag aside to take a seat beside me. "What happened? You look like you've seen a ghost."

A wry chuckle escaped my lips. I saw ghosts every time I closed my eyes.

The chuckle turned into a sob and I buried my face in my hands.

Prae rubbed my back gently.

"Do you need to go home?" she asked. "My friend was going to drive the both of us to the bed and breakfast—Mikayla said the shuttle might be tight and we wanted to be able to leave early if we wanted to. But we can drive you home first."

Swallowing, I wiped my eyes and stared at her. "That's kind of you," I said. "But no, I... Where's Tia? Do you know? Or Orin?"

The two of them had some explaining to do. If they hadn't needed me, they wouldn't have ever involved me.

They couldn't do this without me—but they had to know now they weren't going to do it *with* me, either.

Prae's face darkened, her eyes brightening, and it took me a second to realize Orin's name had likely elicited that response in her. "I haven't seen them in a while."

"But Tia plans to come to the bed and breakfast," I said. It was sort of a question, but last I'd known, she'd told everyone that. Whether she'd meant it or had just said she'd go to keep Mikayla off her back, I didn't know.

If she'd thought tonight I'd get Joel to do my bidding on the dance floor, she wouldn't have thought it necessary to tag along.

Well, she'd have to if she was going to chase me. It was easier than trying to find either of them—or having them come to my house.

I gripped Prae by the hand. "I still want to go. Can you and your friend take me?"

———

We were the first three to arrive at the bed and breakfast, having left hours before the dance was over. Prom Committee was supposed to help with the cleanup—but that wouldn't be until late tomorrow. The school had suspected we'd want to go to after-prom parties like everyone else.

I'd expected a sinking feeling in my stomach to assault me as we'd pulled off the Interstate into the town around Fowles University, but nothing could exacerbate the already sick sensation plaguing me since the kiss. Alone in Prae's friend's back seat, I rubbed my lips as I stared out the window.

The turn of the road was familiar, as was the empty road leading to the bed and breakfast all by its lonesome on a dead end. But the building that rose into view was nothing like I'd remembered. Instead of a two-story house, it looked more like a small apartment building, sleek in design with straight lines, like some gentrified mass housing in small scale.

Even the front yard looked different, the empty grass now full of picnic tables and young, uniform trees, planted in the last decade.

There was a small parking lot now, too, that took up a corner of what had once been the yard. If I remembered right, we'd just parked along the street.

"This is it," said Samar.

Prae leaned forward in her seat, the crisp material of her prom dress crinkling with the movement. "Nice." She looked over her shoulder at me and I smiled.

"Yeah. Totally different from when I was here last."

She frowned. I wondered if she knew my history with this location.

Samar turned off the car and the door to the trunk opened behind us with the touch of a button on his key fob. We all followed suit, stepping outside. The air was fresh, the fish odor of the humanmade lake somewhat strong.

Samar fished our overnight bags out of his trunk and shut it with another click of a button.

"Let's get checked in," said Prae as she and I went to pick up our bags from the pavement.

There wasn't a porch anymore, and as Prae held the door for Samar and me, I had this sinking feeling that everything I remembered about it had been erased. The last remnants of what had happened here had been bulldozed over and forgotten.

That was how it should be, right?

That was how it had to be, if even the smallest hope was now tainted and taken from me.

Before I stepped inside, a waft of something like lavender hit my nose, and I dropped my duffel bag just inside the door.

"I'll be there in a minute," I said, gesturing over my shoulder with my thumb. "I just... need a little fresh air."

"Okay," said Prae, though her eyebrows scrunched up tightly.

I gathered my skirt and picked it up so I could jog away before she thought to stop me.

Rounding the side of the building, I came to the back yard, and the nearer I got, the more my head pounded.

This... This hadn't been bulldozed over and forgotten.

In my mind, I could see the battle going on. Mermaid against vampire, attacking one another in the yard while the rest of us battled it out inside.

Only it had been late fall, then, and all the trellises had been bare, the plants sheltered and covered for the cold winter ahead.

Now it was almost summer, and the garden between the building and the slope leading straight down into Fowles Lake was in bloom.

Even in the moonlight, the colorful garden glowed, the greens and purples and reds twinkling in the night air. I blinked, making sure I wasn't imagining it, but it was simply the gentle moonlight reflecting off the lake hitting this garden, casting it in a silver sort of spotlight.

My feet took me closer to the garden before I realized. My hand reached out to touch the entryway trellis, a tall arch covered in vines that dangled down all around me, little bean sprouts hanging down everywhere.

I stepped inside, just letting the warm night air caress me. I didn't know how long I stayed there, the rustle of the gentle breeze against the flora, the soft movement of the lake the only sound to fill the night.

"The garden is the only part from the original b&b that they kept." Prae's voice carried out into the night behind me and I startled, hugging myself tightly. She smiled sheepishly and gestured behind her at the new building. "That's what the owner told us. You doing okay?"

"Yeah." A loose strand of hair had fallen out from my braids and I tucked it behind my ear as I moved to join Prae under the bean sprout archway. I slipped my arm through hers, surprising even myself with the ease of the gesture. "Thank you so much for coming with me early. I'm sorry I ruined your prom."

Prae laughed and we started back for the b&b. "Are you kidding me? If we'd stayed at the dance any later, we wouldn't have gotten here until three A.M." She gazed around her, taking in a deep breath. "Besides, now we get the place to ourselves for a bit. It's peaceful. After all the work we put in for the past few weeks, it's nice to just relax." We got to the front door and I held it open for Prae.

"Samar went upstairs to one of the boy's rooms," Prae said. "Mikayla figured the couples might want to bunk together, but she also left three rooms for the rest of us to divvy up how we like. I thought you might like to bunk with me."

"Sure," I said, smiling. It felt nice to have a friend. One I could meet up with in person.

"We took your bag upstairs," she said, leading the way ahead of me.

I clung to the staircase. Orin had carried a slumped-over Noelle over his shoulders down stairs in just about this area, but they looked so different now. The angle was off, the design more streamlined and less homey.

I thanked Prae for her help and she shuffled across the upstairs hallway—a long, red carpet with flower patterns draped across the hardwood floor—and opened up a room.

It was slightly bigger than my room at Dad's. Two twin beds sat in opposite corners, and there was a small, pale green couch to the side of the window that overlooked the back yard.

"Nice view, huh?" said Prae. "Samar got the room looking out over the front yard, but I thought I'd prefer the one with the view of the lake and garden." Prae folded her hands together. "The couch pulls out—we might have a third join us in the night, depending on how many people wind up taking Mikayla up on her invitation."

I tried to smile. "I wonder what time they'll get here." Would Mikayla invite any of her friends? Otherwise, there was just her, Alan, and Tia... If the faery showed. She'd extend invitations to Wyatt and Ellie for being on Prom Court, but I doubted either didn't already have plans.

And Joel and Estelle... There was no way they were showing their faces.

Prae laughed as she picked up her duffel bag and tossed it on the foot of one of the beds. "Checkout time is noon, so I hope sometime before then." She started pulling clothes and a toiletry bag out of her stuff. "I'm going to head to the bathroom and take a shower so I can get some rest and explore the area by the light of the day. Want to take a walk after breakfast?"

"Thanks, but I might just stay in." I sat on the couch next to the window and looked outside. The plant life swayed in the breeze.

"Okay. I have Samar with me, so we'll go together." She gathered up her stuff. "There's only one shower, so I better go before Samar gets in there. He takes forever. I'll try to hold him off when I'm done so you can get in, too."

"Thanks."

She left me alone in the room.

I sat there for a moment, clutching my skirt, just letting my mind empty.

A subtle buzzing rung out throughout the room, and I jumped, for a moment unsure of the source of the sound.

My phone. I hadn't checked it all night, not even on the car ride over—it had been in my duffel bag in the trunk.

Dragging my feet, I grabbed my bag and set it down on the couch, fishing out my phone.

After scanning my thumbprint, I swiped through the messages. Ember wrote to have me check in with her about the night and to make sure I got to my "hotel" safely. I hadn't told any of them exactly where I'd be staying.

I'm here, I wrote. *Getting ready to take a shower. I'm fine.*

I dismissed her message and found a series of messages from Ivy, asking me to do the same thing.

Except it ended with a message that read, *Do you know what's up with Ember? She called me and sounded worried in her message. Dean and I were out and I didn't notice. She said it was about you in the voice mail and now she's not picking up.*

I frowned. So she'd tried contacting Ivy after all? She'd promised not to!

I'm fine, I wrote back. *I'm at the b&b.* I hit *send*, then facepalmed. They were all supposed to think I was at a hotel.

Sighing, I dismissed another message that popped up to check on Ember's string of messages. She hadn't read my reply, and her last message had been sent hours ago, about two hours after the dance had started.

My stomach plummeted. Wasn't that about the last time I'd seen Orin or Tia?

Ember, are you there? I checked the time. It was past midnight. To be fair, she could just as easily have been asleep.

I let out a deep breath. Of course she was asleep. She'd probably changed her mind about tattling on me to Ivy and that was why she hadn't called her back.

Ivy's reply popped up. *Hope you had fun*, she wrote. *Any idea why Ember left that message? What b&b? Dad said you were going to some place by Fowles U.*

Didn't sound like Ember had let anything slip.

I didn't reply. Ivy wasn't finished.

Not THAT b&b, right? Does that place even still exist? she wrote.

Chewing on my bottom lip, I scrolled through my other messages. PonyFan had sent a message. *We should probably talk.*

I cocked my head. Okay? She'd probably sent that to the wrong recipient. All we *did* was message one another.

PonyFan started typing again, I assumed realizing her mistake.

Another message from Ivy popped up. *Autumn? You still there? I googled it and it said the place was rebuilt, so I'm wondering...*

Yeah, same place, I wrote back. Admitting that might take care of any of Ivy's worries about Ember's apparent message, too. *Ember found out and freaked. That's probably what she wanted to tell you. But it's totally rebuilt, like you said. I just wanted to be with my friends. Gtg.*

I turned the phone on *silent* and shoved it back into the bag, taking out my pajamas and the bag with my toothbrush and all the makeup remover Noelle had given me to pack. My face went scarlet as I brushed past the tube of lipstick I'd never used to the sheet of condoms.

Best to get rid of those here. I dropped them in the trash bin, then, thinking better of it, quickly pulled out a bunch of tissues from the nearby box to use and hide the stash with. If anyone needed any, well, that was not a conversation I wanted to have with anyone regardless.

I stood in front of the floor-length mirror in front of the closet door and startled. My mascara had run just a little bit, giving my sleek cat's eye look more of a raccoon touch. Sighing, I slipped several sheets of makeup remover out of the package and went to work removing the makeup on my face.

Next, I removed the bobby pins, letting the stiff, crinkly hair down and unbraiding it bit by bit. Even just unbraiding it made me feel like the clumps of stiffened hair might snap.

I looked back at the mirror, at me. Bare faced, hair down and messy, almost wild. A pretty green dress.

For a moment, I felt as if I were about to bring green light to my hand, to fire out a vine with all the might of the champion of bloom. My eyes narrowed, my hand flexing, that feel of magic running through my palm still a memory fixed in my mind.

I looked powerful. Beautiful, even. But also terrifying.

There was a knock on the door. "Autumn, you ready for the shower?"

"Yes," I said quickly, gathering my things off the bed. "Coming."

As I rummaged around in my bag one more time for the slipper socks I'd forgotten, I noticed my phone blinking with a new voice mail message.

But that could all wait for tomorrow.

CHAPTER TWENTY-SIX

When I opened my eyes, sun streamed in through the curtains. I blinked, realizing the bed was a bit too soft, the blanket a bit stiff over me, waiting for my brain to remind me of where I was. Once the fatigue left my limbs, I looked across the room to the other bed. It was a little imperfect, clearly having been slept in, but Prae had made some effort to sort of fix it back the way she'd found it. There was a note on the bed, and I got up, looking around. The couch was untouched. No one had joined us.

The note said I'd looked tired, so she'd let me be. The bed and breakfast had a little buffet downstairs, but if I got up after eight, she'd probably already be walking to the downtown area along with Samar. I looked at the clock in the room. It was after nine.

Tossing the note into the recycling bin beside the trash, I stretched, lifting both arms over my head. The place was quiet. The others had probably gotten in a lot later than we had, which would explain why they may all have still been in bed.

Still, part of me had expected to find Tia on the pullout when I'd woken up.

Or maybe her hovering over my bed like a specter in the middle of the night.

I decided to get dressed before I went down, not in the mood for Alan and whoever else had shown up to see me in my PJs, or even just the bed and breakfast owners. I shuddered at the memory of Orin's parents posing as the previous owners briefly, after they'd fed the real owners to the faeries looking to dine on human blood.

Faefolk were the progenitors of vampires, after all.

I slipped into jeans with a white belt, a plain white T-shirt, and my bright green cropped spring jacket. It was a bit bolder than I tended to wear these days in front of my classmates, but I'd picked it out last summer during a clearance sale, drawn to the vibrant color. The morning this time of year brought with it a chill and I didn't think I could do without it.

Quickly brushing out my hair, I made for the bathroom and freshened up for the day. Not a single soul greeted me in the halls at any point, before or after.

Setting off down the stairs as quietly as I could, I approached the entryway to the house and folded my hands together, unsure of what to do.

The invigorating smell of fresh-brewed coffee and something that was tinged with cinnamon melted the tension in my shoulders and I headed down a hallway, though memories of a darkened hallway and the basement it led to halted my steps. There was a door here, about where that door had been. It looked different—with a shiny gold handle, whereas that one had had a dark color, a paler wood where that one had been oaken brown—but I wondered if the basement foundation had been kept in the re-development.

"Good morning," said a bright, chipper voice.

I turned toward the light at the end of the hallway. A figure darkened by the halo of brightness all around them waved over at me. "Come and have some breakfast."

As if to emphasize their point, my stomach rumbled and my feet picked up, heading to the source of light.

As I stepped into it and the person beside me grew clearer, I startled a bit. I didn't know her, not really, but with her high, sharp cheekbones, the smooth oak color of her perfect skin, the coiled dark brown hair...

She sure looked familiar. And she seemed thirty at most.

She smiled broadly. It was difficult for former faeries to smile like that, though. Orin only smiled slyly and Tia hardly smiled at all.

Then again, she'd smiled to disarm strangers who hadn't a clue to her history.

"Take a plate," the woman said, gesturing to a small buffet table she'd set up. "It's all you can eat."

Humming, she stepped into a kitchen, and I took a look around.

No one was here but me and her. That didn't seem to be a good sign. The dining room was meticulously clean, decorated real modern, industrial style. The crisp white tablecloth on the eight-person table didn't have a wrinkle out of place.

Would it surprise me if one of the faefolk who'd escaped the orb's destruction had settled here, under Orin's direction and resources? Why wouldn't he show an interest in the site where they'd lost so many of their kind, where it had all come to an end?

Hadn't I wanted Orin and Tia to find me?

Besides, there was still a chance this woman had nothing to do with them at all.

Then again... Orin hadn't wanted to do his parents' bidding in the end, but he'd proven again and again he couldn't be trusted.

My hunger winning out over my suspicion, I took a plate and opened the first metal serving dish. There was a small flame flickering on a burner beneath it and the contents steamed. Scrambled eggs.

Orin wasn't, but Tia was a vegan... Wouldn't the faeries who'd just become human in the past ten years be more likely to eat the vegan diet they'd been used to as small, magical creatures?

Then again, they'd indulged occasionally on human blood. I wondered how that'd fit into Tia's vegan lifestyle.

"Are any of the other young people ready to join you?" said the woman from behind me.

I jumped and stared at her.

She laughed, a carafe in her hand. "Forgive me for startling you. Coffee?"

I smiled nervously. "Please." She seemed so nice. "And no. I guess they're all still asleep."

I scooped some eggs on my plate and moved down the line, heading for the dining table and the steaming cup of coffee the owner had poured for me. When I looked at my plate in front of me, I realized the fact that I hadn't eaten a thing since that sandwich before prom might have made my eyes bigger that my stomach. French toast, hash browns, sausage, eggs, fruit, and dumplings all competed for space on my tiny plate.

The owner's dark eyes sparkled as she put a hand on her hip. "Prom can work up an appetite, huh? Did you have fun, hon?"

I stretched my lip muscles again trying to put on a smile as I reached for the little dish full of creamer in front of me. "It was certainly memorable."

"Well, that says a lot... and nothing much at all." She chuckled. "Let me get you some water. Orange juice?"

"Just water, thank you."

I dug in as she headed back into the kitchen, her humming ringing out into the dining room all around me. When she came back in a few minutes later with a glass of ice water, I was already a quarter finished with my plate. Practically choking, I took the glass from her with both hands and swallowed down.

She laughed full-bodily again, and I couldn't picture her working side by side with the likes of Orin and Tia.

Though Tia had been as sweet as pie at the diner—and she'd charmed hundreds of people at school into voting her Prom Queen, though no one might ever know the truth of that.

My stomach sank and I cradled the mostly empty glass in front of me. Ice clinked against the sides as I thought about what school might be like these last few weeks, if people would compare notes and the whole Prom Court debacle blew up at me. And for what?

All I'd learned was that my plans had been ridiculous—impossible. And they'd put Joel in danger.

"Something wrong, hon?" the woman asked. She leaned a hand

on the back of the chair beside me. "That doesn't look like you had the *fun* kind of interesting night."

"No, it's..." I set my glass down and stared at my food. How much could I possibly vent to her? This potential faery? Or potential human who couldn't know the half of it? "I'm fine," I lied, picking up my fork.

"Well, why don't you finish that up and then go for a walk in the garden? It's nearly fully bloomed. Didn't dare disturb that part of the yard when we were rebuilding the place."

I chanced a look at her and her eyes looked glossy as she stared overhead.

"It's beautiful," I said.

She smiled at me. "That it is. Go take a walk and refresh yourself."

She started humming again and went over toward the buffet table, picking up the stray bits of food I'd let fall from the serving spoons in my quest to fill my plate to its capacity.

"Did my friends swing by?" I asked. "The first ones to check in last night?"

"Oh, yes," said the woman. "First to eat and then they asked about the best places to go downtown. I told them there was more to see than they could in just a morning, but they were off to some of my favorite shops near the university."

She hummed for a while longer and when I was three-quarters finished with my plate, I realized I couldn't hold any more of it. I put my fork down and picked up my coffee. "How many more showed up last night?"

The woman turned and tilted her head just slightly. "Not sure who to expect?"

I shrugged. "I know Mikayla wanted to invite a bunch of people."

"Oh, I know her. She and that lovely young boyfriend of hers showed up near three in the morning. I'd told her in advance I'd wait up for her, but I have to admit, I didn't get a lot of shut eye because of it." She yawned.

I winced on her behalf, the sweet coffee swishing on my tongue and sending a boost of warmth throughout my body.

So no Tia, then?

"I thought my other friend might show," I ventured. "Tia?"

As I took another sip, I watched out of the corner of my eye for any strange reaction. But the owner was focused on my plate. "You finished, darling?" she asked, as if the name meant nothing to her.

"Yes, sorry I took too much."

"Don't worry about it. I tend to eat with my eyes more than my stomach, too." She winked at me and headed toward the kitchen. "You finish that coffee up and then go for your walk. Any of your friends come down, I'll tell them where you are."

So either she knew nothing about Tia or she was cleverly side-stepping the subject. She also seemed quite insistent I head out to that garden.

Taking one last gulp of my coffee, I set the mug down and decided to see if she'd send Tia my way.

I stepped out the front door, not wanting to wander around to find the back way to the yard. Samar's car was still in the parking lot, but no others had joined it. The ride share would explain the lack of other vehicles.

The air was a bit chilly this near to the lake, humanmade or not. It was that time of year when days could be hot and then the next day could be borderline freezing. This promised to be somewhere between the two, but it would take a few more hours of sunlight before the temperature got comfortable enough to go without my jacket.

The grass was soft and dewy beneath my feet, the moisture sinking through the tops of my tennis shoes. When I got to the back yard, the scent of lavender and other flowers caught on a breeze and I took in a deep, rejuvenating breath.

Reaching out, I let my fingers trail across the beansprouts in the arch welcoming me to the garden, my hand resting on my bloated stomach as I inhaled slowly and let out a deep breath, letting the beauty sink inside me.

I stepped inside, imagining myself in my own secret garden—which was easy to do, surrounded by all the greens and bright colors.

I took my time rounding the pathway, smelling the roses literally and figuratively. Not once did dark visions of the battle that had taken place here pop into my head. I didn't find any evidence of plant life trampled or replanted. In the past decade, this place had taken on a life of its own.

And after a while, the warm, nostalgic feeling budded out from my fluttery stomach and to my extremities. I curled my right hand into a fist, then flexed my fingers, almost feeling the warm glow that I could summon once, that power. That ability to bring forth *life*. It had always been more potent, somehow, than the champions of blood's and water's abilities to cause decay and destruction.

"Didn't you read my message?"

I twirled on my heel, expecting to find any host of people, though my mind should have known the voice didn't match a single one of them.

Orin or Tia. Ember. Even Ivy or my parents.

But it was Joel who stood there, his hands tucked into his khakis, his dark, wavy hair dangling entirely over one eye. The creamy white sweater he wore was too soft for his stern, grim expression.

"I said we needed to talk."

CHAPTER TWENTY-SEVEN

I blinked. Then a strange sound, somewhat like a choke and a sob, poured out of me. I felt some of my overly large breakfast threaten to push its way back up.

"Your... Your message?"

My mind raced wildly over the contents of my phone and I reached for it in my back pocket instinctively, only to remember I'd left it in my bag—purposely. I hadn't even checked today's messages, and I should have. I obviously should have.

But more than that... "What are you doing here?" I snapped. It was confrontational and I hadn't meant it to be. But I found as he took steps closer to me, I was shuffling backward. He needed to stay away from me. Right? Being together would cause him harm and do me no good.

Joel smiled wryly. "Mikayla invited me, remember? Prom Court?"

"You came?" I said. "But you—when you found out I might be here, you said *no*."

"I said a lot of things I regret." Joel reached a white wooden bench in the middle of the walkway and gripped the top of it.

I scoffed sourly. "I'm getting a lot of mixed signals here."

Joel took another step toward me and I took another step back, but soon I was pressed against a bush, the twigs poking my back, and there was nowhere else to go. "Wait," I said, extending an arm toward him. My fingers grazed his chest. "You told me you could die."

Joel swallowed, his eyes to the ground. "That's what my parents told me."

"It might be true," I said. "But I didn't know that, I swear."

"I believe you." Joel sighed. "I just have a hard time reconciling you with the FreeFallFly I've known for years."

I blinked. Had he just said what I'd thought he'd said?

"You know my old screenname?"

"You really didn't check your messages." Joel grimaced, but it turned into a sly smile. No matter what he did, he remained suave and charming. "I'm PonyFan42U."

A fluttery feeling pervaded my body. "You... You... But PonyFan told me her name was Scarlett!"

"I said that a while ago." Joel rubbed the back of his head. "I was embarrassed to be a boy into ponies—not that I'm really into them anymore, but I didn't want to shut down the account because then you might stop talking to me when you found out I was really a guy. So I gave you the name of my celebrity crush—"

"Scarlett Johansson." I swallowed, all sense of what else to say lost to me. It wasn't that I couldn't respect an online friend's right to privacy, but we'd known each other for years, and I hadn't had a clue.

And then for him to meet me in real life and not say anything —ask me out to the park that one night and *still* not say anything.

"But PonyFan still talked to me when you were giving me the cold shoulder!" I gasped. As if *that* were the important point here.

"My parents don't know I still have that account." He shrugged. "It's hooked up to an old phone number of mine—you know how a few years ago, it was recommended you get a new number to acti-vate the ProtectID thumbprint technology—and my parents never deactivated it from the family plan, so..." From a cargo pocket over his thigh, he fished out a phone. It was thicker than most phones were these days, one hunk of plastic that wasn't foldable.

"Were they monitoring your real phone?" I asked. I wasn't wrong about the hostility I'd felt pouring off his dad that day I'd tried visiting his house.

Drooping his shoulders, Joel slipped the phone back into his pocket and sat on the bench. "Will you let me explain things?"

Chewing my bottom lip, I shuffled my feet and sat next to him. At the opposite end of the bench. As far away as I could get from him.

"Let's be honest with each other," he started. "What do you know about me?"

I chuckled dryly. "Let me start then with what you might not know *about me*." I glanced at him to see if he'd object, but he had nothing to say. I'd never told PonyFan this. It had seemed too ridiculous. "I was the champion of bloom once, ten years ago." I nodded toward the rest of the garden. "The battle against blood and water came to a head here, actually. My sister had a college visit, and we all tagged along—and by *all*, I mean every faery, vampire, and merperson around. We battled it out and my sister Ivy, the champion of blood at the time, won. But only because... Because I shouldn't have been in it to begin with." I scuffed the toe of my sneaker against the cobblestone path in front of us. "I was manipulated by the faery prince and I didn't see it."

"You were just a kid," he said, not commenting on the fact that all of this sounded so unbelievable. His hand reached across the bench to cover mine. A tingling sensation branched all the way to my core and I had to take a deep breath to focus.

I slid my hand out from under his. "Yeah. I was. Don't know what my excuse is now."

"What do you mean?"

"You accused me of trying to use you," I explained. "And I guess... I guess I was in a way." I looked him straight in the eye. "The faery prince—former faery prince—told me you were our only hope. And though I don't trust him and would be the first to admit he could guide me to act how *he* wants without me even knowing, despite the ten years I've had to grow up and think about everything he could do—I did want the same thing he did. So I accepted his help."

"The Prom Queen thing," Joel guessed. "You didn't actually win?"

"Yeah. Tia was supposed to win second place—and she's a former faery, too, by the way, and couldn't care less. They came up with that idea on their own. If I'd have known I could have just pled my case to *PonyFan* without even seeing you in person, I would have left you alone." It wasn't until saying that just then that his revelation was really sinking in.

One of my oldest friends, one of the only people I'd vented to before all of this—well, minus the whole faeries-were-real thing—was sitting here right beside me.

My crush. My best friend—because who offline could match PonyFan in my book?

Both were the angel standing between me and a lifetime of never-ending regret.

"I'm glad we had that dance, despite everything." Joel's smile flittered. "But what do you mean, *former* faery?"

That was the part he got hung up on? "Did you know about supernatural beings?" I asked.

He laughed wryly. "My family's full of them. I just... didn't believe it until I saw it, really."

"Yes, well, about that... When my sister and the vampire prince claimed victory, they wished for all supernatural creatures to become human. So any of the faeries and merfolk who hadn't vanished into the ether lost their magic."

He frowned, staring off at the garden in front of us, clearly thinking. "But my family didn't lose their abilities." He gestured at himself. "My parents haven't had powers my whole life, but..."

"And yours weren't activated at the time?" I ventured.

He shook his head. "I still thought they were stories my parents made up to tease me. I should have known better. They're too no-nonsense to try to inject their son with a sense of whimsy."

"So that's it. You weren't technically a supernatural creature who would then become human—you were a human who hadn't yet become a supernatural creature."

He stared at his hands, flexing them in front of him, as if he could find the answers inside them. I stared at my own right hand and moved it in the air much the same, remembering the feeling of magic like that tickling, aching sensation when your limb goes numb.

"My parents hoped this would never happen," he said, curling his hands into fists and resuming staring in front of him. "I didn't really believe it when they talked about fallen angels and a long line of succession. But it warmed me as a kid who enjoyed things like *My Little Pony* and magic and adventure." He cracked half a smile. "Still, I figured it was something like Santa Claus—not real, but something your parents wanted you to play along with and believe. Santa Claus isn't real, right?" He side-eyed me.

I clamped my lips together, biting back a smile, and shook my head.

He shrugged. "I don't know. Vampires and faeries and mermaids exist, right?"

"They did."

"Well, they told me when two lines of angels descending from the seraphim had a child together, there was a... *potential* their powers would surface. Their DNA would be encoded with every-thing needed to make them a genuine fallen angel."

So Orin's research wasn't wrong about that much. "And you are that genuine fallen angel?"

"You knew that, didn't you?"

"Orin... The faery prince told me you were."

Joel nodded slowly for a bit, then continued his tale. "Both of my parents inherited a feather," he said. "From the original fallen angel in their lines. When a genuine angel's power resurfaces—"

"The feathers turn red."

Joel looked at me, wide-eyed. "You *have* done your research. People without angel DNA aren't supposed to even be able to *see* the feathers. I thought that was a joke, too, when none of my parents' co-workers would admit to what was staring them right in the face in my parents' offices, but I started to wonder if they really couldn't see it. How did *you* know?"

I cringed. "Again. Faeries." Was it time to tell him the feathers' invisibility had a fatal flaw, showing up in reflections? But that would just lead to me explaining how Tia and Orin had been spying on his parents at work, and I didn't need that complicating things when we were finally laying it all out there.

"Right. Well, both of my parents' feathers have been partially red for years, and they have been watching them like hawks to make sure the color doesn't change completely."

"They started turning color years ago? Since when?"

"Since..." He pulled out his old phone. "Since I started feeling like FreeFallFly was my friend."

I thought about what that meant as a butterfly floated by. "Do they know that?"

"No," he said. "I think they assumed it was someone at my old school. Ironic that they made the real mistake moving here, but they explained to me recently that their aim was to move to lands where magic was thrumming deep within the soil."

"The consummate lands," I explained. I gave him a quick run-down of how the lands had become steeped with magic at the end of the first clash between faefolk and merfolk a thousand years before.

"Ah, well... That was why my parents were attracted to the place, I guess. They assumed whoever would bring my powers forth had been where we physically were at the time—in Vermont. They couldn't have guessed it was my online friend. Neither could I. I hadn't known there was any secondary reason behind our move. I'd thought it was just my parents taking better jobs. They didn't tell me all of this until a couple of weeks ago. I didn't put two and two together about the one they'd been trying to run from being *you* until the feathers grew redder still."

"When was that?"

"The night you saved me from drowning." He flexed one hand. "The night my powers activated and I healed both you and me."

What was it, then? The closer he got to me, the closer he got to becoming a fallen angel? "When did you know FreeFallFly was me?"

"You told me your name years ago. And it wasn't a lie. Then there was the fact that you told me you had a crush on a guy who was 'out of your league,' but you bumped into him at lunch that day, peppering his shirt with spaghetti sauce... You didn't actually get any on me, by the way."

My face flushed. I'd been spilling my guts, exaggerating my story, *to that very guy*.

"So you didn't know until then?"

"How could I? I barely knew you existed—the real you, I mean. At school. I didn't remember ever seeing you before, but you caught my attention that day. In more ways than one."

I winced. "I don't like attention. Not since..." I gestured around me. "Not since the days of all this, anyway. Kids laughed at me for believing in faeries, even though I *knew* it to be true."

He squeezed my hand against the bench seat. "Well, you know I'll never laugh at you for that."

We sat in silence a little while, the breeze brushing softly against the lake somewhere beyond the flowers and bushes.

"Did you know my powers only activate when I feel true love?" he said softly.

My heartbeat grew sluggish. "That's what the faeries told me. So I figured I had no shot of making that happen."

Joel slid closer to me on the bench, leaving only a small space between our thighs, a space across which the very air seemed to crackle with anticipation and energy. "You're wrong." He flourished his right hand in the air, and it glowed soft white. "This is proof of that."

"But you hardly know me—"

He lifted his old phone up again. "I know you as well as anyone, I hope. Though you never told me those stories you used to write about faeries and warriors were based on lived experiences."

Well, they hadn't been true to life, but they'd been one coping mechanism. "Because I didn't think you'd believe me." I caught his eye, and my insides melted. My heart was thundering too fast. This felt wild. We were too young, still too much strangers to one another... A lock of my hair slipped past my shoulder, swinging across my face in the slightly warm breeze.

"I was never out of your league," he said, tucking the hair back. "You were out of mine."

I chortled, then, ugly laughing as I leaned back. But he just frowned.

"You're serious?" I shook my head. "It's just where I grew up since my dad remarried. That house is steeped strongest in the magic of the consummate lands. It's why my sisters and I were sought after to be champions. Nothing special about us particularly—well, not me, anyway."

"Don't say that." Joel moved even closer, reducing the foot between us on the bench to an inch. "It takes a special person to give a fallen angel what they've always sought."

I turned my head, my lips a hair's breadth from his. The air between us was especially warm, fragrant with lavender. "And what is that?"

"Real love. A love worth giving it all up for." He cradled my face with his hands and pushed his lips to mine.

A wave of bright white light washed over me, even behind the darkness of my closed eyes. My limbs tingled as I moved to embrace him with shaky hands, deepening the kiss with a quick and gentle probing of my tongue. The thunderous echo of my heart overwhelmed my ears as I lost myself in the bliss of the moment.

This was like... magic.

I shoved him away. A kiss should have felt wonderful, sure, but this... This had felt like magic.

"What have you done?" I asked.

Joel's face fell, his grip shifting to the top of my arms. "I wanted to grant you your wish."

"*No*," I said. "It isn't worth it if it hurts you!"

"My parents warned me that the more I use my power, the closer I'll be to death." He pushed a smile onto his face, but it was faltering. "But I don't care. Autumn, it *killed me* to see you walk away from me last night. To see you so hurt."

"But I... But you... I haven't even told you what I would have wished for!"

He tilted his head, studying me. "But it's done. You were so lonely, hiding from the world because no one believed you, so I assumed you wanted..." He swallowed visibly.

"*What's* done? Joel, you can't just—"

He leaned forward and kissed me again, and for one small fraction of a second, my anxiety eased as I slipped into the comfort of his kiss.

I never heard her approach.

"So I guess that explains these." A dry, raspy deep alto.

I yanked backward, whipping my head around, for a moment taking note of Joel's unnatural stiffness as he gazed at the ground.

In the walkway, shadowed under the beansprout arch some distance behind her, stood Estelle, and in her right hand was the giant pack of condoms I'd shoved into my room's trash bin.

CHAPTER TWENTY-EIGHT

For a moment, my brain couldn't decide what was the most important point here.

Joel had brought Estelle here. Even if she had been his date to the prom, there was that whole incident of her making out with Wyatt. But then again, they were "just friends" anyway, so maybe he hadn't cared.

Then there was the fact that she had *fished through* the garbage *in my room* to find those.

And the most pressing fact that Joel had granted *whatever he'd thought* was my wish.

I stretched the fingers on my right hand, the numb, tingling feeling getting hard to ignore.

"Your little perfect sweetheart had these in her room." Estelle tossed the condoms onto the garden walkway and crossed her arms. The crinkly, plastic wrappers looked so wrong in the midst of this carefully cultivated patch of nature.

"That's not... Why did you...?" I couldn't put my thoughts into words, not when I realized Joel was staring straight into my soul, his chest hitching. "You didn't know I was coming."

My jaw dropped. It took a second too long for my mind to process what he'd said.

He'd wondered if I'd brought them along... for him?

And now that he was certain I hadn't, he was accusing me of bringing them along for someone else.

That was a whole lot of assumptions on a level I really wasn't comfortable with. "No, but... But you..." I spun on Estelle. "What are you doing, rifling through my room? In my *garbage*?"

"So you admit it. They are yours!" Joel jumped to his feet, focusing on entirely the wrong thing here.

My pulse quickening, my throat dry, I darted my gaze from Estelle to Joel. Estelle smirked. Joel looked less angry with me than devastated, as if I'd broken his heart and smashed it to pieces.

Devastated? *Devastated?* After weeks of ignoring me, after not even letting me explain a thing and his *friend* violating my privacy?

I jumped to my feet, too. "They're not mine!" I shouted. "I mean, yes, I brought them, but my step-mom had dumb ideas in her head and forced them on me—"

"Ideas about you *and D*?" Joel snapped.

Was that what he was thinking? That I'd packed them for D and me?

"You don't know a *thing* about me," I said, flinging my arm out to the side of me. "Not if you think I willingly packed those because I was hoping to get lucky with D. I only agreed to go with him because I thought it might give me a chance to talk to *you*!"

"That doesn't make sense." His nose wrinkled.

"You were avoiding me!" I shouted.

"As he was supposed to be," Estelle added.

I whirled on her and glared. She didn't so much as shirk.

"And you thought I'd talk to you when I saw you with D?" Joel said, ignoring his friend.

"Saw me with D doing what?" I asked. "He and I didn't even dance together once." My right hand felt warm, almost on fire somehow. "You're giving me whiplash, Joel—PonyFan—whatever!" Estelle cocked her head at that but didn't ask.

I flexed my fingers, that nostalgic sense flinging out from my palm. "Forget being in love with me—you're not even a nice friend! You *lied* to me. You left me alone, and every time I tried to reach out, you just put up a wall." Tears were building now in the pressure behind my eyes. "Then you let me in again, and you turn on me the second someone else interferes! You don't trust me, you don't *talk to* me—and what do you mean, it's too late? You never even asked me what I was sincerely hoping for, you—"

A vine shot out from my right palm, clear across the garden, and sticking straight into a bush.

Gasping, finding myself suddenly short on breath, I flicked my fist like it had a spider crawling on it and got the vine to fall out.

"No..." My voice was soft, a hoarse whisper. "You didn't." I gaped, looking to both Joel and Estelle.

Other than a slight arch of her brow, Estelle was... unperturbed.

Joel's mouth twisted into a grimace. "You wanted magic back, didn't you? Supernatural creatures to exist again?"

"No!" I shouted. "That wasn't what I wanted at all!"

Joel recoiled, his jaw clenching as he ground his foot into the stone tiles below him, as if I'd slapped him and then he'd been determined to offer me the other cheek.

Estelle laughed. Actually laughed.

Her strange behavior made my blood run cold. Why wasn't she freaking out?

"Come," she said, reaching a hand out toward Joel. "You see how she scorns you, throws your gift back into your face."

Joel shuffled backward toward her, his eyes not leaving me. They were glossy, wide, like windows to the soul.

"I've alerted your parents to this little... mix-up here," she said. "And they're almost here to get us. You were told to stay away from her, and you assured them she wasn't even coming to the prom, let alone your afterparty." Joel was at her side now, letting her slide her arm through his. "I'll take the blame." She pet his arm soothingly. "I just wanted you to see her. Truly see her. To put an end to your longing."

"What is going on here?" I said, clenching my fist at my side and taking deep breaths as I felt the familiar build-up of energy in my right palm.

Estelle offered me a thrust chin and a curled lip. "You're not so special. I have angel DNA. I may not be full seraphim, but I'm as close to one as Joel may ever find. Any children *we* have together will be strong enough to overcome his curse."

"Curse?" I asked, my mind trying to process twenty things at once. "The more power you use..."

"The closer to death I'll be." Joel just stared straight at the ground. "If I'd never truly fallen in love, I never would have been in danger."

Estelle grimaced, the first sign of discomfort she'd displayed since showing up and butting in, tugging on his arm to lead him away. "We'll have a child, and the curse will pass off to them. Then it's just a matter of protecting them, keeping them from making the same mistake as you, *away* from vile temptations—"

"Do you hear yourself?" I shouted. "Have a child to pass your *curse* onto them? Are the two of you even *human?*" What a stupid question.

Joel sent one last longing look my way and let Estelle shuffle him away, out from under the beansprout arch, into the yard, and around the b&b, trailing out of my sight.

My feet were rooted to the ground, my right fist hot with power that shouldn't even have been there in the first place, let alone back now.

"This place is a right mess, innit?"

My spine prickled at the familiar voice, the Cockney accent. I turned on my heel to find Orin bending over to snatch up the sheet of condoms. His nose wrinkled as he crumpled it up to slip it into his jeans pocket. He'd managed to change since last night, sliding into a green checkered short-sleeved button-up shirt as if he were out for a stroll. There were flecks of green and gold all throughout his hair once more, just like there'd been when I'd been a child.

"Thank you, love," he said, grinning.

"*Thank you?*" I spit back at him. My fist clenched at my side. "Where have you been? Do you even know what's happened?"

"Nearby, watching, as you very well know I do." Orin twirled his right hand in the air, a subtle breeze picking up the few fallen petals and bits of grass from around us and twirling them around his hand like in a mini cyclone. "And I'd say *yes*, even without the fallen seraphim shouting it from the rooftops, I'd gather what had happened. As would all faekind." He stepped back, closing his eyes as if stepping into a warm, tropical rain after a week in the desert. He even spread both arms to either side, as if to embrace it.

"What are you...?" I started, but then I slammed my mouth shut.

The sound. I'd heard it before. I'd never *feared* it before, not outside of my dreams.

Like a swarm of insects flapping their wings. From high up above and drawing closer. Closer and closer.

Glowing, green lights flittered down into the canopy of plant life, spreading out throughout the garden like holiday lights hung out in the spring. They blinked, the tittering of small wings still carrying out all around me.

"But they can't..." Of course they could. I'd heard what Joel had *risked his life* to grant me. Something I hadn't asked for.

Mere moments ago, I'd been lost in his kiss, filled with a euphoria I'd never expected.

How had everything gone so bad so fast?

One of the floating green lights hovered in front of me and with a *pop* transformed into the bed and breakfast owner. Just as I'd suspected.

Grinning, she rushed forward and hugged me. "Thank you, dear."

Caught unawares, I patted her back as I looked around me. At the scores and scores of faeries in the garden. I stepped back from her numbly.

Another floating green ball of light *popped* into human size right next to Orin. "Got what you wanted from that cabin of yours." Tia cocked her head. "Sort of came to life on the drive over, that's how I first knew." She held something in her hand: a glowing ball that at first I mistook for another faery, considering a third of it was green.

But it was equal parts blue and red, too.

"Oh, no, no, no..." I said.

The orb that denoted the champions of blood, bloom, and water. The one Ember had been worried about, but I'd brushed aside.

It consisted of what seemed like three shades of glass fused together at the center, perfectly round, like a rock worn away by the tide. It only lit up in each color when all three champions were active.

I stared at my hand, and as if on command, it elicited a soft, green flow.

"I can't be..." I said.

Orin smiled as he took the orb from Tia and tossed it back and forth from one hand to the next. "Keep your powers, love. Enjoy them. With my parents gone, we don't need more bloody pointless wars. We just wanted our powers."

"But you—" I swirled on Tia, but she shrugged one shoulder. "You both! You wanted the lost faefolk brought back, just like I wanted!"

Tia rolled her eyes. "You cared more about bringing back the merfolk than the faefolk, even though *we* were your warriors."

"That's because..." A vision flashed before my eyes, Ember in tears as Calder faded away in front of her. "No, I wanted the faefolk back, too. But not like this! As humans!"

The bed and breakfast owner took a step back, staring at me coldly, all joy dropped from her eyes.

Letting out a great sigh, Orin slipped the orb into one of his oversized pants pockets and put a comforting hand on the faewoman's shoulder. "She doesn't understand," he said simply. Then he brushed past her and turned to me. "We'd have taken them back—so long as my parents weren't among them, I'd be happy to see a few more cousins and the like back with us." He looked over his shoulder and Tia approached, an unspoken conversation between them. She approached a nearby bush blooming with lavender and waved her hands over it, the air filling with the slight tinge of a pale green light.

"But now that we have our powers back, we can give birth to a generation anew," Orin said.

A blossom—an infant one, a floret—grew beneath Tia's fingertips, the petals curling and unfurling until a small, marble-sized green ball of light emerged.

Tears in her usually impassive eyes, Tia reached both hands out toward it, cradling it between her palms as if holding a newborn child.

And then I realized—she truly was holding a newborn *faerie* child.

My foot slipped backward as my heart thundered, taking in the sight of the green lights all around me. My hand glowed green as if in response.

"Easy, love," said Orin. He chuckled. "You or that foolish bird boy's obliviousness, his kind's overprotectiveness, whatever was responsible—you made this all easier for us than ever."

Tia nudged her little green ball against her cheek and for a moment—a fleeting moment—I felt for her.

"We planned to get you to have him wish us back into power once you had him wrapped around your little finger," Orin said. "After you brought the fallen faefolk and merfolk back, however you pleased." Orin tilted his head and shrugged. "Unlike the orb, the angels aren't limited to just one wish—so long as it's of a healing nature."

"But Joel told me he'd grow closer to death the more he used his power," I said, my voice a harsh whisper.

Orin seemed unmoved. "As did the others we discovered in our research. Seems to be their destiny. Fall in love, experience what angels all fell to Earth for, and poof, your time is over. You didn't notice the pattern of them all dying tragically young? I wasn't even really hiding it."

I clenched my fist. He was right. I'd been too busy looking for some hidden message in his notes, desperate to find out how he'd been tricking me, that I hadn't seen it right in front of me.

"But we'll take what we got." He nodded toward my palm. My bright, glowing green palm.

Orin took a careful step back, his hand out in front of him while he fished out the orb from his pocket with the other. "But remember what happens if you or your sisters surrender to one another. You need this to make a wish, yeah? And even if you wish *fast*, friends are sure to start vanishing before you get your wish out. Is it really worth the risk?"

I stumbled, my hand halfway up, a vine slithering out slowly from the expanse of space between my pinky and thumb. My sisters? Of course. The blue and the red on the orb, which were glowing, too.

They'd gotten their powers back.

"You can't..." I started.

My voice was overpowered by the sudden tittering cheers and the flapping of wings all around me. Tia's little green marble of light flew up into the air, and the larger green balls gathered around it, all heading to the sky. Tia spared one look at me, the joy on her face melting to impassiveness, but she nodded, as if offering me that one acknowledgement for the role I'd played in it all.

The role she'd helped trick me into playing.

With a *pop*, she turned back into a little faery, her green ball of light flying off to join the others.

"Enjoy yourselves," said Orin, clutching the orb to his side. His expression was grim, almost determined. "Say *hello* to our fish foes and bloodsucker children for us. Tell them we want no quarrel."

Before I could respond, Orin popped into a green ball and headed up to join the swirling mass above us—the flittering storm flying off into the bright midday light.

CHAPTER TWENTY-NINE

"Did you get any of this breakf—whoa, where's the fire?"

Alan nudged Mikayla after she spoke, a plate in front of him easily three times as overflowing as Mikayla's beside him. They were both in pajamas, standing at the buffet in the dining room with a clear view out into the hallway as I sped by.

"PTSD from the gas explosion?" suggested Mikayla. I didn't know what else she said. I was taking the stairs two at a time up to my room.

"Autumn!" she called after me. "Autumn Sheppard!"

I shoved open the door to the room I'd shared with Prae and slammed it shut behind me. Nothing inside indicated Prae was back yet. The only thing disturbed was the tipped-over garbage can, and I knew who'd been responsible for that. Maybe I hadn't buried it deep enough and she'd noticed the embarrassing strip of wrappers poking out from the garbage can. Or maybe she was just *really* nosy.

My phone was vibrating from my bag. I was surprised Estelle hadn't bothered to snoop around in there. But she'd found what she'd wanted.

Something to tear Joel away from me.

And him, the *fool*...

I put my thumb to the screen and worked my way through the

messages. Too many to read. There were some from PonyFan, yes, but I couldn't bear to look at them just then. Then there were some from Ivy, from Mom, from Dad...

Uh-oh.

Ivy was in the middle of calling, an alert with "twenty-two missed calls" at the top of the screen.

I stumbled to actually answer the call at first. It'd been so long since I'd done a non-video chat.

"Hello?" I said into the phone.

"*Finally!*" shouted Ivy into my ear. I had to pull the phone away a couple of feet. "Why haven't you been answering your phone?!"

"I've been... *busy*." I winced.

"I bet you have! Ember told us everything! And now... Now..."

"She's all right, then?" I asked. With everything else going on, I hadn't had time to worry about her going silent.

"Yes," came Ember's voice over the phone. Ivy must have had it on speaker. Wait, *speaker*? Maybe it was a shared call. I checked the screen. Nope.

That meant my sisters were physically together. Had Ivy flown in from Seattle since last night?

Ember kept speaking. "Though considering you were the only one who knew Orin was back up to his old tricks, I might have appreciated you letting someone in on that information to help find me—"

"*You've* known for weeks and you didn't tell us, either!" said Ivy.

"I was just... Autumn and I..." Ember cleared her throat. "Well, Orin *invited* me back to his cabin last night." He had? When? After I'd... I'd asked about the orb. He'd guessed immediately what I'd been up to. Why did I fail at *everything* I tried? "I wanted to know what he was up to, see if he still had the orb—"

"Which he did," Ivy added.

"But then he left me there this morning, and I struggled to find my way back. Then that girl he was with—"

"Tia?" I ventured.

"She never introduced herself. She showed up and snatched the orb from me." I wondered why Orin hadn't just brought it himself to begin with if he'd just been at his cabin the night before. To keep Ember occupied and away from the rest of the family? To give her something to focus on, some sense of hope? "She led me out of the woods and then took off with the orb, driving like something was on her tail."

She'd helped her out? Why? Had that been against Orin's wishes?

Whatever the reason they hadn't left her to languish in that cabin, the faeries had always hoped to get their powers back. And they'd known they couldn't let the orb fall into our hands if they intended to keep the magic. Not when the three of us champions would all work together.

"Meanwhile, Dad and Noelle are freaking out," added Ivy. "Because even if Ember usually lives alone, it's, like, common courtesy to let the family you're staying with know when you're going to be out all night, right?"

"I hadn't heard from her." A new voice. Journey? Great, how big was this party?

Ember let out a nervous laugh. "I should have at least told Journey, since I'd hinted Orin had been up to no good, but I knew it was a night James was going to be home and I didn't want to bother her—"

"*Bother me*," Journey said. She let out a strange sort of hiss. "Considering everything, I think it's better I know."

That hiss made my blood run cold.

It was familiar, like a sound out of a long-recurring nightmare.

"Yup, Dante's got it, too. He's calling me," said Journey. There was the sound of a phone ringing in the background and she answered it, her voice growing quieter, like she was turning away.

The sound of an engine revving drowned out her first few words.

"Anyway, long story short, Dean and I caught the red eye back here and arrived just as Ember managed to get out of the woods," said Ivy.

So Dean was the one driving, perhaps? He'd been quiet so far.

Driving? Driving to—

"Are you on your way here?" I asked.

"Yes!" my sisters called out at once, as if it were obvious.

"And don't try to tell us to turn around and go home—" started Ivy.

"No. That's good. I need a ride," I answered, shocking them into silence for a moment. Journey's soft voice continued in the background, but I couldn't make out what she was saying.

"Ten minutes," came Dean's stiff, formal tone. He'd lost a lot of his black-and-white movie accent.

A pounding came on the door behind me. "Autumn?" Mikayla asked. "You all right?"

I raised my voice so she could hear me. "Yes! Family emergency. Need to go home. My sisters are coming to get me."

"Oh, I'm sorry." Mikayla went quiet. "Anything I can to do help?"

"No, but thank you. I need to pack."

"Right. Well, just let me know how it goes." Her footfalls carried across the hall.

"So Mom and Dad know?" I said into the phone as I crammed my crumpled pajamas into my duffel bag. My dress was in my garment bag, my dress shoes at the bottom of it. I was pretty much good to go.

"We'll keep you updated," Journey said, and I realized she was talking into her own phone. Then she spoke louder, addressing me. "Kind of hard to hide it when Dean and I turned into vampires right in front of them."

Crud. I'd thought that might be the case—for Dean at least. But Journey, too? I'd barely remembered she'd even turned right at the end of the battle.

Rubbing my neck over the faded wounds where Ember had once bit me, I wondered if it was some form of sympathy pain coming through.

"We have our fire and ice powers back," Ivy said simply. "Could probably change into mermaid vampires, too, but we didn't bother to give it a shot."

Ember hurried on. "I don't really keep in touch with the

merfolk for the most part, but Bay friended me a while back. He got married a few years ago." Her voice cracked, like the thought of a merman moving on—when his own boyfriend had vanished alongside Ember's—reminded her too much of what she herself had not done.

"Well, if he's not currently swimming or taking a bath, maybe he wouldn't even notice," said Journey. "But yeah. Dante turned into a vampire in the middle of rehearsal and is hiding in his dressing room. I had to remind him that he can put on sunglasses and go out in the sun so he can go home until we know what we're dealing with. He still thought that 'turns to ashes in the sunlight' myth was true." She laughed wryly. "I suppose this means Devam turned, too? He'd probably be happy about it."

"And Raelynn?" offered Ember. "But she and Lyric broke up ages ago. I don't know what she's up to these days."

"We need to worry about ourselves first," Ivy said. "Good thing we packed a few extra pairs out of habit." It sounded like she'd zipped open a bag and rifled around. "Here, Ember. In case you turn mermaid vampire and need the eye protection."

"Thanks," she said. "And it's vampire mermaid."

I could practically imagine Ivy rolling her eyes from here.

"Oh," said Ember. "Bay *is* messaging me." Everyone gave her a moment to scroll through her messages. "Yup. Laguna noticed it first. They have their merfolk abilities back."

"So about that," said Dean, his deep voice smooth and unpanicked. "Autumn, kiddo? You know anything?"

I let out a deep, tight breath. "Yeah. I'm not in danger—but I know what happened. I messed up."

The sound of a vehicle pulling into the parking lot out front told me they'd arrived.

"Just give me a minute to run to the bathroom and I'll be right down. I wouldn't come inside—a faery owns the place. Though I think she took off to the skies." I grabbed the pen off the nightstand and quickly scribbled a *thank you* to Prae on the note she'd left behind, telling her I was heading home early with family.

"We'll be waiting," said Ivy. The amount of unsaid pressure in that sentence was enough to light a fire under me.

———

Halfway home, I'd told them everything I knew.

Everything, down to the most embarrassing moments of condom packs and true love and my brief hopes that it could have been real for me, and how those hopes had been crushed again as Joel had so easily believed the worst of me.

If it were just my sisters, maybe—and even Journey was like a nice cousin who'd hung around more than a few times. But I never would have confessed so much in front of Dean if things hadn't been dire.

If my major goof-ups hadn't led to him becoming a vampire again.

He had a right to know.

In the back seat of Dean and Ivy's rental car, I was crammed beside Ember, with Journey on the other side of her. Ivy was in the passenger's seat upfront beside Dean, who was driving as I'd suspected despite the dark, dark sunglasses he had on.

"He doesn't want a war, does he?" Ivy cracked her knuckles in front of her. "Well, wars often start one-sided."

"He has the orb, though," I pointed out. "No sense in any of us 'surrendering' to one another without it, without being able to make the wish."

"Can't we just ask your angel boyfriend to unwish it?" Journey suggested.

"He's not my..." That wasn't the important part right now. "I have no idea where he's gone, but if I had to guess, he retreated back behind his parents' overprotective defenses, and he won't see me. Besides, I can't ask him to undo this—not if it affects his life-span. I don't know if his 'healing' magic *can* undo this. Being able to 'heal' the supernatural abilities we all lost kind of makes sense, but undoing it? That's a wish for the orb."

"Which the trickster prince has squirreled away to who-knows-where." Ember snarled. "I can't believe I let him lead you around for weeks! I can't believe I hoped—" She cut herself short and Journey rested a hand on her shoulder.

She'd hoped I could bring Calder back through all of this.

"If it's any consolation, I think Orin *did* want the lost faeries back," I said. "But he wanted his powers back, too. Probably more. And if that was what Joel gave us first, then Orin was forced to show his hand and hide the orb away from us."

The car went quiet for a bit, the purring of the engine filling the silence. It was one of those fancy electronic sports cars, which was partly why there was so little room in the back seat.

"I'm not sure I like the idea of what you were *really* trying to do," said Ivy softly after a moment. "Maybe I'd feel differently if it were Dean. Well, I didn't hate Calder or most of the other merfolk, not in the end. But it's just... It's just not natural."

"And fangs retracting out of my mouth with venom dripping from them are?" Journey snapped.

"They shouldn't have vanished like that," I said softly.

Ember took my hand in hers and squeezed. "It wasn't *your* fault they did."

"In a way, it was." My eyes welled with tears now. Ivy turned around and waited for me to speak, not saying a word. "If I hadn't been manipulated into becoming the champion of bloom..." I stared at my right hand and let out a dry laugh. "And don't say I was just a kid because it's been ten years and I thought I'd changed, but here I am again. The champion of bloom, manipulated by a faery prince."

"It sounds like there were also some misunderstandings afoot," Dean said, piping up for the first time.

"Even when I *try* to be smart and not let the faefolk trick me, I still mess it all up."

"I think we all know by now that faeries deceive as naturally as they breathe." Ivy turned back around. "And they've been around a long time. I don't think any one of us has a chance."

"If it means anything, I believe Orin when he says he doesn't want to fight," said Ember softly.

Remembering my "big brother," the games we'd play, the movies and books he'd loved to talk to me about, I had to agree.

But were his faery powers that important to him—the loner who'd walked away from his kind for a thousand years?

Or was it...

"He's afraid of dying," I said bluntly. "Growing old and someday passing. He saw what happened to his family who vanished, but more than that, even those left were doomed to die—after a lifetime of humanity."

Dean gripped the steering wheel tighter. "I have to admit it's... hard. Sounds foolish, I know. I was *tired* of immortality. Ready to be human again." He dropped one hand from the steering wheel and took Ivy's, which rested on her lap. His smile was bright in the rearview mirror, even with those blood-red lips against ghastly pale skin that should have made it frightening. He put his hand back on the steering wheel, and I realized Ivy's cheeks were pinkening. "And I just had a little under a century to get used to eternal life. The faeries have known nothing but that since the dawn of time."

I frowned as Ivy buried herself in her phone, seemingly trying to look busy.

For a moment, I felt empathy for Orin and Tia. Who were we to decide that supernatural creatures shouldn't exist because they'd involved us in their little proxy war?

Then I remembered the faeries sucking on the blood of those bed and breakfast owners.

"Zelda's worried about Leopold," Ivy said, looking up from checking her screen. I didn't remember everything about the vampires, but that I did remember. Zelda had been dating Leopold since the 1940s, but she'd broken up with him when they'd become human. She's actually been on Ivy and Dean's side when they'd decided to wish supernatural creatures away. "He and Herbert and Ruby... I'm not sure they'll handle being vampires again responsibly."

"*I'm* not sure I can explain this to my family. What about my job? Do I just show up with sunglasses from now on? Work from home? How do I explain this to my baby?" Journey's voice went hoarse. "Some of us can't turn it on and off."

I clenched my fist as Dean stepped on the accelerator, as if we had a destination in mind, a plan to see through.

Journey was right. Zelda, Ivy... I didn't know which of the merfolk who'd survived had been all in favor of flooding the planet, but this was just too risky, unleashing these powers back into the world.

"We're going to talk to some angels," I said. "We may not know where the faefolk have gone, but we do know where a healing seraphim lives. And we're going to find out exactly what he wished for—and how it might be undone."

I didn't want Joel to have to risk any more of his life, but this was about more than him, more than me.

Unleashing this magic again could have dire consequences.

Ember slapped a hand to her face. "I forgot. That means my dad's a vampire again, too." Grumbling, she started tapping at her phone screen.

We needed to undo this before it all got out of control.

CHAPTER THIRTY

Dean pulled in front of the gated house. It was late afternoon and the sun had retreated behind a mass of clouds, the gray sky hanging ominously over the large house like some kind of omen.

"They look ready for anything," muttered Ivy as she took in the place. "You're sure the angel boy went back here?"

"No, but it's a start," I said.

"What if his parents are home?" said Ember. "You remember how cold his dad seemed. At least Angel Boy would be more likely to listen to you."

"His name is Joel, not 'Angel Boy.' And he's rarely in the mood to listen to me." I leaned between the front two seats to get a better look. Beyond the towering gate, down the long driveway...

"That's his car, at least," I said. "Estelle said his parents were coming to pick them up. I doubt they would have taken him anywhere else, and if his car's here, that means he hasn't left."

"Maybe let's just start by asking?" Journey was massaging her temple. I wondered if vampires could even get headaches. Though looking at the sunlight without dark lenses seemed to cause them a searing sort of pain.

"I doubt they'll let us in," Dean pointed out.

"Well, too bad for them. Their son gave us back our powers."

Unbuckling my seatbelt, I twirled my right hand and got out of the car. I tapped the security screen near the driveway gate and it lit up, a pulsing pink light on the screen and a ringing signal to let us know the call was going through.

After what felt like forever, Dean's rental car running idly behind me, the pulsing light stopped and a clicking sound occurred, like it had been answered.

"Hello?" I said into the silence. "Joel, we have to talk. You can't keep running away from me, especially not after what you did."

I heard a woman's voice, soft and almost distant from the speaker, like she was speaking to someone else inside the house. "What did you do?"

So Joel was there. As suspected.

It had been a while since I'd tried it, but I delved deep inside, remembering that feeling, that *control...*

"Open the gates," I said. My voice flooded with meaning, with *intent*. A command. I swallowed dryly, remembering how wantonly I'd used this ability as a child, but surely, if ever there was a time...

"Open the—" I started again, but I jumped at the sound of metal rattling. Ember had walked to the gates and was trying to *pull them* open with her bare hands. "Ember, stop!" I cried out.

She did.

"I don't think that trick is going to work over an intercom," said Ivy. Journey stood on one side of her, but Dean remained in the car.

"Trick?" said the higher-pitched voice from over the intercom. There was still no visual on the screen.

Rats. The one time that wouldn't have been too egregious a misuse of power... Ember shuffled back beside Ivy.

"Joel made me a champion again." Floral abilities it had to be, then. Summoning the growth from a spark somewhere deep inside me, I curled my fingers as a vine curled out slowly from my palm. "So unless you want your fancy high-tech gadgets shredded beneath nature's wrath at a thousand times the speed of natural growth, I suggest you open that gate and let us inside."

"Why should we do that?" asked a deeper, colder voice. Joel's dad.

"Because some of the vampires and mermaids and mermaid vampires Joel recreated are here." I gestured behind me. "And more are out there right now, probably about to wreak havoc, because your son wished it so."

The screen crackled with a sudden snap and the image indicating for visitors to press the pad appeared once again.

Then something like chains rattling drew my attention. A second set of gates drew shut across the first, blocking the driveway.

Oh, no. They weren't retreating farther into their shell.

Dean revved the engine on his car, rolling the window down. "Should we ram it?"

Ember, Ivy, Journey, and I all stilled, staring blankly at him.

Then we burst out laughing.

"Save yourself the insurance claim." Stepping back, I directed him to the street. "Go park." I squared my shoulders and faced the gate. "We're getting in *our* way."

I heard Dean pull back and out of the way. I was already facing the driveway, holding both hands out in front of me, though only one would grow a set of vines.

"Can fire or ice help?" Ivy asked, examining the gate. Her right hand was flexing beside her, a red light slowly growing brighter, an occasional shot of violet amidst the red.

"Or crackling fire icicles?" Ember offered, tensing her bright blue hand. There were tints of purple in hers, too.

Journey took a step back behind us.

"We'll see." With a flourish, I shook my right hand and vines started pouring out of them, starting as one vine and growing off sideways up and around the gate. The sound was like the constant rubbing of a pair of rubber waders in motion, the little thinner ends that broke off growing into blooms.

I had to focus to keep the florets contained, remembering that rush of power I'd used to teleport the faefolk to me.

To teleport the faefolk to me.

I let go, realizing both my sisters were shooting crackling purple icy flames almost in tandem on either side of me, straight at the hinges on the gates.

They stopped when I did. The gate in front of us was a mess, the hinges burnt and melting, encased in purple slush, the rest of it covered in what looked like decades' worth of vine growth, though the plant life was bright and green and new.

"I can summon Orin—or at least some of the faefolk—with my vines!" I said. "Remember? The florets can teleport them."

The three of us exchanged a look, as if weighing what to do next.

The angels or the faeries?

The healing magic or the orb?

Dean's harried footfalls joined us on the pavement behind us. "Might be good to have some angels on our side first," he pointed out. The dark sunglasses gave him a polished look, though since he'd left the 1940s-style suits behind in favor of tan three-quarters pants and a red polo shirt, he looked more like a tourist than the suave vampire from my memories. "*Encourage* them to help undo the mess Mr. Angel Boy created."

"If they can forgive the mess you made of their driveway gate first," said Journey wryly.

Ember looked over her shoulder. "Do you think the neighbors are seeing this?"

"Should we care?" Ivy offered. "Let the angels explain it."

"Hmm," said Ember. "Autumn, any chance you learned to fly as a faery?"

I shook my head. I'd never fully transformed into a faery on command the way Ember and Ivy had both become vampires and mermaids at times—or mermaid vampires when they'd mastered both forms. My gaze trailed down the sidewalk, looking for any spectators, but then it crossed... "The side gate!" I said, running over there. My hand was already shooting out another set of vines, which wove through the slats with the coordination of the best synchronized swimmers. No extra gate had come out to block this one, and once my vines were tightly wound around the metal, all it took was one mighty heave, forcing more and more energy through my palm and outward, to drag it off its hinges and down to the ground.

"That works," said Dean as the rest of the group stumbled to a stop behind me.

We were in.

A siren rang out from the house a few dozen feet away, the incessant bell ringing from the tripped alarm drilling into my head.

Ivy and Ember pushed around me on either side, both determined to walk through before me. Journey and Dean held up the rear, though I knew Journey's experience with vampire abilities was limited.

I let my sisters go in first, but then it was my turn to put them behind me. "This is my fault," I said. "Stop thinking of me like a kid and let me take the lead."

"I don't think—" started Ivy, but Ember shook her head, stopping her.

No time to argue.

I picked up my feet and ran forward, the perfectly-manicured lawn crinkling beneath me with each step. When something popped out from the ground, I flung a vine straight at it, cutting the growth off like a spear.

"I think that was just the sprinkler system coming on!" shouted Ember from behind me.

Sure enough, another set of mechanical heads popped out from all around us, clicking rapidly before starting up their shower.

"Head for the driveway!" Ivy screamed.

Journey's shriek was loudest, and I spun. Steam poured off her and Dean's exposed skin like red smoke slipping through a sieve.

Did the angels know about the vampire's weakness to water?

Ember and Ivy, not transformed at all, were blasting at the individual sprinkler heads with their crackling purple icy fire just as Journey and Dean made it to the pavement. Journey shrieked again and Dean blinked in and out of existence, his vampire time-pausing power making it seem as if he traveled seven feet in half a second. He spread his arms wide and took a shot of sprinkler spray straight to his face to protect Journey.

The red steam grew so thick, it was like he'd been buried in fog.

Letting out a wild roar, I ran toward the sprinkler, shooting a vine toward it and willing that thing to rip straight out from its root. It did, allowing Dean some peace to collapse to his knees, the steam fading, but I wasn't done. I commanded the vine to spread out, travel along the little pipes fitted into the dirt and grow, grow, grow, destroying every sprinkler head on the front lawn in one mighty, devastating blow.

The air grew quiet, even the tripped alarm no longer screeching. Ember was at Journey's side, sliding out of her spring jacket and using it to wipe as much of the moisture off her as she could. Ivy stood over Dean, her right hand glowing in a gentle red flame as she waved it over his face, drying him.

I turned back toward the house, clutching my fist. I didn't know how much water it would take to really hurt a vampire, but the fact was, any bit of it caused them pain.

They'd hurt my friends. My *family*.

I whipped my hands out and shot another wave of vines, grinding my feet into the soggy sod under my soles, surprised at the amount of energy I had, though well aware of the way my limbs were beginning to tremble. The vines bashed against the double front door, gripping the handles, ready to tear the thick wood apart, but then the doors pushed open, sticking against the plant growth.

"Wait!" shouted a familiar voice. Deep, once cold, but quavering now.

Joel's father?

I pulled on the vine growth, yanking the doors open and experiencing no resistance, the wood slamming against the balusters.

In the doorway, dressed in fine silk clothing, black pants and white tops that were almost a matching set, were two middle-aged people. One was familiar—the man I'd spoken to on the screen a few weeks back. The other shared much of her son's look—the angle of the nose, the set of the cheekbones, though her hair was thicker, even curlier, gathered over one shoulder into a loose pony-tail with a white silken scrunchie. She wasn't as tall as her husband, but she was as willowy, with firm muscles and far too lean a physique. The two of them looked about to fly away in a breeze.

I flexed my fingers. Perhaps that could be arranged, considering Orin's own talent for winds. I'd struggled to master it, but I'd managed a time or two.

I approached the porch, taking slow, careful steps.

"Our son rests," said the woman. "And if you push him further—"

"You will be responsible for his death," finished the man.

CHAPTER THIRTY-ONE

I faltered.

He'd warned me of the price of his powers.

Then he'd gone and done something I hadn't even *asked* him to do and now...

"He was fine when I saw him a few hours ago," I said, standing straight. "Please let me speak to him." I was careful not to color my words with that sort of intent that would force them to do my bidding. Yet. I would if I had to.

Assuming angels weren't immune like vampires were.

"No," said Joel's father quickly. He actually leaned forward as he spoke, his arm out, as if ready to tackle me should I charge at him.

I didn't know whether to find the idea humorous or to actually take him as a threat.

I sized the two of them up. They didn't appear to have any special powers—unless their slightly uncanny disarming beauty counted.

I checked over my shoulder out of the corner of my eye. Ivy shuffled forward with her arm around Dean, Ember and Journey in a similar position as they made their way closer.

It was five against two, and whatever their powers may have been—if they had any—I'd take my chances.

Thank you, Joel, for that.

"Step aside," I said. This time, it was a command.

I picked up a foot, pushing down the feeling of guilt that plagued me as they both complied. That didn't stop them from reacting. The mother frowned, her husband sneering menacingly at us.

"What did you do to us?" he said.

I froze, fighting back nausea. I'd done this before—carelessly, cruelly. Orin might not have thought anything about ordering people around, but I was human.

"Another one of my powers your son returned to me."

Mr. Serafin stepped forward again, blocking my way. Had my wavering resolve freed him? Or had my command been once fulfilled and his own will restored?

"We cannot stop this now," Mrs. Serafin said quietly, standing beside him. Her husband deflated at that. "We tried and look what happened. We brought our son right to her."

My chest grew tight. They were making me out to be some temptress, some vixen.

"I never wanted to hurt him," I said. "I didn't even know being with me *could* hurt him."

"It's not being with you that hurts him, but granting your wishes that does." Joel's father growled. "But unfortunately, you being who you are to him—he can't help himself. Like the others, he..." He looked down, unable to finish.

"Like the other pure-blooded seraphim who fell before him— he will die young," said the woman.

"Seems the easy way to prevent that would be for those with seraphim DNA not to have kids with one another." I scowled. "But if you did that, then you couldn't just get rid of your curse and dump it on your kid, could you?" I remembered what Estelle had told me.

Joel would lose this ability to grant me wishes if he had a child with another seraphim. Only that child would then have the potential to exhibit the magic.

His parents both blinked, the woman's elbows tucking into her sides, the man taking a deep, pained breath as he gazed down.

"Did you have true loves, too?" I asked. "I don't mean each other—did you have a child together to avoid the temptation of granting some other person's wishes?"

They didn't answer. Instead, Joel's mom stepped back, gesturing inside. His dad drew his eyebrows together but shuffled back also.

I didn't move. I hadn't forced them to let me pass by again. I didn't trust the invitation, though it was something I'd been demanding. Now it was coming too easy.

Joel's mom clasped her hands in front of her, not looking at me as she spoke. "You're right. We did have a child together to avoid the temptation. We located a promising family of partial seraphim blood here, counseled our son to do the same as we had—pass the curse on to the next generation."

"And yet before he even had a chance to graduate from high school, you've put him in this position," said Joel's father. "We have plans for our son. Going to college, medical school, like we did, and then have a child—"

Mrs. Serafin held up her hand. "And we never asked Joel if that was what he wanted."

Mr. Serafin's lip flared. "An angel's vocation is to heal. You know as well as I do that our professions helped us stave off some of the calling... to... to go out there, to explore—"

"To fall in love?" Joel's mom lifted an eyebrow. "To really *experience* emotion as our ancestor angels gave it all up to do?"

"We've experienced—" started Mr. Serafin. But he stopped himself, seemingly lost in some sort of memory.

That was enough. If they were agreed on letting me through, if I didn't have to command them anymore, I needed to seize the opportunity.

"I'm not trying to take your son from you. All this talk about true love—I'm still in high school, too." I clutched my fist tighter against my side. "All I wanted was to undo a mistake I made years ago."

"It wasn't *your* mistake—" Ivy started, but Ember cut her off with a hush.

"And now—now it's Joel who made a mistake that needs undoing. I don't want to hurt him, but we can't let vampires and faeries and merfolk run free." I glanced over my shoulder at the others. "They had lives as humans. And some others can't be trusted."

Mr. Serafin started to speak, but Mrs. Serafin just nodded solemnly, looking at the floor. She knew I was right. "He's upstairs."

I rushed through at last, my sisters and their friends trailing behind me. I grabbed for the bannister in the wide, open and bright-white space. The house hardly looked lived in, more like a model, as unblemished as if we were the first ones to take a tour of the place.

"I have to do this alone," I said, turning my head just slightly so everyone knew I was speaking to them.

Ivy's voice carried up from behind me. "But he might freak out or this could be a trap."

"Let her go," said Ember quietly. I wondered if she still had hope I'd get Joel to resurrect her friends—or if she'd accepted I couldn't risk the additional wish hurting Joel any further.

I flew upstairs, my wet sneakers squeaking roughly against each step.

No one followed me.

The hardwood hallway was covered in a long, white carpet. My sneakers left small clumps of brown and green, the muddy grass from the front yard corrupting the perfection. A door at the end of the hallway was open, the bright early evening sun filtering through a window and out onto the carpet.

A woman's humming grew louder as I approached, and I should have guessed who'd be there beside him, but the soft, melancholy tune and the sweet voice were too at odds with the raspy alto I was used to associating with her.

Estelle sat in a white chair beside Joel's bed, trailing fingers over his forehead.

She didn't give any indication she noticed me hovering in the doorway behind her, but she spoke—and it wasn't to Joel. "Do you know why angel families tend to decorate so much in white?"

I didn't respond, my brain still catching up to the fact that she was speaking to me.

"It's comforting to us. Reminds us of home—that ancient home none of us has ever set foot in." She turned over her shoulder and offered me a wry smile. "Then again, we like black, too. A contrast to our original nature, a reminder of the sin of falling." She gestured at herself, at her entirely black outfit. "Some of us are bigger fans of the original sin of our kind than others."

"Is he...?" I asked, taking cautious steps toward her.

"Asleep. For now." She shrugged. "He started getting weak on the way back. He was too worried about you to sleep, and when you showed up on the security camera..." She rolled her eyes. "His dad injected him with something to get him to go to sleep. He had to carry him up here."

She didn't stop me as I approached the bed covered in a white bedspread, soft and fluffy, no doubt filled with down. It was tucked tightly up to Joel's chin, his face impassive as he lay on his back, his breath coming in and out, causing a steady rise and fall of the comforter.

I reached out to caress his face, all logical thoughts forgotten.

"You know," said Estelle, "even though I knew being Joel's true love would hurt him, I'm still jealous it was you, not me. Not saying I was sitting in the corner crying—especially since all of our parents figured his best shot of a long life was marrying me anyway. But part of me... just wanted it to be *real*. What he felt for me."

I turned on her, my hand falling to my side.

"Jealous?" I said. "You actually *know* him." I bit my lip, thinking over all of my conversations with PonyFan over the years. I knew *them*. But I didn't know Joel. PonyFan was just a part of him. "He spends time with you. Him thinking I'm his true love has led to nothing but disaster."

Her eyes darted to my closed fist, and I realized it was glowing green, growing brighter as my mood darkened.

She chuckled darkly. "I don't know. Seems that's proof it's not him just *thinking* anything." She studied me. "If it were me, I might have wished for him to grant me some kick-butt powers, too. Seen where that took me."

"I didn't *wish* for this," I snapped. Joel twitched in his sleep beside me. Taking a deep breath, I stretched my fingers and willed the energy to stop forming.

"That's odd," Estelle said. "He shouldn't have been able to *help himself* from giving you what you wanted if it was within his abilities, not if he kept spending time with you."

"He misunderstood," I said simply. Why did this remind me of commanding someone to do my bidding? I should have commanded him to stop, to fix this all then, in the garden. I'd just been so overwhelmed. I hadn't understood what he'd done until it had been too late.

Joel tossed in his sleep, and I wondered what kind of drug his father had injected him with. My stomach roiled at the idea that his parents would drug him—even if it was to keep him safe. From me.

I spoke to Estelle, but I couldn't keep my eyes off Joel. I shouldn't have felt so drawn to him. I wasn't the one with seraphim DNA and some kind of magical force compelling me to throw it all away for him.

Estelle cackled. Actually *cackled*.

I spun on her. "I'm glad you find this so funny. If you were so keen to marry him and have a kid to pass his curse onto and deal with protecting *them* until they could do the same, why didn't you stop him from following me to the bed and breakfast?"

That wiped the smile off her face. She bit her lip, rubbing some of the deep purple lipstick off. "He wasn't going to let you go. We tried. His parents, my parents... He'd led a normal life before he'd decided he couldn't *stand to* stay away from you anymore. So I thought if he granted your wish, he'd get sick and see there were consequences—"

Before even realizing what I was doing, I chopped my hand

through the air and a blast of wind flew across the room, pushing her chair backward against the wall.

Estelle's eyes widened, her chest heaving for a moment as she gripped the armrests tightly. But then she composed herself. "The condoms were a nice touch. I thought if he knew you were going to screw somebody else—"

"I wasn't!"

She shrugged. "But if he thought you were."

Tears welled in my eyes as footfalls echoed out beyond the open door. Ivy's voice carried out down the hall. "Everything all right, Autumn?"

"Yeah. I'm fine." I used the heel of my left hand to wipe the burgeoning tears away.

The footfalls retreated—there'd been more than one pair. But I knew they hovered nearby, ready to jump... And do what? Stop me from using my powers on this girl? It wasn't like she could do anything to me. Anything but deepen my heartache with every barbed jab of her words.

What was wrong with me? There were so many reasons I couldn't be with Joel, and it shouldn't have mattered. It *shouldn't* have.

"Just out of curiosity's sake, what *would* you have wished for?" Estelle asked, standing up from the chair.

I shook my head. "Nothing. Not once I learned using his magic drained his life."

Estelle drew closer, her arms crossed as she tapped a finger against her bicep. "I don't believe you."

I scowled at her. "Well, now I *do* need something from him. I need him to undo it. Make all of us human again."

The flash of anger across Estelle's eyes sparked to life and then faded. "A seraphim's magic heals. There's no 'undoing' this wish. You can't *heal* a supernatural creature by stripping it of its powers."

So my fears had been founded. My throat went dry. A small part of me rumbled with joy at the thought of not asking this of Joel, of not putting him in further danger by asking for a wish, but...

But if he couldn't do it, then that just left the orb.

The power of champions.

The battle.

And even with my sisters on my side this time, we still had to fight the faefolk to get the orb.

And they were *not* going to give it up lightly.

And if we won, what would I wish for? Supernatural creatures to no longer exist again? That would just mean more deaths—merfolk *and* vampires this time if I was the one to make the wish.

How could I wish everyone back into existence, stop more from vanishing because their sides had 'lost' the battle, *and* get rid of our powers all in one wish?

I collapsed onto the edge of the bed, my hand reaching for his knee beneath the comforter behind me.

"I should have never tried to befriend him," I said quietly. "He had the right idea—keeping me at arm's length." I leaned toward him, knowing he couldn't hear me but feeling it best that we part this way, where my thoughts and feelings couldn't tempt him anymore. My face hovered over his. This wasn't his fight. "I'm sorry I ever dragged you into this."

My eyes met Estelle's guiltily. "He probably couldn't have granted my real wish, anyway. But I'd never ask now—now that I know it hurts him."

"What, pray tell, was it?" Estelle arched a single eyebrow, as if expecting me to wish for the moon.

Maybe I was.

"To bring back the merfolk and faefolk who vanished with the champion of blood's wish."

Estelle opened her plump mouth, shaping it into an 'O,' surely about to ask what I was even talking about, but Joel let out a low groan from behind us, stealing both our attention away as he thrashed under the covers before he cast them aside. A white glow emanated from all around him, casting him in a holy, ethereal light, and he lifted off of the bed just slightly. I realized with fascination —with not the smallest bit of horror—that he wasn't just floating.

Large wings unfurling from his back tore through his sweater and pushed upward.

Red feathers. Just like in the images from the Serafins' offices.

An earth-shattering scream traveled up the stairs and along the hall from down below.

CHAPTER THIRTY-TWO

It was Ember screaming, I was sure of it.

My feet moved without me thinking, headed for the door, then ground to a halt as I stared at Joel suspended in the air over his bed.

Which way do I go?

Estelle tried to touch him, but she kept pulling her hands back at the edge of the light around him.

His torn sweater slid off him, slipping down his arms as Joel moved from the area over the bed to the middle of the room, his socked feet still hanging three feet or so from the carpet. The wings were giant, rounded near his shoulders and spreading out so long, they would have reached his ankles had they fallen straight down.

Voices carried out to me from down below, the pounding of feet down stairs, across the hardwood floor. A door opened somewhere and then there were more footfalls—only these grew louder, a pair pounding up the stairs.

"What have you done?" Mr. Serafin gripped the edges of the doorway leading out into the hallway, Mrs. Serafin hovering behind him.

Their eyes widened, their complexions paling at the sight of their son—still unconscious—his red-feathered wings flapping behind him.

Estelle stumbled back, a wing just narrowly missing her face as she slammed into the armchair still up against the wall.

I was unable to tear my eyes from Joel. His bare, trim chest, decorated with fine hairs, the broad wings, the warm, bright glow. He looked stunning—but also terrifying, his red wings somehow so wrong, his drooping head making it clear that despite the beautiful glow all around him, he wasn't doing this. Something was doing it *to him*.

Mrs. Serafin put her hands over her mouth and strangled a harrowing cry. "You've killed him," she whispered.

I'd... what?

"He used too much of his power." Joel's dad rushed past me, knocking me aside. I stumbled against a dresser, too stunned to react to the hard edge slamming against my spine. I stared at Joel. With his head lolled, his limbs loose, he did look... He looked...

Dead.

Even if those wings, that glow, brought some kind of unearthly life to him.

Joel's dad reached for him, gripping him by the thighs. "Son? Joel? Wake up!" He shook him, and one long, red wing shot forward, knocking him to the floor.

Mr. Serafin scrambled back on his backside. His wife seemed to find her strength, rushing forward to her husband.

"We're too late," he said, clutching her hand that wrapped around his shoulder. "Too late," he said again, softer, sadder this time.

Was Joel dead?

But how? Why? He'd been asleep! I hadn't asked anything of him. I'd—

I'd spoken my wish aloud beside him. Even subconsciously, his desire to please me must have kicked in.

I was of two minds. I wanted to run downstairs, see why my sister had screamed, why all those voices were outside. They sounded tense.

Joel's head snapped upright, his eyes shooting open.

He was alive!

A warm, heady feeling expanded outward in my body from my chest.

My hand reached out to him.

But he shot toward the window, his red wings folding around his head and body like a cocoon as he smashed headfirst into the glass.

His parents screamed his name. Estelle just screamed, covering her head as shards of glass sprung backward in his wake.

Still near the door, I was too far to be caught up in any of the destruction, but the sound of the crash and then the tinkling, crackling fallout was like stabbing little shards into my brain.

I ran out into the hallway and down the stairs, my footfalls leaving a thunderous echo in my wake.

The front door was wide open, the sounds from the front yard a mixture of voices, shouting and screams. I reached the doorway and froze, my feet taking me the last few steps down the porch and to the driveway, though my gaze was locked on the mass of people out on the lawn before me.

No, the mass of *merfolk*—I recognized some of them now. Far off at the edge of the lawn, sprinklers I hadn't reached for with my vines were still spitting out water, and near them, some merfolk flopped around on the grass like fish out of water.

And above them were shining, floating green lights.

The buzz of an insect's wings overhead snapped me back to the moment, and I looked up. A flittering faery soared above me. I reached for it with my right hand, the hand glowing green, and then yanked the hand back, sucking on my finger. The little faery waved his wooden spear around. He'd stabbed me.

"Joel!" Mrs. Serafin's voice grew stronger behind me. She and Mr. Serafin and Estelle practically barreled me aside as they made their way out to the yard. They stepped around merfolk, who watched them curiously, but the couple paid them no mind, keeping their focus on their floating son.

"Autumn!"

Ivy waved me over to a spot to the side of the lawn.

She, Dean, and Journey stood to the side of the yard, just out of reach of the spray of one of the sprinklers I hadn't damaged. Just beyond them in the spray was a set of figures getting soaked. I recognized Ember's almost-white blonde hair as she clutched tightly to someone else, rocking.

He came into view. Calder Poole. Short-cropped blond hair, a muscular upper physique completely bare—and a dark blue merman tail that flopped lazily amidst the grass and the water spray.

I bolted toward them. Ember's sobbing grew more distinct amidst all the other noise, her shoulders shaking as she clutched on to Calder as if he'd fly away the moment she let go. Her nails were raking gashes into his bare back, but he didn't seem to mind. He returned her embrace—though not as tightly. His head kept turning as he took in the scene around him. His gaze locked on Ivy and Dean a few feet away.

"What... happened?" he asked as I pulled up beside my sister and the vampires. A small bit of the spray splattered at my feet.

"You were gone." Ember sobbed, barely choking out the words as she pulled back from him. "For ten years!"

"Ten *years?*" Calder asked. He took Ember by both hands, and I realized she'd been holding them out in front of her, offering them to him readily. They stared into each other's eyes, an unspoken conversation passing between them.

"I-I see," he said, trembling.

With a start, I wondered if he literally *had* seen. The merfolk had been mind readers through skin contact, my sisters had eventually told me.

I studied him a moment, his face beside Ember's. My stepsister had barely aged in the past ten years, but there was something more to her that she'd been missing at my age. A spark of maturity—of grimness. Grief had hardened her just a little, but the barriers she'd put up against those thoughts were crumbling now, her emotions spilling out freely from her face.

I couldn't tell if he'd aged. He still looked the same as I remembered him, but my memories of those days were clouded with revulsion and playacting. It had all been a game to me then, and over the years, those bright imaginings of fairy-tale-like adventures had been clouded with the reality of the damage my mischief had caused.

"You did it," said Ember, sparing a quick glance up at me. "You got him to bring them back!"

I turned, following the sound of Joel's name on the wind. His parents were still calling for him, Estelle having reached the edge of the fence and slumping against it—but all three looking up.

Up at the red-winged angel flapping far above, the green orbs of light darting this way and that around him.

"I didn't ask him," I said. "I thought he was asleep. He did this, but I... I wasn't going to put him in danger."

"You've killed him." His mom's words echoed in my head. He still looked so limp.

"Ember, I still don't fully understand," started Calder. "And where are we?" He turned over his shoulder, barely able to move out of Ember's grip, taking a look at the other merfolk on the lawn. "Mother?"

I swallowed. That was right. The leaders of the faefolk and the vampires had all been killed in the battle before the champion of blood had claimed her wish. But not the leader of the merfolk. She'd vanished into dust along with the rest of them. And now she was here, on the Serafins' lawn.

She stood on trembling human legs, her long, auburn hair tumbling over her bare chest to offer her some modicum of modesty, but not enough. She stood straight and flicked her hair back.

The other merfolk—the ones not getting doused with water— saw this and stood as well, like newborn fawns on trembling legs unused for a decade. I recognized some—one girl had been at our house for Thanksgiving that fateful year, and the pale, lanky but trim redheaded boy beside her had been in the... in the basement.

Beside the dead human bodies. With water spilling out from the water heater, the smell of blood in the air. The redhead had

had dark circles under his eyes, feebly flapping his blue fin in the treading water.

My heart thundered in my chest.

"Cascade and Llyr," said Ivy quietly beside me. She'd been their comrade once.

Calder swiveled, still holding on to Ember, though looser than she held on to him. He positioned himself to get a better look at the mess of the lawn and the standing merfolk all gathering at the center of it, the few stragglers like himself stuck at the edges beneath the sprinkle of water.

He closed his eyes tightly, and then with an almost tearing kind of sound, his tail morphed, ripping into two pieces, the fins forming feet, the scales sliding away until he had two human legs even with all of the water raining down on him.

Ivy paraded down the driveway straight to the mass of merfolk. There had to be at least two dozen of them, including a small child.

I lost my breath for a moment in a gasp. The child had to have been around eight at the most—and he'd vanished along with the rest of them. And he certainly hadn't aged ten years in the meantime.

Tears fell unbidden down my cheeks as I choked out another breath. For one fleeting, beautiful moment, I felt like I'd done the right thing.

"You've lost, Nerida," Ivy practically sneered as she approached the mermaid queen. Dean trailed tall and stiffly behind her. "Long ago. *Years* ago. So don't get any ideas."

"What is she doing?" Ember asked. Her grip on Calder finally slipped as she realized he was trying to stand. She helped him to his feet, and the two stood side by side under the sprinkler, utterly soaked but Ember the only one looking out of sorts because she had on sopping clothes.

I flushed as I turned away.

Journey brushed past me to jog after Dean and Ivy, and Calder and Ember moved to do the same, but Ember let go of Calder and hugged me for a moment. "Thank you," she said. "For bringing him back."

Him, more than them. It was always about him alone for her.

Between those words and the child, I was starting to feel warmer and warmer, a sense of serenity washing over me.

Calder studied the two of us quizzically but didn't ask, giving me a quick nod—I wondered if he even recognized me—and slapping his bare, wet feet against the pavement as he approached his kind. Ember let me go and followed after quickly.

I moved slower, whatever insults Nerida and Ivy were volleying at each other growing clearer the nearer I came.

"Stay back, traitor!" Nerida called. "I don't care where we are or what is going on, but you will *not* be the end of my kind!"

"I already was." Ivy waved her purple, crackling fiery hand above her. "You're only back here because my sister felt sorry for you." Nerida's eyes flicked to me—whether she recognized me or not, my hand was glowing green—and her steely brow softened as she swayed. Perhaps she did recognize me and realized the passage of time.

Ivy continued, not giving the woman time to process anything. "That's right—the champion of bloom. So you can stop acting like merfolk are in any position of power here—"

"Ivy, stop," said Ember quietly but firmly. "We're not enemies. Not anymore."

Ivy turned her head slightly, her nostrils flaring. "They want to flood the world!"

Ember put a hand on Ivy's shoulder, adding pressure to get her to lower the arm slightly. "They can't. They won't. And they also are still in the mindset of that final battle ten years ago, just let them—"

"*You*," said Nerida. She took a step forward but ignored my sisters, aiming her wrath on Calder, her own son. "You did this to us! You killed us, took us away for *ten years*!"

Dean chuckled wryly. "It was more Ive and me than him if you're about to point fingers."

Nerida whipped on him and scowled. "But you couldn't have done it without his blessing—you needed merfolk blood! And he gave it to you. Just like your stupidity killed your father, you threw it all away for this temperamental temptress!" She gestured wildly at Ember, then pulled back her arm as if about to slap her son, though he towered over her. Calder just looked to the ground, turning his cheek to take it.

Two things happened then.

Opening my mouth to command her to stop, I found myself also shooting a vine out to grab the woman's arm. Just as Ember with a *pop* used some of that champion of blood power that still lingered in her system even after becoming the champion of water to step between them.

Tugging on the woman just in time, I saved Ember from receiving a blow.

Screaming, Nerida turned on me, and before I could drop the vine and let her go, the other merfolk gathered around and let out a loud roar that could only be described as something like a battle cry as they all rushed toward us.

CHAPTER THIRTY-THREE

"Mother, stop! It's over." Calder stepped around Ember, putting himself in front of her, but she brought her own hand up, letting the pale violet light crackle at her palm.

"Get behind us," Ember said to Journey, who complied. Dean and Ivy took their places beside Calder and Ember, but the mermaid queen's wrath was focused entirely on me.

"Stop!" I shouted, but my heart was thumping loudly in my ears, and I realized with another jolt of panic that anxiety was eating away at me, taking from me the sense of poise and command I'd need to order anyone to do anything.

Letting the vine fall, I ran, barreling toward Mr. and Mrs. Serafin, who had still been distracted staring straight up at their floating, comatose son until the sound of the merfolk crying out and chasing after me drew their attention.

"*You*," sneered Mr. Serafin as I skidded to a stop beside him. "What are you doing? Leave us out of this mess you created. Unlike *you*, we care more about our son—"

But that was just it. I'd realized without thinking I'd run for my best shot. Above me, floating all around the red-winged angel, were the faefolk my wish had brought back to life along with the merfolk. I knew none of them but Orin, and the one I'd encountered had poked me to thank me for what I'd done, but my instinct at the sight of a horde of merfolk after me had been to run to seek their aid.

I wasn't alone. Ivy volleyed blasts of her crackling purple fire after the merfolk, exploding more at their feet. Dean popped in and out in the fading sunlight, his disadvantage about to retreat beyond the horizon as he wrestled one merperson to the ground after another, baring his fangs and sinking his teeth into a muscular man's jugular.

But then another dove for a spray of water from an untouched sprinkler, his tail emerging in a flash, and like a break-dancer, he spun on his arms, flicking the stream of water toward Dean.

The vampire hissed, the red steam sizzling off him. His sunglasses knocked askew, and he let out a scream as the dying light hit his eyes.

As I stood there transfixed, something wet dripped on my cheek. I wiped it off—it was red.

I looked up. The faefolk—who were supposed to be on *my* side—were using their little spears to jab and poke at the unconscious angel.

My stomach sank.

And my mind grew clear.

We could not let powers like this continue. Not for the faefolk, not for the merfolk, not for the vampires. Some had been moving on with their lives, and others... Others couldn't be trusted.

I zeroed in on my unconscious angel and realized I could save him too—so I hoped.

He didn't have the magic to end supernatural creatures' power, and even if he did, I couldn't let him make that wish for me.

Even if he could. Up there, I wasn't sure how much longer he had.

But I could wish for it—like Ivy and Dean had. So fast, no one would vanish before the wish was made.

I just had to make sure the orb had the blood of the vampires and merfolk on it. Calder and Dean would surely volunteer again.

"Get back!" I shouted to Joel's parents. They seemed about to protest, but Estelle stepped forward and tugged them back.

Letting out a roar, I turned to face the merfolk headed my way and sent vines soaring out of my palm again, as fast and as thick as I could muster them. They grew left and right, up and down, little leaves and thorns springing to life, building a wall between me and any advancing merfolk. Above me, the flittering of the green orbs grew louder, the faefolk drawn away from my floating angel and down toward my vines—toward the florets, opening up and producing light.

Closing my eyes, I ground my heel into the sodden mud beneath my feet, wishing for the faefolk to return—for Orin in particular. *We're under attack*, I thought to the power that surged through my veins. *You have a duty to protect me.*

They'd probably disagree on that point if they had a choice, but the magic of the consummate lands nearby, the magic that flowed through my veins, would not give them that choice.

Letting out a gasp, I opened my eyes to find the dozens of florets of all varieties upon my vines—roses, lilies, lavender, daisies, flowers that had no business growing on vines—blossoming into full-blown blooms, opening up and discharging a bright green glow from each and every flower. The wall of flora towered overhead, at least three times my height, wild and jagged, the plant life often leaving gaps to see through that were nonetheless too small for any human to attempt to squeeze through to pass. It was like something out of a fairy tale. Pulsing, alive with growth.

The scream emitted when one orb crackled and a human-sized faery fell to the ground was jarring enough to halt every approaching merfolk. In the lull, Dean fixed his sunglasses, his own cries quieted even as red steam continued to pour off his exposed skin.

Another green light crackled and Orin appeared full-sized on the other side of the vines, standing upright. He was still wearing his jeans and green-checkered shirt, at odds with the faery beside him, who crumpled to the ground in a green dress woven from long blades of grass. He leaned over to the faery figure who'd collapsed before and I realized it was Tia.

She jumped up and spun on me, gazing at me through an open

hole in the lattice of vines. "We told you we wanted no more fighting!"

Two glowing balls of light from above flew down beside her and each crackled into human size. A pair of faeries in dark brown, patchwork leather-like attire appeared beside Tia. Both regal and tall, oak-brown complexions with curly black hair falling off their heads in waves. "Daughter," said the woman.

Tia turned on them and growled again. It was as if every bit of decorum she'd exhibited over the past few weeks had been butting against a dam about to break. "You won't take her from me!" she shouted.

The pair of faeries—Tia's parents, I presumed, however a pair of faeries decided they were parents to a child born from bloom—exchanged a look.

"You have given birth to a new fae?" the father asked.

I moved forward, cautious, the weave of vines still between me and them, though I had a clear view through one giant gap.

Tia's mother frowned as she put a hand on her daughter's shoulder. "There can only be three hundred faeries," she said. "You know if a new life is created, someone must die."

Tia slapped her mother's hand away.

"Yeah, yeah, we know the rules," said Orin. In his shirt pocket, there was a large lump. It gave off a soft, multi-colored glow. "Moot point, it was, when the whole lot of you were gone anyway. Plenty more chances to create new life." The corner of his lip curled up in a smile he offered his cousin. "Cheer up, cuz. With my parents good and dead, some more fallen before the rest vanished, there's room for your girl and then some."

Tia's eyes blinked rapidly, as if only just realizing this.

No one ever had said anything to me about a finite number of faeries.

Not that I'd have objected. Bloodsuckers, most of them. And literally.

Orin tapped his cousin's shoulder until she stood on two feet. I realized that across her breast, a bright green ball of light glowed.

With the way Tia cradled her hand over it, it must have been the faery child she'd created. She stared out at the mass of merfolk, naked but unafraid as they gathered together in one line, the last of them with tails transforming back to human legs so they could stand beside them. The edges of the lines were doused with sprinkler water, but they didn't blink, undisturbed by the falling moisture.

I couldn't see behind them, couldn't find my sisters and Journey.

Orin hissed over his shoulder and I realized he was speaking to me through the vines. "We told you, we don't want a war."

I gripped on to some of the vines separating us as if it were the bars to a jail cell. "And I'm supposed to care what you want after you tricked me?" I poked my arm through the hole. "Hand me the orb, and let me wish this over with."

Orin turned his head at that, his eyes widening. "Are you having a laugh?"

I flicked my palm open and closed, summoning all my will. "Give the orb to me."

"*No*," he said, turning back to the merfolk in front of him. So he wouldn't respond to my commands. I'd had to at least try.

Orin's eyes flicked upward, and he didn't say anything at the sight of the red-winged angel. The remaining floating green balls of light flew on either side of the small line he was forming with Tia and her parents in front of the vine wall.

"Well, if it comes down to it, I think we can take a bunch of fishfolk without a lake to jump into and a couple of straggler vampires. Didn't think to get the whole gang back together for this final fight?"

"It's not *going to be* a fight," I said. "If you just let me make a wish—"

"And lose our powers again?" Tia said. "I don't think so."

"Don't be ridiculous!" I said, reaching farther through the hole and just barely grazing Orin's shoulder. "Orin, you have to do this. You have to understand!"

With a final click, click, and spritz, the few remaining sprinklers turned off, leaving the merfolk with no further simple way to transform again.

Not that their tails offered them too much advantage in a yard, especially against faefolk, who had no weakness in water.

What had I done?

"Well, if that ain't a sign, I'm telling porkpies," said Orin. "Faefolk, advance! Let us end this once and for all!"

I clutched his shoulder tighter. "No! You can't kill—you can't! It's a battle between champions, remember?"

He spun on me even as the flittering wings of his kind soared overhead, divebombing toward the row of merfolk. The merfolk screamed, a woman with the child darting quickly to the side, the first to break ranks, even as some of the more determined merfolk —Cascade, Llyr, some of the more muscular men and women— roared and slashed out empty hands at the prickling spears of faefolk above them.

"That's *if* we care about making a wish." He grimaced. "I told you with my parents dead, we won't turn the world into a forest paradise. I just asked you to leave us alone." He flicked my hand off his shoulder. "But you couldn't even do that."

"Oh? And I'm supposed to trust that your kin suddenly lost their thirst for blood?"

Orin shirked. "Never cared for it myself."

We locked eyes and I let my right hand fall back beneath the brambles, a plan formulating in my mind before I even stopped to think of it. Keep him talking.

"Orin, it's not you," I lied. Well, it wasn't *just him*, anyway. "I can't trust these merfolk with their powers—or many of the vampires. I can't let Journey and Dante and my sisters' other friends who became vampires back then suffer life as the undead." My right hand glowed softly, I hoped not too brightly, as a small, thin vine went to work, growing straight downward into the soil beneath my feet. "It's... It's Joel, too." I looked up. My red-winged angel still floated there, his wings flapping, his head lolled. Small bits of blood dripped down his bare torso, streaking his skin in rivulets of red. "I need to give him a chance to live—as a human. Please."

Orin rolled his eyes. "Spare me the yarn about true love. Weren't you the one who insisted you couldn't feel such a thing? Too young, it was all too fast, etcetera, etcetera."

I reached through the gap in the vines with my left hand to grab him by his sleeve, the rough material wrinkling beneath my fingers. I tried my best to ignore the sounds of crackling and popping as faefolk became full-sized and small again, as Dean and even Journey, I saw now, were engaged in battle with jabbing little faefolk behind Orin. My sisters' fiery purple crackling ice glowed brightly in the dying sun.

"This isn't about true love," I shouted. "This is about a fair chance at life! Your kind has lived longer than any of them, and you could still have a human life ahead of you—just let this go. Please! I can't stand for there to be any more death."

"Oh, please." Orin brushed off my hand again. "What was one little girl's trauma compared to the loss of my magic?" He narrowed his eyes on me. "I've had enough trauma to last a hundred lives. I'm not going out now."

"Then I'm sorry," I said.

He opened his mouth to speak, but the thin vine I'd wormed through the soil shot up and went straight for the pocket on his chest.

"No!" he shouted, dancing backward, the air around him crackling as he fought to transform into a smaller size. But my vine had already ripped open his pocket, removing the orb just as Orin became small, practically disappearing from sight.

I whipped it to me through the hole in my vine wall, panting, finding myself out of breath after so much use of my power.

Holding it in my hands, I marveled at the warmth of the glassy orb practically bringing the smooth stone to life in my palms. The green, the red, the blue...

Time for the blood of our "enemies."

I just hoped I didn't need my prince to make the wish with me.

Tucking it under my left arm like a football, I darted to the edge of the lawn, looking for a gap in my vine wall. It looked weak near the fence around the property; with a gust of wind, I could probably break it down. I kept up the pace, realizing that there was a wave of fluttering wings behind me. I checked over my shoulder—faefolk, of course. The vine wall wouldn't stop them. At least I'd drawn most or even all of them away from the merfolk.

"Ivy!" I screamed, having no idea if my voice would reach them across the vines. "Ember!"

I couldn't make the wish until they surrendered, until I had their princes' blood.

I didn't watch where I was going until I was yanked behind a tree, between the wall and a line of bushes.

I screamed, and Estelle pulled me down to crouch on the dirt. "What are you doing?" she snapped. "And how will this help Joel?"

Chewing my lip, I looked up, but I could only partly make out Joel's figure in the sky past the leaves in front of us.

"It's a long story, but you need to go—we're about to get pummeled by a bunch of stinging faeries."

Sure enough, the leaves around us shook as fluttering green globes started bombarding the bushes, tiny, jagged sticks poking through the branches. Estelle let out a yelp and covered her head with both arms. Instinctively, I moved to do the same, then real-ized I needed to fight back.

Closing my eyes, I flung out my arm, and a gust of wind sent the balls of light flying back.

"Can you save him?" Estelle asked, her breaths ragged.

"I'll try. All I need is—"

Estelle clamped a hand over my mouth. "Don't say it. Don't even *think* it." She pointed above us.

I sat up straighter, risking poking my head above the bushes to get a better look.

Joel's wings were beating in a consistent, faster rhythm than before. His wings were... Well, if possible, even darker. A deep, deep red, so red, it was almost black.

"If Joel senses you want one more thing that's within his power to grant, he's a goner," Estelle said. "Then you'll get to see what a real fallen angel looks like." She swallowed, her lip trembling.

I wanted—no, I *needed* to get to my sisters and their princes. That wasn't something healing magic could handle. Not unless he could *heal* the lawn and restore it to how it'd been before I'd made a mess of it, before the vine wall could separate us. But even so, with just a little work, I could take the wall down here at the edge myself. I just—

With a *whoosh*, Joel flew out over the wall, his wings flapping as a white glow emanated from his entire body. For a moment that went on too long, I felt warm, serene. Relaxed.

"You idiot! He sensed something you wanted, something he could give you—" said Estelle.

I snapped back into the moment and jumped to my feet.

No.

The vines retreated, fading to dust, the scuff marks all over the lawn re-sodding and being replaced with perfectly-trimmed grass.

I didn't want this. I hadn't wanted—

Joel's wings turned pitch black as they flapped and flapped, and then they wrapped around him and he fell, head-first, to the ground.

"No!" I shouted, shooting a vine out from my palm. It grew and grew and grew as the seconds passed, but he was so far away. Too far away for me to catch him.

The flittering of faery wings swelled, but instead of calling upon the wind to brush them away, I closed my eyes.

I had milliseconds to do this. There could be no failure.

Clutching the orb tighter under my arm, I asked it for strength and with a crackling pop, shrunk down to the size of a faery.

CHAPTER THIRTY-FOUR

With no time to marvel at how much bigger the world had gotten—or more accurately, how much smaller *I* had—I darted forward. The orb, tiny as well, was snug against my side as I soared and soared, moving faster than I knew possible.

The falling winged form was gargantuan above me, but that didn't matter. All that mattered was I'd done enough damage. He would not die because of me. Not when I was so close to saving him.

I popped back into my full size as I hovered beneath him, then shot out vines below us, weaving them to a cushion of brambles.

And then we both crashed into it.

Part of his wing landed on my thigh with a stinging not unlike being whipped, but other than that, we landed side by side, without him crushing me.

Twigs dug into my side, a thorn scraping against my cheek. I stared at Joel. His black-feathered wings had taken the brunt of the impact, cradling his body so only his hair was mussed up with long, thin brambles.

I reached out to cup his cheek. It was cold, pale. His long, dark eyelashes fluttered over his closed eyes, but just barely.

I leaned forward and touched my forehead to his. "I'm sorry," I said. "This is all my fault."

Voices cried out. Screaming. Shouting. Crackling and crashing, fluttering. But Joel's black wings wrapped around me, drawing me closer.

In the cocoon of his wings, I was the warmth giving life to Joel's frigid skin. And he, glowing softly white, was feeding it all back to me, nourishing me, as if *I* were the one in need of his strength.

His seraphim DNA would really give and give to me until he could give no more.

But then the light grew wan, darker, and I grew cold, too. Behind my eyes, flashes of visions took over, bringing with them a sense of dread, of failure, of guilt beyond measure.

Noelle almost tumbling off the upstairs railing.

The bodies in the basement, the water trickling.

Blood—green and blue and red—as battle broke out all around me.

And then what I knew could have been had I not stopped myself.

I sat on a throne made of wood, but it wasn't neatly sculpted. It was more like it had grown out of a tree, veiny, gnarled, and full of sprouts and roots breaking off in every direction. I looked at my hand and saw it was small, as if I'd never aged from those days in which I'd become the champion of bloom.

Still, I *felt* older—aged. Wretchedly so. I gazed around at the endless forest. Bright green balls of light flittered all around me like dancing starlight. It was beautiful... But then I noticed the broken, snapped door, the shattered window. The vines had overtaken a home, consumed it, leaving behind little pieces of it like a rusted bicycle I'd once seen in a photo around which a tree had grown.

I took a step, finding my feet covered in leathery brown, the angles of the seams all crooked and poorly woven together, the thread dried stalks of grass.

The sliding glass door was forever open, the wind flying through it whistling an eerie tune. This was my home.

My father's.

Only I knew then that he was dead. Mom. Ivy. Ember. Noelle... The twins were just a possibility cut short.

The whole world was gone, replaced by endless, endless forest.

I screamed and closed my eyes, slamming a palm against one of my eyelids.

I went to move the other but hesitated. My arm was warm in this cold place, clutching something... something I couldn't let go of.

Shouting, I opened my eyes and found myself back in Joel's arms, the light around him gray and threatening to swallow me like a shadow.

"Autumn!" It was Ivy somewhere beyond those black feathers.

The orb. The orb was still against my side.

Quickly, I landed a kiss on Joel's cold forehead. His lips were turning blue.

"I'll save you," I said, not ready to acknowledge that it might be too late.

I pushed at the wings keeping me cocooned, not wanting to hurt him but realizing I had no other choice. I kicked at them, shoving them, finally bending them just enough to wiggle free. Outside of the wings, something pushed back. Thumping, thumping, jabbing and poking.

A flurry of green lights bombarded me, sharp spears prodding at my hands, my cheeks, wherever they could reach me.

"Enough!" I shouted, whipping wind at them. The row of faery lights fell back, right into a crackle of icy purple flame that sent them careening sideways.

My sisters were below me, Calder, Dean, and even Journey circling around them with their backs to them, keeping the merfolk and faeries at bay.

"Hurry!" I shouted, taking hold of the orb with both hands and lowering it to Ember, who stood nearest. "Surrender to me and share some vampire and merfolk blood."

"You're going to make the wish?" said Ivy. She flung another volley of power at a bulky merman who'd taken a step too close.

"It'll take out some merfolk, but some vampires, too." She leaned her head toward Journey and Dean.

"The merfolk aren't acceptable sacrifices, either," snapped Ember.

Ivy tilted her head, her breaths heavy. She bit her lip, clearly stopping herself from saying something in particular. She knew Ember was right, as angry as she was at the merfolk—even if they were still ready to flood the world. Without Ember, they never would. "Fine, yes, but it's the *faefolk* we need gone." Ivy spun and unleashed another crackling fireball, this one skyward toward a mass of green lights. "And the champion of bloom making the wish will take out exactly zero of them."

"Not to mention your prince." Ember looked over her shoulder, as if she could somehow spot Orin amidst all the flittering lights.

I looked behind me at Joel, passed out—or worse. "I have mine," I said. "I don't need the prince of the faery—it's the *champion's* wish, not his."

Somehow I knew... Yes, Dean had been there making the wish at Ivy's side, but it hadn't been a necessary part because he was a "vampire prince." What was "royalty" amidst the vampires, who created their offspring from humans? Dean had once been a merman prince long ago—it wasn't his vampire power that had helped Ivy.

It was the strength of the bond between them.

"Please!" I shouted, shaking the orb at Ember. "Please just trust me."

Ember and Ivy exchanged a look, then nodded. Ember took the orb from me and held it out to Calder, who cautiously stepped backward to stand beside her.

"Calder?" she asked.

He looked from her to me and then back to the orb. "I don't get exactly what's going on, but I know we don't have time for you to explain it. I trust you," he said, more to Ember than to me. Walking nearer to the vines I still sat cushioned upon, he slit the back of his forearm against a jagged thorn. Blood trickled outward and he smeared it over the orb.

"Everyone, back!" Ember shouted. Journey and Ivy complied, Dean hovering just out of the range. Right. The blast that would follow this. She turned to Ivy and Dean. "We have to work *fast*," she said. Ivy and Dean held hands and nodded, clearly ready with a plan.

If the champion of water surrendered first, it would be the merfolk who started vanishing before the vampires. More of the faefolk had vanished than the merfolk last time—because I had been the first to surrender.

Ember placed the orb on the ground a few feet beyond the cushion of vines and stumbled backward. Calder caught her and guided her far away.

Ember looked up at me. "I surrender to you, Autumn. To the champion of bloom."

The blue light grew bright—so bright, it drowned out the last of the sunlight entirely, and with a boom, it echoed outward, a wave of light like a sonic boom washing outward.

Calder and Ember stumbled in the wave, the air sending Ember's hair flying, but they were all right. Ember grabbed on to Journey with her free hand and the three huddled tight.

Beneath me, the vine cushion rocked and wavered, the very bottom catching on fire. My eyes widened and I let out a string of curses, but before I could say anything, there was a series of pops in the air. In one second, in two, in three, Ivy and Dean, hand-in-hand, moved closer to the orb on the ground.

With a roar, Dean flicked his sunglasses off and turned his head to face the very last of the day's sun. His eyes sizzled and out poured blue venom—the vampire's equivalent of blood. He wiped his hand with the stuff, then wiped the orb, holding it out. Without being told, Ivy grabbed it and looked up at me.

"I surrender to you, Autumn, the champion of bloom." Then she let it go as if it were on fire.

Grabbing Dean's hand, they popped and popped away, but their third attempt didn't get them quite far enough as the orb exploded outward with a blinding flash of red light. They tumbled, but the arc of light soared over their heads, ruffling their clothes in the turret of wind but causing them no visible damage.

Ember, Journey, and Calder were far enough this time that they weren't affected—but the merfolk were advancing on them, Nerida shrieking a terrible, hypnotic song.

No. I caught sight of the merboy child huddled with his mother by the wall, away from the battle. Mr. and Mrs. Serafin were beside them, Estelle, too—just looking at me.

Waiting.

Expecting.

I had not a second to spare.

I transformed into a faery, as if it were old hat, then dove down the vine cushion to reach the orb. I popped back into full size to grab the orb but tumbled on the landing, rolling across the grass. My hand reached out for the orb, two-thirds of the magic stone blackened and the green the only color left glowing. But Orin was there, full-sized too, his foot atop the orb.

"I won't let you," he said.

"You have to." My voice croaked. I scrambled up to my knees, not letting go of my grip on the orb. I attempted to pull it out from him, but his foot remained firm. "There's no time—"

He laughed. "Why? Because vampires and merfolk are fading? Their own fault for not leaving well enough alone."

If his words were meant to make me hesitate, they had the opposite effect. I wouldn't let *one* person fall because of this. Not even a faery. I'd asked my sisters to trust me.

I blinked back into faery size, and to my utter relief, my grip on the orb transformed it to small size, too. Clutching it tightly, I soared upright.

With a deafening crackle, the giant Orin shrunk down to my own size and soared—faster than I could, flittering his wings to catch up with me.

For a moment out of time, the sight of him arrested me. Glowing green, little faint wings—he was an ancient prince in modern clothing.

"Do not take this from us," he whispered, all trace of accent gone from his voice.

"Joel!" I screamed, my little faery voice probably nothing to his ears. "I need you! Not something *from* you—I need *you!*" It wasn't a command, but I injected the words with my will all the same. Maybe it did something. Maybe his own need to satisfy me kicked in.

Either way, with a typhoon-like strength, Joel's wings flapped, the black feathers molting off his monstrously large wings.

I cried out, reaching my free hand toward him, then transformed back to his size.

I grew up and into his arms, his eyes blinking open.

This might be the very last of his strength, but for this brief moment, he was here. He was mine.

He caught me in his feathery cocoon, but the wings were bony now, thin skin and membranes with just the slightest bit of feathers left. I shoved the orb toward both his hands.

"Wish for it," I said quickly, willing him to know what I meant this time. Willing him to understand, to not hesitate to comply.

Before, he'd sensed maybe a part of me *had* wanted to be able to prove I hadn't made up the faeries, the merfolk, and the vampires. I'd never have asked for that wish, but deep down, he'd known.

I'd wanted my powers again. At least one small part of me had.

And he'd sensed my other wishes when I'd focused on them.

He would know what I wanted again.

"We wish," we said as one. Joel looked to me, taking his cue. "We wish to return those who've vanished from the orb's magic, for supernatural creatures to no longer exist, and then for the orb to disappear." We spoke so quickly, my mind pouring all of my command into it, it was as if willing these multiple wishes to become one.

But it worked. Our hearts were so in sync, our words so fast, it would be done.

The wedge of green grew brighter, the orb growing warmer in our hands. But neither of us flinched, letting the wash of power radiate outward as the smooth glass-like stone turned to dust against our palms.

And with a sigh, I collapsed into his chest, his thin, membrane-like wings dissolving into nothingness as we both fell to the ground below.

"Signing your cast is so much cooler than signing a yearbook." Mikayla flicked a lock of her blonde hair over her shoulder. It contrasted boldly with the dark navy of her graduation gown.

I swung my legs against the brick wall I sat atop near the entrance to the gym, staring down at Mikayla's cap. She'd decorated it with the year and angel wings with little green vines and purple flowers, in commemoration of the angel-forest prom theme. My heart soared at the sight, like somehow our bizarre mash of themes was a sign that the champion of bloom had always been destined to cross paths with fallen angels.

"Are you going to even keep that once it comes off?" Alan wrinkled his nose. He looked a little too big for his graduation gown, which dusted just below his knees instead of at his ankles. "It'll probably stink."

"Gross, Alan." Mikayla playfully slapped him on the chest. She took hold of my arm and blew on my cast, practically yanking me down off the wall as she did so, then, satisfied, capped the marker and handed it back to me.

Autumn Sheppard, Prom Queen, you rock.

I winced. No one had ever bothered looking into that mix-up, though it had led to more than a few stares my way over the last few weeks of school. The fact that I'd been walking hand in hand with the Prom King after that had drawn more of their attention, though.

Though some of the gossip I'd overheard when in the bathroom stall had had to do with me cheating my way to get that dance with him all in my brazen, hussy plan to seduce him to date me before school let out.

They weren't entirely wrong, and I didn't care at this point, so I let them talk, waited them out, and didn't even bother to try to correct them.

"Hey!" Prae popped up behind Alan from the direction of the gym. The graduation ceremony was over and everyone was milling around inside and outside, talking with friends, posing for pictures with family.

My own family was somewhere inside. The twins had had to go to the bathroom, and somehow that had turned into an entire circus of bathroom visits and wrangling. I'd slipped outside before any of them had even noticed.

The fresh air was nice in my lungs.

"Congrats, grads," Prae said, grinning.

"You, too." I smiled at her. I felt like I really owed her one after she'd helped me post-prom. But I'd been light on details when she'd asked about the "family emergency" and how I'd wound up dating Joel. Mikayla was curious, too, I could tell, but she seemed to pride herself on not prying too much.

Too often.

"So..." Mikayla clutched her hands together in front of her. "Are you finally going to spill about how your big dance led to you snagging Joel Serafin?"

"Kayla." Alan nudged her, but just then someone called his name.

In the parking lot, his diminutive older sister trotted over from a car with a toddler in one arm and a diaper bag on the other shoulder. "Alan, help with your nephew, please!"

Alan's expression grew pinched. "Where's Parker?"

"With the baby," she said, her sandals clomping against the

sidewalk as she approached. She dumped the toddler in his arms and the child giggled, tugging on the tassel on Alan's hat.

Paisley, one of Ivy's oldest friends, had shorn her hair pixie-short, dyeing it bright red, and she sported an orangish tan that seemed like the type you got from a salon or maybe a bottle. "Someone needs his diaper changed," she said, making a cutesy face at the boy in Alan's arms and booping his nose.

The boy with the dark curls and rosy cheeks laughed.

Alan's lip curled. "Ew. You could've told me that before you handed me him."

"The baby, not Grey J," she said, rolling her eyes. "He's three. He's potty-trained."

The first kid was named Grey Junior, if I remembered right. She'd had him with her first husband but had gotten remarried a year ago. Ivy had flown back for the wedding.

Had *anyone* I knew wound up in a long-term relationship with their high school sweetheart?

"How's it going, Autumn?" Paisley asked, straightening the diaper bag over her shoulder. "I spotted Ivy earlier. Haven't had a chance to say *hi*." She frowned, looking at my cast. It covered my left forearm but luckily left my elbow free to bend. The hairline fissure from the fall had been confined to the forearm. We'd been cushioned by the vines, but I'd tumbled off the edge and fallen sideways. "What'd you do?"

"Playing around in my boyfriend's yard." It wasn't entirely a lie.

Paisley cocked her head and her phone buzzed. "That would be Parker wondering where I am. Follow me and you can drop him off with Mom and Dad," Paisley said to Alan. Then she stopped and looked back at me. "And you—no more roughhousing."

I laughed nervously and did a Scout's honor salute with my right hand. "I'm done with everything like that."

She nodded, though a curious light hit her eyes. Then her phone buzzed again and she dragged Alan behind her, Grey J in tow. "See you around," Alan said to me and Prae. "Kayla, you coming?"

"In a sec!" she said.

She waited until Alan and Paisley had gone inside. Then she turned to both Prae and me.

"My friend Nora saw Tia at that old rundown bookstore off the Interstate—you know it?"

Prae smiled. "Yeah. Her cousin owns it."

Mikayla cocked her head, processing the information, then seemed to dismiss its importance. "She. Had. A. Baby."

"Who?" Prae asked. "Nora?"

"*No*. Tia!" Mikayla shook her head. "She was taking care of a baby and amusing it by getting some cats to play in front of it—Nora said it was real unreal, like those cats were *trained*—and Nora asked if the baby was her sister or something, and Tia said, 'No. She's mine.' Hers! She had a baby!"

Prae gasped. My throat felt dry. I hadn't spoken to any former faery since that day.

"There's no way. I mean, she hasn't come back to school since prom, but..." Prae left the rest unsaid and looked to me, as if I could explain things.

I shrugged. She'd given birth to a faery baby the day after prom, but I wasn't about to explain that.

"No, it makes perfect sense. I know she totally didn't look preggo, but that's easily explained—Nora said the baby had to be at least a few months. She probably dropped out of her other school to give birth and then tried to pick up where she left off again." Mikayla flicked her hair over her shoulder. "Then she dropped out again. No wonder she didn't graduate. And all those people thought she was so cool."

I frowned. "She's cool. She can be, anyway." It was strange to find myself defending her.

"Yeah," said Prae. "Don't hate on teen moms. I think it's admirable she tried to go back to school—and I don't blame her for needing more time to get there." She nodded, as if it all made sense to her now. "I wonder if her parents had the baby at first, if they kicked her out and that was why she went to live with her cousin. I should text her."

I jumped down, my sneakers slamming against the sidewalk. I

had a dress on with a pair of sneakers beneath the graduation gown. It was more comfortable that way.

"I say just give her some time," I told Prae. Hopefully, by the time Prae remembered, she'd be busy at college and not follow up with her too closely. If Tia even deigned to respond to her. "If she'd wanted us to know about all of that, she would have told us."

Something like a realization hit me then. That was the nature of faeries—and presumably always would be, even when they no longer *were* faeries at all.

They'd existed outside of humankind for so long, had thought themselves separate from us.

They'd never been my friends, had hardly been my allies. If they'd gotten what they'd wanted from me back then, humanity would be gone.

And what Orin and Tia had wanted from me. Well, I hoped Tia had gotten to hold on to at least one thing she'd wanted from all of that. Her baby may have been human, but it was still hers. I was sure she'd grow up to be every bit as beautiful as the kind that had spawned her. And maybe, as the firstborn to a human life entirely, she could teach the rest of them a thing or two about appreciating what life on Earth as humans had to offer.

"Watch it, sport." Dad's deep, dulcet tones carried from behind me and I knew somehow I'd been busted. "I saw you leap off that wall. Are you trying to break your other arm?"

Sheepish, I turned around to find Dad with Noelle and Mom, each dressed up in corporate casual. The only difference was Mom had a morning glory in her hair.

"Sorry," I said, to three equally disapproving looks. "I'll be careful. Promise."

"Hi, girls." Noelle brightened. "I recognize you both from the Prom Committee photo."

"Yup," I said, reddening. Noelle had had the thing framed and hung along the staircase. "Mikayla and Prae."

"I hope you'll stop by sometime this summer before you all go your separate ways. You girls off to college?" Noelle was all business, and Mikayla jumped at the chance for a shot in the spotlight.

"Yes! My top pick! I was on the waitlist, but then the whole Prom Committee experience got me in." She started prattling, drawing Noelle's attention as Mom and Dad each came to give me a big hug. Mom planted a kiss on my head. She smelled sweet and fragrant, like a garden in a summer's day.

"Congrats, baby," she said. "We're so proud of you."

"And even if you're thinking of transferring next semester for *some boy*—" started Dad.

"*Easton.*" Mom slapped him on the chest with the back of her hand.

Dad was not deterred. "Even if I think it's foolish to be transferring schools in January over some boyfriend who'll probably dump you as soon as he gets on campus—"

"*Dad!*" It was my turn to playfully slap him.

"I'm glad you're thinking about a bachelor's degree. Ivy took the long road, but well, we're so proud of her, and I don't want you to be stuck here for years."

"She wouldn't be stuck here." Mom gave me a side hug. "My baby is always welcome at *my* house."

Dad stiffened. "Mine, too." I wondered if Noelle would have something else to say about that. Visits, sure, but living there much longer...? "I just mean, well..." Dad rubbed the back of his head. In the sunlight, his wrinkles seemed more pronounced, and his eyes sparkled. "I don't know what I mean. Love you, kid. And don't *ever* keep secrets from us again? Nothing like that sort anyway."

He gave me another hug as Mom murmured her agreement.

"I promise." I squeezed Dad with my right arm, settling for just lightly patting Mom with my cast.

I'd had *quite a lot* to explain in the hospital while the ER had patched up my arm. The explanation had continued long into the next day. At least my sisters had had my back.

"Where's everyone else?" I asked.

"Ah, the kids wanted a tour of the school," said Dad. "Your sisters obliged."

"I told them not to take too long." Mom looked over her

shoulder as she dug her phone out of her purse. "I wanted to get pics."

"I guess I should find my own family. See you, Autumn!" said Prae, stepping back from speaking with Noelle.

"Swing by the front of the school before you go and maybe we can get more pics," added Mikayla.

I waved to them both and strangely found myself saying, "I hope you *will* stop by this summer! Or we can hang out someplace!"

"Sure!" said Prae, beaming.

Mikayla winked. "Yeah, or maybe I'll see you and Mr. Sexy at parties around town." She and Prae giggled as they headed inside.

"Mr. Sexy?" Noelle asked, amused.

Dad blanched.

"They're teasing me," I said quickly.

My phone buzzed in my pocket—Ivy always told me to look for dresses with pockets—and I pulled it out. There was a message from PonyFan.

Mom and Dad ran into some doctor they know. Bored out of my mind. Missing you. Where are you?

I rolled my eyes and typed back. *We've only been apart twenty minutes. And why did you bring your old phone with you?*

Because Mom has my new one in her purse. Something about being all in the moment today. But now she's the one totally oblivious to the fact that I've snuck off. But also, 'only' twenty minutes? You wound me. That's forever, princess. He added a series of black and purple hearts.

Well, get used to it, I typed back. *I can't get into your school until next semester.*

I can always stay here. Go to community college with you.

No, I wrote back. *We'll survive the time apart. I promise. There are always weekends and holidays.* I waited to write more, though PonyFan was already typing back.

But you're already spending a month in Seattle this summer! When will I even see you?

You will, I typed. *I just want to take this slow. Dad said you'd cheat on me and dump me before I transferred. I want to prove him wrong.*

PonyFan sent a series of exclamation points. *Never! Did you explain the true love thing?*

And angel DNA? Sure. But you're not an angel anymore, Joel. You've got your whole human life ahead of you. I don't think the true love thing needs to stick.

Me being human doesn't change how I feel about you. You didn't wish ALL magic away.

I thought about that. If Ivy had wished it all away to begin with, none of this would have happened. No one would have come back, and Joel... Well, I wasn't sure what would have happened to Joel. Perhaps his parents would have made him marry Estelle and have a kid with her anyway because they wouldn't have known he was no longer at risk of dying by granting one lucky young woman's wishes.

I'm going to find you, he wrote, not even waiting for me to explain where I was.

"Autie!" I pulled up my graduation gown to slip my phone into the pocket of my dress, just in time for Hyacinth to body-slam into my torso. "Congrats, Autumn!"

Ashwood shuffled his feet on the sidewalk behind her, clasping his hands behind his back. "You look pretty today," he said. "And smart. Pretty smart."

"Thanks," I said, pulling him in for a double twin hug with my right arm. I looked up as the twins pulled away.

Ivy and Dean approached, arm in arm, Dean's eyes missing the vibrant shade of blue I'd known had filled his irises that day.

And beside them, Ember with Calder, her arm through his. There was still a little something off about the picture—Calder had been sixteen, a junior, when he'd vanished, and he hadn't aged a day. But Ember looked young herself and they were taking it slowly.

Ember had reddened when I'd asked her about it. She reminded me she had her months-long job in the Atlantic Ocean anyway, but she'd postponed joining the team to stay back for my graduation.

And spend some more time with Calder, catching him up to modern day.

Bay, his best friend, and Bay's husband had taken him in somewhere in Chicago. He'd taken in Cascade, too, since she was his cousin. Llyr, brokenhearted, had gone to live with his parents and sister. Llyr and Bay had dated in high school, and Llyr had still been in love when he'd blinked back into existence—well, as soon as he'd gotten over his bloodlust like the rest of them.

But Bay had moved on. And, as my dad would be the first to tell me, some high school romances weren't meant to last forever. Some.

Calder's mother wasn't speaking to him, wherever she and the other merfolk had settled.

I wasn't worried about it. They were only human.

"Congrats, kid." Dean nodded at me.

Calder winced. "I can't believe you're graduating before I am."

Ember looked up at him, her face brightening. "You have time. All the time in the world. Bay's helping him with his GED." She said that last part to our parents more than anyone else.

Dad grimaced but didn't say anything. Whether it was because Ember was his step-daughter and he'd only helped raise her one year or because he recognized the special circumstances, who could say, but I knew he was holding himself back from making some comment.

His daughter was older than the boy in question this time. He couldn't exactly accuse him of taking advantage.

He cleared his throat and said something anyway. "Well, I think that's great. I know you two just got reunited, but keep some space." He eyed Ember. "Give him a couple of years to catch up." He left the rest unsaid.

She flushed crimson red. "I wasn't planning... I mean, of course..."

"*Okay, then,*" said Ivy, resting a sympathetic hand on Ember's shoulder. "Should we take that picture?"

"Let's head over here," I said, leading the way. We stood in front of a tree I knew had been near where I'd last left Joel. I'd eaten a lot of lunches by this apple blossom tree during my high school years. Today it was particularly beautiful, bright white petals flittering on the breeze.

I spotted Joel a short distance away as soon as I arrived. He was chatting with Sabine, Rick, and D, along with a bevy of adults I didn't recognize. Estelle was nearby with what were probably her parents and grandparents, but she was stuck in a conversation with Wyatt and his family, dryly looking over toward her own friends from time to time, but quickly looking away whenever one of them made eye contact with her. Though it was never Joel.

Estelle had thanked me once after all of that. Just once. Then she'd walked away and hadn't spoken to Joel or any of her friends since.

D looked my way and nodded at me, his hands stuffed into his pockets. I offered him and Sabine and Rick a timid wave. Joel was bouncing on his heels, about to dart away. Sabine nudged his shoulder with hers, saying something to him.

He turned around. The awe transformed his face. It grew brighter, as if this were the first time he'd seen me in years. Or ever.

As if I were the most beautiful person he'd ever laid eyes on—instead of vice versa.

My family shuffled in around me, Noelle barking out orders and conferring with Mom about how many shots to take with each phone. She looked over her shoulder for someone to step in and take the picture, no doubt, her grin growing mischievous as Joel made his way over.

"Joel, just the person we need." She shoved her phone at him and gathered Mom's too. "Take our family photo?"

Joel's face fell and I winced, but I couldn't stop the smile from forming on my face. I mouthed, 'Please?'

"Okay," he said. He sounded grim.

Noelle, Dad, and Mom took their places on one side, Dean and Calder on either side of my older sisters, who flanked me.

I gripped on to Hya's shoulder in front of me and stared straight ahead.

"Okay, on the count of—" started Joel.

"Here, let me."

My mouth dropped as someone tapped Joel's shoulder, that Cockney accent unmistakable.

Joel turned and his hands went limp enough for Orin to scoop up both phones.

"Now wait a minute—" started Dad.

Ivy reached across Dean to put a hand to Dad's chest. She nodded tellingly toward Ash, whose shoulder she held. He and Hya looked up at Dad curiously. "It's just an old *friend*," Ivy told us. "Right?" She offered Orin a tight-lipped, grim and obviously fake smile.

He laughed. "A *very* old mate, that's me. Thought I'd stop by and say congrats, all right?"

"Thank you." The words came out through grinding teeth. But I took a deep breath. Human life wasn't treating him too badly, was it? Sounded like he was back at the bookstore, at least long enough to play with his cats and give his cousin someplace to show off her baby.

"Hey, Orin," I said. "Why the accent?"

Everyone looked to me.

"Sorry, love?" Orin cocked his head.

"I know you don't have a British accent," I said. "You spoke to me like an American... that day." I gripped Hya's shoulder tighter and she looked up at me quizzically.

His shoulders bounced a little. "I hate to tell you, but American *is* an accent. More than one of them too, yeah? And I'm free to do as I like. Got a bucket list and all that. Only so many years to do and see everything I want to. I'm working on getting the whole family round to my way of thinking."

He displayed a wide grin at me, and, defenseless, I smiled back. He hadn't really answered my question. Typical Orin.

But when it came to him saying he wanted to bring his family round, I believed him. Even if he was lying to me, even if he wasn't fine with it deep down, I would choose to believe him.

He wasn't my problem anymore, and he never really should have been.

Still, I was glad... to at least have reason to think they were going to be okay. All of them.

Joel, who'd never known the faery prince's trickery firsthand, dismissed him quick enough, melting with joy evident on his face as he scooched in between Ember and me, giving Hya a little rub on the head as he passed her.

"Hey," she said, fixing her hair again.

"On the count of three!" said Orin, not giving us much of a chance to get ready.

"One, two—"

On the count of three, like we'd read each other's minds, Joel pressed his cheek to mine and I pressed mine against his.

When the flash finished, we both turned our heads at once and shared a kiss under the apple blossom tree.

ABOUT THE AUTHOR

Amy McNulty is an editor and author of books that run the gamut from YA speculative fiction to contemporary romance. A lifelong fiction fanatic, she fangirls over books, anime, manga, comics, movies, games, and TV shows from her home state of Wisconsin. When not editing her clients' novels, she's busy fulfilling her dream by crafting fantastical worlds of her own.

Sign up for Amy's newsletter to receive news and exclusive information about her current and upcoming projects. Get a free YA romantic sci-fi novelette when you do!

LOOK FOR MORE YA SPECULATIVE
FICTION READS FROM SNOWY WINGS
PUBLISHING

Snowy Wings
PUBLISHING

Parker Mills has it all. She's the two-time winner of the Miss Divine Pecan Pageant, head of the 8th grade dance committee, and a secret psychic empath. Since she absorbs strong emotions from those around her, Parker has committed herself to finding short-cuts to happiness. Whether acting as a tutor, coach, or matchmaker, Parker knows that when others are happy, she's happy. Granted, all that fixing other people's drama means her own crush has no idea how she feels, but it's still a win-win so long as her psychic method remains a mystery.

At least, that's how it always worked until Mia came to town. With her mysterious past and dark cloud of depression, Mia's moods threaten to rain on Parker's happiness parade. After Parker's usual shortcuts fail—even after bringing super cute Josh on the scene—she's forced to kick things up a notch or two. But when Parker's psychic power goes haywire, dangerous secrets unravel... starting with her own.

"The story moves at a fast clip, with numerous subplots expertly knit together. Each strand builds on the complexity of the tale until its explosive, intense culmination. *Shortcuts* is a memorable speculative novel that begs for a sequel." – *Foreword Reviews*, starred review

ANGEL DOWN
MICKY O'BRADY

Ten years ago, the Founders, angel-like creatures, arrived in their spaceships and conquered humanity. Seventeen-year-old Lea Akiyama knows all their rules by heart, especially the Eleventh Commandment: Thou Shalt Not Touch Those Descended From The Heavens. After all, breaking that rule got her parents killed.

Unfortunately, she does touch a Founder. Okay, she saves his life, but still. It would be eighteen-year-old Jamie's right to kill her. Instead due to a weird twist of fate they both end up doing the bidding of the human Resistance.

Trapped and forced into cooperation, Jamie is the last person Lea expected to bond with. Granted, he's definitely hot thanks to those uber-perfect Founder-genes, but he's still one of them. Yet, as Lea and Jamie begin a dangerous double game for their freedom, the sparking tension between them becomes impossible to ignore.

Desperately trying to keep their distance from each other, Lea and Jamie uncover the Founders' biggest secret—a secret that could change the course of the world and puts Lea in mortal peril not only by the Founders and their commandments, but even more by the boy she is falling for.

READ MORE FROM AMY MCNULTY

"The story is fun and engaging, featuring a female protagonist who will resonate with young teens." -School Library Journal

"...A whirlwind of time-bending adventures that immerse readers in a maelstrom of plot twists and allusions to "Beauty and the Beast" and other fairy tale love stories, while Noll's understanding of gender-based social and cultural dynamics develops." -Publishers Weekly

Nobody's Goddess (Book One in The Never Veil Series), <u>winner of The Romance Reviews Summer 2016 Readers' Choice Award for Young Adult Romance</u>:

In a village of masked men, each man is compelled to love only one woman and to follow the commands of his "goddess" without question. A woman may reject the only man who will love her if she pleases, but she will be alone forever. A man must stay masked until his goddess returns his love—and if she can't or won't, he remains masked forever.

Seventeen-year-old Noll's childhood friends have paired off and her closest companion, Jurij, found his goddess in Noll's own sister. Desperate to find a way to break this ancient spell, Noll instead discovers why no man has ever chosen her. She is in fact the goddess of the mysterious lord of the village, a man who refuses to let Noll have her right as a woman to spurn him.

Thus begins a dangerous game between the choice of woman and the magic of man. The stakes are no less than freedom and happiness, life and death—and neither Noll nor the veiled lord is willing to lose.

FALL FAR FROM THE TREE DUOLOGY

Terror. Callousness. Denial. Rebellion. How the four teenage children of leaders in the duchy and the neighboring empire of Hanaobi choose to adapt to their nefarious parents' whims is a matter of survival.

Rohesia, daughter of the duke, spends her days hunting "outsiders," fugitives who've snuck onto her father's island duchy. That she lives when even children who resemble her are subject to death hardens her heart to tackle the task.

Fastello is the son of the "king" of the raiders who steal from the rich and share with the poor. When aristocrats die in the raids, Fastello questions what his peoples' increasingly wicked methods of survival have cost them.

An orphan raised by a convent of mothers, Cateline can think of no higher aim in life than to serve her religion, even if it means turning a blind eye to the suffering of other orphans under the mothers' care.

Kojiro, new heir to the Hanaobi empire, must avenge his people against the "barbarians" who live in the duchy, terrified the empress, his own mother, might rather see him die than succeed.

When the paths of these four young adults cross, they must rely on one another for survival—but the love of even a malevolent guardian is hard to leave behind.

BALLAD OF THE BEANSTALK

A Library Journal Self-e Selection.

As her fingers move across the strings of her family's heirloom harp, sixteen-year-old Clarion can forget. She doesn't dwell on the recent passing of her beloved father or the fact that her mother has just sold everything they owned, including that very same instrument that gives Clarion life. She doesn't think about how her friends treat her like a feeble, brittle thing to be protected. She doesn't worry about how to tell the elegant Elena, her best friend and first love, that she doesn't want to be her sweetheart anymore. She becomes the melody and loses herself in the song.

When Mack, a lord's dashing young son, rides into town so his father and Elena's can arrange a marriage between the two youth, Clarion finds herself falling in love with a boy for the first time. Drawn to Clarion's music, Mack puts Clarion and Elena's relationship to the test, but he soon vanishes by climbing up a giant beanstalk that only Clarion has seen. When even the town witch won't help, Clarion is determined to rescue Mack herself and prove once and for all that she doesn't need protecting. But while she fancied herself a savior, she couldn't have imagined the enormous world of danger that awaits her in the kingdom of the clouds.

A prequel to the fairy tale *Jack and the Beanstalk* that reveals the true story behind the magical singing harp.

www.ingramcontent.com/pod-product-compliance
Lightning Source LLC
Chambersburg PA
CBHW061315190726
48288CB00002B/507